# COLLIDED

## BELLMARE HIGH SERIES

## MARY

# BELLMARE HIGH BOOK ONE

# Contents

# Trigger Warnings

The book contains emotional and physical abuse, grief due to the death of a loved one, trauma, panic attacks, anxiety, graphic violence, and mention of domestic violence and cancer.

# SYNOPSIS

**Bad boy meets good girl.**

*Shy. Sweet. Smart.*

Hope Hanson has fictional characters where most people have friends. A loner at school, she thinks love is as fictional as the stories she reads. Real-life love shattered her parents' marriage with punches and screams, resulting in her Dad leaving them. Three months later, her new fractured reality is turned upside down when her Dad returns and Hope becomes his new target.

*Grumpy. Sarcastic. Angry.*

Heath Travon has almost everything. He's intelligent, rich, and the daydream of the girls at Bellmare High School, but all he wants is to be left alone. Beneath his cold eyes and icy attitude, he's mourning a devastating loss that has him both fighting for every breath and wanting each one to be his last.

By accident they collide in the hallway. One look at her and he finds himself intrigued.

Heath sees the tears she doesn't shed, the bruises she desperately hides, and the truths behind her lies.

Hope sees his buried pain, as well as the thoughts he doesn't reveal and isn't fooled by his tough persona.

As Hope's home situation worsens and Heath's grief spirals, both are determined to help each other. He is adamant about protecting her and she is adamant about saving him.

# PLAYLIST

*I DON'T LIKE DARKNESS* — Chase Atlantic

*stuck in my head* — BLÜ EYES

*One Day* — Tate McRae

*Lonely Eyes* — Lauv

*Uncomfortable* — Chase Atlantic

*Brown Eyes, Brown Hair* — Caleb Hearn

*Broken Home* — 5 Seconds of Summer

*X&Y* — Coldplay

*Something About You* — Eyedress, Dent May

*ocean eyes* — Billie Eilish

*Come Down Soon* — Lizzy McAlpine

*400 Lux* — Lorde

*What You Do To Me* — Blanks

*Labyrinth* — Taylor Swift

*This Side of Paradise* — Coyote Theory

*Today Was A Fairytale (Taylor's Version)* — Taylor Swift

*Night Changes* — One Direction

*To the people who read this story on Wattpad.*
*You guys have changed my life.*

# 1

## HOPE

AT BELLMARE HIGH SCHOOL, EVERYONE FITS IN, EXCEPT FOR ME.

Treading the crowded hallway, no one bothers to look at me, let alone talk to me, mainly because of two reasons. First, I'm the nerd with straight A's in every subject. I always know the correct answer, and you know how people tend to stay away from those. They only talk to me when they're desperate and need my help to pass a test—those instances don't happen often. Second, and I take the blame for this one—my nose is always buried in a novel. It'll sound dramatic, but the world could be under attack, and my first instinct would be to find a safe corner to read peacefully. I only need books to survive.

As I walk toward my class I keep my head down. My eyes peruse the words of a fantasy-romance novel with great interest to know what happens next.

Reading is escapism for me. It flies me to places and lets me experience the lives of others like it's my own. It creates a bridge, connecting my world to theirs. The best part is no one can break it. Between the pages, I find more connection than I ever could in the real world, and with the characters I feel more at home. I'm never lonely with them.

With no siblings and friends, I'm always on my own, and the hobby has turned into an addiction. In every fleeting minute of the day, I try to skim the pages. I know I'd never be able to read every book in the world in this lifetime, but I want to read enough.

Sometimes, I wonder how people go on in life without reading the stories trapped in books. For as long as I can remember, books have been my only comfort. My tunnel to another universe where things are good, and people are nice, unlike my reality.

I'm in my senior year, and I've never had a friend.

*Do fictional people count?*

I step into the boisterous classroom, and take a seat at the back, because I'm shy and an introvert. Sitting at the front and feeling the attention of the whole class on my back gives me anxiety.

A minute later, Mr. Carlie, our Chemistry teacher, walks in. He's in his mid-fifties with a bald head that shines– something that elicits jokes among students– but he's always too nice to chide them. Out of all the teachers, he's my favorite.

"Good morning. How is everyone?" After hearing a string of replies, he scribbles the topic on the whiteboard with a black marker.

I reluctantly set aside my novel, when through the window something catches my eye—or rather someone.

A tall, lean guy stands under the sycamore tree, with a phone pressed to his ear. The old branches create a magnificent bower over the side of the parking lot. I watch a leaf break off, and slowly glide through the summer air of August as it falls, missing his head by a fraction. He walks around with his back toward me. I run my mind through the faces I know at school, but I can't put one on his back—I mean his hidden face.

*Who is it?*

As if to answer my question, he turns around. Heath Travon. The infamous bad boy of the school who's always getting into fights and skipping classes. Last year, he transferred here. At first, people gawked at him because he was the new student, and we don't usually get them with how small our town is—I've been with the same classmates since kindergarten. Within the first week, he got into a fight with one of the players on the football team, Jason, who cornered him and said something that made Heath lunge at him. He landed punch after punch until he was a bloody mess, and the principal had to come and separate them.

The only punishment Heath got was a one-week suspension. Since then, he became big news—and bad news.

I've seen girls fawn over the ground he walks on, and guys hate him for stealing attention. However, he's never once interacted with anyone. Enough time has passed, but his popularity is still the same—the frequency of fights too. Perhaps it's because he's mysterious, quiet, and angry. It all adds to this appeal.

Dressed in a black T-shirt and jeans, he looks deadly. Raising his hand, he runs his fingers through his dark strands. His mouth moves as he talks, but when his eyes lock on me he stops talking. Even from afar, I feel his piercing stare before it narrows into slits and burns me like a scorching flame of fire.

The embarrassment of getting caught makes me break eye contact, but I feel his stare pinned on me like a laser.

Oh God. I hope he doesn't recognize me.

Who am I kidding? He surely doesn't. I'm invisible to people.

I let my hair shield the side of my face. The flaming sensation disappears, but not his stare. It's very much still there, but I don't dare to look back at him.

If it were any other girl in my position, she'd be thrilled about the bad boy of the school staring at them, but I'm not. I want to keep a low profile and pass the next few months, so I can get away from here.

I skim over my notes that I made last night of the topic that's currently being taught. I didn't have a new book to read, and it was too late to go to the library. I had to kill time somehow. Fortunately, the library opens early. I managed to grab a book on my way here.

The class ends with an announcement of a test, and everyone whines. Piling up the papers on top of my folder, I join the sea of people in the hallway.

While arranging the papers in my folder, I feel the strong vibration of my phone in my back pocket. I balance the pile in one hand and then reach for it. I see five messages from Mom. An immediate pang of worry hits me in the chest. She's drunk again. I already know what her messages will say.

Regardless, I open the thread. Before I can read the messages, I collide with someone and stumble back at the impact. I anticipate meeting the floor, but an arm circles around my waist and saves me from my fall.

"I'm sorry—" my words die when I find Heath inches away from my face.

*Oh my God.*

*How did he get here?*

My gaze drifts to the striking features of his face. Fair skin that's smooth and clear, sharp nose, defined jawline, and eyes that are deep blue like ocean waters.

He's beautiful. And his eyes...they are unlike anything I've ever seen before.

We stare at each other, much like before, but this time I can't seem to look away. He's the most beautiful guy I've ever seen.

At once something flickers through his eyes, and he averts his gaze. Clearing his throat, he steps back and his hold on my waist slips away. I Immediately miss the heat. For some strange reason, my skin is always cold. I don't know why.

"I—" My eyes move down, and I gape at the scene. All my papers are strewn on the floor and people are walking on them with no care. I grumble at their blindness.

Slipping my phone into my pocket, I bend down and quickly collect the papers from one side. Then turn, only to find a hand stretched out with the rest of my papers and the empty folder.

I glance at Heath, who's crouched down in front of me, with his intense eyes fixed on me.

I'm so stunned, I can barely move a muscle. I wasn't expecting him to help me or save me from the fall for that matter. He's someone who ignores your existence rather than helping you in any way.

Thrusting the folder and papers into my hand, he stands up. I carelessly put all the papers in the folder and bring it to my chest, feeling awkward and shy all of a sudden.

Heath towers over my five feet eight inches frame with his tall and lean build. The strands of his dark brown hair fall over his forehead as he looks down at me with a grave face.

Without saying a word, he turns around to leave, but I block his way. Annoyance crosses his face, making my heart race and my hands clammy from nervousness.

*Here it goes.*

*You can do it.*

*He won't bite your head off even though he looks like it.*

I smile at him. "Thanks for your help. I'm sorry for earlier. It was a mistake. I was just busy—"

His expression hardens as he cuts me off, "Next time, look where you're going. Perhaps, then no one will have to save your sorry ass and collect your fucking papers."

I did not expect such a venomous reply. "Excuse me?" I ask. He frowns.

"You heard me," he retorts in an icy tone.

"I told you it was a mistake."

Giving me one last look, he disappears into the crowd that watches him with interest. A few questioning looks are sent my way, but I'm already walking to my next class.

That was my first interaction with Heath, and I'm already regretting it.

The school day ends. I don't see Heath in any of the classes that we share.

All day I couldn't forget his cold eyes and icy tone. I've never spoken to him before, but now that I have, I'll be staying far away. I don't want trouble, and he seems exactly that. Too volatile to handle.

Besides, I have other things to worry about. Like how my home life is a mess.

Dad walked out on us three months ago. That was after he almost killed Mom.

A shiver runs through me at the memories that sneak back in. It was terrifying. I thought I'd lose her.

I should've seen it coming, though.

That night was the ending point of years of fighting. It started when I was ten—perhaps, even before that, but that was when I started noticing—and then it became a regular thing. Not a single day went by without them arguing over the tiniest things like TV, laundry, money, and meals. From screaming at each other to Dad hitting Mom, every dinner would end the same way; him leaving and my mother being hurt. It looked foreign to me at first, but slowly I got used to it. It got to the point where it felt strange when it wasn't loud in the house. The silence creeped me out more than the noise because I knew something big would happen soon. The wait gave me anxiety.

Weekends were the worst. The three of us would be home and my parents would have more chances to fight. Money was the reason why my parents fought all the time. Dad worked as a receptionist at a small law firm that was on the brink of bankruptcy. What he earned wasn't sufficient to run a house. Mom offered to help, but he refused and later blamed her for being useless and hit her. Every night he'd come home and release his frustration out on her, but never with me.

I wished he'd hit me, so my mother could be safe. Whenever he'd yell at her and raise his hand to her, my body became paralyzed, and I couldn't move. I never moved. I never saved her.

Which is why I'm glad that he's gone. What he did to her that night scarred me for life. It was the first time I feared him. I saw him as a monster and not as my father. That image of him still haunts me at night. I wonder if it'll ever go away.

A two-story house surrounded by two months' worth of herbs appears. I've asked Mom to cut them, but she always brushes off the topic to save the money.

I unlock the door and step inside. The hallway separates into three rooms: the living room, kitchen, and my parent's—now Mom's bedroom. At the end is a staircase which leads up to my room.

I open the refrigerator and find a plate of spaghetti. I put it into the microwave, which only half-heats because it needs to be repaired, but Mom has no plans to spend money on it, or anything really. When I have stuffed myself with food I go upstairs.

My room is a tiny, poor place with chipped cream walls, creaky wood floorboards, and a broken window. A study table rests next to the window with my stack of textbooks and stationery on top. In the center of the room is my iron bed. To the right is a huge wardrobe and the bathroom.

Nothing in the room means more to me than my book wall that's across the foot of my bed. It's a stack of twenty books that I've been able to buy over the years.

Removing my shoes, I slump onto my bed, adamant to finish the book tonight. Strangely, my thoughts fly to those mesmerizing blue eyes.

I'm intrigued by Heath. Everyone at school says he's trouble. I don't believe the rumors, there's always more to a person. It's one of the many things books have taught me. You don't really know someone until you're in their head.

Something tells me Heath is like that. A part of the ocean no one's ever dared to dive into.

# 2

## HEATH

THE SMELL OF THE CIGARETTE LINGERS AS I STUB IT OUT WITH THE HEEL OF MY SHOE.

My chest should feel less tight, and my mind should be less crowded, but nothing changes.

I need one more. Then I'd feel fucking better.

"Where the fuck was your ass?" Sebastian approaches me with a scowl.

"Why? Are you fond of it?" I lit up my third cigarette. The prior two have been fucking ineffective at numbing the anger coursing through me. It never truly goes away, no matter what I do. Over the past year, it's become a permanent part of me, and I want nothing more to get rid of it.

He smirks playfully. "Unlike you, I have someone who's got a *fine* ass I can fond over for eternity."

"Touché. My ego is hurt." I exhale the smoke that fades Sebastian from view. But the sharp glare he's sending me tells me he's right here.

He's fucking stubborn. He doesn't know how to leave me alone—not that I want him to. He's the only person who's keeping me from drifting into the darkness. My best friend.

Sebastian clears the smoke with a wave of his hand. "Your ego should be the last thing hurting, considering, your grades are going to fall if you keep up this

act. You can't come to school to *skip* classes and *smoke* until you're high as fuck."
He agitatedly paces in front of me like a mad father.

I sigh. "My grades are fine, and I don't miss classes *that* often."

He arches an eyebrow accusingly. "Really? Because this is the third time this
week and it is only Thursday." Annoyance covers his face. "You're better than
this, Heath. Inhaling poison won't numb anything, and you fucking know
that," he says every word with a finger pointing at me.

*He's so wrong.* Getting high helps to quiet my thoughts and numb my emotions. There is calm for a few minutes, my body stops vibrating with pain and
anger. I crave *that* feeling. That's what makes me smoke.

"Except it *does* help, Bash," I say placidly, the chemicals start to work into my
system.

*There it is.* The temporary calm to my relentless storm.

"One of these days you're going to regret ever doing this. Like me." The
warning slips past his mouth like a bullet, but it doesn't hit me. It never does.

My best friend thinks I'm afraid of death. That's the best thing that could
ever happen to me. I *want* it to happen to me. I've got nothing to gain or lose
from life. Not anymore. Not since last year.

"I won't." Resenting the look of concern on his face, I throw the cigarette on
the ground and smother it with my shoe. It's already done its magic.

Folding his arms over his chest, he joins me by leaning against my car. His gaze
filled with concern. "Now tell me."

"Tell you what?" I rake my fingers through my hair as uneasiness bubbles
under my skin. My hands aren't occupied which makes it hard to hide the
shaking.

"What the fuck is wrong? You don't smoke unless there's a reason. And
there's always a reason. So, tell me what it is or else..."

"Or else what?" I ask.

"I'll delete your Fortnite account." The mischievous glint in his eyes tells me
that he'll do it.

"You wouldn't fucking dare," I hiss. I've spent long hours to reach the 'cham-
pion' rank. I'm so close to becoming 'unreal' which is the last and highest rank.

Sebastian is 'diamond.' Marie, his girlfriend, is higher than him. She is 'elite.' She's better than him, but he doesn't mind.

"Trust me, I would. And hurry up. She'll be coming out any minute now. I can't cater to your grumpy attitude around her."

I steal some air to breathe out my next words. "Dad called."

Two words. They are enough to make Sebastian understand why I'm in a sour mood and why I was smoking. That man gets on my nerves like no one else. And when he tries to control me, it's even more aggravating.

Last week, I got into a fight and broke a guy's nose. He provoked me knowing I don't like it when there's anything said about *her*. Like a pussy he reported to the principal, who then called my father, who then called me. Our six-minute call today ended with me cursing at him, and then hanging up. I was so close to blocking his number—an urge that frequently crosses my mind—but I didn't. Like every single time, I didn't have the fucking guts to do it.

"Oh fuck, man. You okay?" Sebastian asks in a soft tone that irks me. I don't need his pity.

"I'm fine." *I'm not fine. I will never be.*

"What did he say?"

"Usual stuff. Freeze my credit cards, stop my allowance, and ground me. As if he can do any of that. I earn enough to support myself." I look away and catch a glimpse of the girl who bumped into me earlier.

"Look I know—" Sebastian speaks, but I hardly hear a word. All my attention is centered on *that* girl. The pretty girl with her prettiest eyes.

My eyes follow her. Holding a book in front of her she paves her way aimlessly, as if telling the universe to clear her path because she's too busy reading. At this rate, she'll end up bumping into another guy, and he might not be kind enough to help her.

For fuck's sake. She needs to be careful.

"—you could've attended the last three classes. Two of them were free anyway." Sebastian finishes just as she disappears around the corner.

It takes me a minute to construct a reply. "I was pissed, especially after some girl walked into me. I had to collect her papers and folder for her." I shove my hands into my pockets to not reach for another cigarette. I'll get lectured and I'm not in the mood for it.

Sebastian's eyes grow big. "You *helped* her?"

I'm surprised too.

"It wasn't a big deal." I shrug carelessly.

He chuckles. "Yeah right. I see you helping girls every day."

"I don't help anyone."

"Then why did you help her?"

"Because she needed it," I say, running a hand through my hair, wishing this conversation would end soon.

He arches an eyebrow. "You sure about that?"

Sending him a glare, I ask, "Why *else* would I help her?"

"What does she look like?"

*Is he fucking serious?* "Why the fuck are you asking me that?"

He puts a hand on his chest. "Tell me. You're entitled to tell me everything." If it isn't obvious already, my best friend is dramatic.

"Don't bullshit me. In no form of words, I *ever* want to hear you talk about fucking your girlfriend."

Sebastian gasps. "I wanted to talk about *my* feelings."

"Feelings? You told me the seven fucking ways you fuck her to Sunday."

I was traumatized by those gruesome details. No one needs to hear them. Least of all me. I don't need to be reminded of what action he's getting when I get none. Not that I'm looking for sex. My hand does the job just fine. Besides, I might get addicted to it just to fill the emptiness in me and end up with a baby. Thanks fucking not.

"I mentioned how *I* felt while doing it. So, it counts." Sebastian shrugs like it's no big deal that he injected explicit images into my brain.

"Just don't talk about *it* to me ever again," I warn him.

He sighs loudly. "I hope you get so choked up in feelings that you ask *me* about sex and feelings."

*That would never happen.* "Not a fucking chance."

"We'll see." Sending me a smile, he snaps the hair tie on his wrist that his girlfriend gave him for anxiety. I often find him snapping it when he's stressed, but occasionally, he does it out of habit. It helps him to not get lost in his head.

Only someone who knows him from the inside out can tell when it's serious and when it's not. Right now, it's not serious.

"You didn't answer, Heath," Sebastian prods.

"For fuck's sake," I mutter, earning a chuckle from him.

"C'mon tell me. It's not like I'll talk to her or anything."

Strangely that idea lights fire under my skin

"Why the fuck would you do that?" I pin him with a glare.

With a smile he says, "I'll figure it out." That's his catchphrase. Four words that mean trouble.

"Hey guys." Marie, his girlfriend, skips up to him with a grin so bright it could compete with sun. She is a goddamn sunshine. If the light of a thousand suns was trapped in a human form, it'd be Marie Anderson. The five-foot-seven who's got a six-foot-two wrapped around her finger so pathetically I wonder if she's a witch behind all that light.

"That's no way to greet your boyfriend, babe." Sebastian wraps an arm around her waist and pulls her to him. "You know the right thing."

"I do." With a giddy smile, she stands on her tiptoes and kisses him.

One kiss turns into a make-out session. I have to clear my throat to pull them apart. "You'll get plenty of time to continue."

Marie breaks the kiss and turns to me. "Not really. I've got tons of homework. Also, we have a chemistry test next week. I barely understood the topic. The concepts are so weird. Like puzzle pieces scattered and nothing makes sense. I asked Mr. Carlie to explain to me again, but he said he couldn't repeat a whole forty-minute lecture. But I really need the help. Besides—"

"You talk too much, Blondie." After a year I still haven't gotten used to her ramblings. How does she find so many words?

Marie beams. "I know, but Sebastian said it's okay and you don't mind. You just tell me otherwise."

I shoot him a curious look and he pins me with a 'you better agree with that, or I'll kill you' look. For her, he will.

"Of course," I mutter and earn a smile.

Fuck. What's there to smile about in life?

"You could ask someone to help you," Sebastian suggests, caressing her cheek with his knuckles.

She blushes under his touch, and continues, "I did. Mr. Carlie said I should ask Hope. She's extremely smart and offers help. I'll look for her tomorrow."

Hugging her from behind Sebastian kisses Marie's cheek. *Twice.* As if once wasn't enough.

"You'll do great," he assures her with another kiss.

She tilts her head to face him. "I hope so. I don't like it when I score below C. It's not a bad grade, but I feel—"

"It is bad." I put her rambling to stop.

She faces me. "No, it's not. It's an okay grade. Meaning you can improve if you work hard."

I don't know if she's saying it because she believes that, or she's seen the C on my Biology test. The only subject I don't get an A-plus in.

"Heath met a girl." Sebastian changes the topic.

I don't know if I should thank him or punch him.

"*Girl*? Heath met a girl?" Marie looks between us in excitement. She's been waiting for me to meet someone. She hates that I'm a loner.

I do, too. Third wheeling with a couple who are nauseatingly in love isn't fucking fun.

"I'm straight, Blondie," I state in a grave tone.

"You are?" she asks with her hazel eyes peering up at me.

I narrow my eyes. "Why the fuck would you think otherwise?"

"You never talk to girls and hate when they hit on you," she says without skipping a beat.

"That doesn't mean I'm *not* straight."

"Well, I thought... anyway, so, you met a girl. Where did you meet her? What does she look like? What grade is she in? Do you have the same classes? No wait, tell me her name. I wanna know her name. I'll find the rest. But really does she—"

"She bumped into me. That's all that happened."

The hyper-energy whistles out of her like a deflated balloon getting pricked. She leans back into her boyfriend. "So, no talking and exchanging numbers?"

"We didn't go that far." I humor her.

"How far did you go?"

"Nowhere."

"That's a bummer. You should've taken a few steps."

"I stayed put." I'm getting annoyed with this topic. Seriously! So I bumped into a girl and helped her. What's the fucking big deal?

"He helped her by picking up her papers and folder," my best friend adds.

Marie gasps. "Heath helped her!"

Why is it so strange that I helped a girl? I've helped people bef—never mind I haven't. I hate people and do everything to avoid them.

"It wasn't a big deal." I grind my molars in frustration.

"What is she like?" Marie asks just like Sebastian. The two of them are so similar in ways. Like two sides of a coin.

"Pretty," I say without thinking.

*What the fuck? I didn't mean that.*

What the fuck is wrong with my head?

"What?" Marie and Sebastian exclaim, making me grimace. There's no way they missed it.

"Clumsy. I meant clumsy." I correct, as if that'll help my case in any way.

*The damage can't be undone, but good luck with that.*

Marie shakes her head. "No! You said *pretty*. You called her P-R-E-T-T-Y." She spells it out as if my ears didn't hear my mind betraying me. *Fucking traitor.*

"It was a mistake. I meant clumsy, silly girl." Yes. I meant that. Not that other word from any fucking angle.

"No. I heard you." Like her boyfriend, Marie folds her arms and fixes me with a calculated look. "You can't take that back now. It's set in stone."

"I'll set the stone on fire," I say.

"You can't do that. They are made of oxide which is—"

"I'm leaving." Opening the door to my car, I get inside and switch on the engine. Just when my foot is about to press onto the accelerator a knock on the window stops me. I slide it down.

"It's okay, you know," Marie says softly. She tries to sprinkle sunlight on my dark life, but it doesn't work. I'm a black hole that destroys it.

Marie started dating Sebastian last year, and I've spent enough time with her to tolerate her presence. She's my best friend, and I care about her, especially when she's been through so much. I'd protect her from the bad, and ruin anyone who tries to make her miserable—I did do that. I don't show it often. I'm an angry, cold guy, but she knows me enough to not take my tough remarks to heart. She knows I'll be there for her and it's all that matters.

"It was an accident. Nothing more."

"Some accidents are too good to not be coincidences." Her gentle smile doesn't stop me from my crude reply.

"Nothing in my life is a coincidence. Everything is a fucking accident."

I drive out of the school feeling my chest packed with the returning heaviness.

# 3

## HOPE

GETTING READY, I HEAD DOWNSTAIRS. Noise drifts out of the kitchen, which only means one thing. Mom is home. She's a nurse and works five days. She has a four-day on-and-off schedule at one hospital, and an eight-hour shift at another which leaves only two days for her to relax and tend to house chores. I try to do most of them so she has time to rest, but the clean freak in her needs to redo everything.

She started working after Dad left. It's a way for her to bury the worry and grief under work. I often find her staring at their wedding picture and her ring. They got married at a courthouse because my mother's parents didn't like my father. They thought he was a loser with no degree as he dropped out of college in his junior year—for reasons I still don't know. However, Mom stuck by his side because she loved him.

She still cares about him, even though he tried to choke her to death, abused her mentally and physically, and hasn't returned to apologize or make up for his act. Maybe it's a good thing that he hasn't come back because she will take him back, especially after the drunk texts she sent me yesterday about missing him.

All I know about love is what I've read in books. What my parents have is a toxic bitter love. No man should ever hurt a woman, say mean things to her, or call her names. That's not what love is.

"You're home."

She turns around and gives me a weak smile. "I have an hour before I leave."

My mother is a brunette with the same shade of hair color as me. She has those rare gray eyes that lock you under their enchanting gaze the moment you look into them. She's tall and has a svelte figure. Her round face has full pink lips and a small nose. She's stunning. No wonder my father fell for her.

Mom hugs me. I hold onto her tightly. With no one in life, she's the only person I've got.

"Seems like you missed me a lot," she teases.

"Yes, I did." Her schedule allows little time for me to see her.

She pulls back. "Quickly eat those pancakes, and make sure you eat both of them. I don't want you to faint in the hallways again."

"That happened once." I take a seat at the island and start eating.

When I was in middle school, I used to skip breakfast because it'd make me nauseous. One time, I skipped both dinner and breakfast. I was fine in the first two classes. My senses were coordinated, and I was paying attention to everything. By the third class, I had a headache, and my vision blurred. Before lunch break, I fainted in the hallway.

When I got home, Mom spent an hour scolding me. That day I swore to never go to school on an empty stomach. Not only to avoid a lecture from her but also because it's embarrassing. Luckily the hallway was empty, and no one witnessed anything, otherwise, I'd become a joke over something normal.

"I won't be home tonight. I have to do this extra shift," she informs me with a grimace.

The money must be running low again which sucks.

So, I say, "You could go to the city. I bet the pay will be more and you won't have to work so hard."

Mom sighs heavily as she cleans up. "The commute alone would cost me half the paycheck. It's two hours away from here."

I gather the courage to bring up the topic for the hundredth time. "I could work at a diner and help you out."

Anger flashes across her face as she fixes me with a stern look. "Absolutely not! Focus on your studies and work hard because you'll be going to med school. You don't need distractions." The finality in her tone is like thorns being pressed against my skin.

Since I was little, she's decided for me that I'd go to Med School because I'm good at science. I admit I enjoy studying those subjects, but becoming a doctor isn't something I want to do for the rest of my life. I'm uncertain about what path I want to embark on, though I'm certain medicine isn't it. I want to do good, but not by becoming a doctor.

No one talks about how hard it is to choose a career path this early in life when you've experienced nothing. It's this one thing you have to do for the rest of your life. So, you don't want to choose something you hate *and* do it for the rest of your life. What a nightmare that would be.

"I don't think I want to do that." My voice crumbles when she cuts me with her piercing eyes.

"You sound unsure because you don't know. But *I* know, and I'm telling you. Getting into medicine is the right thing for you. You're brilliant. Why waste your intelligence on doing something mediocre?" She sends a pointed glare at my novel. Her disdain for my hobby often pops up in arguments, but since I keep my grades perfect it leaves little room for her to reprimand me. I do not doubt if I messed up one test she'd put a permanent stop to it.

I can't imagine not reading books. They're like oxygen to me. I won't survive without them.

I wish she understood me.

"You're right." I plaster on a fake smile while my heart sinks.

My feelings are invalid. They don't matter.

"I always am, because I'm your mother."

The school is a twenty-minute walk from my house and no bus goes through my neighborhood. There is a bus stop three blocks away and it crosses the route to school. I take it on days when it's raining or I'm not feeling well. With little money in my pocket, I think twice. I could be saving that to buy a book.

I'm afraid it's too late to realize that I'm addicted to books. Is that considered a certified addiction? I hope not. If so, I don't care. I'm not giving it up.

I better not say it at school or people will think of me as a freak.

The white school building appears, and I hurry toward it.

I'm crossing the parking lot when the loud rumble of the engine fills the air. A black luxurious car pulls up. I can't help but stare at it as the sunlight reflects off of it.

The door opens and Heath steps out. Grabbing his backpack, he slings the strap over his shoulder, locks his car, and strides toward the building, ignoring all the eyes that are locked on him. His black T-shirt hides his lean body that is packed with muscle, paired with black jeans and black and white trainers. It's the same attire from yesterday, but he pulls it off effortlessly. I notice a bruise on his left cheek that needs care.

Heath stops, turns his head, and looks straight at me. His intense gaze disrupts the rhythm of my heart, making it skip a few beats.

My cheeks burn with heat. I quickly avert my gaze to my book—to not look like a creep who was staring at him because he's handsome.

God. Twice now. I need to find other things—guys—to look at. However, I don't think I'll find a guy as impressively good-looking as him.

After a minute, I take a peek and he's nowhere to be found.

Since yesterday, I haven't been able to kick him out of my mind. There's so little known about him around the school. People have all these strange theories about him that sound baffling. Some say he's in a criminal gang, while others think he lives on the streets and steals money. All of it sounds absurd. Seriously, who comes up with this nonsense?

I force myself to not do anything about my curiosity. It'll only get me into trouble. Besides, I have to stay focused and get into med school. If I don't, my mother will rain hell on me.

Pushing the doors, I study the hallway that's buzzing with groups of friends.

I'm reminded once again that I have to go to classes alone. I pace like a ghost in the school. Nobody talks to me unless they need my help—which I don't mind, I rather enjoy helping others—but I do feel used because my help is all they need, not me. It's almost like being a tissue. Used then discarded.

I'm alone but that doesn't mean I like being lonely. Living with my thoughts all the time makes me go crazy, especially when they're dark.

Sometimes I think I have no friends because I'm the problem. It makes me sad. Well, it's not like I haven't tried. In the past, I've talked to my class-mates—despite my social anxiety—but they seemed uninterested. I talked about novels, and they thought they were boring. I talked about music, and they commented on my music taste. Everything I like isn't something they like.

I feel out of place here.

Miss Sheila elegantly saunters into the classroom and a hush falls over. She has a skinny figure and always ties her blonde hair in a tight bun, which makes her go hairless from the front of her hairline, but I don't think she cares about it.

Everyone is listening to her, but I'm drawing stick figures in my notebook. I never understand a word she teaches. She makes math complicated.

In the middle of the lecture, Heath comes in. Everyone stares at him, but he appears unbothered.

Miss Sheila glares at him. "So nice of you to join my class. Perhaps next time you can try to arrive ten minutes early."

Instead of answering her, he searches the classroom. When his eyes meet mine, he starts walking in my direction.

*Oh my God.*

*He's coming my way.*

*Look away.*

I sit straight and focus on my doodles, acting nonchalant. Of course, I'm not bothered by him—

The chair next to me screeches against the floor, and he plops down to my left, despite the fact there are many vacant seats.

I'm bothered.

A few heads turn to notice the scene, mostly girls. Under their sharp looks, I want to pull over the cloak of invisibility and sneak out of the classroom into the library. If only the Harry Potter universe was real. I'm pretty sure I'd be a muggle, but that's beside the point. In my head on my eleventh birthday, I get the letter and go to Hogwarts. I became a wizard and have the most amazing friends.

Plucking courage from the depths of me, I sneak a glance at the guy who caused this commotion. He's already watching me, with a pen dancing between his fingers as he plays with it.

'I'm not sure if you noticed, but there are plenty of other seats.' If I were brave I'd say those words to him. But I'm not.

The class continues. I try to ignore him, that's easier said than done.

His presence consumes the tiny space between us.

You can't ignore a guy like him. Everything about him demands attention. I'm sure he's used to it. It must be nice to not be invisible like me.

Maybe I do have the cloak of invisibility.

Lunch usually goes by with me reading in the library. Being surrounded by books makes me feel less lonely.

When there's an emptiness inside of you, you try to fill it with other things. If it could be filled by you it wouldn't be there in the first place.

My emptiness is loneliness. I fill it with books. The company of fictional characters, and the bonds that feel real. That explains why I'm always attached to a book. I don't want to be alone or be empty.

I'm walking toward the library when Heath comes around the corner and I bump into him. My hand latches onto his T-shirt to not fall back, but he's quick. Grabbing my arm, he steadies me.

Deja vu hits me.

I curse at myself and immediately let go of him.

"Do you have a habit of bumping into people?" he says in a rough voice that caresses my skin like gravel.

I meet his curious stare. "You came out of nowhere."

From this close, I study his injuries. There's a bruise on his cheek and a minor scratch near his hairline.

"Yes, I appeared out of fucking thin air," he drawls out in a dry tone.

"It looked like it," I say, finding humor in his words.

The intense look on his face doesn't slip away.

*Awful joke. Got it.*

Lifting his hand, he runs his fingers through his hair. His scraped knuckles catch my attention next. From the looks of it, he didn't apply anything to them which isn't good.

Heath walks past me, and I follow him.

"Wait." I hold my book tightly.

*I know he's going to reject my idea.*

*Why am I even suggesting it?*

*Because you like to help people.*

He tilts his head back with an annoyed expression. "What?"

I point to his knuckles, and he follows my gaze. "I can wrap them up for you to prevent any infection."

"Not fucking needed," he grumbles.

"I just want to help."

He narrows his eyes on me. "I don't *need* your fucking help." He flexes his knuckles and doesn't even grimace, but I do. I can imagine the burning sensation permeating under his skin.

A hard look contorts his face, and his body stands tall with tension. He resembles a wall that can stand anything you'd throw at it. So, if I argue with him he might not let me do it, but if I soften him a little bit maybe he will.

I smile. "You've saved me twice now and also helped me. I want to return the favor."

Something about him makes me want to help him, even though he won't take it.

Before he can change his mind, I rush out. "Let me help you, and I'll try to not walk into you again."

"I don't think you're capable of it." He gazes at me with his blue eyes. For a second, I get lost in them and miss what he says.

"Of what?" I ask, feeling like an idiot.

*Don't look into his eyes.*

"Not walking into me."

A smile tugs on my lips. "Both times it was an accident."

An emotion flashes through his eyes.

Looking away from me, he runs a hand through his hair. When he speaks, the muscles in his jaw clench. "Will you stay away from me if I let you help me?"

"If that's what you want," I say in a quiet voice.

# 4

## HEATH

SHE WALKS BEFORE ME, AND I FOLLOW HER—WHICH IS SOMETHING NEW. I don't follow anyone. I do what I want.

*Fuck.* I mutter under my breath.

She leads me to the infirmary and glances my way numerous times as if I'll ditch her. I'm pretty sure if I did, she'd hunt me down and take care of the wounds that don't even hurt.

When you're hurting all the fucking time, you get used to the pain.

She moves around the infirmary with a level of confidence and finds me a stool.

"Sit," she commands. I glare at her but obey.

She opens cabinets and retrieves supplies while mumbling words to herself. It's interesting to watch her in her element.

While she does that, I take my time to look at her.

Her dark brown hair falls on her shoulders in waves and reaches a few inches below her chest. She has light brown eyes that balance the line between honey and whiskey. A shade entirely new, that I'm sure didn't even exist before her. I run my eyes along her body, she's tall and has a skinny figure. Her face is bony with a sharp jawline and hollow cheeks. She has a button nose, full lips, and cheeks that blush in a pretty shade.

She's beautiful.

I called her pretty in front of my friends, but it was a fucking mistake. I should've said beautiful. A million times over, only then it'd come close to how I see her.

Taking a seat on the other stool, she looks at me as her hands proceed in my direction.

My first instinct is to pull away, but I let her hands hold mine and put them in her lap. Her touch is delicate. She's cautious to not hurt me.

Getting some cotton, she cleans off the blood. As her fingers work on me, I feel her warm skin.

Tiny sparks race up my arm as our skins touch. This is fucking odd.

Her eyes are concentrated on the task while mine study every contour and curve of her face.

She glances up at me. "Can I ask you something?"

"What is it?"

"How did you get these?"

I want to ignore her question and let her believe the outrageous rumors about me. Sooner or later, she'd know I'm no good and she should stay miles away from me. Just a week ago I broke someone's nose.

"In a fight," I answer vaguely, hiding the actual truth that no one here knows.

"Mr. Huxley hates when there are fights in school." That's such a good girl thing for her to say. From the looks of it, she surely is one.

Our principal favors the rich kids and feeds on money. Wealthy families make donations to Bellmare High School to keep up their facade of being good, and to avoid taxes. One of those families is my parents, who also donate millions and are the reason why I haven't gotten expelled no matter how hard I try. The more I want to piss off Dad, the less the universe lets me.

However, all the fights I've been in are because those guys pushed me to the limit. They made crude comments about the people I care about, and I'm not one to take it like a fucking saint. If you come for my people I will bury you alive.

"It wasn't at school," I tell her.

She looks up at me. From this close, I stare into her brown eyes. *Fuck, they're hands down the prettiest eyes I've ever seen.*

"Oh, that's..." she clears her throat while avoiding my gaze.

"What?"

"Nothing." She brushes off the topic and it pisses me off.

Why I want to know her thoughts is beyond me.

"I hate when people do that," I snap.

"Do what?"

"Leave me hanging. If you start something you fucking finish it."

Tucking a few strands of hair behind her ear, she puts away the cotton. "*'That's strange. How else would you end up in a fight?'* I wanted to say that." A lovely shade of pink paints her pale skin.

Fuck. That blush of hers is something else.

Taking some ointment on the tip of her finger, she applies it to my scrapes. A hiss leaves my lips as my skin burns under the antiseptic.

"I'm so sorry." She blows air that quickly carries off the flaring sensation. "Is it better now?"

I nod, too stunned to say anything. Never in my life have I ever been tongue-tied before.

What the fuck is happening to me?

"I fight at an underground boxing ring." That's it. I'm not telling her anymore about myself.

"That sounds super illegal and super dangerous."

A chuckle scratches my throat, I conceal with a cough. *For fuck's sake. Now she's humoring me.*

"It is."

The pretty girl wraps my hands in a gauze and ties the knot. She does it so meticulously as if she's done it before which once again piques my interest.

When she lifts her head, our faces get close. I hear the hitch in her breath. *Brown eyes. Just as pretty as her.*

Clearing her throat, she applies a bit of ointment to the scratch on my head. Then stands up and puts away the things.

"What's your name?" I assess my hands to avoid looking into her eyes.

"Hope."

Wait, is it the same girl Marie was talking about?

*Hope.* I repeat the name a few times in my head until it's ingrained in my memory.

"Thanks," I mumble, not wanting her to hear me, but the way her lips split in a smile I know she did.

"Anytime." Hope picks up her book.

"Have you done this before?" I hate that I appear interested in her. I don't know why I want to know about her.

"No. But I spend my free time either in the library or here. Nurse Anna taught me basic stuff." The more she speaks the more I want to listen to her.

"So, this is your first time doing it?" I inch closer to her like a moth to a flame.

"Yes. Before I just watched her." She checks the time on her phone. "I should go."

I arch an eyebrow. "Aren't you gonna ask my name?"

"Everyone knows who you are," she mumbles.

Anger burns up my body as I think about how people perceive me when they know nothing but shit. "Actually, they fucking don't. My name *can't* exactly tell what kind of person I am."

She nods. "Do you have friends?"

"Yes." Two annoying idiots who make my life insufferable, but I wouldn't want it any other way.

"As long as they know who you *really* are. That's all that matters."

Her words hit me in the chest.

Sebastian and Marie know plenty about me. Enough to look at my face and understand what state of mind I'm in. They know me through and through. If it weren't for them I wouldn't be here. They tolerated me when I was going through hell. Pain that turned to poison and infected them. I've never been good with emotions. I don't know how to talk about my feelings and be vulnerable. All I know is how to hide them behind my cold words and tough act. Still, they stayed. They didn't leave my side when I needed support more than ever.

"You got friends?" I ask.

"It's just me." She shrugs carelessly as if it doesn't matter to her, but the sadness is evident on her face.

Before I can say anything more, she says, "What's your—"

The bell rings.

She shakes her head. "I have a class. Bye."

In a hurry, she exits the room, leaving me in a pool of thoughts.

"Woah. What's that?" Sebastian flops down on the seat next to me and stares at my wrapped knuckles with rapt interest.

"That's called a bandage," I reply in a dry tone.

Sending me a glare, he takes out his textbook. "I know that asshole. I'm wondering *how* it got there. Did Paul haul your ass to the chair and tie it himself?"

Paul is my trainer. A thirty-six-year-old man who's taught me every single thing about boxing and how to channel my anger into something useful. Much to his dismay, boxing doesn't help me with grief. If anything, I fight because I enjoy it.

"No." I direct my attention to the whiteboard wishing for Mr. Nathan, our business teacher, to enter the classroom so I can save myself from this conversation.

"Then?"

"It doesn't matter."

He frowns and stares at me with his inquisitive green eyes, more than eager to get to the depth of what I'm hiding.

Fuck it.

"Tell me," he asks again.

"I said it doesn't fucking matter."

"It does. Just tell me. Wait, are your hands okay? Don't tell me you're hiding broken bones underneath that." Scraping his chair against the floor, he gets closer and tries to take my hand.

I resist the urge to punch him in the face.

"Back off, asshole," I warn him, inching my hands away from him. "What the fuck is wrong with you?"

Sebastian points his finger at me. "Wrong with me? You're the one *not* telling me stuff."

Inhaling air, I try to exhale the irritation out of me.

"Look, Bash, I'm okay," I say, with as much calm as I can summon, which is very little.

He scoots away from his chair and stares at my hands. "Something doesn't feel right."

"I'm fine," I say.

"Now something is *definitely* not right."

I curse at Mr. Nathan for being late. Where the fuck is he?

"You know I'm here for you. If you need anything, tell me."

*Fuck.* I don't want him to worry about me. He already has plenty on his plate. Also, he has a habit of taking care of others before him. He never shares what's bothering him because he doesn't want to burden anyone with his baggage. After the shit show that happened last year, Marie made him understand that it's okay to ask for help. Though, it'll take years for him to let that sink in, much like how it's taken years for him to depend on himself only.

To put his mind at ease, I come clean. "*That* girl did it. Now stop asking me questions."

I pull up my phone and scroll through emails as I check up on my online businesses and avoid facing him.

The phone is snatched out of my hold.

Suppressing a groan, I look at him.

Sebastian looks content now that he has my undivided attention. "Are we talking about the pretty girl? The one you bumped into?"

Fuck. I hate my life. Why did I say anything in the first place?

*It was the truth. She is really pretty.*

I stay silent, but Sebastian doesn't.

"It was her."

I ignore him.

"You are a dickhead."

I want to punch myself.

"Heath, I'm talking—"

This is it.

"Yes, it was her, now shut up!" I snap and a few heads turn our way.

"Jeez, no need to yell at me. I was just asking," he says nonchalantly as if he didn't short-circuit my brain.

"Don't ask." It's questioning how hot and bothered I am because of her. Sebastian and Marie will be on my ass if they know half the things rolling in my head regarding her.

"I'm still wondering how it happened."

I have no clue myself. I was on my way to the rooftop to smoke. I wanted to smother the sick feeling curling in my chest when she collided with me. Again. I had no intention of seeing her, let alone talking to her. Somehow, one thing led to another, and I had a full conversation with her, which for some strange reason I didn't mind.

"She walked into me and—"

"Again?" He smirks. I glare at him. "Fine, continue. I won't say shit."

"She saw my knuckles and offered to help to pay me back. I only agreed because I wanted her to leave me alone. At the infirmary she did this, we talked a bit, and then she left."

"What did you talk about?"

"Stuff. Now that I've told you, stop pestering me."

"You left out a great deal. But it's fine. At least you're finally going to get some pussy."

"It's not like that." I grind my teeth.

He smiles. "Isn't it? You called her pretty, let her take care of your hands, and also talked to her—you never talk to anyone. So I believe there is *something* there."

"It was an accident. I didn't chase her or anything."

He leans back in his chair. "You remember what Marie said? Maybe it wasn't an accident."

"It was. I'm not getting any fucking pussy, because I'm not interested."

He sighs heavily. "God help your virgin dick."

Taking my pen, I throw it right at his face and he shrieks like a girl. "Dammit, you asshole."

"Stop mocking my virginity," I say.

"I'm your best friend. I'm supposed to help you." He puts my pen into his bag.

Letting out a quiet groan, I flex my knuckles to relieve the tension. "If I wanted to fuck, I would. I don't need your fucking help."

"You do know that a little practice won't hurt."

My lips curl up in a smirk. "Only my *dick* is virgin, not my *mind*. I know how sex works."

"You're right." Scrolling on my phone screen he adds, "Your browser history is quite un-virgin."

Moving over, I yank my phone out of his hand and slip it into my bag. "You need to fuck—"

The class starts before I can throw a train of curses at Sebastian.

When I look at him, he chuckles. I give him the middle finger.

# 5

## HOPE

"HOPE HANSON. IT'S YOU, RIGHT?" A CHEERY VOICE GREETS M, AS I COLLECT MY BOOKS FROM THE LOCKER ON WEDNESDAY MORNING.

For a moment, I freeze. Not sure if this is actually happening.

*Someone's talking to me?*

She knows my name which probably means she's here for my help.

For a moment I thought she was here for different reasons. *Stupid me.*

I face her. "It's me."

The girl standing in front of me is an inch shorter than me. She has high cheekbones, hazel eyes, a heart-shaped face, a button nose, and pink lips. Her golden hair is pulled back in a high ponytail, leaving her beautiful face on display. Seriously, she is beautiful.

"Hi," I say with a smile, despite the tornado of thoughts orbiting my brain.

Her grin widens. "Hey! I'm Marie. I'm in the same grade as you. We also share a few classes. Mr. Carlie said you can help me with the test that's coming up next week." She explains in a sweet voice.

There's a certain warmth to her. Like being under the sun in winter.

"Yeah, sure." My voice comes out shaky, which isn't a good first impression. I clear my throat and add, "Meet me in the library after third period, if you have it free."

A frown takes over her delicate features. "Isn't it P.E.?"

One class I try to avoid at every chance. I'm not an athletic person and don't like any sports. Books are the only thing I like, and I'd rather spend a forty-five-minute class reading.

"Yes, but I heard Miss Jameson is absent today, so it'll be free." People are always loud in the hallway, firing information like a news channel.

Marie nods. "It works for me."

"Okay then." I look past her in the crowded hallway. No one pays attention to both of us. We might as well be invisible to them. I get why people avoid me. I'm the nerd, the girl who's always reading books and getting A's. I don't talk and avoid human interaction as much as I can. I'm also shy, awkward, and quiet. All the things people probably don't like.

Marie, on the other hand, she's someone who'll fit perfectly in the popular group. I'm surprised she doesn't already have girls flocking behind her. She is friendly and also beautiful.

"What class do you have right now?" Marie breaks my chain of thoughts.

I don't speak a lot, but my mind is always having full-on conversations. I swear, it's not creepy. I just think a lot. Sometimes so much that I want to escape it and find quiet somewhere.

I take out my phone to check my schedule. "English."

Disappointment flickers through her hazel eyes. "That's a bummer. I have computer science. It's my elective." She explains while I think I've never seen her around school. She said we share classes, but since my eyes are always fixed on a book I might've missed her.

The second bell rings and the hallway gets crowded.

"I'll see you during third period at the library." With that, I leave.

Marie is right on time as she walks into the library. I take in her outfit; a white top and a pink skirt, paired with white sneakers that are decorated with art. Cherry earrings, a gold heart necklace, and beady bracelets complete her look. There is so much color and fashion, which suits her.

She nears me with a dazzling smile.

"Hi." Her smile is her best accessory.

I quickly close the novel. "Hi."

She puts down her bag and takes out a notebook. Her eyes land on my novel. "You read."

I nod.

"That's great. I don't read books, because coding is my thing. I'm always learning and experimenting with it for hours."

"You must be great at it."

She blushes and shakes her head. "My teacher says I'm brilliant, but really I play a lot with it. Coding seems easy to me. I want to do it for the rest of my life. And since you read books, I bet you'd join a publishing house or something. I don't know much, so please don't mind me if I'm wrong."

Mom's words echo in my head. Instantly my heart drops into my stomach in despair.

I answer in a neutral tone, hiding my pain, because what good is there to show it? "It's fine, I don't mind. There are various things you can do besides joining a publishing house. But I won't be able to, because I'm going to med school."

A gasp leaves her mouth. "Med school? That's exciting *and* terrifying."

I agree with the terrifying part. Studying for so many years just to do long shifts. I don't like how absent Mom is from home. Days go by before I get to see her. We spend little to no time with each other. All we have are messages and calls that are too short. I don't want the same to happen to me. I want to do things, read books, and visit places like Hogwarts—the film set in England. I won't be able to do any of that if I become a nurse or doctor. I'll be bound to the hospitals and patients. While it's a noble profession that saves lives, I just don't think it's for me—a high-strung person who gets anxious and lives inside her head.

"I'm good at science," I repeat Mom's words.

Marie beams. "No wonder you are. Mr. Carlie mentioned you've never gotten below A-plus. That's amazing!" She sighs heavily. "Here I am flunking that class when it's the last time I have to study it." She leans back into the chair. "I'm not an overachiever, but I like getting good grades, and it's not because of my parents. They're cool with anything, as long as I'm happy."

It must be good to not feel pressured to follow a certain path and do whatever *you* want to do.

"I can make you some maps that'll help you memorize information." I change the topic to slide away the gloominess weighing on my chest

She nods enthusiastically. "Yes! That would be helpful. Also, I talk a lot, so stop me if I ramble."

*It's the most anyone has ever talked to me.*

I offer her a genuine smile. "I don't mind." I mean it.

For the next forty minutes, I explain the topic to her and fill pages with summarized notes and web diagrams. Once I'm done, we solve a few questions together, and she answers most of them correctly. I help her when she needs a hint, but she does well on her own. I realize her weakness lies in a lack of understanding, and not learning.

Marie slumps back and lets out a dramatic sigh. "All my brain cells are dead."

A laugh bubbles out of me. A sound I haven't heard in a while.

"Thank you for the help," she says softly.

I smile. "You're welcome."

With dread, I check the time. The bell is about to ring any second now. Part of me doesn't want it to. For the first time, I'm having fun with someone, even if it's a study session. She's the only one who's actually talked to me and made me laugh. Usually, I work with people in silence. They need my notes and I... well, I earn the satisfaction that I helped someone. Nothing more, nothing less.

Marie's phone pings. She sees the screen and scowls. It's strange to see her like this.

"I hate how rude Heath is," she mutters under her breath.

Wait. What?

My mood changes drastically.

*It can't be him.*

At the mere mention of his name my heart races.

I can't help being curious, and blurt out, "You mean Heath Travon?"

Marie quickly looks at me and studies me, then says, "Yes."

I hold my breath as I ask, "You–you know him?"

She nods slowly. "Yes. He's one of my best friends. Well, he'd say otherwise, so don't believe him. I'm dating his best friend, Sebastian Hale, so Heath hangs out with us."

"Oh." This is what he meant when he said he has friends.

"But how do *you* know him?" She sounds protective as she eyes me skeptically.

"I bandaged his knuckles. You must've seen them. They were bad," I explain nervously under her scrutinizing gaze.

Marie's eyebrows pinch until something clicks. A grin stretches tugs on her lips, and she cups her mouth with both hands, then points at me. "It's *you*. The pretty girl."

*The pretty girl. What?*

*Heath can't possibly mean that about me.*

*I'm the clumsy girl who bumped into him twice. Yes, that's more like it.*

I shake my head. "I don't think that's me." There's no way Heath said that about me. He was mixed levels of grumpy and annoyed and acted like he couldn't wait to get away from me.

"Holy fucking shit. I can't believe it," she whispers.

Picking up her phone, she furiously types on it, then switches it off.

Leaning over the table, she locks her gaze on me. "What happened yesterday, tell me all about it. Don't skip."

"Uh..." Heath didn't mention not saying anything to anyone, so I think I can talk about it. Also, Marie said she's his best friend—which I find hard to believe, I mean they are opposites—and they must hang out, meaning she should've already known about it.

"You don't have to if you don't want to," she adds in a sympathetic tone.

"Nothing happened," I say.

"You said you tended to his knuckles. How did that happen?"

"I bumped into him, and he saved me, so in exchange, I suggested taking care of his knuckles. He agreed, and I wrapped them up. That's it."

Her eyes widen. "Heath *never* lets anyone touch him, let alone take care of him."

I can see that happening. However, he was pretty compliant with me. He said not a single word. Also, he wasn't cold and angry like he was with everyone else at school.

I purse my lips as those thoughts roam my head. "He did that because I agreed to stay away from him." That was the whole point.

"Wait what?!" Marie exclaims in surprise. Others turn to glare at her.

Standing up, she rounds the table and sits next to me. In a hushed voice she asks, "He said that?"

"Yes."

She curses. "Don't mind him. He's a good guy."

I know nothing about the guy to form an opinion, but if someone like Marie is his friend, and says he's a good guy, then it must be true.

"Do you have friends?"

"No." My hands fidget with each other. God, I'm nervous.

"Would you be my friend? I hang out with two guys. Although, it's fun to be around them. I want female company. And no girl at school likes me enough to be my friend."

My eyes widen.

*She can't be serious.*

I find it so hard to believe. Marie is nice and sweet, even funny at times. It baffles me that she doesn't have an army of friends already.

*Would you be my friend?* It's the first time someone has asked me this question. From kindergarten to this day, no one bothered to like me enough to be my friend. I always thought something was wrong with me. That there was a fault I couldn't see, but others did that repelled them from me. The only reason they approached me was because they were compelled to—they needed the grade, and I could help them get it. But they didn't want anything more from me.

My chest packs with air. I'm overwhelmed with a ton of feelings. A history of flashbacks rolls in front of me. All those times I was alone and everyone had someone.

It's such a simple question, but it holds so much meaning to it.

My voice cracks. "I'd love to, if it's okay with you."

I'm sixteen, and this is the first time I'm making a friend.

Life is full of surprises. One moment you're alone, the next you aren't.

Marie tears up, and giddiness brightens her face. Like me, she's been alone too. I can see it on her, and she can see it on me. It's not difficult to read someone who's like you.

We've both been alone all this time.

Until now.

Marie nods, without a doubt in her eyes. "I'm more than sure about it."

Giving me her phone, I save my number, and she sends a text. "I'll send you my schedule and we can be together in classes."

Just like that a friendship forms.

I take the bus because of cramps. I just know my period is due, and this time it'll be painful.

For me, some months are easy, but some are so excruciatingly painful that I can barely step down from bed.

Mom gave me birth control pills to help with the pain, but my skin started breaking out and I felt nauseous. I couldn't deal with throwing up and seeing my face covered in pimples—I got rid of them by applying a ton of products and it's only now that I have clear skin. I'll take pain over bad skin every day.

When I get home, I find the front door ajar. And no, the lock isn't broken.

I stop in my tracks.

Mom won't leave the front door open. No one besides us has the key, except for one person. Alex Hanson, my father, who can't be here. He walked out on us three months ago.

With caution, I enter the house. The eerie quietness makes my heart beat erratically fast.

I tiptoe into the living room and find no sign of him.

Maneuvering into the kitchen, I gasp at the state it is in. All the cabinets are open. Pots, containers, spoons, forks, and food boxes are strewn on the floor as if a wild raccoon paid a visit. The refrigerator top is a mess— Mom puts emergency cash there.

Taking a stool, I stand on it and search behind the candle box. The money's gone. All of it. There's not a single penny.

I hop down the stool and sit on it as I try to think. There's no way Dad took it. He knows why we put it there; in case we have to go to the hospital, buy a meal when there's no food or fare for a cab.

I take my phone out to call Mom but a knock on the door startles me.

Taking a deep breath, I go outside, and find Nadina, our seventy-year-old next-door neighbor, standing with the help of her cane. For a moment, I'm in shock to see her at my doorstep.

Giving me a smile she breaks the silence. "Hey, dear. You got a minute?" she asks, wrinkles surfacing with each word.

I hold onto the door frame and pull myself together. "Yes. Would you like to come in?"

"No, I have to go back and babysit my grandchild. I came over to tell you, I saw your father earlier this afternoon. He was so drunk he was missing steps and talking to himself. I was going to help him but thought otherwise when I saw how wasted he was. I heard stuff breaking and then he left in a car."

I stay mute, not knowing what to say to her. The woman has never talked to me before, but the way she's looking at me tells me that she knows everything about us. She must've heard everything over the years. After all, walls are thin.

My cheeks burn in embarrassment.

I never wanted anyone to know what happened in my home. My parents went from love to fighting with each other. Affection changed into abuse. The things I heard and saw still haunt me.

I tightly hold the door to not shut it and hide in my room.

"If you need anything I'm only a few steps away," Nadina offers, despite no reply.

My stomach curls in uneasiness. She knows stuff I want to erase from her memory—and mine.

"Thank you." I avoid eye contact and stare at her strawberry earrings and the orange gown she's wearing. She also has bracelets and necklaces on her, and I just know each piece has a story attached to it. Looking at her, I wish I met my grandparents. I wonder what they're like. Both of my parents never mention them or even talk to them, so I have no idea if they're even alive or not.

"No problem, dear. Just remember you're not alone." With a smile, she steps down the porch and looks back at me. "I'm glad you weren't home. That man was not in the state to walk, let alone talk to his daughter."

Something tells me this won't be the last time my father shows up.

# 6

## HEATH

THUNDERING DOWN THE STAIRS, I CROSS THE HALLWAY WHEN THE OPEN DOOR CATCHES MY EYE AND MAKES ME STOP. The room belongs to my sister—dead sister.

My feet stay glued to the floor as I stare at the purple walls with floral murals drawn over them. The bed is unmade from when she last stepped out of it. Even the little things on the nightstand—her phone, Hello Kitty keychain, journal, and purple glitter pen—rest there messily, exactly where she left them. Her study table with books, pens, and a laptop in the same condition.

This is the only place in the mansion where time has frozen, and nothing has changed. While everything else and everyone else has moved on. *Not me*. I'm right where she left me. Both mentally and emotionally.

I think about stepping inside, sitting on the floor, and looking at the photo frame that has our picture. A selfie from when we were getting ready for the fair a few years ago. I took it and sent it to her, not knowing that it'd become one of my favorite pictures after she'd been ripped away from me. I was oblivious to the pain, despair, and loss waiting for me down the years.

If only I had known sooner. Maybe I could've helped her in some way. Saved her perhaps.

Regrets are heavy to live with. They have the power to pull you down and drown you.

Every day, I feel like I'm one second away from drowning. That darkness that awaits me deep in the ocean scares me, but someday, I'll have to meet it.

The laughter pouring out of the living room draws me away from my dark thoughts—each one consists of me blaming myself and rolling in guilt.

Closing the door, I lean my head against it and take a long breath.

*Fuck. I miss her. I miss her so fucking much.*

I join the two people who live more at my house than theirs. They even have a room here.

Sebastian sees me first. "Glad you're finally here. Tell Marie Fortnite is the greatest game of all time."

Before I can say a word, Marie jumps in. "Wait until you play Elden Ring or GTA five. Those are pretty great."

I sit with them on the sofa and take a slice of pizza that I didn't order, but I'm sure they paid for it using my card. "I agree with Blondie. Those games are something else."

Marie beams since I sided with her. "See? Heath is versatile. You can't just play one game and say it's the greatest of all time. You have to try a lot of something to pick one top favorite. Also, open-world games are difficult. I once spent a week doing a GTA mission because I kept getting killed. Elden Ring is ugh! Don't get me started on it. It's on another level. That game is the complicated complicate of complicating." She hums. "That was a tongue twister, but you get the point. It is—"

"We get it. Now shut up, Blondie," I grumble at Marie.

With a sigh, she says, "All right."

"I need to buy a PlayStation." Sebastian pipes up.

"I can get you one," Marie replies excitedly.

Marie's father is a successful businessman, and her mother is a brilliant lawyer. Both of them have made enough money to live off of it for years.

Marie comes from money. So, Sebastian felt uneasy around her at the start, but now he's gotten used to the fact. Besides, she never lets him feel little. She's always trying to help him. If it were up to her he'd be living in one of the houses uptown, the residence area of the affluent families where she and I live.

"Don't you dare! You know I hate when you surprise me with things I want," Sebastian warns her softly.

"Isn't that the point of the surprise?" She kisses his cheek and my best friend sighs.

"Just don't. Get me a T-shirt but *not* a five-hundred-dollar PlayStation."

"Okay." The way she agrees quickly is a dead giveaway that she's going to get it for him.

Before Sebastian can argue with her, she directs her attention to me. "I met Hope today. She's so nice. And you were right. She's pretty. Like *really* pretty."

My heart drops right into my stomach. "You met her?" I croak out.

She nods excitedly. "Remember Mr. Carlie told me to get help from someone named Hope? Turns out she was that Hope. *Your* Hope."

"She's not mine. What is fucking wrong with you two?" I scowl at both of them.

Marie shrugs. "Nothing. You're the one getting antsy—which you shouldn't, I *just* mentioned her."

"Then don't fucking mention her. She's no one."

Her expression turns fierce. "She's *my friend* now and she's *someone*. So, you better be good to her. I don't want—"

"What do you mean friend?" I'm so fucking confused.

"—want you to drive her away. She's my friend. Like you and I."

"I'm *not* your friend. I tolerate you, Blondie." I tell her but we both know it's not true. She's my best friend. I don't want to feed into that because she'll make a great deal out of it. Like, bring out balloons and cake to celebrate friend anniversaries.

Marie ignores my remark and continues, "Hope will be hanging out with us now. It'll be so cool. Now, I can have sleepovers and girl's nights doing girl stuff. I've never had one of those before." She slumps against Sebastian who wraps his arms around her and kisses her neck.

"If someone doesn't hang out with you, then *they're* the ones missing out. You're an amazing girl, Mare. The absolute best." He consoles her as he further pulls her to him. If he could, he'd fuse her into his body to protect her and never let her feel alone like she once did.

Those days are gone now. She has a boyfriend and a best friend. She isn't on her own anymore.

"I know that. It's just hard to believe when no one wants to be my friend and invite me to parties or sleepovers."

Sebastian bends down his head and murmurs something into her ear that makes her body relax and grows a smile on her face.

It's interesting to watch these two interact. They share a bond I've never seen before. They're in love but they're also best friends.

"When Hope said she doesn't have any friends, it made me so sad. I know what that feels like." Facing him, she says, "Can I invite her to our next hang out? Please!" Marie pleads with Sebastian who smiles at her.

"Of course you can. Right Heath?" He pins *me* with a hard stare.

The dickhead had to throw me under the bus.

"Sure," I mutter and eat the fifth slice of pizza.

"I can't wait," Marie chirps.

Sebastian kisses her. He truly loves that girl, even though she's too bright for him. Well, she's too bright for anyone.

Taking the remote, I put on Lucifer season two episode one. Last weekend the three of us were hanging out—much like now—and started the show. Whenever we're at my place we pick a show and watch it together. Before it'd be Sebastian and I, but when Marie joined she shifted our taste, but we don't mind. I mean, I wouldn't watch One Tree Hill and Friends on my own, but together it becomes bearable.

Marie hurries to the switchboard and turns off the lights. I shake my head as she walks past me grinning like she won a lottery.

Like always, she cuddles up next to Sebastian, while I sit at the other end of the sofa like a loner. Not that I mind. I like being alone. But I don't like being lonely. My best friends don't make me feel lonely.

The family dynamic on the show makes me think about the relationship with my parents. *Nonexistent.* One word that perfectly sums up my current status with them.

After my sister's death, my parents left me in this mansion and ran off to Canada to take care of their businesses. Sweeping away the huge loss and pain like dust pushed under the rug. The one week they stayed here, after the funeral, was filled with fights and arguments. I was a walking volcano bursting and firing at anyone or anything, that included my parents, especially my father. He and I argued over everything. I know we were both mourning, but it all wouldn't have happened if he were here with us and played the parental role for once in his goddamn life.

Now that Emery, my sister, is gone Dad is reminded of his duties. Every day he calls me, and every day I ignore his call. It's a cycle that starts and ends the same each day. My mother and I haven't talked for months. To be honest, I don't want to talk to her. She abandoned me in a huge mansion with money and staff as if anything could suffice for the care or attention a child needs from a mother.

I've grown up in this mansion on my own. My parents left me here when I was one and my sister was a few months old. In this maze of ten bedrooms, nine bathrooms, a kitchen, a living room, and plenty more rooms, I've lived my entire life. From childhood to teenage years. My sister and I have spent more than a decade here. While this place has everything a person could wish for, I resent it. If it weren't for Emery, I would've moved out. I would live in a dump, anywhere but here. Her room and our memories here are the only two things she left me with. I want to be as close to them as I can be.

"Heath, you okay?" Sebastian asks me as he rubs Marie's arm who's dozing off on his chest. It's past ten. We've been watching the show for the past two hours.

"I'm fine." My throat grows thick with my lie. I refuse to burden him with my issues. He can't or won't understand what it feels like to lose a sibling who is—or was—your best friend.

Never in my wildest dreams, I'd wish anyone to go through what I did.

Every single day is a battle, every memory is a weapon, and guilt is the enemy.

"Sir, dinner is ready," Derek announces. He's the butler of the mansion. He enters the room dressed in a black suit that he never takes off. Since I was a kid, I've never seen him in informal clothes.

"For fuck's sake, it's Heath. I've told you a thousand times." I narrow my eyes on him.

Derek shakes his head. "Sorry, sir. It's a habit."

"Dinner's ready?" Marie mumbles, rubbing her eyes and looking at Derek. "Oh hey, Derek. How are you? What's for dinner?"

"Good evening ma'am. I'm well. Miss Kelly made chicken casserole and meatloaf."

"Not again," I mutter.

"If you want something else, sir, we can make it," Derek suggests quickly.

"It's fine." I nod, feeling like dick for saying that out loud.

Once Derek leaves, Marie turns to me. "You're such a jerk."

"Eat that dish ten times a month and you'd say the same." I get rid of the empty pizza boxes and dirty glasses.

"I definitely won't. I love food."

The three of us sit in the dining room where the meal is already laid out hot and ready. The rectangular long table is meant to serve twenty people, but it's always just the three of us—or Emery and me before she passed away.

Kelly, who's the chef and the housekeeper, brings over the leftovers on Marie's request.

We all start eating, when Marie says, "You're a princess."

I choke on my bite. "Excuse me?"

She waves around her hand. "You live in a mansion, have a staff for almost everything, and also have the attitude."

"That was good, Marie." Sebastian snickers and I kick him under the table.

I glare at her. "I'm not a princess *and* I don't have an attitude," I grumble.

Marie pins me with an accusing gaze. "You do. We should name you something. Princess—"

"I swear to God I'll—"

"Or not," Marie mutters with a mouthful of pasta from last night.

According to Marie, I get the royal treatment. What she doesn't know is that money doesn't fill the gap in my chest from the loss of my sister. We tried everything that we could to help her. Every expensive treatment that we could avail, we did. But money didn't save her. Since then—her—I hate money. It's the reason why my parents live in Canada, the reason why my sister couldn't be saved, and the reason why I feel hollow for every second of my life. I hate that she died and left me alone here.

*What the fuck am I supposed to do without her?*

*We did everything together and now it's just me.*

*My best friend is gone.*

*My sister is gone.*

It's been more than a year, but the pain is still alive. There's not a day I don't think about her and not mourn her. She lives in my mind and heart. I never want her to die. Even when it comes to holding onto this black hole called grief. It eats me and kills me, but I won't ever let it go. I don't want to forget her or get over her death. I want to keep remembering her. I want to hold onto this grief tightly that still binds me to her. The only connection that's left.

"Hope told me she bandaged your knuckles. They were that bad?" Marie asks worriedly.

Sebastian looks at me and smirks, probably recalling our conversation from yesterday.

"They're fine." I shut down the topic. But it's Marie, she never shuts up.

"Please tell me you didn't break any bones."

Sebastian bursts out laughing. I grip my spoon tightly.

"Am I missing something here?" Marie asks Sebastian.

"No, babe. You aren't missing anything," he says, trying not to laugh, but fails miserably.

She frowns. "I kinda feel like it. He did break his bones, didn't he?" She worries too much. I'm happy that she'll have Hope now and will leave me the fuck alone.

"I'm right fucking here," I grit out.

"I think we should head to the ER and get him checked out."

Sebastian nods. "You're right. While we're at it we should also pick up condoms on our way." The wink he sends my way makes me want to strangle him.

"Condoms? Why would he need them?" She looks at me in question.

"He *will* need them," Sebastian presses.

Marie grins. "Oh, you're going to hook up with someone?"

For fuck's sake.

"I'm not. Don't fucking listen to him." I glare at my best friend who's chuckling.

"Sebastian's right. It's better to be safe," Marie argues.

"For fuck's sake." I stuff my mouth with food.

"You won't be saying that when you have a baby," Marie adds.

"Marie Anderson, stop fucking talking."

"It's Marie Lia Anderson, and okay."

I breathe in some air to calm myself down.

"Should we get a lube, too?" Sebastian asks.

I throw my spoon at him, but he misses at the last second. "Both of you get out of here!"

Sebastian laughs while Marie looks between us.

"Damn, you're extra grumpy today," she says absentmindedly.

"I'm always like this." I run a hand through my hair and grimace when my knuckles get scratched. I shouldn't have removed the bandage, but it kept reminding me of Hope. I didn't like that.

# 7

## HOPE

LYING IN BED, I'M READING ANOTHER ROMANCE BOOK WITH THE DYSTOPIAN TROPE. The genre I mostly pick because I love the adventure, the thrill, and finding love in the middle of the chaos. You're on your own, but you also have someone who'd be by your side no matter what.

Rolling over to my left side, I scoot closer to the lamp I bought yesterday, so I can read late at night without brightening up my entire room.

My phone lights up with a text message.

**Marie: Sit with me at lunch tomorrow. I want to introduce you to my boyfriend.**

I quickly write back.

**Hope: Sure, if you're okay with it.**
**Marie: I'm 1000000000% sure.**

Smiling at her text, I switch off my phone.

Marie and I have become good friends in the past week. One moment she was a stranger to me, and now she's sending me links to TV show quizzes to see which character we are. Most of them I haven't watched, which she noted in her to-do list for us. I've also learned she's a music enthusiast. Our messages are filled with song recommendations she thinks I'll love. I listened to them and immediately fell in love with them. In a few days, she's tied this bond between us that feels real, strong, and important. I can't imagine how I went through life without it. Friendship is such an amazing thing. I used to read about it and now I get to experience it.

I don't realize I'm grinning until my cheeks begin to hurt.

*It's stupid, but I'm happy.*

The door unlocks downstairs, and the thud reverberates in the house. I remember I locked the door.

Sitting up in worry, I swing my legs down and slip into my shoes.

The quieter I descend the stairs, the louder the noise gets in the kitchen, which confuses me. Mom can't be in the kitchen at eleven p.m. She has a night shift and if there was any change she'd let me know. I have no texts from her.

When I enter the kitchen, my spine straightens into a rod.

Dad is rummaging through cabinets, his movements frantic as he searches for something. His hands are shaking, and he's mumbling words I can't hear.

For a minute I stand and stare at him. Fear, shock, and sadness have paralyzed me.

It took him three months to show up. Three months that went by without fights. Three months that were safe.

I'm not happy that he's back. I'm terrified. So afraid of what he'll do now.

Growing up he never attacked me. Maybe because I'd freeze on the spot and wouldn't move a muscle.

There's flight and fight instinct, but there's also a third one; freeze. That was how my body reacted when he'd hurt Mom, and I'd watch it happen. Guilt always visited me later when he'd stop, and she'd ask me to go to my room so she could cry and tend to her injuries. I'd lay in bed and think about it; how I failed her, how I didn't fight him, how pathetic I was.

I still think a lot about those moments *and* him.

My throat is dry, but I push forward the word. "Dad?"

At the sound of my voice, he turns around. Red eyes, messy hair, and weeks' worth of stubble . The plaid shirt he's wearing has torn buttons and is ripped from places, his rugged jeans have patches of dust, and his boots are covered with dirt leaving a trail of footsteps on the floor.

Three months later he looks like he's been through hell. But why is he here? It's obvious he needs money, and from the looks of it, he needs it for alcohol.

"Where is the money?" Those are his first words to me. No greeting or anything. Not that I expected it. We've never been close.

"There's no money. Mom has yet to get her paycheck." I hold my book tightly. I feel safe knowing I have it in my hands.

Dad rakes his shaky fingers through his hair. "She always keeps some here." He points to the refrigerator. "I took the last stash, there should be more."

Since Dad is six foot he easily reaches the top of the old appliance and looks for money that isn't there. He knocks down a few items and anxiously runs his hands through his hair.

Worry clings to my heart at seeing him like that. "Dad, maybe you should sit down. I can get you—"

"Shut up! Shut the hell up. I need a bottle and there's no money," he yells at me, then walks in my direction. Gripping my shoulder, he brings me closer to him. "You must have some for lunch."

What?

He's asking me for the money that I need for school. He can't possibly be that desperate.

"N-no I don't. I swear." Fear wraps around me like chains. Instead of Mom, it's me.

If I had money I'd give it to him, just so he gets away from me.

I freeze in his hold. My stomach tightens in a string of knots that pull my muscles together. It's a dreadful, strange feeling that I used to experience three months ago and now it's back.

"You're lying," he hisses, and I smell his stinking breath. He's drunk.

Panic takes over me like a storm. I start trembling as he glares down at me with his fuming brown eyes that I inherited from him. They hold no softness for me.

"You're a shitty liar." His big hand wraps around my neck and he backs me up against the counter. He pushes me and I knock over the dirty pots and dishes near the sink.

"Give me the fucking money." He squeezes my throat.

I try to pry his hand off my neck, but he's so much stronger than me. His grip closes around my windpipe and interrupts my breathing.

Shaking my head, I croak out the words in mere whispers, "I-I don't have it. Please."

*Please let me go.*

*Don't hurt me like you used to hurt Mom.*

*This isn't that night. He won't kill me.*

*Why is it happening?*

Dark eyes bore into mine. I try to find my father in them, but I don't. This man isn't the father who never abused me. Right now, he's the man who's looking for a bottle and is tuned out.

I always imagined what I'd do if he returned; how things would change, how time and space would give him some perspective, how he'd become a better man and treat Mom better.

This isn't how I imagined it. He's even worse than before.

I didn't want to believe Nadina, but now, seeing him with my own eyes I'm having a hard time trying to grasp the truth.

My hands clamp around his wrist, and I try to get him off me.

My eyes fill with tears and blur my sight. But I keep trying.

"Please," I beg.

Something snaps in him, and he lets go of me. He stands there and watches me, then storms out of the house.

*Oh my God.*

*What just happened?*

In disbelief, I sit down on the floor. My heart is beating so loud.

Opening my mouth, I attempt to inhale oxygen, but I get nothing. It's like smoke is everywhere or all the air has been sucked out of the room, and there's a vacuum around me; something I only studied in Physics but never thought I'd experience in real life.

*What just happened?*

Wiping my tears away, I stand up by holding the edge of the counter, then lean against it.

Dad never touched me before. He always lashed out at Mom but never directed violence toward me. The most I got from him was a mean glare.

When I watched him choke her that night three months ago, I realized, perhaps, he was filled with darkness. Darkness that love can't erase. Whatever he was dealing with at work, he projected it at home on her but never me.

*What just happened?*

My mind rewinds the last ten minutes trying to piece everything together. Nothing makes sense.

My neck hurts, and my throat feels like it's been bruised from the inside.

Picking up the pots I put them in the sink to wash them. One of the dishes is broken, so I throw away the pieces. Turning on the tap I wash everything and then tidy the kitchen. I do everything on autopilot.

A while later, I lie in my bed and pull the covers over me. My novel is long forgotten.

One part of my brain tells me to warn Mom, but the other side screams not to. She'll take him back and he's in no state to return. He's even worse than when he left.

*He attacked me.*

Some sick part of me was happy that he left. We were free of him.

I loved my father when I was very little, but when he started hitting Mom, that love disappeared. Tonight, he tried to choke me, and my heart is just filled with hatred and anger for him.

Is he going to come back?

*I hope not.*

The next day, I go to school wearing a red turtleneck to cover the bruises. I don't own makeup because school, home, and the library are the only places I go to.

Luckily, the weather is a bit chilly today, despite it being August. So, wearing a turtleneck might not make me look like a weirdo. I wear my hair down hoping to hide the marks that peek out from under the collar. The last thing I want is for someone to see them and ask me questions—not that anyone would. Only more gossip will circle the school, and I don't want to be a headline.

Opening my locker I'm about to gather textbooks when—

"Hey!" Marie chirps.

Startled, I drop my novel on the floor, as my pulse shoots up.

*What is happening to me?*

My hands shake a little, so I brush them against my black jeans, repeatedly.

*Gosh.*

*She'll think I'm insane.*

*We've only been friends for a week.*

*What is wrong with me?*

*Fix it.*

Marie picks up the book and gives me a worried look. "Are you okay?"

*No.*

*She knows something is up with me.*

*Damage control. Now!*

Smacking on a smile I say, "I'm fine. Just surprised to see you."

*That sounds reasonable.*

Marie grins.

Together we walk down the hallway as she tells me about her boyfriend. "So, my boyfriend is Sebastian. We've been together since last year. We were friends first, but then he asked me out. I swear he's the best guy in the world. You'd like him right away, he's super nice. Heath is too."

I arch an eyebrow and Marie sighs.

"Heath is questionable, but he's good. He's nice to people once he knows them."

"It's fine. He told me to stay away from him."

"Oh no! Don't listen to him." She flies her hand in the air. "He says a lot of meaningless stuff like that. When you know him you learn he's just full of bullshit."

I smile at her, liking how she knows her friend so well. I didn't know Heath had friends. He mostly wanders alone and ignores anyone who approaches him. That doesn't show he has friends.

We stop by the classroom. Others brush past us without paying attention to either of us. We might as well be invisible to them, or irrelevant.

Marie's hazel eyes light up. "We'll be sitting together at lunch. You'll see how less of an asshole he is."

"He's famous around school for being a..." The curse gets lost in my mouth.

"Asshole. Yes, he is. A big one. A six feet and two inches tall asshole."

I shake my head in amusement. "You guys will be in the cafeteria?"

"Yes."

*It's happening.*

*I'll be sitting with actual people in the cafeteria for the first time.*

*I won't be in the library reading my book.*

"Are you sure it'd be okay—"

"One thousand percent," she says quickly, diminishing all my self-doubts.

"Okay then. I'll see you at lunch."

Marie giggles. "I'm seeing you in the third period, Hope."

With that, she disappears into the crowd of students.

# 8

## HEATH

MARIE STANDS IN FRONT OF ME WITH A SHARP LOOK ON HER FACE. She's a couple of inches shorter than me, but it never matters to her.

"Don't skip lunch. Hope is sitting with us, and I want us all to be friends with her," she tells me in a stern tone. She's taking this friendship to heart. I remember she used to cry because no one wanted to be friends with her, and she just wanted a friend. Something so simple but seemed impossible. All because of a mean trio who bullied her, spread rumors about her and made sure no one befriended her. Thank fuck they got expelled.

I let out an exasperated sigh. "You can't just bring someone into the group, Blondie."

Putting her hands on her hips, she glares at me. "I can *and* I will."

"You're stubborn."

"A little." I arch an eyebrow. "Fine, a little too much."

"Indeed."

Marie picks up her white bag with sunflowers on it that Sebastian painted. It took him a whole weekend, but he was dedicated because he wanted to make her happy. She changes stuff frequently, but the bag is the one thing she uses every day.

"I'm going to find a table. You guys get food." She runs into the building leaving me with Sebastian.

Sebastian chuckles. "Damn. She's so excited that she forgot to kiss me."

"She'll dump your ass soon."

He looks unshaken. "She won't. She doesn't give up on people. And she loves me."

That she does with her entire sunshine being.

I start walking toward my car. "Didn't hear the last bit."

He laughs as he follows me.

I drive to the diner we usually eat at. Sebastian rattles off the order and then pays for it. Two minutes later we sit in the parking lot in wait.

"So…"

I turn on the AC. "So what?"

"Mare told me that you told Hope to stay away from you. What's up with that?"

"Nothing," I say rather too quickly.

*Fuck.*

A smirk curls on his lips. "I see."

He's thrilled with the idea that he can tease me about a girl. God knows I did the same.

"What?" Rolling down the window, I pluck out a cigarette from the pack and light it up.

"You're afraid of catching feelings for her."

That won't ever fucking happen.

I've never gotten serious with a girl. They don't interest me. Sure, I can make out for a bit, but that's about it. I've never taken things beyond kissing. Not because I'm not attracted to girls or anything. It's just my mind doesn't rest when our lips are moving, and my hands are roaming their body. I'm supposed to feel something, fall into lust, or whatever, but I crave to be alone.

I exhale the smoke out of the window. "You're delusional, Bash."

"Call me whatever you want. Deep down, you know I'm right."

I flicker down the ashes and spare him a glance. "Quite contrary to your belief, I won't fall in love with her. She's not my type at all."

He scoffs. "No girl is your type."

"Precisely. I'm not interested in girls."

Confusion flickers across his face. "Is it boys then? Because that would be okay too."

That comment pushes me off the edge and anger makes my blood hot.

He knows I'm not gay. If I were, he'd be the first to know. However, it pisses me off that Marie and he both think there's a chance I'm gay because I don't mingle with girls.

"Shut the fuck up."

He gestures to the cigarette. "This isn't right for your health. You can stop now. You're still young."

"You're one to talk."

He looks out of the window. "It'll get you killed."

"Why else do you think I do it?"

Sebastian has listened to my suicidal talk enough to not fight with me on the matter. Nothing he says will change my mind or the way I feel about life.

People live life, I'm getting pushed through it, because I can't stay stuck at one point in life. Just because I wake up every day doesn't mean I want to.

There's a cocktail of emotions inside of me. Anger, frustration, guilt, sadness, and what fucking else. I can't tell someone what I'm actually feeling. All I know is, I'm not fucking fine. Not even close to it. I'm miserable because of what happened last year. I can't get over the death of my sister.

"How's your mother?" I ask, instead.

"She isn't doing drugs." That's as far as he'd answer that question.

He stares at me, and I already know what he's going to ask. "Did your dad call?"

"Yeah. I had a match, so I missed it." That man doesn't give up. He's been insistently calling me every day, for God knows what. He knows I hate him, but that doesn't stop him from making me hate him even more. Parents are so fucking aggravating.

"I have a match tonight," he offers.

Sebastian and I both fight at an underground boxing ring where bets are placed, and drugs are exchanged every night. That place is a nutshell of gangs, drug dealers, and criminals as free as birds. Every single person there is on a payroll. To fight in that place, you have to be extremely good and also dangerous enough to survive. Every junkie and addict from the town is also there for their next fix. Armed men walk around like it's a playground and weapons are sold like candies. At the right price, you can get anything.

After Emery's death, I was filled with rage and guilt. Enough to drown in it and still swim back up on the surface. It happened to me every single day. Like an endless loop.

Sitting at home, I dwelled on the past and her, more than I was supposed to—I still do—and let myself be gripped with so many emotions that every day felt like I was dying. Until I found that place and learned how to box.

Boxing is a violent game. I get hurt often, but the physical pain numbs the emotional pain. For a little while I'm not drowning. I can breathe something other than fucking emotions. I breathe air.

"You wanna spar after school?" I suggest.

He grins. "You want to get your ass kicked?"

Stubbing the finished cigarette, I throw it away, and then face him. "I kick your ass every single time."

A chuckle bursts out of him. "Shut up. I've knocked you down once."

"Only once," I remind him.

"You're so fucking so cocky. I have no idea why we are friends."

I put the car into motion. "Sure, blame it on me."

"Your ego needs to be put in check."

After getting the bags, I drive us back to school.

Together we walk toward the table situated at the end of the cafeteria hall. Heads turn in our direction, and I sense girls staring at me, but I ignore them. Seriously! I'm so fucking tired of being gawked at. There are plenty of other guys to fuck. I don't want to be bothered. Besides, it's not like I'll fuck them anyway. Sex is the last thing on my mind.

"Hey." Sebastian kisses Marie and sits next to her.

I take the seat next to Hope and find her fidgeting with her hands under the table.

*Look at me.* I don't like anyone else to look at me, but it's different with her. I'm about to ask her what's wrong when—

"Sorry, we got carried away." Marie tames her hair and glances at Sebastian who smiles at her.

"Is there a time when you two aren't fucking?" These two and their PDA remind me that I'd never have that in life. I would never find someone who'd understand me and choose to stay with me, after seeing how dark I am. I naturally repel everyone—which is partly my fault, I admit.

"When we're at your place." Marie hands everyone a burger and also pulls out the fries.

I roll my eyes. "I heard you in the guest room the other day."

"It was *one* kiss," she defends, blushing hard while Sebastian coughs.

"Sounded more than one kiss to me."

"Shut up you pervert." She is red like a brick.

"And the time you were—"

"Stop it, man." Sebastian kicks me under the table.

"Fine."

Marie takes a bite of her burger and says, "What's the plan for Friday?"

"I think we decided to go ice skating," Sebastian answers quickly, then looks at Hope. "Would you like to come with us?"

Before I can open my mouth, Marie jumps in. "You definitely should, Hope. It'll be so much fun. We can get a nice dinner afterward and a karaoke night. Or we can hit the arcade and—"

"Babe, let her think." Sebastian kisses Marie's cheek and rubs her back.

"Sorry, I got too excited. I'm crazy like that."

Sebastian kisses her temple. "It's fine. I love *your* crazy."

I feel sick to my stomach with being a 24/7 witness to the romance between my best friends. I'd say get a room, but it's me who regrets it later because I can hear them.

Sebastian faces Hope and asks again, "What do you say, Hope? Tag along with us. It'll be fun."

Marie clasps her hands together vibrating with her fucking *sunshine energy.* "Yes, please. That way Heath won't be alone. He hates when he's alone."

What the actual fuck?

She did not just fucking say that.

For fuck's sake.

"I don't *hate* being alone," I retort.

"Yes, you do. You told me."

"I did not." I grind my teeth, hating that she's right.

"You did."

"I was drunk." I shouldn't have drunk Vodka. What was I thinking?

"But you swore. And you can't lie when you swear."

"I was out of my senses."

"More like feelings."

"Tell me again, why were you there when I was drunk?" I ask, growing irritated.

"Because I'm your other best friend." She grins proudly.

I scowl and run my fingers through my hair. "I'm not your best friend. I tolerate you."

"That's what true friendship is."

Ignoring her, I check on Hope, but she refuses to look at me. She's also stiff like a board beside me which confuses the fuck out of me.

Is my proximity bothering her?

Is she feeling sick?

What the fuck is it?

*I want to fucking know it.*

For the past ten minutes, Marie hasn't stopped chattering, and I've noticed the lack of response from Hope. She hasn't agreed to come to the ice rink, either.

Something is wrong with her. I can feel it in my bones. I also know it isn't my place to intervene. She's got Marie to talk to. Besides, I told her myself that I wanted her to stay away from me because deep down I know she's trouble for me. Since that day in the hallway, I haven't been able to forget her. She's been at the forefront of my brain. My thoughts keep revolving around her. Her lonely, brown eyes make me weak, strange, and more. I don't know what it is. But I know there is *something*.

Hope is better off without me. I'm no good. I'm rude, angry, and frustrated. No sane girl would want to be anywhere near me.

*Why am I even thinking that?*

"Hope, you're coming, right?" Marie shares her fries with her.

Hope twiddles her fingers in her lap. The movements get hasty as if she's nervous.

"Um, sure. Friday it is, right?" Her voice comes out breathy as she stares at her.

Marie nods. "Yes. I'll even pick you up and drop you off."

"You don't have to," she rushes.

"It's no big deal."

Hope nods. She doesn't touch her burger and instead stares at the table. She wants to make herself disappear. I know that feeling all too well, but I hate that she's feeling it.

When school ends, I go up to the rooftop and smoke a couple of cigarettes. Once I feel at peace, I get to the empty parking lot.

I spot Hope sitting on the entrance stairs. She's holding her head in one hand and staring at her phone.

My first instinct is to call Marie and tell her to get here, but then I remember she left with Sebastian to buy groceries for his home. I swear the two of them are like a married couple.

I spare Hope another glance. *That girl isn't your problem. Keep walking.*

I turn around only for my heart to scream at me to do the right thing.

*For fuck's sake.* Muttering a few more curses, I stride in her direction and climb up the stairs.

The sound of my footsteps gets her attention, and she lifts her head. "Hi." She smiles shyly.

I stand rigid and ask in a rough tone, "Why are you here so late?" I'm agitated with myself for caring when I shouldn't, but I can't help it.

She grimaces as if she's in pain. "I have a headache, and I missed the bus, so I'm booking a cab."

My eyes dart to her phone which is cracked from the top side, then back at her.

"I'm going to grab something for lunch. You can come with me, I'll drop you off." I lie.

*I hate myself.*

Hope checks her phone. "I'm not hungry and my ride is an hour away."

"What?" My voice raises. She winces.

*Fucking dammit.*

"You should go." She avoids my stare.

I want to leave.

I want to stay away from her.

But I just can't.

"Come with me." I jog down the stairs. When I look back she's staring at me with a frown.

The sun rays fall on her and the red turtleneck she's wearing gives *me* sweat. How is she not feeling hot?

Her dark brown hair falls like waves over her front and reaches a few inches below her breasts—*do not focus on them*—and is curly at the ends. The black jeans hug her legs and accentuate her thighs—*stop looking at those curves*—and she has blue Converse on.

"You don't have to do this," Hope says, holding a novel to her chest as she stands up and follows me to my car.

"I know." For some strange reason, I want to.

"Then why—"

I hold the door open for her. She gives me a puzzled look but gets inside. With a deep breath, I get in the driver's seat.

We stop at a streetlight, and I turn on the AC. There's no way she isn't hot under that fucking turtleneck.

"What do you want to eat?" I ask, drumming my fingers on the steering wheel because I'm fucking restless. I've never had someone in my car before. It's my personal space that's now invaded by her.

"Um..." she fidgets with her fingers and refuses to look at me.

Yeah. I don't fucking like it when that happens.

I want her to *always* look at me.

"I'm hungry, so hurry up," I grumble, annoyed with myself. This girl is throwing me off my orbit.

Her cheeks turn red. "I don't have money, so I'll just eat at home."

I stiffen, not knowing how to say the right thing.

"It's just food," I reply nonchalantly.

She meets my gaze. "Food that *you'd* pay for."

"I wouldn't let you pay anyway. It's not the right thing."

"So, you're a gentleman?" Her tone is playful which is better than her shy replies.

*Am I a gentleman?* I don't know. I've never been with a girl before. All I've done is kissing and that doesn't really require mannerism. Also, no girl has ever sat in my car before. It's always been me. Precisely why there isn't any garbage lying around on the floor and stuff splattered on the seats.

I bought this car, a black McLaren 600LT, with my trust fund money—to piss off Dad—two years ago.

When Marie, Sebastian, and I hang out, we either take his jeep or her car. I don't want them exchanging body fluids on my damn seats. As long as they are alive I want to keep my car Sebastian-Marie-sex-free.

Titling my head, I stare at her. "Only for you."

Her cheeks further redden, but she smiles. *Fuck it's a good smile.* The kind that says we have an inside joke.

Moving forward, I turn on the music. Chase Atlantic blasts in high volume. I quickly turn it down.

I glance at Hope.

Our eyes connect and something clicks. It's like the world stops moving.

A car horn blares from behind us and breaks the spell.

I find the light green. Taking a hard right, I speed through the street and pull up into the drive-thru of a local diner I usually eat at.

The woman asks for our order. Hope chooses a small burger. I roll my eyes and order a big one for her with fries and a few nuggets, and then rattle off my order: a chicken wings bucket, diet coke, and extra-large fries.

I pay using my credit card. Then drive down to the next station where the line is fucking long, so we wait.

"You didn't have to do that," Hope whispers.

I face her. "Do what?" I know exactly what she's talking about.

"Order so many things for me."

"It's done now."

She rushes out. "I'll pay you back."

I glare at her. "No, you won't. When you're with me, you're not going to pay for anything."

"Like ever?" she asks with a cute frown.

*Cute? What the fuck is wrong with me?*

"Like ever," I finalize.

I need to put distance between us. Because sitting here with her is suffocating my damn heart. It's beating rapidly. I never knew it could beat this fast.

Picking up the order from the station, I park a few blocks away. Handing her food, I get mine and start eating.

From the corner of my eyes, I watch her open the wrap of the burger and take a bite. I feel content that she's eating when she skipped lunch. I swear, she's so fucking skinny it makes me worried.

"Do you have any siblings?" I ask, out of nowhere.

"No."

It must be so fucking lonely for her to be on her own all the time. I have Marie and Sebastian who are always at my place, but she's got no one.

No wonder why her lonely eyes haunt me.

"What do you do all day?"

She waves the novel at me. "I read books."

"You don't get bored?" My eyebrows pinch.

She laughs. "*Never*. It's so interesting to read about other people's lives. When you open the pages you know nothing about them, but as you keep flipping you get to know the characters so well that by the end it feels like you've known them your entire life. It's almost like you have a friend."

That's the most she's ever talked. It makes me want to listen to her more.

"Huh?" I act clueless so she can elaborate.

She straightens and her eyes fill with fire I haven't seen in her before. "Stand-alone books are great. But when you read a series, it's the best thing ever. If there are six or more books, you feel like those characters are your best friends. How you've gone without them in life makes you question everything. Closing the last page of the last book is the most excruciating experience ever but also so heartwarming and just perfect."

A silly smile takes over her face and her eyes brighten with the light she's always missing.

I realize something.

Hope looks dreamy when she talks about books—the look is pure magic.

"What genre do you read?"

Just like that, the light goes away, and intense blush covers her cheeks. Hiding her eyes from me, she takes a mouthful bite.

I find that amusing and lean back in my seat. *Fascinating*.

"Mostly romance," she replies.

"So, you're a hopeless romantic?"

"I am."

Before I can ask more, she crumples the wrap and puts it in the paper bag. Taking out the fries she starts on them and gazes at me with curiosity. "What about you? Do you have any siblings?"

Suddenly the chicken wings taste like shit in my mouth.

How am I supposed to answer that simple question? I don't.

I shut down. Like I always do.

She stares at me but doesn't say anything. She waits, waits, and waits. She doesn't push me by speaking a single word. I find that both endearing and irritating. Former because she's not pressing me, latter because she's waiting for me to answer, and I don't want to.

I dust myself off. "It's late, I should drop you off."

"Okay."

We put away the bags in a nearby trash can.

The more I drive, the more the tension grows in the car. My hands tighten around the steering wheel as I try to stay calm and not get flooded with emotional pain. The mere mention of my dead sister pushes me into a state of grave sadness. My whole body gets paralyzed, and my mind fills with memories and glimpses of her.

Despite a year getting past, I still get triggered. I haven't learned how to cope with grief.

I don't want to let go of her. I have something to hold onto, even if it's destroying me from the inside out. It's better than moving on and forgetting her, having nothing of hers to keep with me anymore.

"Do you have water?" Hope breaks my thoughts.

I point to the divider between us. "It's here."

I stop the car so she can drink.

"You should put your bag in the back," I suggest as she struggles to balance it on her lap. It looks heavy.

Taking her bag, she leans over to put it in the back, when her turtleneck pulls down and I see bruises on her neck.

What the actual fuck?

Did someone choke her? It sure looks like it.

Rage washes over me and I can't control myself.

"Why are there marks on your neck?" My voice is cold like ice.

Hope freezes. "W-what?"

"*Marks*. Why are they on your neck?" I ask again, my hand curls around the steering wheel as anger seizes my entire arm.

She gulps then says, "Oh...it's nothing."

"It doesn't look like fucking nothing to me."

"It's not what it looks like."

I glare at her. "What does *that* mean?"

"I'm fine."

Two words. The same I use all the fucking time because I can't explain, and no one will understand.

I narrow my eyes on her. "I *saw* them. Did someone choke you? Is someone hurting—"

"It's late. I want to go home." She pulls the collar up to her chin. Her fingers quiver, and her chest is moving rapidly as if air can't be contained inside her.

I'm making her anxious, which is something I *never* want to do. I want her to be comfortable with me, like I am with her. But I can't ignore the fact that someone put their hands on her. *I just fucking can't.*

She won't tell me and if I push her she might end up crying. I don't know how to deal with crying girls.

However, something tells me if she cries, I'll calm her down anyway.

"Address," I ask in a low tone.

She rambles off her street and looks out of the window.

The playfulness from earlier is gone—all because of me. I asked her something she clearly didn't want to talk about.

How the fuck am I supposed to overlook that? I know what I saw. Those were fucking finger marks. Someone tried to choke her.

My heart drops in my stomach when I think there could be more under her turtleneck. Someone did worse than—

*Shut the fuck up. You need to back off.* The warning blinks in red light with sirens blaring in my ears.

I need to back off. She is nothing to me.

I pull up to her block and drive down until she tells me to stop.

Grabbing her bag, she escapes my car like I'll kill her if she spends an extra second with me.

*I'd never hurt her.* If only she knew.

Hurrying up the stairs, she slips inside the house without looking at me.

I stay outside and listen to the silence, just to make sure she's okay. Then drive to my house.

# 9

## HOPE

CLOSING MY EYES, I LET OUT A HEAVY SIGH.

I can't believe Heath saw the marks. I wore the turtleneck to hide them, and he still ended up seeing them.

He was livid. His eyes darkened and the lines in his face hardened. He looked like he was one step away from strangling someone to death. All because he saw the marks on my neck.

I wonder what he'd do if I told—

*I can't.*

I barely know the guy.

Also, I don't want anyone to know. No one would understand. I'm still trying to wrap my mind around it myself.

I hate that I messed up. He saw the marks and now he's suspicious. I don't know how to answer him the next time he asks me questions.

I'm scared, confused, and in constant fear that Dad will return, and things will be widely different. This time, I'll be his target.

I still can't believe he was here. I thought he was gone for good.

Stepping into the bathroom, I stand in front of the mirror and pull down the collar. The marks are there. Tears build up in my eyes and I clutch my stomach to swallow a gut-wrenching sob.

Five minutes later, I wipe my cheeks, wash my face, and tie my hair in a messy bun.

*Breakdown time is over.*

*I won't cry anymore.*

I walk back into my room when something catches my eye. I retrieve the box from under my bed. It contains stuff that reminds me of the days when life was good. I look at my baby pictures, some with my dad and some with my mom. They looked happy when they had me.

I pick up Harry Potter and the Philosopher's Stone, my first-ever paperback. My mother bought it for my eighth birthday after weeks of me begging her. I remember I read the book in a day, then read it all over again. I pleaded with her to buy me the second book, but she didn't. She never did, and I stopped asking. I didn't have money to buy the rest of the series myself and I didn't read it by lending it from the library because I wanted to own it.

Putting the book aside, I look at the bead bracelets. When I was little I used to make them. Since I was alone all the time, I had nothing better to do. My mother bought me a set that had many colorful beads, strings, and little instruments to build a bracelet. Every night, I'd get to work after dinner and stay up until I'd be done.

I pick up the bracelets and look at the size of them. They won't fit me now, but still pull a smile out of me.

The longer I play with the beads, the more my head chants an idea that sounds insane like Hogwarts-existing-in-real-life insane.

Saturday is cleaning day. Mom will scrub the floors, do laundry, and clean every inch of the house. She doesn't rest for a second and keeps herself busy until she's exhausted and passes out. It doesn't take a genius to figure out that it's her way of mourning the sadness that came with Dad's departure. I can't understand how she misses a man like him. All he ever did was hurt her.

It's late in the afternoon when I find her in the living room, dusting the corners to get rid of the cobwebs. She's dressed in an old T-shirt that belongs to Dad and faded jeans. Once she's done, she hops down from the stool. She pauses when she sees their wedding picture covered in dust. Picking it up, she cleans it. Her eyes fill with tears and her hand trembles over the glass.

"Mom?"

She sniffles and wipes away the tears.

"I'm fine, honey." She puts it down, but her gaze doesn't avert from it. "I wish he'd come back. I miss him so much."

My heart skips a few beats.

*This* is the reason why I can't tell her about Dad. If she knew, she'd want him to move back, despite what happened the last time. In the past three months, it's all she's talked about. She thinks he's changed and won't hurt her anymore, because he loves her and will get better for her.

Love isn't abuse. Love isn't tears. Love isn't betrayal.

Books have taught me that love is supposed to be this magical, pure, sweet thing that makes you feel safe. *It* wants you to be better. *It* protects you and keeps you safe. I know it's all fictional and made-up, but even if it is, that's the kind of love I wish for myself. What my parents have isn't the love I want.

Mom composes herself and turns to me. "I want to talk to you about something."

"What is it?"

"Did you take the money from the top of the refrigerator?"

Memories from that evening reappear. I refuse to sink into that sadness.

It's been three days, and the marks have faded completely, but not the event from my mind.

"Yes. I wanted to buy a few books." There's no way I'm telling her about Dad.

She shakes her head in disappointment. "Honey, you *can't* buy books. You know how expensive they are. Why do you need to buy them when you can borrow from the library using your library card?"

A lump grows and constricts my throat. Mom knows I love books, but she always refrains me from buying them and gives me this exact speech every single time.

As a reader, I want to *own* books. Enjoy the feeling of holding a paperback and annotating it. But I can't because I can't afford it.

"I'm sorry," I mumble.

Mom sighs and rubs her temple. "It was our emergency stack."

I fidget with my fingers, something I do when I'm anxious.

"I didn't mean to." I try not to look at her as she glares at me.

"Your focus should be on studies, not on stupid books that are unrealistic and just a waste of time and money." She raises her voice.

My stomach ties in a series of knots pulling my guts together in a painful tug. I shift on my feet as tears prick my eyes. I refuse to cry anymore. I've shed plenty of tears in the past three nights.

"I'm looking out for you, Hope." She softens her tone.

"I know." First, she gives me a blow then rubs it with a balm.

She clears her throat. "Why don't you help me with lunch? I got my paycheck so I'm making something nice."

Just like that the topic ends.

The library is my favorite place in the world. If I could, I'd live here and make it my home.

Sitting on the floor, I lean my back against the shelf and make myself comfortable. I flip the pages of the third book in the series. I've got four more, but I'm already dreading the last book. I'm enjoying it so much that I don't want it to end.

The idea from last night crosses my head, especially after this morning. I can make bracelets. I know how to. Maybe...I can sell them online and make money.

That way, I can buy as many books as I want, and also spend some when I'm out with Marie and her friends.

I was embarrassed when Heath bought me food. If it weren't for the headache and hunger I would've put up a fight.

My phone vibrates. I see Marie's name popping up on the screen.

"Hey. I'm coming to pick you up to go to the ice rink. I'm sorry I had to bail yesterday. I had to run an errand. I'm free now, and so are the boys. So, text me your home address."

"I'm at the library, actually." I close my book.

"Oh, the one near the pizza shop, right?"

There is only one library in Bellmare town and it is mostly vacant. Not a lot of people come here to read. So, the librarian doesn't stock up on the latest and trending releases which sucks big time for an avid reader like me.

"Yes." I put the book back in its place.

"I'm a minute away."

I exit the library and stand outside.

A brand-new white BMW i8 pulls up to the curb. I see Marie waving at me.

Once I'm in, she says, "I missed you."

I smile. "You saw me yesterday."

"I know."

There's something about Marie. She radiates off such bright energy and sunshine that even your sadness and problems dim under her light.

"You don't have a book with you today."

"I left it inside. I'll pick it up tomorrow."

She frowns. "Do you not buy books?"

The question rubs me the wrong way. "I don't. I use my library card to read books."

She grins excitely. "That's great because I can give you books."

I giggle. "That would be the best gift."

"I can also get you bookmarks, pens, highlighters, and so much more stuff."

"A book would be fine, Marie."

Starting the car, she shrugs. "We'll see."

I look around the car and find it littered with empty wrappers and cups.

Marie must've noticed me because adds, "I babysit kids, and they caused this mess. I'm gonna get my car cleaned tomorrow."

"You babysit?"

From owning a BMW to looking like a model, Marie screams money just like Heath. Her outfits are from famous brands, and she changes stuff often. Even her phone cases are different each day.

"Yeah. I don't like being alone. So, I spend time with children and they're the most fun. My neighbors are busy and travel frequently and I babysit their two sons and daughter. They're awesome. There are other kids too. Some in the neighborhood and others here and there."

Marie lets out a short laugh. "Also, my *parents* are rich. I'm not. They bought me this car, but everything else I bought on my own. I live in the uptown, it's a lavish area, as you know. The people are wealthy, so they pay me well. That's how I'm able to afford most of my stuff. But don't get me wrong, I *do* save and only buy stuff if I can't help it. Like there's this computer I'm building and the parts cost thousands of dollars. Lately, I'm saving up, and splurging less. I love pretty things, especially clothes and makeup."

Sparing me a glance she adds, "There's only one life to live. I want to make every second of it worth it. Turn my dreams true and fulfill my wishes. I don't want to have regrets when I'm old and gray. Regrets are heavy. I don't want to live under the weight of them."

*There's only one life.*

*Regrets are heavy.*

*Turn dreams true and fulfill wishes.*

Something snaps in me. I decide then and there that I will give my idea a try. If I fail I don't have anything to lose, and if I succeed good things await for me.

"You're wise, Marie."

"Fuck no. I'm young, dumb, and broke."

I laugh. "You're definitely not broke."

"Well..."

We both share a laugh.

"Tell me about yourself. I want to know everything."

"There's really not much to me." I only now realize how blank I am. If I were a color I'd be white. There's nothing to me. I'm boring, and so uncool compared to Marie who's a rainbow.

"Tell me about your family."

I swallow the confused feelings. "My mom is a nurse and my dad... he left three months ago." *But recently he paid a visit and almost choked me to death.*

"It's all right," she says softly. I get the feeling that Heath hasn't told her about the bruises. If he did, nothing would've stopped her from interrogating me. She cares.

"I'm mostly alone at home. Sometimes I cook food and bake—I'm not good at it. I blame the cookbook."

She makes a turn. "I happen to be a great baker. We can do it together sometime. What do you say?"

"I'd love that."

"Tell me *more*, Hope."

"There isn't much."

She shakes her head. "Huh? I find that very hard to believe. You are nothing but full of surprises."

I'm confused. "What? How?"

She smirks. "You got Heath to talk to you. That guy is always sulking and hates the world."

"He's not that bad." I think about the last time we were together. He turned on the AC for me, bought me food, and drove me home. He did all those nice things for me, and I didn't even thank him. I'll do that the next time I see him.

"What makes you— wait, did something happen between you two?" Marie parks the car and studies me.

I shake my head. "No...yes... I mean..." I stammer like a kid in the principal's office.

She narrows her eyes, eager to know everything. "What did he do?"

I guess I have no choice but to tell her. It's what friends do, right? Tell each other stuff.

"On Thursday, I stayed back at school because I was having a headache. Heath offered to give me a ride. He also bought me food and we talked. Then he dropped me at my place."

"Oh my God." Marie shrieks like that kid on a rollercoaster, the one who'll take it again because it's the definition of fun.

My cheeks burn. "It's nothing."

She gasps. "Nothing? Girl, it's fucking something. I can't believe it. Why didn't you text me? I would've driven to your place then we would've dissected everything."

I can't invite her over with Dad paying random visits. It'll be a disaster if he sneaks in when Marie is there. I'll hate myself if something happens to her, and I can only imagine how much it'll freak her out. I want to protect her.

"Heath and I...I don't know what there is."

Marie's hazel eyes soften. She unbuckles her seatbelt and takes my hand. "It's okay, you know."

I frown. "What is okay?"

"If you're feeling something toward him. I agree he's a dickhead. But he's a good guy and I can see he cares about you. Even if it's a little bit."

"There isn't anything between us. He was just being nice."

"Nice *and* Heath don't go in one sentence." She squeezes my hand. "I won't intervene because you both can handle stuff. Just know it's okay. I'm here if you need to confide in someone. I'm *the best* at relationships and friendships."

I don't know what overtakes me, but I blurt out, "Can I hug you?"

Marie advances and wraps her arms around me. "You don't ask for hugs. You take them."

I hug her back, feeling the world slip off my shoulders. I have no idea why she came into my life. But I like that she's here. She makes me believe in friendships that I read in books—the forever kind.

A knock on her window pulls us apart. Heath and Sebastian stand next to each other, and I notice how they're the same height, but Sebastian is more muscular than Heath.

Sebastian is wearing a white shirt and denim jeans. As soon as Marie locks her car, he hugs her and rain kisses all over her face. She giggles in his embrace.

Watching them is like watching my favorite book couple come to life.

A piercing stare burns my face. I turn and find Heath staring at me.

Like always he's in a black T-shirt, and black jeans, but tonight he's got black Converse on—like me, but mine are blue. I notice the silver chain hiding under his shirt, and the few silver rings on his fingers. He looks intimidating with how his muscles grip the sleeves, and his broad shoulders and chest fill the front. I know he doesn't do any sports, and this physique is because of that underground place he fights at, but he has an incredible lean athletic build.

Coming closer, he towers over me. I have to crane my neck to meet his blue eyes. Lifting his hand, he brushes my hair off my shoulder and caresses the side of my neck. His touch is light like a feather.

"The finger marks are gone," he murmurs.

A trail of shivers runs down my spine from his single touch. The rhythm of my heart picks up the longer his touch lingers on my skin.

I step away to divert the topic. "There weren't any marks."

"I'm not blind, Hope," he says my name in a deep gravelly voice that further increases my heart rate.

This was why I wore the turtleneck. I wanted to avoid interrogation.

"I didn't say you were. I'm just telling you they weren't finger-marks. I burnt myself with a straightener."

Curling my arms around me, I glare at his chest. I see his muscles tightening against the thin material of his T-shirt. He's annoyed at my poor attempt to lie.

"I didn't know that straighteners have fucking fingers," he drawls out in a dry tone.

*They don't.*

*I suck at lying.*

"Let it go. Please," I whisper, if he pushes this matter I might start crying.

He knows something is up. I can't let him believe that. I don't trust him. We're not friends. We are nothing. Not long ago he told me to stay away from him. So his feelings toward me have been pretty clear.

"Guys c'mon." Marie leads the way.

Heath falls in step beside me. Tension rolls off him in big waves and hits me.

The ice rink is a big hall, flooded with bright ceiling lights. In the middle is the wide, shiny ice where people are flawlessly sliding in their skates. An array of benches is on one side of the rink where teenagers sit in groups. Near the entrance is the counter where a guy is handing out skates and also ringing up the customers.

"You two hurry up!" Marie looks back and hollers, her words echo in the room. People stop and give her a look, but Sebastian pulls her to his chest and glares at them. Kissing her forehead, he takes her to the counter.

Heath and I both catch up.

"Hi, Hope," Sebastian says. I give him a wave.

"It's been five minutes and you're greeting her just now?" Heath grumbles.

"I was busy greeting my girlfriend." Sebastian pays for our tokens.

I want to contribute, too. I just don't have money.

The disappointment must be apparent on my face because I hear him speak.

"What's fucking wrong?" Heath asks as we both gather the skates from the counter.

"Nothing. I'm fine," I assure him, but instead, he narrows his eyes at me.

"You're not fucking fine. Someone—never mind."

We sit on the benches and slip on our skates. He's quick with tying the laces while I slowly work through them. It takes me longer, because my hands are shaking, and I can't seem to make them stop.

"Fuck it." Bending in front of me, he takes the laces from me and ties them.

I'm staring at him when he looks up at me and clears his throat. "You were taking forever."

Standing up he gets onto the rink and looks back at me. I wobble on the floor, desperately trying to not fall on my face, and also helplessly searching for something to hold.

Heath sees my struggle and comes over.

"Give me your hand." Before I can overthink, he takes my hands. Electricity sizzles through my blood and hits every nerve ending. I've never been electrocuted, but one touch of his and I know what it feels like.

The warmth of his hand radiates off a promise that he won't let me fall. He'll catch me the second I trip. With him, I'll never know what it feels like to fall and get hurt.

Heath opens the tailgate for me.

I step onto the ice. My feet slip and I reach for his shoulders. "Oh shoot."

Heath's lips quirk up as he gets me to the rail. "So you fucking cheat-curse?"

"Cheat-curse?"

"Make up words that resemble curse words, but it's the same fucking thing." Heath smirks widely as if he can't bring himself to smile.

I can't wait to see him smile or laugh someday. I bet he'd look beautiful. Still, my heart jumps inside my chest. I feel something brewing in my stomach.

*I'm in so much trouble.*

"Are you okay?" Marie skates up to us with Sebastian following close behind.

"Barely," I offer.

She offers me her hands. "Come on, I'll help you out."

"I can help her," Heath interjects.

The three of us stare at him with various expressions: Sebastian with a smirk, Marie with a smile, and me with surprise.

"No! No, it's fine. I'll manage." I tightly grip the rail.

*God this is embarrassing.*

They have to help me and can't enjoy themselves.

*No wonder I didn't have friends. I'm a hindrance.*

Heath glares at me. "It's not fine."

"Heath, I have to talk to you." Sebastian steers him away from us.

"I can't believe it," Marie sidles up to me with a grin.

"What?" I frown.

"Heath is being nice to you. I mean I believed you. But fuck, he's really going out of his way to help you."

"I..."

"It's your choice. If you want, we can swap partners and you and I can skate together. Whatever you're comfortable with." She looks at Sebastian and smiles.

Marie is a good friend to me. I don't want to be terrible to her when she clearly wants to be with her boyfriend. Besides, I need to thank Heath for Thursday.

I decide. "I'll skate with Heath. I need to talk to him."

Marie loops her arm around mine and we skate to the boys who are in a staring battle. Heath looks annoyed and Sebastian looks amused.

"It's decided. You and Hope are going to skate," Marie tells Heath who quickly looks at me.

*You want to?* his eyes ask.

*I want to,* I reply.

Coming near, he offers me his hands. I take them, holding his long, calloused fingers tightly.

"Marie threatened you?" He helps me slide on the ice, keeping a fierce grip so I don't falter.

I give him a confused look. "I don't think she's capable of threatening anyone."

He shakes his head. "She is when it comes to protecting her people."

I can't imagine that. She's so full of light and happiness, thinking there's a blazing fire behind all that is similar to a rabbit having quills. Impossible.

Heath and I skate at a turtle's pace which must be bothering him, but he shows no signs of annoyance or anger. He doesn't let me go, and his grip is tighter than mine is on him.

Silence extends between us and it's not awkward. It's comfortable.

*It's the perfect time.*

*I should thank him.*

*It's the least I can do after I made him pay for my food.*

"I wanted to talk to you," I say timidly.

His blue gaze connects with mine. Worry flashes through his eyes.

"What is it?" His hands tighten around mine, encouraging me to go on.

My stomach fills with warmth. "I want to thank you for Thursday. You bought me food and drove me home. It was nice of you."

"It's nothing." He brushes it off in an it-doesn't-matter way as if he does it for every girl.

*Does he? The mere idea bothers me strangely.*

"It's something."

Our eyes meet and I can't hold my brimming smile.

Heath gulps hard, making his Adam's apple move incredibly slow. It's the most attractive thing I've ever seen. His eyes soften a bit, and he slowly lets go of one of my hands. "You got a hang of it?"

"I think so."

I hold his other hand with both hands and try to skate like everyone else in the rink—like a professional. Right now, I resemble a baby penguin who's learning how to walk on ice and it's not cute at all.

Heath instructs and I do as he says and almost squeal when I don't plant my face on the ice.

"It's working." I straighten with confidence. I like hearing the noise of my skates slashing the ice as I circle the perimeter with him. My speed is more than that of a turtle.

"It is," he says.

Tilting my head, I find him staring at me. His hand squeezes mine and heat runs up my arm and reaches my heart.

"You know I'm a boxer," Heath says casually.

I give him a questionable look. "You told me you fight at an underground thing."

His lips quirk up. "That *underground thing* is dangerous and only the best fighters are there." Pulling me to him he adds, "If someone is hurting you, I can fucking help you."

The color drains from my face. I turn numb.

"No-no one is hurting me," I whisper in a weak voice. I don't sound convincing even to myself.

He tugs me to him and our fronts press together. "That's a fucking lie."

"You agreed to not talk about this." How I manage to say that with our proximity is beyond me.

His face hardens. "I didn't fucking agree to anything."

I slip my wrist out of his hold. "Well, I agreed to not telling, because there isn't anything to tell." My throat suffocates my next breath. "I came here to have fun. Not to talk about *that*. I don't want to..." *think about it or discuss it with you.*

Heath clenches his jaw and rakes a hand through his hair. "I fucking tried. If you don't need help then I won't offer it."

Truth is, I'm barely surviving on my own since that night. For the past two nights, I've been having these vivid nightmares that wake me up. I'm stuck in a phase where I refuse to believe Dad hurt me. So, really I don't want to talk about that incident because I'll get triggered.

Heath follows me around the rink. He doesn't hold my hand which upsets me for some reason. We don't talk, but he doesn't leave me alone.

At one point Marie keeps me company. She talks about going to the nearest diner and I agree.

Nothing awaits me at home anyway.

Mom has a night shift and Dad—I don't have the energy to deal with him.

We leave the rink and go to the diner. Sebastian and Marie take Sebastian's jeep, and I go with Heath.

During the ride, he doesn't say a word to me. Tension is thick in the car, and it consumes us.

There's something between us when there shouldn't be.

Heath is dangerous. He fights at an illegal place and probably hangs out with delinquents. At school, he's famous for his bad reputation. He isn't someone I should hang out with. But he's also nice and notices things that no one does.

He *sees* me.

At the diner, I pick a burger, but he orders a chocolate smoothie for me when he finds me staring at it. I try to refuse but he doesn't listen to me. And when that smoothie lands in front of me, I'm glad he didn't. There are two reasons. One, I love chocolate with my entire being. Second, it helps me calm down.

Marie chatters about her job and all the children she's met. Sebastian joins in too. Heath and I only listen and contribute very little to the conversation.

Later when we're outside, Heath asks, "Do you have a ride?"

"Marie said she'd drive me home."

"Seems like she's busy."

I peek inside the diner and find Marie and Sebastian splitting the bill.

"I'll drive you since her driver took her car home. She'll be going with Sebastian." Heath briefs.

I hesitate, "Are you sure? I can—"

"I'm fucking sure. Let's go."

I shoot a text to Marie.

Once inside his car, I lean my head against the window as Heath pulls out of the parking lot. I catch a glimpse of them still inside and counting bills. They're like a married couple already.

I'm tired, but I'm happy. Today was fun, even though ice skating gave me hell, I still enjoyed doing it and sharing food with people who are slowly becoming my friends.

Dread fills me as we get closer to my house. I don't want to go home, especially when Heath is with me. What if Dad sees me with him? He'd go livid. God knows what he might do to me.

I'm scared and anxious as the car pulls up in my neighborhood.

I search for lights and they're on, meaning someone is home.

*Oh my God.*

*He's here.*

Dad is back.

# 10

## HEATH

I CAN FEEL IT.

The nervous energy radiates from her.

Putting the car into brake, I give her my full attention to find out what's bothering her. I never like it when she's not her usual self. For some fucked up reason, it irks me.

Hope is bouncing her leg, and her eyes are filled with fear.

Questions run through my mind; I ignore them. She doesn't want me to intervene. She's been vocal about it enough.

*I can't just fucking ignore when someone's hurting her.*

My hands tighten around the steering wheel. I try to vanish Hope out of view. It's damn near impossible.

I wait for her to get out. She stays put.

She's stalling and it makes me worried.

"Something wrong?" I finally ask.

"No." She hesitantly slips out of the car. Leaning down, she says, "Thank you for everything."

I nod, too distracted by the lady watching me from the window. She's pulled the curtains away and is studying me with a peculiar gaze.

"Goodbye, Heath." She goes inside her house.

I stay out for a minute then drive away.

I offered her help. If she needs it she'll ask for it.

I come out of the bathroom in a pair of shorts and throw some punches in the air to get ready for my fight.

Sebastian watches me curiously.

"Your girlfriend won't like you appreciating my body, Bash." I tease him.

"You wish. Mine is so much *better* than yours." He gestures to his body that's ripped and filled out with muscles in all the right places. Like me, he spends a lot of time in the gym to be this fit. Also, it helps him cool off and release stress.

I walk deeper into the room. "I found you passed out on the treadmill yesterday."

"I was sleeping!" he says flushed.

"So that's what we call passing out now?"

"For someone who didn't say a word at the diner, you're quite chatty now."

"I didn't have anything to say."

"Huh?" He smirks.

"What's that look for?" I sit down and start wrapping my knuckles with the tape.

He arches an eyebrow. "Are we *not* going to talk about it?"

I know exactly what he means. "No."

"You like her, man."

I have no idea what he's babbling about. I like no one.

"You're fucking delusional." I avoid his stare *and* his presence.

"The only one delusional here is *you*. Why can't you just admit you have a thing for Hope?"

"I don't. I just helped her because Marie and you are too lost in your own world to notice anyone else."

He points a finger at me. "Take that back. It's not true."

"You left us," I deadpan.

"Maybe it was intentional."

"No one asked you to play matchmaker."

Sebastian sighs and picks up the water bottle and downs half of it. He fought before me and won the match but gained a gnash on his forehead and a split lip. Marie will scold him. The thought amuses me. He is more muscular than me, and people get intimidated by him quite easily. However, it's a sight when Marie is scolding him, and he's looking at the ground and watching ants. She hates it when he gets hurt or drinks—something he's given up on since last year.

"We're not playing anything. You're the one who decides to spend time with her. Like tonight when Mare offered to skate with her *you* stepped in. And when Hope sat in the booth, *you* sat next to her."

Denial tastes like poison in my mouth. I chug down some Gatorade.

"I don't care about her." If I say it enough, he'll believe me. *I will, too*

"Then I guess you won't mind if I give Tyler her phone number. He asked me for it at school."

Pure rage flows through my veins. Without thinking I pin Sebastian to the nearest wall.

I get into his face and snarl. "Don't you fucking dare, Sebastian."

Instead of pushing me off, he smiles.

I quickly step back in shock.

"Don't *care* about her? You're such a fucking liar." He strides out of the room when I stop him.

"If you give him her number I'll destroy him."

"You know I won't do that." He looks back at me.

"I'm just telling you." I pick up my towel and wipe the sweat off my neck.

"You know me, Heath. I've got your back and your girl's."

I throw the Gatorade bottle at him, but the fucker escapes before it can hit him.

Left jab. Right jab. Right Uppercut.

My opponent falls to the ground. The referee whistles and announces my win. Men chant in excitement of my victory and the prospect of winning the bets they placed on me.

Yanking my hand away, I hurry to the back room. Getting my gym bag, I change into black trousers and a T-shirt. Ryan, the manager, comes in with a thick wad of cash.

"You were good, kid." He hands me the money. Without counting the bills, I throw them in my bag and turn to leave when he steps in my way. "Mr. Wild wants to talk to you."

Warning bells ring in my head. He's a mobster and a drug dealer with a vast network of suppliers everywhere. He makes millions of dollars every month and has a frightening reputation.

"Tell him I said no." There's no way I'm meeting that man. I'm reckless, angry, and rude, but I'm not a fucking idiot.

I side-step him but Ryan holds my arm to stop me.

I glare. "Let go of me."

Ryan does as I say. Good. Because if he didn't, I would've ripped his arm off.

His lips thin in displeasure. "If he wants to talk to you, you don't walk away."

I know the serious repercussions that could come from ignoring Wild, but I'm not willing to get involved in his games or become his bitch. If he wants a fighter he can find plenty here.

"I said I'm *not* interested. Not now. Not ever."

With that, I leave the building and enter my car. Going over sixty, I speed through the streets and arrive at my house. After taking a quick shower, I get downstairs.

Derek watches me as I take care of my knuckles in the living room.

"Where were you, sir?"

Derek is a sixty-year-old man who has no family or relatives. Thin gray hair that was once black frames his wrinkled face and his black eyes look like pits of darkness. Standing an inch taller than me he is an intimidating man with a lean figure and skeptical gaze. I'm not afraid of him because I've known him since I was little.

"Out," I say.

"Your father doesn't like it when you stay out—"

"I don't give a fuck about his opinion."

"Sir, that's disrespectful."

I glance at Derek and see his usual disapproving scowl. "He deserves nothing *but* my disrespect."

"He cares about you."

I scoff at the ridiculous implication. Does he care about me? Sure. I see him visiting me twice every month.

Xavier Travon, a tycoon in the world of electronic business and real estate is my father. A father I wished I didn't have. He's the owner of multi-million-dollar companies. A known businessman in Toronto who's been featured in Forbes thrice and is only forty-three.

"Because I'm the heir to his empire, not because I'm *his* son."

I leave Derek before he can bombard me with more wisdom. He always ties me up in phrases I can't escape from.

Kelly stirs the ladle in the hot pot. She's a short petite brunette with brown eyes—hers are darker than Hope's, not that I'm thinking about her. Kelly is in her late sixties and has a few grandchildren she asks me to hang out with.

I hate people. I've always been an introvert. Meeting new people and going to new places annoy me. I like my room, my bed, and my loneliness.

The moment I'm in the kitchen, she sends me a smile. "How was your day?"

Kelly has raised me since I was little. She knows me and my sister from the inside out. She's seen me at my highest and my lowest moments in life and tried to help me. I refuse it every single time. I don't want her sympathy or pity.

Everyone treats me like a china plate that will break at any moment. I hate it. I'm not vulnerable or need to talk about my feelings. *I'm fucking fine.*

"Same as old." I sit on the stool at the island.

"Nothing exciting happened?"

I roll my eyes. "No."

She sets down rice with stir-fry vegetables. It's my favorite dish. She knows it.

"Let me grab a plate and we can eat together."

Since Emery's death, Kelly tries to keep me company during meals—not that I need it—and asks me about stuff. It's irritating at times, but it also makes me feel less lonely.

"Whatever."

She makes a plate and takes a seat across from me.

Derek comes in for dinner but doesn't join us. Good. I'd hate to be around that vigilant man who's a pain in my ass.

"What's been going on lately?"

"Nothing." I take a bite. Like always it's delicious.

"Marie was telling me about this new friend. She's in your group now?"

*For fuck's sake.*

"She is *only* Marie's friend." And Sebastian's. Definitely not mine.

She shoots me a warm smile. "I think it's good to make new friends. Don't you think so?"

I glare. "No."

"Your go-to answer to everything." She laughs and I stuff my mouth to not reply. "When you meet new people you get to know their story, sometimes you can even relate to them. I know you don't like people. But I think it's worth a try."

I clutch my silverware tightly. "Only to fucking *lose* them later, right?"

A deadly wave of silence fills the kitchen and creates tension.

Kelly looks at me softly. "You're not going to lose every person in your life. What happened to Emery—"

"I don't want to fucking hear it."

"Sebastian is here."

"I *was* going to lose him last year."

"You didn't. That's what matters," she says with a finality to her tone.

"Maybe."

She switches the topic to my studies. I reply in short answers.

When we're done I offer to wash the dishes, but she pushes me out of the kitchen. She never lets me help her, no matter how persistent I am.

Lying on the couch in the living room, I watch old boxing matches on the forty-inch flat screen. I study the moves and try to memorize them to get better.

Boxing is one thing in life that brings me peace. It also gives me a sense of direction when I feel lost all the time. I don't know what I'm doing or where I want to go in life. But in the ring and fighting my opponent, that's the only time I don't feel lost. I feel like I belong there. I'm meant to do this one thing.

An hour later, Kelly comes into the room with urgency.

I sit up to make space for her. "What is it?"

She clears her throat, her eyes sad. "I don't know if I should give it to you or not."

I frown in bewilderment. She never hides anything from me.

"Just tell me." I insist.

She clears her throat again. "Derek and I were trimming the bushes when I found this in the soil."

Her hand disappears into her white apron pocket, and she pulls out a ring that belongs to Emery.

I snatch it from her and stare at the purple stone embedded in a silver ring. Nothing fancy. She bought it from a cheap jewelry shop, and raved about how it's the greatest place on Earth—my sister was dramatic like that. Then she lost it, and we turned the whole mansion upside down but never found it. Until now, when she's not here anymore.

I close the ring in my fist and fight back the tears that burn my eyes with the heat of embers.

Without saying a word, I jog up to my room, twist the lock, and lean my back against the door.

My room is where my emotions are safe. Where I'm allowed to have a mental breakdown without anyone watching.

I stride toward the floor-to-ceiling glass window that gives a spectacular view of the town that lies below me filled with lights and life. Sometimes I sit here and watch it. It's calming.

Sitting there, I play with the ring, rotating it between my fingers. I remember her wearing it. It was her favorite ring. After two days of endlessly searching for it, we went back to the shop but couldn't find another piece. There was only one, and it was lost.

*Not anymore.*

Emery settled for another ring. She was like that. Someone who wouldn't fret over things too much. To her, people meant more than things.

I'm the opposite. For me things hold meaning. I still have the hoodie from the fourth grade that Sebastian gave me because I was cold, the black mug with butterflies on it that Marie gave me last year, and the silver chain Emery gave me on my fifteenth birthday—the one I wear every day since. I have so many things from all the years that my friends and sister gave me. I'm attached to them. I can never think about throwing them away or replacing them. If I ever fucking lose them, I'll lose my mind.

That explains why I'm reluctant to let go of Emery. She's irreplaceable.

My phone vibrates. I see Mom's name on the screen. Switching on the silent mode I toss my phone on the bed.

Out of nowhere, Hope slips into my thoughts. I remember that woman looking at me from the window. Something about her doesn't feel right. She must be her mother—the person who hurt her. Or it could be someone else. Maybe someone at school.

*Please let there be no more bullies. We dealt with them. I don't want Hope to get through the same shit Marie did. It was hell.*

I have no idea why there's an urge in me to protect Hope. I don't even know the girl. She's a nobody to me, yet there's a pull that tugs me toward her.

*I'm only doing this so nothing bad happens to her.* That's my reason.

Not that I'm interested in her. She isn't my type. Well, I don't have a type. No one interests me to pursue them. The ones who are interested in me only want a good time.

My thoughts steer back to Emery. The ring digs into my palm as I hold it a little tightly.

I feel hollow, lonely, and detached.

After a while I move to my bed, the sorrow pushing me down. It's a heavy feeling, and all of it rests on my chest. The pressure suffocates me.

My chest expands with insurmountable emotions that make it hard to fucking breathe. Air escapes my lungs.

*Fuck. It's happening.*

I think I'm having a panic attack. I get them frequently, so I don't freak out now.

Rolling over, I lie on my back and stare up at the ceiling. The cold metal digs into my skin and diverts the mental pain.

Opening my mouth, I draw in long breaths, while listening to the rapid beats of my heart. The sound is fucking loud as it echoes in my head like a drum.

For the next five minutes, I repeat the same thing over and over.

Breathe in. Breathe out.

Breathe in. Breathe out.

Breathe in. Breathe out.

Breathe in. Breathe out.

Breathe in. Breathe out.

This feels like I'm being punished for not saving my sister. Anxiety and depression—as Sebastian told me—are the rewards I got for my failure.

Maybe helping that pretty girl can help me redeem myself.

# 11

## HOPE

"I saw a guy bringing you home last night," Mom says casually, as she stirs the ladle in the pot.

*Oh my God.*

*She saw Heath.*

*I can't lie to her now.*

With a shaky breath I say, "Yes."

She faces me and arches an eyebrow. "Do you know him?"

I grow nervous under her scrutinizing gaze. In the pit of my stomach, I have a bad feeling about this conversation. *Abort.*

"Yes." *Now this is a lie. I don't know Heath. Not really.*

"How come? Do you two share any classes?" she asks with an edge to her tone. She's never seen me with a guy before. Perhaps that's the reason why she's suspicious.

"A few." I sip water to damp my parched throat, but I end up drinking half the glass.

I had no idea lying makes you thirsty.

"So, you went from not having friends to hanging out with *boys.*"

My mouth opens in shock. There's nothing going on between us. For Christ's sake, we're not even friends.

"It's not like that. He's *just* a friend." Okay, so, he isn't my friend now, but he's an acquaintance who'll later become a friend. I'm shadowing the future here. *This is bizarre.*

"*Friend.* I see how it is." She dries her hands with a washcloth hanging on the oven handle then turns to me. "I don't want that boy around you. Stay away from him. Guys like him want nothing but sex."

Heath would never want that from me. From what I've seen he minds his own business. Girls don't intrigue him. He never bats an eye at them.

"I don't think he's like that." I surprise myself by defending him.

"You aren't sure, and you can't be, because you don't know it, Hope." With a sigh she takes a seat at the table and drinks a glass of Scotch that she bought last night. Drinking has become a norm for her since dad left. "I'm not saying don't make friends but be careful. Even if you want to be around him, just stay friends. No sleepovers or staying out late alone with him."

I nod.

Mom opens her purse and counts the wad of cash she got as her paycheck. She categorizes it into groceries, bills, college funds, and other things. When she's done she rubs her temple and chugs down another glass.

"This isn't much, but I think we'll be able to make this work. If only I could go to the city and get a good job," she muses.

The idea of making those bracelets pops into my mind. I plan to go out today and buy the materials.

"I need money to buy a second-hand textbook from the store. Our teacher said it's a great reference book for those who want to pursue medicine," I ramble off, feeling horrible on the inside.

I hate lying, but I also can't tell her about my plan. She won't understand and call it stupid and the hopeful part of me doesn't want to hear any of that. I'm doing this for me. I can't back down. I don't want to.

"Sure," she quickly agrees and hands me the bills.

I hold the money tightly to my chest. "Thank you."

"It's all right, sweetie. If you need more let me know." She brings the bottle to her mouth instead of using the glass and I just know it's going to be a long night.

The next day, I buy some of the items, for the rest I use the internet at the library to order those. The librarian is kind enough to let me use her computer.

It's late in the evening when I arrive home. I see a shadowy, tall figure trying to open the door with what appears to be a key. The lights are off in the house so I can't make out his face. The door opens, and he switches on the lights. Turning around he closes the door but stops when he sees me.

It's Dad.

Fear possesses me. My hand tightens around the handles of the bag as if my life depends on it.

Dad leaves the door open and gestures to me to come inside.

Everything in me wants to run the other way. It's getting late and the streets are a dangerous place to be out at night. Especially when addicts and perverts roam in the shadows of the alleyways. So, I have no choice but to go inside.

Taking slow steps, I enter, and he closes the door behind me. I'm about to run upstairs when he grabs my wrist and pulls me to him. Leaning over me, he glares down at me with his wild red eyes.

"Where is the money?" he asks. His breath stinks of alcohol.

"There isn't any," I lie.

Dad squeezes my wrist. "Don't lie to me."

"I'm not."

He hauls me into the kitchen and lets go of me. He stomps to the refrigerator and searches for the money but comes up empty handed. Curse words leave his mouth as he bangs his fists against the door of the appliance.

Dread seeps into my bones. I stand like a statue in front of him.

"The money is supposed to be here. Where the fuck did it go?" he asks me in a menacing tone. I cower in fright.

*This won't end well for me.*

"You should know where Mae put it."

I see the Scotch bottle sitting on top of the cabinets. I have no idea why Mom put it up so high, but it looks like a golden ticket for me to get out of this situation.

"I don't know about the money, I swear. But there is Scotch." I point to the bottle, and he turns to look at it.

He takes the stool and stands on it. "You were of some use, pathetic girl."

This is my chance.

I sneak upstairs. From the corner, I watch him leave without looking back at me—not that I wanted him to.

Hurrying downstairs I lock the door—not that it matters, he has the key.

I return to my room. Switching on the lamp, I look at the bruises on my wrist and cringe at the awful sight of them.

If someone sees them, they'll know someone assaulted me. How do I tell them it was my father? The man who's supposed to protect me now abuses me, because he needs money for his booze.

I'm confused, scared and alone. I don't know what to do. How to make him stop from coming here. When he was gone, I thought he was gone for good. I thought it was forever.

I was so relieved. He was done hurting my mother and terrorizing us. *How wrong I was.*

The nights are chilly due to the giant forest and greenery surrounding the town. Tall cliffs and rocky hills add to the topography, you can see the whole town from up there. That's also where the rich people live.

I've always wondered what life looks like when you stand on the top and look down. I imagine it must be beautiful, seeing the lights and buzz of the town.

I pull the edge of the blanket over to my chin and snuggle into it. Picking up the book from beside my pillow I get lost in the words that work like a bridge. They take me from one place to the other.

An escape that I desperately need.

# 12

## HEATH

Night is the most vulnerable time of the day. The darker it gets, the more you're open to feelings and emotions that don't invade you in broad daylight.

It's 3 a.m. Logic can't justify why I'm lying on the floor of my sister's bedroom and listening to the last voicemail she sent me.

*"James! I know you're worried but relax. You called me ten times. Geez. I feel wanted when you never call me. I'm safe. You should stop worrying about me. I promise I'm fine. I'll be back home on Sunday. We'll watch a movie together. I have something I want to tell you. Also, do not touch my controller just because your buttons aren't working. I will kill you if I find out."*

The beeping sound hits, and her voice disappears, but the empty feeling in my chest stays right where it is.

I play the voicemail for the thousandth time and listen to her sweet, worried tone. Emery was fond of threatening me, yet she's the one who left me.

It all happened because of fucking cancer.

My hands go up to my hair. I yank the strands to get rid of the God-awful headache. It's like someone is banging a hammer on one side of my brain.

I need to get away.

Grabbing my car keys, I bolt out of the room.

"Where are you going, sir?" Derek asks from behind me. I swear this guy never sleeps. He's always onto me like my own shadow.

I ignore him and go to the garage where my McLaren is parked. Minutes later, I drive out of the driveway when the sound of another car reverberates in the vicinity. Derek is following me.

For fuck's sake.

Pressing hard on the accelerator, I speed through the narrow streets while also keeping track of his car.

"Motherfucker." I increase the speed to over sixty and make several rounds of the same neighborhood. When I can't see him in the rearview mirror, I turn off the headlights and slowly drive through a network of roads and pull up at the gym.

I find the room already bright with lights. Paul, my trainer, is punching the bag viciously as if he's killing someone.

The noise of my footsteps gets his attention, and he looks up at me with his drenched hair and sweaty chest that's an eight pack. At thirty-six he has more muscle and stamina than any man I've ever fought. From winning bronze to gold medals, he's an impeccable fighter with no one in life, except his German Shepherd, Yale.

"Tough night?" He quirks an eyebrow at me.

"Something like that," I mutter, not wanting to talk to him about my personal matters. He knows about Emery's death, it's the reason why he agreed to train me. According to him, 'boxing is therapy.'

"Hop into the ring," he orders, knowing damn well I hate talking about myself.

Removing my shirt, I look down at my black sweatpants. I don't have shorts, so they'll have to do. Putting on my gloves, I enter the ring and throw some punches around for the fun of it.

Paul tosses me a headset. I roll my eyes. He shoots me a glare. "Safety first, boy."

With a sigh I put it on, he doesn't. "You don't need *safety*?" I taunt.

He smirks and bumps his gloves with mine. "To hurt me you have to hit me first."

Nobody aggravates me like Paul does, but I also know he's the best in Bellmare.

Someone who's a loser knows the true value of winning. That's how Paul is. He worked his ass off to get where he is today—and picked up arrogance on the journey. That aside, he is a good trainer and knows how to kick my ass.

We spar for hours. I throw punches and hooks, but he blocks every hit. His defense is better than mine, but that's because I'm an attacker and he isn't.

Sweat covers my body and my breaths get heavier.

I'm frustrated.

Swinging my arm, I keep trying to hit him, until he rounds his leg around my knees and knocks me to the floor. His hands take a hold of my wrists, and he pins me with an intense glare. "What's the matter with you?"

I scoff and refuse to look at him as the memories from earlier conjure in my brain.

*I'm fine.*

"Nothing," I grit out.

Paul gets off me. I roll over and stand up. Untying the gloves, taking off the headrest, I sit on the mat to catch my breath.

He sits a few feet away from me and stares at me. "It's your sister, isn't it?"

I shake my head and splatter sweat on the mat.

He scoffs. "Yeah, sure. Why else would you be here at five in the morning?"

I look out and see the sky turning bright and flocks of birds flying around.

*How long have I been here?* Clearly more than an hour.

"I should go." Collecting my shirt, I get into the bathroom and take a shower. Cold water flows down my body. It doesn't freeze the damn numbness in my chest or the way my soul aches.

I'm in pain, emotional pain. I don't know how to work through it.

Therapy is out of the option. The mere idea of telling a stranger my inner thoughts makes me want to get hit by a truck.

I don't like being fucking vulnerable. More than that I don't fucking know how to be.

I can talk to Sebastian, but he has his stuff to deal with. Marie doesn't need my darkness touching her light. I'd hate to make her upset. She already worries about me a lot. I hate it.

So that leaves no one.

After a shower, I slip on my clothes and drive to Sebastian's apartment that he's renting all by himself. God knows, he needed to move out of the house where he was living with his mother who loved drugs and brought strange men to her home. Men who hurt her son, but she didn't care.

Using the spare key, I slip inside and turn on the lights.

"You're early." Sebastian comes down the stairs where his room is.

"Yeah." I lean against the nearest wall.

His apartment is too small, but it's his. The living room and kitchen are an open concept and share the same space. There's only one bedroom and bathroom that are both up the few steps of stairs. Unlike me, he isn't a clean freak, but when Marie is here, she either makes him do it or does it herself. She's transformed this tiny space into a home with their photos hanging on the walls, scented candles, decoration pieces and other house accessories that make it a great place to live.

His eyebrows pinch. "Everything okay?"

"Mhm." That's better than lying.

Marie comes barreling down. "My best friend is here. Good morning!"

I cock my head to one side. "Good morning. You're quite cheerful."

Her cheeks turn bright red, and she grins. "You see, I came in a little earlier and Sebastian and I spent the time in his bed—"

I roll my eyes. "And that's all I need to know."

Moving toward the kitchen I open cabinets and pull out the protein powder to make a shake for Sebastian and I. Marie starts on pancake batter, and Sebastian eagerly joins her.

Seriously, he should be helping me instead of sneaking his hand under her top.

Sex freaks.

Once I'm done making the shake, I turn to him only to find him kissing her neck and grinning like a fool.

Fuck. I'm so glad that he's here and he's happy. He deserves this girl and the love she gives him.

As if he can feel my stare, he looks up at me and smiles. "Is it ready?"

I nod, and we both move to the couch in the living room while Marie works on pancakes.

"Did you do the business homework?"

"You need help?" I know he finds business difficult when math is involved.

"Can I copy yours?"

"What do I get in return?"

He leans back on the couch. "How about the list of boys asking me about Hope?"

"What?" I burst out in rage, which earns me a scolding from Marie to keep my voice down because it's early in the morning.

Sebastian swallows the drink before laughing hard. "God. You pathetically like her."

Excuse me? I don't like her. Yes, I'm intrigued by her and want to help her, but that's only because I don't want her to get hurt.

"I. Do. Not," I insist.

"Yeah sure." He grins.

I want to shove a brick into this mouth.

"You're a piece of shit."

"Don't insult me like that. You're the piece of shit for lying."

Fuck the manners.

Taking the glass of water, I splash it onto his face.

"Heath you fucker! I'm going to kill you," he roars behind me. I enter the kitchen where Marie would step in and stop him.

"Step outside you dickhead," he says coming around the island, but slips and falls onto the floor with a thud.

"Oh my God." Marie rushes to help him.

I can't hold my laughter and grip the island as I laugh loud. My stomach hurts as I watch him sit at the stool while holding his back.

"I'm going to kill you," he warns me in a cold voice, but I keep laughing.

"Heath stop it or else he'll come for you," Marie warns me.

I flex my jaw to not laugh again. "Good luck with not falling."

"That's it." Sebastian comes at me, but Marie gets in his way.

"Stop it you both and eat breakfast. We're getting late for school."

"It doesn't start until eight, babe." Sebastian bends to kiss her cheek and also shoots me a glare. I give him the finger.

"It's six already," she reminds him.

Rolling his eyes, he sits at the island and starts stacking up pancakes.

I carefully take a seat next to him. Retrieving a fork, I dive for his pancake.

He slaps my hand away. "Stop eating my food."

"It was one fucking bite."

Marie serves me next then goes upstairs to tidy up the bed and gather their things for school.

Silence settles in. I feel uneasiness in the pit of my stomach. It wasn't this quiet when his mother was around and making a mess around the house, screaming and cursing at him, or fucking men in her room down the hallway.

"I think someone is abusing Hope," I blurt out.

Sebastian stops chewing and narrows his eyes on me. A deep frown that will grow wrinkles on his forehead.

He'd look so fucking ugly.

"What the fuck, Heath?" He hisses at me.

I clear my throat. Feeling completely no edge with how my intestines curl and twist in discomfort. Maybe this wasn't a good idea. But Sebastian is my best fucking friend. I can tell him anything.

"I know it sounds fucking delusional. But I'm telling you *something* is wrong."

His fork clatters on the plate. "How do you know?"

Anger surges through me ferociously. My fingers dig into the palms as they form into fists.

For some unknown reason I feel violent at the thought of someone hurting her enough to leave marks. Her neck had finger-like fucking bruises that were put there and weren't from a fucking straightener.

"I—" something in me stops me from mentioning those marks. I want to keep *that* information to myself because it seems too personal.

I look at my best friend who's watching me with piqued interest.

"She's skittish and keeps her distance," I say, instead.

"Maybe because she's shy. Or we intimidate her."

I want to slap his fucking face.

Sebastian is one stupid asshole.

"Right because we look like fucking monsters from the movies." I sarcastically comment.

Sebastian shrugs. "I wouldn't disagree. I mean look at me. I'm quite tall and big."

I want to bang my fucking head against a wall.

"We're the exact same," I say.

"You're not quite as muscular as me. That's why I'm better than you at boxing."

I chuckle dryly. "Wanna test that later today?"

Sebastian grins with his blond mess covering the forehead. "Sure. What do I get for winning?"

"Nothing because you are *not* going to win. However, if I win, you're going to give me that fucking list you were talking about."

Sebastian laughs and elbows me in the stomach. "Pathetically like her."

# 13

## HOPE

It's downpouring heavily.

In the morning, the sky was clear, but by fifth period, a dark gray carpet had rolled over with turbulent winds sweeping the school grounds and banging on the windows.

Earlier, I checked my locker for an umbrella, even though I knew there wouldn't be one. I used it the last time and forgot to bring it back to school.

Now, I've been standing near the entrance for the past thirty minutes, waiting for it to stop.

Queues of cars drive out of the school. Some catch rides while others walk through the rain with umbrellas.

Marie and Sebastian ditched school after lunch because of something. They didn't elaborate and left as soon as they could.

Heath probably skipped, too. I didn't see him in the two classes we had together.

I check the time on my phone. 4:30 pm. It's getting late.

Letting out a sigh, I slip my novel into my bag and step into the torrential downpour.

In a matter of seconds, I get drenched. Water seeps through the soles of my Converse and my feet get wet. Like glue my clothes plaster against my body.

Bringing my bag to the front of my chest, I try to prevent the winds from slicing me into two halves.

I start walking in the direction of the bus stand. The bus will drop me four blocks away from home. At least, that is better than walking miles, especially when it's raining so hard.

A cold breeze sweeps past me. I shudder due to the chills that spread all over me.

I reach the bus stop and study the schedule. Bus 106 - 4:00 PM

I missed the bus.

This is my sign.

Luck isn't on my side.

It probably hates me.

I sneak shelter under an awning and stomp my feet at my bad luck. There's no way I can walk home like this, wet and cold, but I also can't stay here. Soon it'll get dark, and I don't want to walk home alone.

I look left and right in search of a cab, but there's not a single one in the vicinity. The roads are empty, and no one is around except me.

A black car rolls out of the school gates and stops beside me.

I know who this car belongs to. Heath Travon.

The passenger door opens, and he looks at me with his cold blue eyes. "Get in the car."

I hesitate for a moment, but do as he says.

I put my bag on the floor and hug my shaky arms as I inch closer to the fans that emit hot air.

Heath reaches out and turns all the fans in my direction.

Tucking the long strand of my hair behind my ear, I turn and find him already watching me.

"Thank you," I murmur, feeling embarrassed for getting a car ride from him. Again.

I wonder, what was he doing so late at school? I thought he left.

Heath drives to the drive-thru he took me before. "Are you hungry?"

I shake my head but my stomach grumbles.

Shoot.

If it wasn't raining, I would dig my own grave and fling myself in it.

My cheeks flush. "I'm fine."

"You don't need to fucking lie to me," he says in a low, gruff voice.

At the station, he orders a burger and chocolate smoothie for me and gets a bucket of chicken tenders for himself.

Like before, he pays using his credit card. I watch him tip the lady who shoots him a smile, but he doesn't acknowledge it. So I return it, and she grins at me until Heath closes the window.

I pick up the cold chocolate smoothie and sigh in pleasure as it goes down my throat. I stir and take a long pull when my eyes meet his.

"You like chocolate?" Heath asks, opening his Diet Coke can. His gaze doesn't steer away from me.

My smile grows. "I *love* chocolate."

"Of course." Slowly, his gaze drops to my body.

I follow and see the prominent outline of my blue bra showing through my top. Quickly I cross my arms and turn my body away from him.

*Oh my God.*

*I want to die.*

*Preferably a quick death.*

How could I forget that my clothes were wet?

I flashed him the sight of my bra. And also, the sight of my nipples poking through the material.

"It's all right." I hear him speak.

I close my eyes and mutter a few not-so-good words.

"I can see you through the side mirror."

*He's bluffing.*

I check, and sure enough, he can see me.

"I'm sorry." I reach for my bag and hug it to my chest. I've never been more embarrassed in my life before.

"There's nothing to be sorry about."

"You just saw my—"

"Yeah," he says in a deep voice.

"I didn't mean to flash you... or whatever."

"It doesn't matter." My chest tightens.

Right, of course. He must've seen many nipples, so it makes sense. He must've also touched them and kissed them.

Clearly, I know a lot, thanks to books.

"I should go home," I suggest.

Heath drives me home in the rain that refuses to slow down. The pitter-patter of the rain is the only sound in the car. He parks on the side of the curb and shuts off the engine.

"Let's get inside," he says.

I try to form the word 'no', but it doesn't leave my mouth.

Taking our bags he runs to the porch. I follow him. Pressing a button on his keychain he locks the car and waits for me to unlock the door.

Stepping inside I leave the door open for him. "I'm going to change."

He nods. His gaze doesn't move to my chest that I'm hiding behind my bag. Still a tornado of warmth spirals in my belly.

Going up to my room I take a quick hot shower and change into something nice.

What are you doing? It's not a date.

I cringe when I pick a cute dress that I haven't worn since I bought it. I mostly wear jeans so I can carry cash, keys, and my phone without worrying about pockets.

Flipping through the hangers I decide on a simple white top and denim jeans that fit me tight. I brush my wet hair, so it looks tame and not frizzy. To look more presentable, I apply moisturizer on my face and lip balm. I contemplate mascara but decide against it at the end. I don't want Heath to think I'm trying too hard. Especially after he's seen my nipples. *God, I'm not forgetting that ever.*

When I get down, I find Heath in the kitchen, scrolling on his phone in boredom. The moment I enter the room, his hand pauses and his eyes run all over me like he's seeing me in a new light. My stomach turns upside down. He stares at me, then clenches his jaw and averts his gaze from me.

*He checked me out and he didn't like what he saw.*

*That does something to my self-confidence.*

*Whatever. I know I'm not pretty, so it doesn't matter.*

*I'm on Earth to read books. That's the sole meaning of my existence.*

"It's getting cold," he complains as he opens the bag and puts everything on the island, making himself at home even though it's his first time here.

I walk deeper into the room and reach for his wings. "I can heat it," I suggest.

"It's fine."

"Let me do—"

He directs a glare at me. "I like the crisp."

A laugh bursts out of me and his gaze softens. Out of all the things in the world, I didn't expect him to say that. It makes him normal.

The tones of my laughter fill the room while he remains stoic.

With a shake of his head, he starts eating. "It's not funny."

"I didn't expect you to say that." I stifle my laugh.

A dark look crosses his face, and his eyes look sharp as he slowly swallows. "There's a lot you don't know about me."

"You can share if you want."

He pauses in surprise, then recovers, and asks, "With you?"

"Y-yes, if you're okay with that. I'll listen to anything you want to talk about. No topic is off-limits," I rush out nervously.

There's something about him that makes me nervous, the kind where I stutter and my stomach gets all fuzzy and warm unlike my father, who ties my stomach in a rope of knots. I hate that feeling.

"I didn't know there were off-limits topics."

"Uh...everyone has those."

He's quiet for a long moment before he mutters, "Yeah. You're fucking right."

I take a bite of the burger. "I told you."

"Won't it be unfair if you know about me, but I know nothing about you?" There's a playful hint to his voice.

"What do you want to know?" I sip my smoothie.

Heath fires off the question quickly. "Do you live alone?"

"I live with my mom. She's a nurse and works long shifts."

"That means you're alone most of the time."

"Yes." I nod.

He opens his mouth, but I stop him with my hand.

"My turn."

"Fine."

"Why do you skip classes?"

He arches an eyebrow. "*That's* what you're fucking curious about."

I grin in reply.

Tearing away his gaze from me, he stares outside. "I can't... concentrate." He whispers the last part as if he didn't want to say it.

"Why not?" I probe, eager to know the answer.

"There's always a lot on my mind."

Those words sink into my soul like claws. I've also been losing focus in my classes since Dad's visits. It's hard to occupy your mind with something else when there's already so much. The closest analogy I can draw up is filling an already filled jar.

"Do you wanna talk about it?"

"No," he replies in a dead-serious tone, marking an end to the topic.

The air shifts between us. I can feel him closing off and hardening the shell around himself. There's more to him like how a shore is just the beginning of an ocean.

Tension builds as we clean up. Neither of us says a word to break it or make it easy for the other. When there's nothing else to do, I walk him to the door. It's only then I notice that the rain has stopped.

Suddenly a strident blast comes from somewhere nearby and all the lights in my house go off. Darkness blankets the space around us and a hush falls around us.

My heart accelerates and goosebumps rise over my arms. On instinct, my hand reaches out and grabs the first thing I can get a hold of. Which is him.

"What the fuck was that?" Heath asks roughly.

"I don't know," I whisper, fear clawing my insides.

Without thinking, I inch closer to him just as he switches on the flashlight on his phone. He puts it on the side table near the door. The light brightens the room a little, making it easy for me to see him.

Looking down at me he says, "It's okay." Then inches closer to me.

His proximity doesn't bother me. I know he won't hurt me.

"Is there a generator or something?" I shake my head. "I think it's a power outage, so you might be out of electricity for a few hours."

I pull back from him to not bother him, but his fingers wrap around my wrist. Using his phone, he sheds light on the area where Dad held me last night. The bruises are on display.

"What the fuck is this, Hope?" His tone is deadly as it makes my spine straighten like a rod.

"I-it's-nothing." I try to wriggle my wrist out of his hold, but he keeps me in place.

Stepping closer, he towers over me. Our eyes meet and he keeps them locked with his intensity.

"Did someone fucking touch you *again*?" The darkness in his voice is dangerous as if he'd go out at this hour and search for the man who hurt me.

I'm surprised to see him like this.

"It's not like that," I whisper. *It's exactly like that.*

My heart races with anxiety. If he pushes the matter, I might end up blurting out everything to him.

He puts back his phone on the table.

I relax, thinking he's going to leave.

"Look at me. *Please.*" His voice is much softer than before.

Tilting back my head, I meet his gaze. There's no escape when his entire attention is on me.

Anger blazes through his blue eyes. "Someone is hurting you. Tell me the fucking name and I'll take care of them."

*Take care of them? As in I won't get hurt again?*

Tears cloud my vision when I think of him getting beaten by my dad. He'll do more damage to Heath than he could ever do to him.

"I'm fine," I say the words, hoping he'll believe them.

His fingers start caressing my knuckles. "I don't believe you."

I smile at him. "I'm fine, really."

"You have no idea what I'm fucking capable of. If you just tell me, they won't hurt you ever again." There's a promise behind his words.

"It's nothing." I brush it off again.

With a sigh, he looks away. His gaze stops at the stairs that lead to my room.

"Show me your room," he commands and my feet start moving. He follows me closely as I lead him upstairs.

I light up an old candle that I found in one of the drawers and close the windows.

When I turn around, I find Heath standing so impressively tall in my room that he makes it small. His eyes run over every inch of space as he takes it all in. I don't even want to know what he's thinking.

Regardless of how this place looks, I love it. I feel safe here. I'd never have this feeling anywhere else—maybe the library.

I quickly get rid of the textbooks and stationery that are on my bed from last night's study session and straighten the bedsheets.

"You can sit here," I offer, not that there is any other place where he can sit in this room.

Heath sits on the bed that squeaks under his weight.

My cheeks flush from discomfort. I think about what he's thinking and that further upsets me.

Pushing those thoughts away, I realize this is the first time a guy is in my room and sitting on my bed. A guy who must visit these kinds of rooms every night. I've never seen him with a girl before, but there's no way he's a virgin. That face. Those eyes. He probably wouldn't even have to ask them for it and just *do* it on the bed, against the wall—I need to *stop* thinking.

"So, you read books?" He gestures to my book wall.

"Yes." I smile.

He leans back against the wall and gets comfortable on my bed. He folds his arms behind his head and stares at me with golden specks flicking through his eyes.

"Your romance books?"

*He remembers.* "Yes."

"What are they about?"

*Oh God.* I never prepared myself for this question. How am I supposed to tell him the plot without sounding like an absolute hopeless romantic? Someone who's in love with the idea of love and everything that comes with it: whether it's complexity or simplicity.

"People," I say vaguely.

Heath quirks up his lips in amusement and glances at my books.

I stand in his path to block the view. If he reads the titles, he'll know exactly what they're about, and I'll never be able to meet his eyes again. There are some outrageous ones that I've turned toward the wall.

"Nothing special," I add, but my cheeks burn and that's a dead giveaway.

He stands up. "Nothing special, huh?" His height overshadows me and against his muscular body, I look like nothing.

While maintaining eye contact with me he starts walking toward me. For each one of his steps, I take two back. Soon my legs hit my book wall.

He bends down, then stands up.

I see a book in his hand, and I try to retrieve it, but he raises his arm in the air.

"Give it to me, please." I lift my arm to reach him, but he's just so tall.

"You're always reading. I want to know why."

He flips through the pages.

My heart rate drops. I think I'm going into cardiac arrest.

*He can't read the words on those pages.*

*Do something.*

*NOW!*

I push against him to reach my book, and we move backwards. He stumbles and falls on the bed with me on top of him. Our faces get close, and my hands are splayed on his chest where I can feel his thundering heartbeats. His heart is beating so fast. Just like mine.

My eyes fall to his lips. The heat in my stomach doubles until an inferno lights up in there.

I've never felt like this before. No guy has ever made me feel like he does. There's something about him. I can't pinpoint it. The reason why I'm drawn to him. The reason why my heart beats so fast when he's around. The reason why he makes me want to tell him everything.

Is it stupid that I'm aching to trust him when we're only strangers?

"Hope," he whispers painfully.

I watch his throat move incredibly slowly. The movement does something to me.

It's then I feel him against my thigh.

"I—sorry." I get off him, rip the book out of his hold, and hug it to my heaving chest.

*Oh my God. I... was that...did he...*

I can't think at all.

Heath sits up and opens his legs. Leaning over on his knees he rests his elbows on them. He then hangs his head low and closes his eyes in pain.

He must have been when I was sitting on top of him or perhaps... My body turns warm.

"I'm sorry. I didn't mean to—"

"It's fine. Give me a fucking minute," he grits out.

During that time, I arrange my textbooks on my study table and then put all my notes in the folder. Marie loves them since they proved to be quite helpful in the recent test. She didn't ask me, but I'll give them to her anyway.

Five minutes later, he finally speaks. "What's that?"

I find him pointing to the stuff I bought for making bracelets. "Something."

"Something?"

I sit next to him on the bed, with my knees drawn up to my chest. I put my chin on them to make myself small. "I'm..." my voice flatters.

It's hard for me to open up when I've been alone all my life. I don't know how to share things and tell someone about my interests, hobbies, or anything really.

When you're alone for a long time, it becomes a permanent thing. Almost like a scar that'll never go away.

His stare doesn't move away from my face. He's waiting for me to tell him even if it takes me ages.

I take a deep breath. "I'm making bracelets to sell them because I need the money."

It's not an unknown fact that Heath is rich. The car he drives looks expensive. Also, he lives uptown.

His eyebrows pinch. "You know how to make them?"

I nod. "When I was little, I used to make them. They're not that hard to make, to be honest."

He studies the supplies with new interest. I grow nervous around his quiet thoughts. Even his face is blank. I can't see what he's thinking and it's driving me crazy.

My overthinking brain starts to question whether I did the right thing by telling him. I wasn't even planning on telling Marie. But I've told Heath.

I just got this feeling that I can tell him about this.

When he doesn't say anything, I rush out. "But I can't do any of it. The back camera of my phone is broken. I tried with the front camera but it's hard to take pictures with it."

It's been a real hassle.

When he doesn't say anything, I grow even more nervous. I stand up to put away things in some safe corner when Heath grabs my hand. Warmth shoots up my arm and pours directly into my heart.

A cluster of fireworks explodes when he makes me sit next to him. I'm reeling from what just happened when he says, "You can use my phone."

*What?*

*He's offering to help me. But why?*

"No. It's all right," I reply quickly, and take my hand back to fidget with my fingers.

He stiffens before saying in a cold tone, "I'm not asking for permission. I'm telling you."

I frown at him. "And I'm telling you that I don't need your help. I'll figure it out."

"What's wrong with me trying to help you?"

"We're not friends."

He rolls his eyes. "I don't have to be your friend to help you."

"No, you don't have—" *He's right.*

"I want to help you," he tells me softly.

Those words hit me in the chest. Air escapes my lungs, and I clutch the ends of my top to understand the simple concept that's lost on me. No one has ever tried to help me before. It's always me helping others.

"But why?" I whisper.

There has to be an ulterior motive. A guy like him won't help a girl like me. No one has before.

He arches an eyebrow. "There has to be a fucking reason?"

"Yes."

"Then my reason is, I don't fucking know. I just want to." He looks deep into my eyes as if he might find the answer in them.

The dim light brings out the sharp edges of his handsome face. A glint of candle fire flickers through the black dot of his eyes and makes them look magical.

My heart flutters like a trapped bird inside my ribcage wanting to reach him.

The chiseled edges of his face appear so fierce and uninviting, but then there are his eyes, soft and blue, and so welcoming.

"You don't have to."

He ignores me. "You can come to my house, and we can work out the location to take pictures."

Slipping his hand into his pocket he pulls out his phone. "I've got the latest model. The camera is brilliant."

I salivate over his sleek, dark gray phone. It looks new and expensive with a big screen. His iPhone doesn't have a home button, unlike mine.

I badly want to hold it. I'm not into phones, but the latest iPhones make me weak.

"Do you want to test it out?" He advances his phone in my direction as if he can sense my eagerness.

My eyes widen. "What? No! It must work fine."

*I don't want to make a fool of myself by dropping it.*

He puts his phone in my lap. "Try it."

I switch on the phone and swipe up the black lock screen when the password screen pulls up. He tells me the password and I put it in. The black home screen appears with all the apps arranged in an order with hundred plus notifications.

I open the camera app and aim it at him. His eyes stare at the lens darkly and he barely eases his facial muscles when I snap a photo. I open it in the gallery.

"Satisfied?" he asks as he moves closer to me.

"Very."

Even in the photo, he looks insanely beautiful. I've never met a guy who looks as stunning as him.

"Wait for me after school tomorrow. I'll take you to my place."

I nod and hand him back his phone.

A yawn escapes my mouth and my shoulders sag with exhaustion.

"You should sleep."

I stand up. "I'll see you out."

"I can stay until the light comes back."

I shake my head at the prospect of Dad breaking in. "No, you can't."

He studies my face. When he doesn't get a read on me, he lets me walk him to his car.

The neighborhood is blacked out and quiet, creating an eerie surrounding that makes me shiver.

"I think I should—never mind." Getting in his car he drives away.

When I'm back in my room, I crawl into my bed and pull the blanket over me.

The candle will run out any time and then I'll be alone and scared in a cold, lonely house.

A selfish part of me wanted Heath to stay. The other part knows that if he did, he'd know about the secret I'm keeping from him.

# 14

## Heath

Pushing out the rusty iron gates, I follow the path leading deep into the cemetery that is as old as this town. It's situated at the foot of the hills with an enormous forest attached to the back of it. Clouds hang over the hills and slopes covered with trees.

A ghostly silence whirls in the air turning my blood cold. I come here often, but the serenity and quietness haunt me for hours later.

Slipping my hands into the pockets of my jeans, I approach Emery's grave. The hollowness in my chest expands into a black hole, and despair and sadness settle in and weigh on my chest like a rock.

I glare at the tombstone, reading the details for the millionth time. I've stared at those few lines for so long that by now I've memorized them.

She was only sixteen when cancer killed her. In a matter of months, it progressed so aggressively that chemo and radiation did not affect it. It was past the stage of treatment. Instead, a deadline hung over her head.

In her last days, she was positive. Her light circled her so brightly. I wished I'd soaked enough in it so it'd last me a lifetime.

Every single day down to every minute, I spent by her side. There was peace listening to the beeping sounds of the machines and watching her breathe when she was sleeping.

I wish I could stretch those moments for several years more because letting go of her so soon broke my fucking heart—something that feels empty now.

Some moments in life alter the whole course of your existence. They are like shooting stars. You never see them coming but when you do, it's too damn late. They are gone so quickly.

Sitting on my toes, I put down the bouquet of fresh lilies I bought on my way. It was her favorite flower. She always wished someone would buy them for her.

Words die on my tongue. I used to talk to her for hours when I first visited her grave, but with time lack of response burrowed a hole in me. She is on the other side of the world. Maybe it's time I believe it and stop holding onto her like she's a ghost and roams around. That'd be crazy to believe anyway. I want her to be in the afterlife, not here, even if that means I'll never see her or talk to her.

I turn to leave when I catch sight of Denrick. When he sees me, his eyes go wide, and he freezes into a damn statue. I breathe fire seeing his ugly face.

Before I know it, I'm striding over to him with heavy steps. "What the fuck are you doing here?" I seethe, gripping him by his collar and yanking him over to me.

"The same reason why you are here."

Lifting my arm, I punch him across the face and his face whips to the other side.

My veins are close to bursting as adrenaline mixed with rage flows through my blood.

"I told you to stay away from here." I kick him in the stomach.

Denrick falls to the ground and doubles over in pain. A groan leaves his mouth as he clutches his stomach and rolls to one side.

"Stop it," he wheezes out, eyes glistening with tears.

My eyes fall on the scar I gave him. When I found out about him, I slammed his head into the wall to kill him, but the fucker survived. He was Emery's secret boyfriend, and she'd told no one about him—not even me which annoyed me. Later, I asked why she didn't, and she told me I'd be mad at her. It was a valid reason. I wanted to protect her from everything and everyone. Denrick was the first person who noticed the signs of my sister's failing health, but he didn't do anything about it. Because of him, it was too late.

*You were as ignorant as him.*

Fuck. I was.

I should've paid more attention to Emery. I should've noticed how her health was worsening when I thought she was just exhausted from school. It was fucking naive of me.

One mistake led me to this moment.

"I should fucking kill you for what you did." I grit in anger as my body vibrates with the desire to just do it. But I don't. Because I'm also to blame.

After the cemetery, I spend the rest of the day at my secret spot. My mind is a tangled web of thoughts and memories. I like visiting her grave, it brings me closer to her because she's physically there, but it always takes a toll on me.

I go to this dark place that makes me want to die.

Sadness weighs so heavily over my chest that it hurts to breathe. Panic attacks also happen, and I wish for one of them to end me, but I survive every time.

I think about Sebastian and Marie. The two people in my life who'd be devastated if something happened to me. In moments of pure chaos, where my mind overtakes my body, their faces peek through my paranoia and stop me from attempting something.

It hurts.

It hurts a fucking lot.

I want the pain to stop. I want to feel better. I want to breathe.

But the reminder that my sister, my best friend, my favorite person, isn't in the world anymore keeps coming back.

I drive to school after smoking a bunch of cigarettes. My car reeks of the pungent smell, but at least I'm not feeling chaotic anymore. My mind is quiet and calm.

I'm waiting for Hope outside the school when my phone pings.

**Sebastian: You missed school again.**
**Sebastian: Is everything okay?**

My best friend worries too much. Especially after he's come out of rehab and therapy. He thinks he can help me, but he can't. There's nothing wrong with me. I'm fucking fine.

**Heath: Everything's fine.**

A knock on the window pulls my attention. Sebastian is standing next to my car holding his phone with my text on screen.

I unlock the door, and he quickly gets in.

"Where were you?" he asks in a tone laced with worry.

"No greeting for me?" I tease him to move over this question.

He faces me with the expression I'm-not-letting-this-go.

*Fuck.* Now I'm going to get fucking lectured. Fucking great.

"Stop dodging the question and tell me where you were."

If I told him he'd worry ten times more, and I don't want to cause him distress. Since last year he's tried his best to help me in whatever way that he can. He was there for me more than he was there for himself. Something I'll never forgive myself for. I was somewhat privy to his struggles at his home, but he didn't tell me how fucking bad they were. He's always been someone to take care of others and not think about himself. He's the most selfless person I know. For once, I want to be like him. Deal with my shit on my own.

Instead of answering him, I search for Hope in the crowd.

A pretty girl reading a book. Where is she?

Sebastian sighs heavily. "Heath, stop ignoring me."

"I'm not."

His expression hardens. "Where were you?"

I sigh, knowing he won't let go. "I was at the cemetery."

A frown dips between his eyebrows, and his eyes fill with sorrow.

Fuck, not that look. I want to dig a fucking cave in the hills and never come out, just to avoid this pathetic look. I don't need fucking pity or sympathy.

Yes, my sister died. It doesn't mean I'm a fragile, broken person who needs assurance, nice words or a fucking hug. I need nothing. I don't want others to worry about me, especially Sebastian. I hate when he stresses over me.

Why don't I just die already?

He watches me closely. "Your knuckles are red. Did you punch a tree or something?"

"Denrick was there."

He curses. "Heath don't tell me you—"

My gaze finally locks on the person I'm looking for. "Get out of my car."

He pauses, then says, "Excuse me!"

I glare at him. "I have something to do, and I need you to leave this second."

"What the fuck does that mean?"

*For fuck's sake.*

He sniffs the air, then narrows his eyes. "You were smoking, weren't you? How many times—"

"Sebastian, leave."

I see Hope nearing my car with Marie who's talking to her in her animated way—moving hands and smiling like a sun. But she's not why my heart is almost beating out of my chest. It's the girl next to her.

Hope is in a plaid skirt that has her long, thin legs exposed and a cream sweater that fits her skinny frame perfectly. Her brown hair falls on her shoulders in soft waves that make me want to run my fingers through it.

*What the fuck?* I did not think that.

I must be staring at her because Sebastian follows my gaze.

"You're picking her up, aren't you?" He shoots me a teasing smile.

I can barely speak. I'm stunned by how fucking beautiful she looks.

He chuckles and I have the urge to smash his fucking face. "This is interesting."

Hope and Marie stand next to my car engrossed in a conversation that makes Hope laugh and hold her book tightly to her chest. She looks even more beautiful up close.

I gesture to Sebastian to get out, but he leans back in the seat. I swear if he doesn't get out I'll kill him with my bare hands.

"Sebastian—"

"Fine, okay. No need to growl at me."

He opens the door. Marie bends down and kisses him, then turns to me.

"Hi." She waves at me with a grin.

"Tell your boyfriend to get his ass out of my car," I order.

Marie turns to Sebastian, who whispers something to her that makes her smile big.

Sebastian steps out and shakes hands with Hope which makes me want to punch him. He could have waved or smiled. No need to *touch* her. They start talking when I beep the horn, and he bends down and grins. I actually hate him.

"Hope get in the car," I say in a tense voice.

She gets inside quickly. She puts her bag on the floor and her book on her lap. I notice her red cheeks that make her look so fucking pretty.

My hands tighten around the steering wheel. I try to extinguish the feelings burning inside of me. But when I see her, my stomach curls in a weird feeling. What the actual fuck is this girl doing to me?

"Hi," she says with a hint of a smile.

"Hi," I say looking into her beautiful eyes.

"Um, thank you for last night, and also for picking me up." She tucks a strand of her hair behind her ear and peeks up at me.

My palms turn warm.

Is it fucking hot in here?

Why is it fucking hot in here?

Summer is over. Why the fuck am I sweating?

I turn on the ignition and pull out of the school.

"It's nothing," I grumble.

"It's something," she says sweetly.

That fucking smile. I swear I'd do anything for it.

"Are you hungry?"

Hope is so skinny it makes me want to feed her. I haven't seen her under her clothes—I imagine it sometimes—but I bet she's all bones and no skin. Something about it unsettles me because I know how it ended when I ignored it.

"No." She fiddles with her fingers in her lap.

I know right away she's nervous, so I make the decision. "I'm gonna grab food from the diner."

At the station, I make the usual order and pay for it. When we pick the bags from the next station I put hers on her lap and mine on the back seat. I knew she wouldn't eat unless it was for me too. So, I did it for her. Which is odd. I've never done things out of kindness or care for anyone except for my friends and sister.

"You didn't have—"

"It's already done."

"Thank you." She smiles at me. *This* smile is different from before. It's the kind that makes me want to buy every item off the menu and have it in front of her.

*What the fuck is going on with me? Why am I feeling like this with her?*

Pressing hard on the accelerator, I drive around while she eats. My playlist plays in the background that's filled with Chase Atlantic and The Coldplay songs. The two artists I listen to the most.

Once she's done I drive us to my place. Punching in the passcode, the gates open of my house, I speed down the driveway and park in the garage.

When I cut the engine, I notice Hope scan the room in awe. I watch her with strange amusement.

"Do you like cars?" I ask.

"Who doesn't?" She stares at the white Audi that my sister owned. I haven't driven it since her.

My heart squeezes into a ball. I push down the despair and focus on the girl beside me.

"That one isn't mine," I share.

"Oh." She purses her lips. "Who does it belong to?"

I fight with myself whether to share the information or not. I know she'd feel sorry for me and try to tip-toe around me like I'm broken—which I'm fucking not—and some selfish part of me doesn't want that. I want her to see me like she does right now. Just a normal guy, who feels strange things when she's near him.

I step out. "We should get inside."

Hope stares at the foyer with big eyes, taking in every inch of the walls and ceiling. Fascination and wonder cross her face as if she's seeing a mansion for the first time in her life.

Compared to her house, mine is a work of art. There are plenty of rooms, bathrooms, and hallways with a private garage. Also, a garden of one good acre of land, with an array of trees and bushes. The staff and security are also present.

My parents wanted Emery and me to grow up in a nice house, but not a loving home. This place has everything a child could wish for, every luxury you could desire for, yet it lacks warmth and sweetness. Something I felt when Marie invited Sebastian and me to her place. Her house feels like home. Maybe it's because she has parents who love each other and adore their daughter.

"Let's go up to my room."

I should give her a tour. Maybe later.

We take the stairs and walk down the long hallway that has my room at the end of it. I open the door for her and let her in.

She pauses in the doorway. "Wow."

My room is my sanctuary. I spend most of my time here. From breaking down to having panic attacks in the middle of the night. This place feels safe for me to be myself and not have someone else witness the worst moments of myself.

She gapes. "You have a really big room."

I give her a gentle push to enter. "I guess."

"My room can fit in here fifty times."

I cough the chuckle that threatens to leave my throat. "Don't you think that's too much?" I fold my arms over my chest.

Her gaze immediately cuts to my arms, then back at me. "I'm sure."

I gesture to the couch, and she follows.

I contemplate whether to sit at the other end of the couch or beside her. The decision is easily made when she looks up at me with her brown eyes. I can't resist being away from them.

Cursing at myself, I join her and watch as she retrieves different bracelets from her bag and spreads them on the coffee table. They all look impressive. Beads, clay objects like flowers, circles, butterflies, cubes, and stars, in various colors and sizes fill the strings with each one having a silver clasp.

I have no idea how she came up with this, but she's fucking brilliant and creative.

Because of Emery, and the little jewelry that I wear, I have an eye for good stuff. Without a doubt, Hope makes good stuff. Amazing stuff.

She watches me with a tiny smile and flushed face. She's embarrassed.

"This is beautiful," I find myself saying. My true, honest opinion.

The crimson red in her cheeks suffuses more, and she refuses to make eye contact with me. "Thank you. I made these—" picking up a good amount "—last night."

"You didn't sleep?" I ask quickly.

"I couldn't sleep."

I notice the quiver in her voice. I want to ask her about it.

Something tells me that she'll shut down. Like last night. The way she told me 'Let it go, please.' I'd be a fucking asshole to push her again.

Deciding not to ponder over it, I take out my phone and hand it to her.

For an hour, we take tons of pictures using the coffee table as a prop. Afterward, I help her make an Instagram account and teach her a few things about marketing. The more I tell her, the more she's captivated. I find it fucking cute.

*I'm losing my fucking mind. That's what's happening.*

By the time we wind up, the night covers every inch of the sky with clouds flying in different forms.

Besides me, she posts the photos and closes the app in a hurry. "It's done."

"Nervous?" I ask as she hands me back my phone.

She nods. "Very much. I don't know if anyone will buy it. It's nerve-wracking."

"The very first thing our business teacher taught us was 'every opportunity in life is a risk.' You either win or you learn."

She rubs her arms. I immediately know she's nervous.

It's puzzling how easily I read her. Her body language speaks to me. I can't help but store every new thing I learn about her because I want to.

"You're right. It's not like I have anything to lose."

"This will fucking work," I assure her, so she doesn't look sad. For some strange reason that frown and worry swimming in her eyes tug the strings of my numb heart.

A smile dances on her lips. "Thank you for helping me. I wish I could help you back in some way."

"I don't need your help."

"There could be something."

I lean back and turn my head toward her. "Don't fucking dwell over it."

Mimicking me, she leans back and turns her head toward me. "I'm not used to kindness."

"You should get used to it." *I'll be offering you a fucking lot of it.*

"You're a good person."

I don't say anything.

Deep down I know that I'm not. I hurt people with my icy tone. That's not something a good person does.

"That car belongs to my sister," I explain.

Surprise washes over her like an unexpected tidal wave.

I gulp hard to swallow the brimming emotions. Why the fuck I shared that with her?

"You have a sister?" she asks quietly.

I nod and avoid eye contact.

"Is she around? I should've greeted her." She stands up to go search for her. If only she were here.

Taking her hand, I pull her down and she falls over me. Those light brown eyes peer up at me in confusion, but otherwise, her body stays relaxed in my hold. Good. I don't want her to fear me.

"She's dead," I state in a gravel tone that scratches my throat in the most agonizing way.

A gasp leaves her, and her eyes fill with tears. The sight should annoy the fuck out of me, but it doesn't. I see her feeling my pain and understanding me.

"W-when? How?" Her questions are better than sympathy and pity.

"Cancer. Last year," I brief, my voice monotone due to repeating those words a dozen times. At this point, I can even write them down in my sleep.

Hope stares at me with such despair and sorrow, my hand itches to comfort her. I just don't know how to do that. I barely know how to comfort *myself* on nights when I'm crying like a toddler while curled up on my bed.

My mind is trapped in a haze, which explains why I don't react when arms circle around my neck, and a warm body presses against mine in a fierce hold.

My heart beats loudly.

I stay frozen in her hold. I want nothing more than to return it, but I can't fucking move.

Emery's face laps around my mind. She's all I can focus on. The fact that she isn't here anymore. It hurts. It hurts a lot.

"I'm sorry for your loss," she whispers in my shoulder, bringing my attention to her.

I take a deep breath. Her lavender scent enters me and takes over me like a storm without warning. She tightens her arms around my neck with unspoken words. *I feel your pain and I want to take it away.*

"It's fine." The words are just words.

Hope doesn't say anything. She just keeps her arms around me.

For the first time in my life, she's all I can think of instead of my sister.

"You didn't need to hug me," I say.

"You looked like you needed a hug."

Fuck me.

Someone knocks on the door making her scramble off me. It opens, making me want to kill the person on the other side for interrupting us *and* my hug.

"Dinner is ready, sir." Derek flits his gaze on Hope. I can already read the suspicions in his head and the news traveling to my dad. I really don't want that to happen. I want to keep every aspect of my life hidden away from my parents because their opinions don't matter to me. *They* don't matter to me.

"I should go. I didn't think it'd get this late." Hope tosses everything into her bag.

"Stay," I end up saying and it surprises us both.

She clears her throat. "I'll eat at home."

I stand up. She's a couple of inches shorter than me and reaches my chest.

"Eat dinner with me, then I'll drive you home," I suggest.

Her teeth gnaw at her bottom lip and the action makes my insides twist and turn.

"Are you sure?" she asks in a low voice.

"Yes," I reply in a heartbeat.

"I'll stay then." She smiles.

# 15

## HOPE

*"You don't ask for hugs. You take them."*

I blame Marie for my actions. It's the only plausible reason why I ended up hugging Heath.

After he told me about his sister I couldn't help but console him in some way. He looked concrete like a wall, but I could see it in his eyes, the way he missed his sister. He didn't shed a tear, but that didn't mean he wasn't crying on the inside.

He was in pain. I saw it.

I can only imagine how he carries the weight of such sorrow with him every day. It must bury him some days, or perhaps every day. I know so little about him. Like a puzzle, there are so many pieces to him. With each encounter I gather a new piece, hoping to fit it somewhere in the giant picture. That day in the hallway when I first met him, he was rude and angry, now he's helping me. All the rumors and whispers I've heard about him in the past are like jagged, imperfect pieces that don't belong.

Lying in my bed, my mind keeps revolving around the guy who's the total opposite of the person I expected.

Heath appears so tall and muscular when he's standing next to me. He can snap me in half if he wants to, but with him being near I don't feel scared. I feel safe and comfortable.

I open the windows. Chill air sweeps in like an uninvited guest and greets me. I embrace it as I sit on the windowsill.

Dinner at his house was quiet. We didn't talk, even in the car when he dropped me off three hours ago. Since then, my mind has been replaying him.

Musky wood scent. Blue eyes. Dark hair. That's all I focus on for the rest of the night.

"Hope, did you know..." Marie prates about the game tournament she participated in with Sebastian and how they won second place. The rest of it fades into oblivion when I see Heath. He is leaning against his locker, with one strap of his bag slung over his shoulder as he stares at me.

"...we might participate another time." Marie stands in my way. "What are you looking at?"

My cheeks burn. "Nothing."

She turns around and we both look at Heath who's listening to Sebastian, but his gaze is on me.

A smirk appears on her lips. "I see now. It's Heath."

I fold my arms and don't answer.

"Did something happen between you two?"

"No."

Her eyes narrow. "My lie detector is catching signals."

"It *can't*. I'm not lying." I tightly hold my book that I haven't touched since yesterday.

She takes my wrist and leads me to the bathrooms which are empty. Closing the door with a thud, she blocks the path and stares at me with interest.

"Tell me. What is it?" She taps her foot impatiently.

*Should I tell her?*

Marie must've seen my reluctance, she steps closer with a soft expression on her face. "Someone taught me the rules of friendship. There are fifty of them.

I'll teach all of them to you, though it'll take me a while. Anyway, one of them is, 'Friends tell each other things.' That is if you want to."

"I want to, Marie." I lean against the sink to collect my thoughts. I never thought I'd find people who'd want to know about me. The reason why it's so hard to talk to them about myself and my feelings. I'm not used to it.

For the past sixteen years, I've been on my own. No friends. No cousins. No aunts and uncles. No grandparents. I've had very little contact with people. It's bewildering now that I'm thrown into a friend group that is close and tight. Some part of me doesn't want to be lonely anymore, but I don't know how *not* to be. It's ingrained in my DNA.

However, I need to take the step. I don't want to be the same lonely girl anymore.

I brief Marie on yesterday, excluding the fact Heath told me about his sister, wanting to keep that to myself. I bet she already knows.

"Oh my God. Heath made you an account and is helping you!" Marie shrieks in excitement.

My face burns up to a hundred degrees. "Yes."

"What's the account name? I need to follow you." Marie follows me and likes every single post. She also shares it to her account. "Why didn't you tell me? I could've helped you."

"I didn't know how to tell you. Heath and I were just talking. Somehow I ended up telling him. I wasn't going to tell anyone. I don't even know if it'll work."

She grabs my shoulder and demands my attention. "*It'll work*, I promise. I'll make sure it works." She speaks with such conviction even I manage to find some confidence in myself.

"Thank you, Marie."

"Always. Are you and Heath friends?"

I laugh in disbelief. "No."

"That's a bummer."

"He's *just* helping me."

She nods. "He helps people at the community center every weekend."

Disbelief fills me. "He does?"

She rolls her eyes. "Of course not. He's not that kind of person." Joining me against the sink she says, "I think he's got a thing for you."

I can't hold my laughter. "I don't think so."

"That's what everyone said when Sebastian was spending time with me."

Her words make me think, but I instantly block the process.

I don't want to believe in something and then lose my faith in it. I'd be delusional if I think Heath has feelings for me when he's never entertained a single girl in school. No matter how persistent they are he ignores them like plague. It's kinda contradicting as most guys with bad reputations are also involved in bed with multiple girls. Heath is nothing like that.

It'd be so easy to read his thoughts if there was a book about him. I'd be able to understand him better and find out if he has any feelings for me or not.

"It's not like that."

She smiles. "Time will tell." Taking my hand she adds, "I know you're not used to friends, but you can talk to me about anything. I'll never judge you or not listen to you." A sad look crosses her face, but I don't indulge in it. Mainly because I don't want to push her.

"You can tell me anything, too. I'll be there for you."

She pulls me to her, and I hug her back. It's the hug that reminds me of all the quotes I've read in books regarding friendships. Marie makes me believe in friendship.

Suddenly a group of girls walk in, and we separate.

"Is that Heath Travon outside?" One of them squeals.

"I think so. Let me check." The brunette peeks outside and turns around with a beaming smile. "He's still there. God, he looks so fucking hot. I wish he'd look at me."

"He wouldn't look at you." The tall blonde girl, Shian, walks to the mirror and adjusts her hair. "I bet he's waiting for me."

"They're so delusional," Marie whispers, then she says to them. "he's *definitely* not waiting for you."

Shian spares a condescending glance at Marie. "Who the fuck are you?"

"I'm Marie Anderson, his best friend." Marie folds her arms in a confident manner and doesn't back down.

Shian laughs and looks back at her friends. "Yeah sure, weirdo."

Marie takes a step forward, I pull her back. "We should go."

Taking our bags we exit as they whisper behind us. I've watched these girls being mean to others, but after a group of famous girls, just like them were expelled, people stopped bullying. There are strict repercussions if a single complaint is filed.

Heath straightens when he sees us. Like every day he's wearing all black and brooding like he hates the world.

His blue eyes fall on me and his face hardens. "I need to talk to you."

I look over at Marie and she's not there. I search the hallway, but she's gone. *How did she get away so fast?*

I check the time. "Class is about to start."

"You don't even listen to Miss Sheila," Heath deadpans.

"That's not true!" *How does he know that?*

A satisfied smirk curls on his lips. "I saw you doodling in your notebook."

I assault my lip to come up with a reply.

"C'mon." He takes me to his car outside. We pass the sycamore tree. I remember it was right here where I saw him that day. We've come so far now.

Opening the door for me, he gestures to me to get inside and then joins me.

"The whole night my phone was buzzing with notifications." His face turns cold.

I wince. "I'm sorry for that. I'll download Instagram and then you—"

"I'll put it on silent next time."

I purse my lips and fidget with my fingers. "Did you get any sleep?"

Heath pauses. "I don't sleep much."

That's all he's going to tell me.

As someone who's been struggling with sleep lately, I understand how hard it is when your mind is running a thousand miles per hour. There are so many directions your thoughts take you. I always end up with anxiety and fear. Two emotions that I hate feeling.

"You got some orders." He hands me the phone. I see messages from two people.

"That was fast." My spirits lift. I admit I didn't think this would work, but it looks like there's a chance. There's a little hope.

*Not my name being a literal feeling. Arghhh.*

"Your account is new. It'll be best to post daily if you want it to grow."

"I had no idea." I know so little about social media. My whole world revolves around books, books, and books. Sometimes music.

"I own a few accounts, so I know." He briefs in a monotone voice.

I don't ask him what he does with them—not that he'll share. He is private and keeps his secrets close. Even after weeks, I know so little about him. Not that I mind. I just think he'll tell me when he feels comfortable. Like yesterday.

I read the orders and write down their information in the back of my notebook.

"How exactly are you going to mail them?" Heath turns on the car and aims the AC fans in my direction.

"Mail."

"Do you have the money for that?" he asks skeptically.

"Yes. I sent them the item price plus delivery, so I won't be at a loss."

One side of his mouth quirks up. "Smart girl."

Two words and my entire body floods with heat.

I look everywhere but him, though he's focused solely on me. His attention makes my cheeks red and increases my heart rate.

"I'll pick you up after school to go to my place."

"I can get there on my own." I'm embarrassed that I have to take rides from him, and I don't give him back in any way. He's helped me so much, but I can't say the same.

His eyebrows furrow. "How would you do that? You don't have money for anything."

What!

*He...did he really say those words to me?*

*I...*

*Why does my chest hurt?*

Those cruel words pierce through my heart like a sharp knife meant to tear you apart.

I open my mouth to say something, anything, but no words come out.

All this time he was nice to me. I forgot he's known for being rude.

*I'm so stupid. So stupid.*

Without saying a word, I exit the car.

# 16

## HEATH

"You said *those words* to her?" Sebastian stares at me with his grass-like green eyes.

"It was the fucking truth." I throw away the dirty towel over the bench press and get on the treadmill to run myself to exhaustion.

My best friend joins me, not showing any signs that he'll let go of this topic. He's always been a persistent one.

"Heath, what you said was condescending," he reprimands me.

"It wasn't." Turning up the speed I run as if my life depends on it.

I want the pain in my muscles to numb the pain in my chest.

"You're an asshole."

"I've been called worse." I meet his gaze in the full-length mirror covering the entire wall of the home gym in my house. Well, not my house technically. My parent's house.

He scowls in displeasure, clearly irritated with my carefree attitude. "Then you need to work hard because being an asshole is getting old."

I ignore him and increase the speed. I need the fucking pain in my chest to disappear. It's been there since I said those words to Hope. I stepped over the line with her. I hurt her—which was the last thing I wanted to do.

For fuck's sake.

"You need to slow down," My best friend says from beside me as he runs at six mph while I'm at eight mph.

"I'm fine," I heave out, my breathing ragged.

Pain starts to descend into my muscles with the force of a meteor, but nothing is comparable to Hope's teary eyes and sad face. I might've ripped her heart out with how forlorn she looked.

*Fucking damnit.*

Our last interaction takes over my brain and kicks out every other thought until all I can think about is her. I've hurt people a lot of times, but this is the first time there's a weight over my chest that refuses to move no matter how hard I try. Her face keeps swinging in front of me like a pendulum.

I feel like shit for hurting her.

Those tears in her eyes were because of me. I'm such a fucking asshole.

When my legs can't take it anymore, I get off the machine.

Silence fills the room with the force of a dark sky. Tension ripples through my bones.

"You need to apologize to her," Sebastian says in a strained voice that I've only heard him use on me a few times.

"If the truth fucking hurt her, that's her problem. I didn't mean to." I feel awful for hurting her, but I don't have the courage to approach her and apologize. She might not even want to see my face after what I said to her.

Fuck. It was mean. I'll deserve whatever she hits me with. Probably a book.

Sebastian puts his hand on my shoulder. "You're wrong here. You need to do the right thing if you want to keep her close. Girls are sensitive. You have to be aware of not hurting them, but they're the best damn thing that could ever happen to you. I know from experience." He grins, definitely thinking about Marie.

I wipe my damp neck and then hunch over my knees trying to catch my breath. When I close my eyes, I see her face and the weight sinks deeper over my chest.

Why the fuck I'm feeling this way?

"I won't apologize, Sebastian. Forget it."

I need to stay away from her. I hurt her today and it's eating me alive. I don't want to do it again. I'm as volatile as a volcano. My fire should never burn her.

The next day at school, I attend all my classes for the sake of keeping atten-dance. The way I fuck up things around here, only two things keep me here. One, the handsome donation my parents make to the school, and second, my grades and attendance.

As much as I don't want to be here, I also don't want to be a dropout.

"Heath." A silvery voice nears me.

I take a long inhale of the cigarette and ignore her. This is not the first time a girl has approached me. I'm used to their flirty tactics, I just never indulge myself.

A petite girl with brown hair and blue eyes stands in front of me. She's dressed in a skirt that's too short and a top that's too tight. Every part of her is accentuated to grab attention, specifically when she crosses her bare leg.

I exhale the smoke, the cloud wafting in the space between us. A clear sign to leave me alone, but she's adamant about not going away.

For fuck's sake.

She wears a whimsical smile. "I saw you outside the girl's bathroom yesterday. Did you want to talk to me about something?"

*What the actual fuck?*

I look at her from head to toe. *I don't like her.*

"I don't know who the fuck you are." I take a drag and search for Sebastian. School ended five minutes ago, what the fuck is he still doing inside? He's supposed to shoo her away. Maybe I should text Marie. She'll come to my rescue.

I stay silent hoping she'll go away. I thought fucking wrong.

"I know you." She steps closer and arches her back pushing out her big breasts in my direction.

My eyes meet her in iciness. "You don't know a fucking thing about me."

For fuck's sake. What's her problem?

"I know your sister died—"

The cigarette hits the ground as I inch closer to her. "Don't you fucking dare speak about her." I take a breath. "Leave me alone. I have no interest in you."

That's how I am with every girl who approaches me. They irk me. I can't look at them, let alone think about touching them. They either think they can fix me or give me a good time. I want neither.

The girl steps back with a scowl. Disappointment blazes through her eyes. "Gosh, you're so rude and angry. What's your fucking problem?"

I frown in confusion. "My problem is, you're wasting my fucking time."

"Well, you're lucky that I'm even sparing you a few minutes." She crosses her arm.

Slowly, I spell it out to her. "I. Don't. Care."

"Fuck you!" Stomping her feet she walks away but stops when Hope gets in her way. That girl has a serious problem with walking into people.

"Get out of my way, nerd." The crazy girl screams in her face. Hope quickly side steps.

After a minute, she moves in my direction, holding onto her book that has a bookmark wedged between its pages, and a pen stuck to the cover.

At the sight of her, my anger begins to dissipate. She's in black tights and a maroon baggy top. Her hair is tied in a braid with a few strands flying around. She looks fucking pretty.

"Hi." She looks at me with her brown eyes.

"Hi," I reply softly.

She holds the book tightly to her chest as if gathering courage from it. "I need the password to the account. Marie said she'd help me."

Marie said what? I'm the one who made the account, and I know plenty because I've studied marketing. Marie only knows coding and other computer shit. Nowhere qualified enough to manage a business.

"She isn't equipped to help you," I say in a rough tone, trying to conceal the unknown fury curling inside of me.

*She's staying away like I wanted.*

*Well, I don't fucking want it anymore.*

"We'll figure it out then," she replies with a determination that I've never seen in her before.

*Yeah. I don't fucking like it one bit.*

*I don't want her to stop talking to me.*

*Apologize!!!*

Emotions cloud my mind and blur the lines of logic. "No, you won't."

A frown creases her delicate features. "Excuse me?"

"You heard me." I step closer to her. Her lavender scent catches my senses. I'm surprised at how much I like it.

"I need to use it. I can't if you have it," she protests.

Something is seriously wrong with me because I can't seem to focus on anything but her eyes. *Fuck.* Have they always been so beautiful or is it just today?

"Did you send the packages?" It's strange how I was thinking about it at midnight.

Hope gets puzzled by the change of topic, but nods. "Yes. I didn't make much money, but it's just the beginning."

"You need to look at some trends and figure out what's selling." The advice spills out of me quickly. I don't hold back because I genuinely want her to succeed. And to see her smile.

For fuck's sake.

Shock flashes through her eyes. "I'll s-see what I can do."

"You can come—"

Her face turns serious. "No. I don't want to. And please give me back the account. I told Marie and she's eager to help me without reminding me about my social status." Her voice gets quiet toward the end. I feel like a prick for letting her believe that.

An apology is sitting on the tip of my tongue. I can't get it past my fucking lips.

When did speaking become so difficult?

Sorry. It's one fucking word.

Taking out my keys, I unlock my car and get inside. Rolling down the window I say, "I told you, I'm not giving it back."

She glares—or she tries to, but it's definitely not a glare—at me. "It's my account."

"That *I* made."

She shuts up and eyes the passenger seat, then straightens in stubbornness.

"I'll make a new one then," she announces, surprising the fuck out of me.

I clench my jaw. I didn't expect her to stand her ground and make me feel ten times worse than I already do.

Pretty girl might be bad for my health.

Turning on her feet she walks away and leaves me in a fucking foul mood.

# 17

## HOPE

Heath is a big ogre who's rude and mean.

*Okay, that's not true.*

*Just because I'm mad at him doesn't mean I should compare him to that ugly thing.*

I can't believe he's withholding my account just because I refuse to work with him when he's the one who insulted me. He doesn't even have the decency to apologize to me. If anything, he's full of pride, arrogance, and other bad things.

I shouldn't have accepted his help in the first place. Why did I?

*You were desperate.* I was. I am. I made six bucks minus the delivery charges. It's not much, but it's something. However, at this rate, it'll take long before I can earn hundreds.

Standing outside the huge, black metal gates I search for the doorbell but don't find it.

Don't rich people have a doorbell?

Making a fist I knock, and cup my hand when it throbs. Geez, how hard is that thing?

A bodyguard in a fine black suit comes out and scrutinizes me. "Who are you?"

I squirm under his hard gaze.

However, I can't back down now. I walked thirty minutes to get here. I won't go back until I have that account.

"Hi. I wanted to meet Heath. We go to the same school."

The man studies me and speaks into his intercom, probably to call for backup to throw me out. I mean he doesn't have to. He'd been fine alone with his massive body.

Chills dance on my spine and weaken it, but I refuse to let him intimidate me. There's only one person who scares me. My father. From plaguing my reality to my dreams, he's everywhere. I can't escape him. My nights are spent wide awake because I'm scared of him moving back in which won't happen. Mom won't let him, especially when he's drinking. Or maybe she will. The probability keeps me up day and night. After all, love conquers all, even abuse, toxicity, and addiction.

The bodyguard escorts me inside. I stand on the front porch when a familiar man greets me and asks for my name. I've seen him before when he came to inform Heath about the dinner. Seeing all the staff, bodyguards, and the luxurious mansion, I'm astounded. This is something I've never seen before. Only read in books.

People are rich. Heath is filthy rich.

I wait outside as he leaves to get Heath.

The enormous mansion is magnificent. I look like an ant in front of it. In ways it's intimidating. The garden and the array of flowers bordering it is a beautiful sight. Also, the open property gives a marvelous view of the setting sun.

The door opens. Heath steps out panting hard *and* half-naked.

*Don't look.*

*Don't look.*

*Don't—*

My eyes trace his face before dropping to his *very* naked chest and torso. Oh my God. He's ripped. His body is toned and filled with muscles that make a perfect six-pack. With each breath he takes, his chest moves, and my gaze notices every time. He's in black shorts that expose his beautiful, muscular, and strong body. He's tall and built like a professional player.

Heat curls in my stomach. I lift my eyes to his face that's equally gorgeous. He's straight out of a book with all this beauty and perfection.

"I can come back later." I try hard to not stare at his sweaty, hard chest.

He shakes his head, "No. Come in." Holding the door open, he widens the space for me to walk in.

This time I'm not flustered by the extravagance of his home. The architecture is modern and sophisticated, and the interior design is in soft tones of colors.

We stand in the foyer with a beautiful chandelier hanging above our heads that must cost a fortune.

Heath watches me for a minute then says, "Give me a few minutes to change."

I see his bloody knuckles. "You're bleeding."

"It's nothing."

"I can wrap them for you." I dislike myself for being nice to him, but I can't help it. That's just how I am to the core. I like helping people.

"No need." With that, he leaves.

I stand in the foyer alone until that man in the uniform arrives like a ghost. I gasp and he gives me a crooked smile. "Ma'am, let me take you to the living room."

"Please call me Hope."

He nods and takes me down the hallway to the living room that could fit an army in it. It's spacious and well-lit with chandeliers and golden lights. Expensive sofa sets, imported rugs, and thick curtains complement the aesthetic of the room. Magazines and a vase sit on the coffee table in front of the fireplace.

"Do you need anything?" he asks.

"No, thank you." I expect him to leave me alone, but he lingers in the doorway and watches me curiously. His black eyes feel like they can see through me. "I'm good. You don't need to stand there."

He doesn't look away. "I wanted to ask you something if you don't mind."

I gulp. "Sure."

"Do you and sir share classes?"

"Two classes."

"Are you his *friend*?" There's an edge to his voice that I can't shake off.

"Not really. We're in the same friend group."

The man steps further into the room and sucks the air. "You know his friends?"

"Yes. I know Marie and Sebastian. Marie is my friend," I explain, hoping he'll step back and leave me alone.

The man creeps me out with his intelligent eyes, wrinkled face, and straight posture. "May I ask—"

"Leave her alone, Derek." A booming voice carries through the room as Heath comes in. "I'll let you know if we need anything." Then his stare falls on me, checking to make sure I'm okay before settling on my tote bag. My backpack was filled with textbooks and notes. It was getting late, so I opted for the second option. "Let's go up to my room."

All the way I can feel a steady gaze at the back of my head drilling holes. It's clear Derek does not like me. He might even kill me and make it look like an accident.

*I'm being delusional.*

Once inside Heath's room, I turn to him. He looks at me with the same cold and tense features.

"I wanted to take a look at the messages." I fidget with my fingers and refuse to meet his eyes.

"There's my phone. You know the password." He gestures to the nightstand.

I get his phone and quickly open my account. I see a few notifications, but no messages.

Disappointment hits me like a gust of wind that knocks away my dreams and wishes.

"Nothing?" Heath is right behind me.

I put down his phone. "No."

"You haven't posted in two days. It's important to be consistent."

I bite my lower lip. "Maybe it's not going to work."

Heath eliminates the little distance between us. His intense gaze burns my face as I look down at the floor. I can't meet his stare when I want to hide away and roll in my failure.

"It's going to work as long as you want to do it," he tells me softly.

"I want to but—"

"Then don't make excuses."

Anger flares through me. I lift my head. "I'm not making excuses."

"It sure looks like it."

Another new thing I've learned about Heath is that he loves to get on my nerves, bringing out a side that no one has brought out before.

I get to the coffee table and lay out all the bracelets I made in the last few days. I don't need to say anything. This is me not giving up on chasing freedom and wanting happiness that money can buy me. It's small, but it means everything to me. I want to hoard books and pay for meals when I go out with him and his friends. I want to do nice things for Marie because she's such a good friend to me. My first real friend. I need to do this. I need to make this work somehow.

Heath joins me, and we quietly work.

"What are you doing?" Heath leans against the pillar on the porch. It's past seven p.m. and we're outside in the dark. Well, it's not exactly dark. There are lamp posts along the driveway.

"Calling a cab." I gesture to my phone.

A deep frown embeds between his eyebrows. "No, you're not."

*God. He loves to tell me what to do.*

"Too late. It's already on its way." I shrug, feeling content that he can't do anything.

With a smirk, he looks over at the bodyguard standing a few feet away from us. "Don't let any car in." The man nods and speaks in his earpiece.

Surprise grips my body. I stare at Heath in disbelief.

He starts walking in the direction of the garage.

With growing agitation, I follow him. "Heath, what are you doing?"

"Hope, I'm driving you home." He spins the car key on his finger.

"I can get there myself because I have the money." My voice carries a subtle edge, intent to cut the words he said to me before.

Stopping in his tracks he faces me. "Look..." running a hand through his thick mesh of straight, dark brown hair, he continues, "I didn't fucking mean what I said."

My feet come to a halt. Those words trip me off my axis with such force I'm unable to think.

His blue eyes set on me. "I'm sorry for what I said. It was wrong of me."

"It was," I agree, reminding him of his mistake.

He does another round with his hair. "It won't fucking happen again."

My mind goes blank. I stand and watch him with surprise. I never expected an apology from him.

"You don't know that," I reply.

"I swear," he softly promises.

"It hurt me, you know," I whisper.

He steps closer. "I know. I shouldn't have fucking said it. I hurt people with my words all the time, but I don't want to hurt you."

"Why?"

He touches my hair. "We should leave."

In the tight space of his car, I breathe in rich leather and the musky wood scent of his cologne that consumes me like a drug. With each inhale he captures more and more of my attention.

*Has he always smelled this good?*

Going over sixty, he speeds through the roads and stops at a diner. Looking over he unbuckles his seatbelt. "Are you hungry?"

Since I have money I nod.

At the counter, I read the menu and do the math for the prices.

"Hi. What would you like to order?" The old woman asks with a smile and eyes focused on me.

My mouth goes dry, and my hands turn clammy under her undivided attention.

Human interaction makes me nervous. The reason why I don't order food is because picking up a phone and reciting my order gives me chills. They ask so many questions and you have to reply quickly. It makes me nervous. I always hang up and ask myself why I'm like this.

"Girl, what do you want?" she asks in a stern tone, making my pulse accelerate.

*Oh my God.*

*She must think I'm crazy. I'm not.*

*I just don't like ordering.*

Heath looks down at me in confusion.

I get it. It's not every day people freeze at the counter before ordering because they get anxious.

*God. He must think I'm a freak.*

Bending down a little, he asks in a quiet voice, "What's wrong?"

"C-can you order for me?" I beg him with my eyes while fidgeting with my fingers.

Instances like this I need to have something to ground me. Something to keep me busy, otherwise I start to grow restless. My fingers are the perfect option to do something.

He studies me for a moment, then asks, "What do you want?" He notices my hands. I don't care if he sees my turbulent state. I'm too stuck in my head to care.

I tell him and with a nod, he says, "Get a table."

Luckily, I spot a booth in the corner of the room and quickly claim it. I put my phone on the table, but it clatters as my hands shake. Taking a deep, long breath I put my hands under my thighs, but my leg starts bouncing.

*Oh no. This can't happen here.*

*Why?*

*Just why?*

*Take control of yourself.* I tell myself, but those words hold no power over me.

Suddenly my breathing shortens to shallow breaths, and my throat begins to close around me.

*Oh no.*

*Why is this happening here?*

*Why? Why now? Why here?*

One side of my brain yells those thoughts and the other shoots logical reasoning to get this under control. Trapped in my breakdown I don't register when a hand settles on my thigh and clamps it down in a vice-like grip.

Heath stares at me with a puzzled face and curious eyes that feel like they're evaluating me. Under his stare, I feel emotionally naked.

I gape at him.

"It's okay." He applies more presses until my leg stops bouncing. Tiny tremors race through my legs.

"I'm fine," I say, but he doesn't take his hand away from my thigh.

After a minute those tremors turn into sparks that flow straight to my stomach. A ball of heat forms.

"I can see that."

I take my first breath which doesn't nearly bury me.

"This all happened because of the order thing?" he asks.

I nod, feeling vulnerable for sharing a piece of me. However, I can't lie when he's already seen me like this.

"You don't like to order?" he asks without removing his hand from my thigh.

"I just get really nervous. They ask all these questions and stuff, and I freeze." I lean back and try to make myself small, but with Heath's steady gaze dawning on me like the sun. I know he sees me.

"You could've told me," he mutters.

"So you could mock me later?" I counter back.

A glare is sent my way. "So, *I* could fucking order for you the next time."

"What makes you think there will be a next time?"

With a roll of eyes, he says, "You and I will be seeing each other a lot since Blondie has befriended you."

Wait. What?

A smile appears on my mouth. "You have a nickname for Marie?"

"Indeed."

"That's cute." I put my elbow on the table to cup my chin.

"It's certainly *not* cute," he grumbles with a scowl.

I smile.

He glares.

A teenage waitress puts our food on the table and then turns toward Heath with a friendly smile. "If you need anything else, tell me."

Heath doesn't even glance at her and completely ignores her.

When she walks away, he steals a fry from my basket. In return, I take a chicken tender from his basket, and he sends me his signature scowl.

"What? You stole first."

With a sigh, he looks away, but his mood isn't sour like it is always.

# 18

## HEATH

What the fuck am I doing?

Why am I sharing a meal with a girl and having fun? Okay, scratch the last part. I'm not having fun.

*Liar.*

"—are so beautiful. I wonder how they make it," Hope rambles about something as she sips her chocolate smoothie. She loves that shit.

How do I know? It's her eyes. Whenever she sips it, her eyes spark up in delight.

"Make what?" I ask.

She gulps the smoothie. "Maps in books. They're so pretty."

Of course, she's talking about books. She loves them more than anything else in the world.

"There are fucking maps?" I have no idea about books.

She nods. "In fantasy books, there's world-building, so there are maps to navigate as you read. A whole world resides in a book. It's amazing."

I watch the way her lips move as she explains. Her vibrant smile is like a final brush stroke just before a masterpiece is complete.

"You must have a favorite," I say, not hating the fact that I'm making conversation. I want her to speak more because she looks entranced when she talks about books. A look I've never seen on her face before, one I'm starting to like on her face.

*Fucking dammit.*

Hope chews her bottom lip in thought. Something visceral and primal shifts within me by that act. Something that has never happened before with another girl.

*What the fuck is this?*

Finally, she replies, "The Harry Potter series. I've only read the first book, but it was enough to get me hooked."

From the corner of my eye, I catch a guy staring at Hope with a look that makes me want to bury him in the ground. *Keep your fucking eyes off her, asshole!*

Turning in my seat, I shield her view and glare at him through the faint image on the window. He sees me and cowers away. *Good.*

"Why haven't you read it?" I distract her so she doesn't notice.

Just like before her hands fidget with each other. I know right away she is uneasy. The question is why.

"My mother isn't a fan of me reading books, so she doesn't buy me the series. I tried saving up money to go to the city and look for them in a bookstore. The fare alone would cost me more than a hundred bucks, but that's my best option. The library here doesn't have it. The librarian always gives them away in schools or some kid is always reading them."

I don't like her mother.

A gloomy look passes over her face and her eyes further lose their light. She looks sad.

My heart claws my chest in an ache I haven't felt for anyone in a long time. Not after all the shit that went down last year. This is different and more personal. I have no idea *why* it matters to me.

Hope is just some girl. I shouldn't feel like this toward her—this need to take away her sadness or protect her from danger. Whenever I am with her, she calms the chaos within me.

"Someday I'll read it." With a smile, she shakes off the sadness like it's a speck of dust.

Once we're done at the diner, I drop her home and then drive to Sebastian's place with a heart that refuses to settle down. All my thoughts circle back to the girl who's fucking up my emotional equilibrium.

The only emotions I feel are anger, guilt, and more anger. That's how I function. Every day I wake up with a storm of rage that consumes me all day, and at night comes in the wave of guilt that lulls me to sleep.

Out of nowhere Hope came around and disturbed everything I've been feeling since last year. I don't like it one bit. I like being in control, but with every interaction with her, I feel like I'm losing the ropes of my restraint.

I get inside his apartment using the spare key and find him playing a video game.

"Hey, what are you doing here?" Sebastian spares me a glance before turning back to his game.

I shut the door. "I need to talk to you."

He switches off his game and faces me. "So, you apologized to her, didn't you?"

I scowl at his twinkling smile. "Yes."

That damn smile splits into a grin. "Will you look at that? My best friend is becoming a softie."

I roll my eyes as I take a seat beside him on the couch. "I'm not a softie."

Heat crawls up my neck as I think about it.

"You like her."

I glare. "I don't like her. How many times—"

"You're turning red, Heath." He folds his arms and smirks arrogantly.

I don't think I can deny it anymore. *Fuck it. I'm done lying.*

Leaning over my knees, I hang my head low. "There's something fucking wrong with me. Whenever I'm near her I can't seem to pull away. Her voice. Fuck. It does something to me. There's also the instinct to protect her because I know someone's hurting her."

"You mentioned that to me before. Why do you think that?"

I think of lying to him. It won't help given things might get worse. I'll need help to bury a body. He needs to be by my side.

Looking him dead in the eye, I say, "You can't tell Marie."

Sebastian stiffens. "You know I can't do that. I'm always honest with her."

"I'm not telling you to lie to her. I'm just saying don't mention it to her. That's *different*."

"It's the same to me," he replies curtly.

Times like these I want to strangle him.

"It's important, Bash. You know how Marie is. She won't think and jump headfirst and force Hope to tell her everything." I take a deep breath. "Once I'm certain we'll tell her."

That's the closest I can get him to agree to this. If I'm going after that person who's hurting Hope, I need my best friend with me.

He lets out a groan. "Fine. Now, tell me. I have to cook dinner as well."

"What are you making tonight?"

"Pasta."

He prepares a container of pasta and sets it on the stove. Getting two knives and a slicing board he hands me the vegetables.

"I'm not your fucking maid," I grumble but get to work.

He chuckles as he joins me. "So, what is it? You're creating so much suspense and haven't said a word about it."

"Someone is hurting Hope."

Sebastian gives me a side-eye. "This again! What makes you say that?"

Images fill my mind. I refuse to focus on them knowing I'll do something reckless.

"I've seen fucking marks on her. Someone choked her hard enough to leave bruises, and a few days later she had them on her wrist. I believe someone is physically abusing her. I just don't know who that person is." I let it all out.

"Are you sure?" he asks slowly as if he can't grasp the gravity of the situation.

"*I'm sure*. I know what I saw. Since Emery I'm…" my throat grows thick. I hate myself for getting weak. I can't get past that tragedy—I never will. "Believe me."

The pasta boils and he starts to make the sauce. Like robots, we work around the kitchen.

"We should tell Marie," he mentions again.

"Seriously, I don't need your pussy-whipped brain right now. As I said, we'll tell her later."

"Then we should get someone else involved."

"Like who?"

"Issac Anderson?"

I glare at him.

Marie's dad holds a sweet spot for Sebastian and is always trying to help him in whatever way he can. Marie is the driving force behind it, but in the end what matters is that her dad is like a fatherly figure to Sebastian. A hole my best friend has been trying to fill for years because his dad walked out on him.

I also have a hole in my chest residing next to the enormous gap my sister's death drilled in. My parents walking out on me and not wanting me hurts. I never got to experience love and care. All I know is how the house staff takes care of a kid as their own. Kelly and Derek have raised me. They're more of parents to me than the ones who brought me into this world.

"Not until we're sure, Bash," I tell him as I dump the vegetables in the pot.

"Fine."

Ten minutes later we sit on the couch with the plates full of pasta in our laps.

"So, we were talking about someone hurting Hope?"

I nod. "*And* not telling Marie."

"I agreed to that?"

"You fucking did," I assert with force.

"If it's true then Marie would be heartbroken. She loves Hope already. She's finally found a friend. She won't think twice before getting to the bottom of this."

"All the more reason to keep her away."

He ignores my warning. "Until we find out who's behind it."

I hum in response, not giving him a definite answer purposefully. "I asked Hope, but she refused to tell me."

His fork clatters on the plate. "What the actual fuck?"

"What?" My eyebrows raise.

With a loud sigh, he continues, "You can't ask such fucking questions, Heath. Not with such straightforwardness. It's not right. Things like these take time to tell someone else."

"I don't fucking get it."

"Have you told her about your sister?"

I nod.

His green eyes widen into saucers and his mouth opens in bewilderment.

How am I supposed to tell him that talking about my sister to Hope was the easiest thing I've ever done? When it was supposed to be anything *but* that.

That girl is fucking with my body chemicals. I'm not functioning normally anymore.

"What the fuck?" He gapes at me like a chimpanzee.

"Shut your mouth for fuck's sake."

"You do know that it's a big deal. You don't go around telling people about her. Christ, it took you weeks to even speak about her to *me*. I'm your bestest friend—"

"Best friend," I correct.

"—and you told Hope. Damn. She's really got you by the balls."

"Funny."

"It is."

I divert the conversation before he can hear how loud my heart is beating. "Her mom seems off to me. I haven't met her, but the way Hope talks about her. She could be the one hurting her."

A glare is sent my way. Clearly, he doesn't like my opinion.

"Don't you go and accuse her of abusing Hope. It would fuck up things. For both Hope and us. If she is the one, then we need proof or something to hold her accountable."

"So we wait?" I spit out in anger. He can't be serious.

"Yes."

"She could do much more damage to Hope, Bash. Do you have any idea—"

"I know, Heath. You know I do." A multitude of emotions flash across his face and his eyes darken in color, rich with the animosities he had to endure.

I shut up knowing damn well he knows better than me because he's been through something similar. For fuck's sake. I hate that he went through it.

School and police are out of the question. Marie was bullied every day for months by a trio of mean girls and the teachers and the counselor did shit to help her. She reached out in the hope that someone would help her, but no one did. It got worse until Sebastian met her and learned about it. He shared it with me to look out for her. I wasted no opportunity to chase those girls away from hurting Marie. How she is today is nothing like the girl I met last year. There was no self-confidence, courage, or bravery. She was weak, terrified, and malleable. Those girls snubbed her at every chance they got, and Marie didn't do anything—mainly because she couldn't. I hate both the teachers and the students at school for being fucking cowards and idiots. There's no way I'm telling them a thing. They won't do anything. Useless fucking bunch.

Police on the other hand might drop Hope into foster care if her mother is found guilty of abusing her. That scenario creates an ache in me that I'm sure I won't survive. I don't want her to be fucking away from me. I like it when she's close to me. I like it a lot.

There has to be another way to keep her safe. I will find it out.

"Heath, don't tell me you are—"

"What if I am?"

His face hardens. "We can't just barge in and swoop her out when you aren't even sure it's her mom. Besides, she must be under eighteen, so she'll be thrown into foster care. You have no idea the horrors that occur there."

Agitation wraps around me like a vice as I burst out, "What I'm supposed to fucking do then? Leave her the fuck alone?"

Shaking his head he gives me a tender look that simmers down my anger a bit. "The only thing you can do is be her friend and try to be there for her. There's a big chance that she'd tell you or ask for your help. Then we can think about doing something."

Frustration swirls like a tornado inside of me and gives rise to the brimming fire of helplessness.

"I can't be her fucking friend."

Sebastian watches me with an amusing smirk. "Of course, you can't be. You *like* her."

I shoot him a glare, but his smirk morphs into a grin and he wiggles his eyebrows at me. "Cat caught your tongue, James?"

"You fucking know all about that, huh? You friend-zoned Marie because you were a pussy to admit your feelings."

Shaking his head he says, "I didn't want to ruin our friendship."

"So you watched her date other people."

"It was two dates for Christ's sake."

I smirk. "Two dates that got your balls twisted. It was fun watching you roll in misery over some girl."

"She wasn't some girl then and she isn't some girl now. She's always been special."

I scoff in amusement.

Feelings are pathetic, especially love. It's a misconception, made up by the world turning people into fools. A disease that plagues minds and hearts leaving only ruins in the end.

"Be her friend, Heath. Sometimes that's all a person needs."

"I don't do friendships with girls."

"Hope is not some girl."

*No, she isn't.*

# 19

## HOPE

Descending the stairs I feel the shift in air before I hear the hushed whispers coming out of the kitchen.

With blood gushing through my veins, I near the door and take a peek.

I turn cold at the sight in front of me.

Dad sits at the island. Mom serves him breakfast, smiling and staring at him like all is well. *It isn't.*

She looks tired in her blue scrubs, but there's a glow to her face that radiates further when Dad picks up her hand and places a kiss.

My dinner rises to my throat with such force that I'm seconds away from puking my guts out.

*What is happening here?*

*Does she know he's not sober?*

*Is he sober?*

*Why is he even here?*

Dread mixed with fear seeps into my soul like a poison and turns everything bitter.

*Is this a dream?*

*Please let this be a dream.*

My heart sinks in my chest. I don't think I'll be able to hold it inside any longer.

"You make the best coffee in the world." He pulls her down for a kiss.

My stomach rolls in disgust. *Is this real?*

I can't fathom why Mom is letting him touch her. The same hand that was going to land her six feet deep four months ago. Here she is acting like nothing's wrong.

I pinch myself and suppress the wince. *No. It isn't a dream. This is very much real. As real as it gets.*

My parents are together—as it appears so. The fact should make me happy. It doesn't. All I feel is anxiety in the pit of my belly that multiplies crazily.

Hundreds of questions circle my mind like planets around the orbit. With the addition of my thoughts, I find myself on the whim of toppling over the axis and falling into space.

When they pull away, she catches me watching them. A look of surprise washes over her face.

"Hope, you're awake," she says breathlessly.

"It's time for school."

"School, right," she mumbles.

I meet Dad's gaze and resist the shudder. Icy, sharp shivers glide down my spine like balls of spikes.

The longer he stares the more my body goes haywire. The knots in my gut tighten by ten folds making it almost painful, but I speak my mind. "What is *he* doing here?" I'm able to hide the quiver in my voice.

Mom shoots me a glare. "That's not how you talk to your father. Be respectful, Hope."

I don't back down. "I don't know any other way when he used to abuse you—"

"Good morning, Hope." Plastering a sick smile, he stands up and sucks every bit of air molecule out of the room.

My heart drops to the floor and my soul is on the pedestal of leaving my body. *I'm scared. So scared.*

I take a deep breath—it doesn't help because my lungs hardly hold anything.

Striding in my direction he watches me with a strange glint in his eyes that further rolls the massive ball of anxiety inside me.

I back away from him to protect myself. He notices my move but chooses to ignore it.

Like a mask, he puts on a sorry face and says, "You're right. I don't deserve respect. After all, I'm a bad person."

*Bad* isn't even the word to describe him. He's way past it. So far away from the word that now it's a dot, especially after all the encounters that left me with bruises.

I open my mouth, but my throat is dry like a desert.

Taking my silence as a cue he proceeds, "I've made up my mind. I'm going to change. I'm going to prove to your mom I'm not a bad person. She's willing to give me a chance, right Maedrian?" He looks back at her and she cheers up.

"Of course. What happened was a mistake, now that you're back we can move on," she says enthusiastically.

What happened was a mistake.

You're back.

We can move on.

What is going on?

My brain is on the verge of exploding as I try to comprehend the situation.

"Exactly, sweet." Dad grins at Mom.

I put my hand on my stomach to calm down the wild creatures bombarding inside with their nervous energy.

"Hope, your dad is going to move back in and he's going to change. Aren't you happy?" Mom looks at me with an expected smile.

I just stare at her dumbfounded.

Never in my wildest dreams, I imagine her believing the lies he's spewing with such confidence.

I realize it now. Telling her about the encounters would mean nothing. He has her under his spell. She's trapped in whatever fantasies he's been feeding her. She won't believe me or do anything. After all, she loves him, and she wanted him back ever since that night despite what he did.

That realization digs a hole in my chest so deep I feel it in my soul.

"I am," I lie to her.

"I'm even looking for jobs." Dad chirps in.

Mom sends me a pointed side-eye. "See? He's trying."

"In no time I'll be on my feet, and you won't have to work so hard, sweet."
He goes to her and pulls her into his arms. She leans into him as he plants kisses
on the side of her neck and rubs her arms.

Clearing my throat I say, "I should leave."

"Hope—"

I'm already out of the door and running down the street. Once I'm a few
blocks away I stop and lean against the wall of an alley.

*Dad is back.*

*He'll be living with us.*

The reality of the situation grazes and ruptures my entire breathing system.
Air escapes my lungs like someone has punctured huge holes in the muscles.

My vision blurs. Objects and people dance in front of me like a hazy dream.
Holding onto the wall I inhale—it doesn't help.

*He is back.*

*He is going to hurt you.*

*This time things will be worse.*

*He'll be onto you.*

*More fights and arguments.*

*He'll choke you.*

*He'll hit you.*

*He'll—*

The voices in my head get louder, drowning my own little voice that was
assuring me before. I *can't* hear it anymore. It's gone. Instead, I keep hearing
words that make me scared.

I've solved complex equations in Math, drawn difficult structures in Organic
Chemistry, and practiced lengthy derivations in Physics, but I can't think of a
single thing to help me at this moment.

A trail of shivers travels down my backbone and the hairs on my back rise. I'm
losing control because of my doubts and fears.

I'm not sure how to be okay.

A hand grips my wrist and tugs me. I try to slip out of the hold, but it tightens, not to the point of leaving a bruise, but enough to not let me get away.

"Hope, hey!" I hear a strong masculine voice that sounds familiar. I can't pinpoint it.

*Where have I heard it before?*

"Hope, it's me," he says as his thumbs wipe away my tears.

Heath. I see him now. His face, his *handsome* face, is right in front of me.

"What's fucking wrong?" he asks.

I can barely speak.

"Are you okay?" Heath asks with his cold face.

I clench my fingers, but I can't seem to stop them from shaking.

He releases my wrist and instead takes my hands in his. The warmth and size of them engulf my coldness and anxiety.

"It's okay. You're safe with me," he says.

"Are you sure?" I whisper.

"Yeah."

We stay like this for a few minutes until I'm feeling better.

I half expect him to walk away; he doesn't. He waits for me to calm down.

"You good?" His thumb draws circles on my wrist.

I give him a shaky nod—it's all that I can manage.

"Come with me." He opens the car door for me. "Do you want to go somewhere else?"

I slowly nod. There's no way I'd be able to concentrate in school. With how fuzzy and unsettled I am, I'll only be experiencing breakdowns with an audience that would make fun of me. Becoming the headline news isn't on my to-do list today.

Heath drives in the opposite direction of the school. The speedometer increases with every passing second, but the car is under his control as he maneuvers the turns. I'm impressed by how great of a driver he is.

I lean back and let tears fall down my cheeks in an endless river.

My head is turned toward the window, but with the way Heath keeps glancing at me, I know he knows I'm crying. There's no point in hiding, still I can't bring myself to be vulnerable around him.

*It's your second time already.*

I feel embarrassed. Whenever he's near me all my walls start crumbling down. Whatever armor I wear to keep everything inside of me breaks.

He takes the route that leads to the forest. A strip of long road leads up to the hills with acres of tall trees on both sides. Branches create a canopy over us, shielding the sky and the sunlight that seeps in and out through the openings. No buildings or people are in sight, and I love it—being away from everything.

Fifteen minutes later, we're parked near a rocky hill cliff. The town lies beneath us with life and noise spilling out of it at eight in the morning.

I lean on the hood of his car as I observe everything. It's so beautiful up here. I've always wondered how it'd look to be on one of these hills and watch the town.

Drawing in a deep breath, the brisk forest air clears some of the haze in my head.

The silence stretches between us. He's beside me and looking ahead. It's comfortable to be here with him. So far he hasn't bombarded me with questions, he's giving me time to collect myself which is thoughtful of him.

When I look over, he's fumbling with an unlit cigarette. His fingers tip the stick up and down in a rhythm only he knows.

"You smoke?" I haven't seen him smoke. There was one time when his car reeked of the scent, but I wasn't sure that it was because of him.

"Sometimes," he says lowly.

"Why?" For all I know it's dangerous for health and tastes like trash—I read that online.

He glances at me. "It helps to clear my mind."

"It does?"

The side of his lips quirks up as if he finds my question comical. "You have no idea."

A cold breeze of air sweeps past us, cutting the tension. I wrap my arms around myself to gain some heat. "I've never skipped school before," I say to distract my body from feeling cold.

"I bet." Amusement is reflected in his words. "Such a good girl."

My cheeks redden. *I'm sure he doesn't mean it in the context I usually read it in.*

"Maybe I should go back."

He scoffs. "What's the point if you can't pay attention?"

"They'll call my parents."

"They won't."

"Why not?"

"I asked Marie to tell the office you're sick and won't come in today."

Surprise hits me hard. *He did that for me.*

"When...why...how?" I sputter nervously.

"Am I supposed to answer all those fucking questions?" He drawls out in a sarcastic tone.

"I'd like that."

He sighs, probably annoyed. "I texted her *when* you were crying. I *did* that because I assumed you would get a lecture at home. I don't have the answer to *how*."

My mood lifts a little. I bite my lip to hide the smile. "You didn't have to do that but thank you."

Ignoring that he asks, "Are we going to talk about what happened back there?"

I concentrate on the beauty in front of me. The rich blue sky and the white clouds hanging on it. The view is serene and beautiful. Hundred times better than what I see from my window.

"You get panic attacks?" Heath presses.

I hug myself tighter to make myself small. "I don't know."

"You can talk," he says in a grumpy tone.

"To you?"

I feel his stare on me. For a minute I ignore it, hoping he'll look away, but he doesn't. The undivided attention makes me cave in. I turn and find his eyes on me, trying to peek at the secrets I've been hiding lately.

"To me," he says softly, but his expression stays hard.

"I don't know how to do that. We're not even friends—"

"Let's be friends."

My mouth opens and closes like a fish. "What?"

He leans back on his hands. "Marie considers you her best friend already. We'll be seeing each other a lot. It's only fair that we become friends."

"You-you want to be my friend?"

"Yes."

"Are you sure?"

He arches an eyebrow. "Do I sense hesitation?"

"No! I'm just... shocked." I pause. "You don't seem like the person who befriends people."

"I don't, but it's *you.*"

"Me?"

He stares deeply at me. "Yes."

I never thought I'd be friends with the bad boy of the school—that's what *everyone else* says. The idea doesn't appall me, maybe because I've started to know him a little.

"I guess we can be."

Heath holds back a chuckle with a cough, but I see the hint of his smile.

Tilting his head he looks down at me. "*You guess?* How sweet."

I only smile.

Maybe being friends with him won't be such a bad idea. After all, there aren't any feelings involved, and there never will be. Yet, my heart races just thinking about him.

# 20

HEATH

I've lost my fucking mind.

That's the only plausible reason why I've brought Hope to *my* secret place. I'm talking to her while my heart jumps and sinks inside my chest like I'm having multiple heart attacks all at once.

*Is that even fucking possible?*

*Apparently yes when she's around.*

We're sitting together—with no body parts touching—but I can feel her heat and lavender scent—don't even get me started on it—swirling around me and consuming me.

What kind of fucking sorcery is this? I've never been affected by someone's perfume, but for fuck's sake, her flowery scent is driving me nuts. It's soft and sweet—not my type—and I can't get enough of it.

For the past hour, all I've been thinking of is pulling her into my arms and burying my nose into her hair—what the actual fuck is wrong with me? I've never thought about a girl in this way.

This is all because of Sebastian. That fucker fed me weird shit about feelings, now I can't think about anything else but seeing her naked—

*I'm going to hell.*

"...head back."

I catch a snippet of her sentence. "What?"

She looks nervous. "I think we should head back."

"To school?" It's past ten. There's no point.

"Yeah. We can attend the classes after lunch."

"Marie said you're sick. It'd be strange if you show up," I argue, partially because I don't want us to leave. It's nice here with her.

"I don't want to go home," she mumbles.

I choose to not say anything about it. I'm sure she didn't expect me to hear that bit. But It's stored in my mind for later. "Do you have your bracelets with you?"

"I keep them in my bag."

"Good. Because you've got orders to mail."

A beautiful smile takes over her face and erases every ounce of sadness from earlier.

*Good. This is better.*

"Really?" she chirps.

"I don't lie, Hope."

"Do you know how many?" She jumps off the hood excitedly.

"I didn't check." I most definitely did. But the way she's excited to see it for herself isn't something I want to steal away. It's her moment and she deserves to have it.

"Can I have your phone, please?"

I hand it to her and watch as her brown eyes fill with light.

I'm certain I've never seen someone look this utterly beautiful when they're happy.

Fuck. I want to see this look on her a thousand times more.

"Heath, look at this." She comes to my side and scrolls the screen. "There's fifteen of them. I got fifteen orders. That's the highest I've ever gotten. Can you believe that?"

My eyes don't steer away from her eyes. I'm afraid that if I look away I'll miss this pure joy that sparks in them.

This rare sight steals my breath away. I'm breathless over this pretty girl.

"We've got work to do." To distract myself I breathe some air that isn't lavender scented, and it bothers me.

*For fuck's sake.*

"This is so good. I can't believe it." With a bounce to her feet, she slips inside my car as I open the door for her.

I linger, watching how she replies to everyone with a smile. The quiet organ in my chest beats crazily. It's like she gave life to it.

I clench and unclench my fist to get rid of the tension coiling around my body. This isn't how it's supposed to be. I just agreed to be friends with her. I can't feel like this.

*Get a fucking grip.*

Shutting down whatever I'm feeling, I get behind the wheel and start the engine.

Hope looks at me frantically. "Wait! Don't drive. Let me make the packages so we can mail them at the post office."

"We could do that at my house." Derek would be on my ass and call Dad.

"Wouldn't your parents ask questions?" she asks slowly.

"They would ask questions *if* they lived with me, which they don't," I reveal more than I was fucking supposed to.

"Oh." She picks up her bag and retrieves the bracelets, brown paper, and twines. No wonder she's doing magic on me. She uses twines for fuck's sake.

"Do you need my help?" I ask, only because I'm bored, not because I have any intention of lending a helping hand.

I don't help people.

*But you help her.*

I want to punch my inner voice after hearing that.

She gives me a nod and smiles. "Yes. I'd love that."

Together we pack the bracelets. I cross-check the orders with her and then write the names over the packages so we can send them to the right address.

While working, I ask her the question again, hoping she'll answer me this time. "What happened back there?"

Her hands freeze over the twine that she was tying a knot on. Clearing her throat, she says, "I didn't have breakfast, so I had a vertigo."

Fucking bullshit.

"I didn't know that's what we call panic attacks these days."

Her eyes quickly find mine. "You know what they are?" The way she watches me closely makes me want to book a flight and never return to this godforsaken fucking town. She's getting past the wall that hides my secrets.

"I've heard of them." *And experience them almost every other night since my sister's death.* They are useless since they don't cause fatal death, but they're pretty good at making you believe you're nearing the end.

"I...I've never talked to someone about this before." She works on the next package as if she can't bear to sit idle and talk about her feelings.

It's insane how well I can read her *and* relate to her.

"I won't fucking judge you if that's what you're worried about."

"It's not that."

"Then?"

Not knowing what's bothering her frustrates me. I want to know what's wrong and fix it for her. I don't want her to have panic attacks. I know how awful and weak they make you feel. If I can do anything for her, so she doesn't have them, I'll do it in a heartbeat.

A forlorn look touches her face. "I've never had friends. Since kindergarten, I've been alone and now I'm a senior. It's years of loneliness that I can't erase just because I have someone now."

"You've had me for a while now," I whisper.

I try to see it from her perspective. She's not wrong. It must be hard for her to suddenly be thrown into a tight group. Sebastian, Marie, and I all have been through a lot. It doesn't matter that Marie joined us last year. With the way she's supported us and been there, is like how Bash and I have been for each other for years. We two have grown up together since second grade. We shared everything until Emery got sick and I fell into depression, and he fell into alcohol because of how things were at his home.

Nonetheless, I've always had someone. But Hope truly has been alone all this time.

"I already know things and I haven't judged you. You can trust me with anything," I add.

She stays quiet for a whole minute, then says, "I don't know what happened back there. It was like my mind couldn't stop thinking. Every thought had its branch that kept growing with more voices. Before I knew it I couldn't breathe, and my heart was beating so fast. It was like I was stuck in—"

"Chaos." I complete it before I can stop myself.

She watches me keenly, before nodding. "Yeah. That's exactly how it was. I was so afraid. I've felt fear before, but this was different. It was like I'd die."

"You *were* having a panic attack."

"How do you know that?" she asks with a frown like she's worried for me.

"I've read about it."

She studies me skeptically. Then chews on her bottom lip, and says, "Thank you for helping me. If you hadn't, I don't know what would've happened."

My chest tightens.

This girl does strange fucking things to me.

Once we're done with the packages, I drive us to the post office. Hope pays the money, and we walk out onto a busy street. People around us go about their lives throwing little attention at us.

It's past noon and the sun is shining brightly. The phase of summer air slips away as August comes to an end.

Hope and I are quiet, knowing now we have no reason to hang out.

Obviously, that doesn't sit well with me because I blurt out, "Do you wanna grab something for brunch?" Knowing damn well I'd feed her, it doesn't matter what her answer is.

She smiles. "Sure."

At the diner, I order the food. The last time she did, it made her anxious as fuck. I don't want to put her through that. So, I ask her to find us a booth.

This little thing has sort of become our routine. I used to eat alone at diners but now she accompanies me which I don't mind. In fact, I enjoy her company.

When I sit across from her I see her reading a book with an illustrated cover of a couple. I know right away it's a romance book, which she seems to love too much.

"Is that a romance book?" I tease her.

Hope abruptly shuts the book and hides it under the table. "Huh."

"It is, then," I observe how her cheeks redden like a rose.

*Rose.* That's it. She reminds me of a rose. Especially how the color is the same as when she blushes.

She puts her book on the table and meets my gaze. "Okay, fine. It is."

"What is it about?"

She adjusts her hair. "Oh, um, I haven't finished it yet."

"How far have you read?" I eye the bookmark which is a strip of paper taken out of a notebook and folded many times to make it thicker.

For a book nerd, she doesn't own many book-nerd things or whatever they are called.

"A little." She tucks a strand of her hair behind her ear as if she's nervous.

*Do I make her nervous? I better fucking not. I want her to be comfortable with me.*

"What's happening so far?"

A waitress interrupts us by putting down our milkshakes and assures us that our food will be there in five minutes.

Hope quickly reaches for the chocolate milkshake and sucks on the straw. "Nothing."

Explicit images of her doing something *very* inappropriate fill my mind. I have to look away.

This friendship won't work once she knows what goes through my mind.

"So, you're telling me you're reading blank pages?"

Hope chokes on the drink. I'm seconds away from making sure she's okay. After coughing a few times, she clears her throat. "You'd get bored if I start talking about it."

She could talk about animals and nature for hours, and I wouldn't get bored. I'd listen to every word like an addict clinging to every particle of his fix.

"I won't," I assure her.

"Well..." she starts talking about her book and doesn't stop. I believe she's reciting every word with how detailed she gets. She paints the picture so well

I find myself getting invested in the story, even though I have zero attachment toward Adrian and Eleanor. ". . .they go to a party, and she has fun."

I realize I'm mesmerized by how sweet and dreamy her voice sounds.

Fuck. I'm in so much fucking trouble.

"When will you—"

"Oh my, you guys are here." Marie half-screams across the room. Hope and I both turn to see her.

Taking quick, hurried steps she approaches our table and slides in next to Hope. Throwing her arms around her she fires questions. "Are you okay? Is everything okay? Why weren't you at school? I missed you. Mr. Carlie spent an extra fifteen minutes, and I wanted..."

I zone out Marie's rambling and glance at Sebastian who watches her with a look of someone who's whipped.

"No need to stare. She's all yours."

He smiles. "It's hard to believe it sometimes."

"Put a ring on her, then."

"Soon."

I stare at him in surprise, but he just smiles.

The waitress from before leaves our food and asks Marie and Sebastian for their order. Marie is too busy bombarding Hope with questions, so Sebastian orders for the both of them.

Once done he turns to me with a sick smile. "So, you and her, huh?"

I glare. "There's no her *and* me."

"Right, of course. There's an *us*."

"Fuck off." Because of him, my brain can't think of Hope in an innocent way.

"Excuse me? What did I do?"

I lean closer so the girls can't hear us. "Feed my brain the idea that it's *good* to be friends with her. I can't be her friend."

"Why the hell not?" My mouth sews shut. "Wait a sec. You asked her to be your friend. When did this happen?"

I pop a fry into my mouth. "This morning. We were on the hill, talking, and I fucking asked her."

"Hill as in your secret place where no one is allowed, *even* me." Bash puts a hand on his chest as if he's offended.

He can be as offended as he wants. I don't care. Sometimes I need silence to quiet the chaos in my head.

"Yes," I mumble.

Surprise contorts his face. "Woah! I didn't think you would. I'm offended."

I roll my eyes. "It's not a big deal."

Sebastian slaps his forehead and everyone in the room looks at him.

Fucking great. More attention. Exactly what I needed.

"What happened?" Marie's eyes bounce between the two of us.

"Nothing, babe," Sebastian convinces her with a smile but shoots me a mean glare.

Marie nods. "I'm hungry. Do you want something?"

"I already ordered for us, babe." Sebastian winks at her. Marie grins like a damn fool.

This is what I've been subjected to since last year. Third fucking wheeling.

My gaze flickers to Hope who's smiling at them. At once her eyes find mine. She blushes and looks away.

Clearing my throat, I turn to Sebastian who's smirking at me. "Not a big deal, huh?"

I shove him and eat my burger.

I check on Hope and she's eating nuggets. Relief washes over me that she isn't fucking starving herself.

"So how was today? What did you two do?" Marie watches us closely. She looks suspicious as if we visited the unicorns and didn't invite her.

"We...um...talked," Hope stutters and refuses to look my way.

Could she be any *less* discreet?

"About what?" Marie pushes her. I kick her under the table.

"Ouch! Sebastian." She winces.

He raises his hands. "I didn't do it."

Marie looks at me and she leans over the table. "Something you wanna share with us?"

"Not with you, Blondie," I say in a cool tone.

She turns toward the one person who won't lie to her. "What about you, Hope?"

Hope's eyes widen. "Um, what?"

Marie folds her arms and puts on her interrogation face. "Where were you two?"

As much as I love to see her growth in confidence, in instances like these I hate it. She can be a real pain in the ass when it comes to matters revolving around the two of us—Sebastian and I—and now Hope too.

When Marie narrows her eyes, Hope cracks under the pressure. "We were on the hill talking about cigarettes, panic attacks, being friends, and bracelets."

A moment of silence stretches between the four of us before the chaos begins.

"Bracelets!" Sebastian and Marie speak at the same time.

"Um..." Hope gives me a shy smile and I glare at her.

"Heath and bracelets. What? How?" Marie asks.

"Panic attacks and cigarettes?" Sebastian jumps in without skipping a beat.

"Here's your food. Enjoy." The waitress puts a pause on the enthusiastic couple who can't wait to get to the bottom of this.

The two of them watch Hope and me. I don't blame her for cracking under pressure. She's got a long way to go with these two.

Marie points at the two of us. "You both start talking."

Hope caves in, while I sit back and watch.

What a fucking mess.

# 21

## HOPE

"I can't believe it. Why didn't you tell me you were going to skip school?" Marie asks.

We're sitting in her car, eating ice cream and watching the sunset in an empty parking lot. I've told her about how I skipped school with Heath, but not *why*. I wouldn't be able to share that. I had a panic attack in the middle of the street. Luckily there weren't many people around, otherwise, they'd think I'm a lunatic. It was embarrassing.

"I didn't know how to," I murmur.

"Why not?" she asks softly.

I swirl the spoon in the melting ice cream, wishing it was easy for me to talk about myself. To say the words that wouldn't sit like rocks on my tongue waiting to be let out.

The situation at home is a burden I'm carrying every day. I don't want others to bend under the weight of it. Knowing Marie I know she'll worry about me, and I don't want her to. I like the way she shines so brightly. My sadness diminishes under the light of it. When I'm with her a stream of happiness flows through me.

I stare off at the view. "I've never shared things with anyone. Before you, I didn't even have a friend. So, keeping things to myself is all I know." I meet her concerned gaze. "I'm sorry if that bothers you. It wasn't—"

She waves her hand. "Don't say sorry. Before you I didn't have any friends either. Well, a girlfriend, I mean. Sebastian is my best friend and Heath too, but sometimes only girls understand girls, you know." I nod and she continues, "I know how to talk about my feelings or stuff because Sebastian taught me that any secret is safe between friends. However, we're new to each other, so it's fine. Just remember I'm here for you today, tomorrow, and always."

*Today, tomorrow, and always.* My heart swells inside my chest. Even when it's hard for me to believe those words, I try to lock them away. Perhaps someday when I'm ready I can talk to her.

"I'm here for you too. Today, tomorrow and always." Tears fill my eyes, but I keep them at bay. It's surreal that I'm *not* alone anymore.

"Don't make me cry." Leaning over, she embraces me in a tight hug.

"I'm sorry." I tighten my arms around her.

"Don't be," she assures me with confidence.

Moving back, she wipes her eyes. "So, you and Heath make bracelets, huh?"

"Yes."

Marie reaches for her ice cream that has melted into a puddle. "I feel like I'm in a dream world where that happens."

I laugh. "It's quite real."

"Tell me more."

"He helps me with the marketing aspect, drives me to the post office, and helps me in any way that he can." A smile grows on my face.

"This is so sweet."

"It is," I say, "Now we're friends,"

Her hazel eyes grow big, and she shrieks in joy. "Oh my! You're friends. That's great. I'm so happy. My ship is sailing."

"What?"

Does she ship me and Heath? We don't have feelings for each other. He is just my friend—who makes my heart race—and I assume he considers me just the same. He doesn't ever look unsettled when he's with me. I'm a mess when I'm with him. Not because I'm nervous. It's a mixture of giddiness and excitement. The kind I read about in books.

His proximity, blue eyes, voice, touch, and every other little thing lingers in my head long after we part ways. I've started to think about him more than my fictional characters, which is a first.

Marie gasps. "What ship? I didn't say any ship. I meant my shell is sailing. You know how seashells get carried away in water. That's what I meant."

I know she's covering up, but I don't call her out.

I close the door behind me with a smile on my face.

*I have friends.*

*Not fictional ones, but actual ones.*

A warm feeling stirs inside of me, and my smile widens to the point my cheeks hurt.

"What the fuck are you smiling about?" The sharpness in his tone pierces through me.

My body whips around and my smile drops faster than an object falling through free fall.

Dad takes a step forward. "Where the fuck were you today?" He stares at me with such authority and power. For once, he's sober, still the way he's looking at me is similar to when he's intoxicated—there's not a trace of love or affection.

"Out with friends," I say in a feeble voice.

He frowns like it's a ridiculous excuse. "Friends? You don't have any fucking friends, Hope."

"Things have changed," I say.

Striding forward, he backs me up against the door. Air knocks out of my chest and gets lost in the cloud of tension between us. In seconds, my hands are shaking, and tremors are running up and down my arms. I start panicking.

*I just want to go to my room.*

"You're a liar," he spits out in anger.

"No, I'm not. I do have friends now," I mumble, looking into his dark eyes that swallow most of the white. It's a frightening sight.

"I've known you since you were a kid. You've always been a loner. No one talks to you."

"That's not true." Telling him about Marie is at the tip of my tongue.

"Your mother was the same. She didn't have anyone aside from me."

My eyes widen at the information. "I was out with friends. I swear."

Dad wraps his hand around my neck and presses my head against the door with a thud. Pain shoots like tingles in the back of my head. *That. Hurt.*

Closing my eyes, I hold back my tears. I refuse to cry in front of him. I don't want him to think I'm weak. That he holds any power over me.

*He does hold power over you.* A small, scared voice whispers.

"Don't lie to me, you bitch!" He squeezes my throat, enclosing my air column on the verge of collapsing.

I wheeze like a dying animal for its last breath.

"Ple-please," I beg him as my hand holds his big one.

For a moment, I think my touch will bring him back—he'll let me go.

I only learn how stupid I am.

He squeezes harder and my head starts to get dizzy. His voice is distant as he talks, my ears hardly register a word.

Dots appear in front of my eyes. I'm seconds away from passing out.

Flashbacks from today run through my mind. I realize how serene I felt with Heath when we were on the hill. I told him things I've never told anyone. I shared a part of me, even though it was a very tiny one. I talked to him like friends do. I let myself be vulnerable.

*I felt safe with him.* Exactly what I don't feel right now.

"...lie to me again," Dad spits those words in my face and lets me go.

I sink to the floor and hold my aching throat. I open my mouth and try to breathe.

I hear footsteps receding and the television playing loud in the living room. The path to my room is clear now. I sneak into my room and throw on the door bolt for safety.

On the bed, I curl on one side and let the hot tears fall down my cheeks.

Time is a distant thought as I cry my heart out and empty the wells behind my eyes. Once I'm done my pillow is soaked, and my cheeks burn from the sting of the salt streams. If that's not enough, I have an excruciating headache.

Out of nowhere, Heath slips into my mind. His blue eyes, muscular body, tall height, and beautiful face. He's so handsome but in a grumpy way. He only ever scowls, smirks, and smiles—those are tight-lipped smiles that don't count. I've never heard him laugh or seen him happy. He's always cold and distant like he's mad at the world.

I should stay away from a guy like him. A guy who skips classes, smokes, fights at an illegal place, and is always mad. Despite all those reasons, he's the one I feel safe with. He's the one I can talk to, and he listens to me. When I'm having a panic attack he helps me instead of leaving me. I'm a nobody at school, but he makes me feel like somebody.

Maybe I'm losing my mind or gaining feelings for him. I don't know what it is. All I know is, something is there.

*Safety. Comfort. Friendship.*

When I thought of setting up a small business I knew I'd land nowhere. I don't have a good camera to take pictures with or know how to do social media. Then Heath stepped in, and he's helped me in every way that he can. Also, he encourages me.

One thing is for certain. If he weren't there for me, I'd have failed miserably.

I don't pay him. Maybe I should. He deserves to have a proportion when he tackles every aspect. I know he won't take my money. He doesn't even let me pay for food.

At the reminder of food my stomach grumbles.

Looks like I'm skipping dinner again. There's no way I'm going downstairs.

I caress the side of my throat and wince when I imagine the marks I'll find there in the morning.

I can't go to school tomorrow, but I also can't stay at home.

Heath will ask me questions, Marie will worry about me and Sebastian will watch me quietly. They'll know something is up. I have no idea how I'll avoid their suspicions.

Maybe it's time I invest in makeup. I believe it'll become a regular thing in the coming months.

# 22

## HEATH

Two days later Hope and I are sitting in my room making bracelets—she's making them and I'm handing her the beads. Why I'm doing this is beyond me.

I've stopped thinking about why I do stupid things around her. There's no point in looking for a reason when there isn't any.

I just *do* things for her.

Hope is wearing that fucking red turtleneck again when it's sweltering hot outside. It's September for fuck's sake.

The sun has set, but the summer heat is moving with humidity. Fortunately, the AC is working, and she isn't sweating.

I'm certain her neck has bruises. This is the second time I'm seeing her wear this fucking red article. She also missed school for two days.

My mind is a ticking bomb. I'm seconds away from interrogating her, but I'm holding my tongue.

Sebastian said that she'll talk to me if I become her friend. After our conversation at the hill, I know it'll take her some time to give me the name of the person who's hurting her. Until then, I have to resort to clenching my fingers a million times to unwire the cords of tension wrapping around my arm.

I'll call Ryan and ask him to set me up for three fights. I need to direct this fucking rage somewhere else.

"Heath," she says in her sweet voice.

My stomach churns strangely. What the fuck is wrong with me? She just *said* my name.

"What?" I gruff out.

"There's something I wanted to ask you," she says hesitantly, as if she's afraid. She doesn't have to be.

I'm here making bracelets with her. At this point, she can make me agree to *anything*.

"I don't have time to wait until next year," I remind her after a minute of silence.

A soft laugh bubbles out of her and hits me right across the chest. I stare at the delicate lines of her smile and the glint of humor in her eyes. She's just so fucking beautiful.

Taking a deep breath, she meets my gaze. "Would you like to have a small commission out of every sale I make? It won't be much, but still."

*Not happening, Rose.*

I harden my gaze. "I don't need the money. I've got plenty already. Besides, you should save as much as you can and invest it somewhere."

"I know you have plenty, but it feels wrong to me because you help me so much." Her gaze softens.

I arch an eyebrow. "Why don't you gather my proportion and buy a new phone? I'd like that very fucking much instead of making these."

Hope watches as I pick up beads, line them for her to put through the string, and make the bracelet.

"I didn't know you disliked doing this," she mutters.

"No fucking guy likes doing this," I grumble.

"I can ask Marie. I bet she'd—"

"No need," I add quickly.

If she does this with Marie, then she won't need me. And I can't let that fucking happen.

I hate having anyone in my room, except her. When she's here I don't feel alone. We don't talk much but it's better than me sitting around and smoking as I kill time.

"But you said—"

I give her a sharp look. "Focus. I'm hungry and I want to get it done soon."

She bites her lower lip.

Blood rushes from my chest to my dick. I curse myself.

For fuck's sake. Maybe it won't be that bad if Marie helps her.

By five p.m. Kelly brings us tacos and nuggets. If it isn't clear already I love nuggets and chicken wings.

She lingers until I send her a glare and she scurries out of the room. Between Derek and her, there's less chance of her calling my father and feeding him gossip. But that doesn't mean she won't question me later.

I switch on the TV and flip through shows. "What do you wanna watch?"

Hope looks at me with wide eyes. "I-I get to pick?"

I roll my eyes. "I asked you, didn't I?"

"I'm fine with anything."

I browse and settle on Lucifer. "How far have you watched it?"

She stares at the screen. "I've never watched it."

I jump to season one episode one. I don't mind watching it again for her sake.

Ten minutes later she asks, "Can I dim the lights?"

I stand up and do it for her. It reminds me of Marie and how it always annoys me, but I don't mind doing it for Hope.

Yeah, shit is different when it's with her.

Settling back on the couch, I end up sitting close to her. We both look at each other. I'm about to move away because I don't want her to feel uncomfortable, but she shoots me a shy smile and turns back to the screen.

My heart beats crazily fast inside my chest and I can hardly breathe. At this rate, I'll fall head-first in love with this girl. It's a stupid, crazy thought, but it lingers somewhere in the back of my mind.

One episode turns into six. When I check the time it's past ten.

"Isn't ten your bedtime?" I look at her for the hundredth time. She looks cute with my black blanket on top of her as she's curled up on the couch in comfort.

I barely watched the show. I kept glancing at her to make sure she was enjoying it—that she did. She smiled, laughed, and even talked to me about who could be the suspect in every episode.

Surprise flits across her face.

"What?" She scrambles off the couch and checks the time on her phone. The color drains from her face and her eyes widen. Her whole body freezes.

"Oh my God. I'm...dead," she whispers before starting to throw things in her bag like a maniac.

I turn on the lights and observe how her hands are trembling. She's fucking anxious.

"I'll drive you home." There's no way I'll let her take a cab at this hour.

She slings the strap of her bag over her shoulder and shakes her head. "No. I'll get home by myself."

Like hell, she would.

"It's past ten at night. You won't even find a cab." I step closer, but she steps back.

"I have to go." She rushes out of my room. I chase after her but she's already outside.

Briskly walking down the driveway, I turn her around by gripping her elbow. Her body tenses in my hold and a gasp leaves her lips.

What the actual fuck? She's never reacted like this with me before.

I assess her stiffened body and feel my heartstrings pull in worry.

I don't like this one fucking bit.

She's safe with me. I'll protect her.

"Hope, look at me." I loosen my grip, but don't let go of her, knowing she'll flee away.

The pretty girl shakes her head and looks down at her shoes. A pair of rugged blue and white Converse she wears every day.

"Hope." I hate how much it bothers me that she isn't looking at me. I can't read her.

"I need to go home," she mumbles brokenly and spares me a glance. It's enough for me to catch a glimpse of her teary eyes and quivering lips.

For fuck's sake. I'm a second away from killing the person who makes her feel this way.

"I'll take you home in no time," I promise her.

She meets my gaze and nods.

"Wait here for me," I say.

I run to the garage and drive my car to where she is. She gets inside and hugs her shaky arms.

I don't know what the fuck is going on, but it's bothering me. More than anything ever has before.

I turn on the AC so she's not sweating in her fucking turtleneck.

Pressing hard on the accelerator, I go over sixty on the speedometer to keep my promise.

Hope is quiet beside me, gazing out of the window and rubbing her arms.

*Stay with me.* The words sit on the tip of my tongue, but I don't possess the courage to say them.

In a matter of weeks, she's become someone who knows which strings to pull to make me feel something. I've been distant and unemotional for the past year. To the point it feels like I've become heartless. Now here she is, making my heart go above the usual number of heartbeats in a minute.

I can't describe what I feel toward her. With one look in her eyes, I feel like she understands me. She sees *me,* not the reputation that's built about me.

Slowly and quietly this girl is getting under my skin, I can't do anything about it. Or maybe I don't want to.

Much to my dismay, I pull up into her neighborhood and switch off the headlights.

"Just park here." Hope points to the curb.

"That's ten houses down from your house." I stare at the long stretch of deserted road.

"I know."

Before I can argue, she's out of the car and running down the street.

I follow her and watch her go inside her house.

I wait for a few minutes, but nothing happens. However, my gut twists and turns like something bad is supposed to happen. I try to shake off the feeling, but it grows.

"Fuck it!" I switch off my car and get out.

Stealthily, I go around the side of the house and look up at the window to her room. There's no light or shadows, which is fucking odd.

Concern scratches my insides like barbed wire and my curiosity spikes high. *Go check on her.*

Looking around, I search for a trash can. Putting it under her windowsill, I climb up and peek inside. I find her lying on her side. Her back is toward me and she's reading a book under the little light of the lamp. *She's okay.*

# 23

## HOPE

*This is a bad idea,* my mind complains as I stare at the gym building.

I tightly hold the bags and try to muster up the courage to go inside.

*Open the door. You've come this far, might as well go a little beyond.*

I repeat for the millionth time, but hesitation holds me back. How do people just *do* things?

A man steps out. He pauses when he sees me standing like a fool in the parking lot. Tall, lean, and sharp-looking, he approaches me, causing my pulse to drop.

*Oh my God.*

*How do I go invisible?*

*I need the invisibility cloak. NOW!*

"Hey. What are you doing here?" He rubs the little stubble covering his jaw.

"Hi." I heave a breath. *Here it goes. Don't stop.* "I'm looking for Heath. His best friend dropped me off saying he'll be here. I need to see him if that's okay. But I can come back later if he's busy." I look anywhere but his eyes.

The man smiles. "He's free now. We just had a spar. I'm his trainer, Paul. You can go right in. Take the door number seven. That's his room."

*Wow. Heath has a personal trainer.*

*No wonder his body looks so hot and—*

*Stop thinking about his hot body.*

I thank him and walk ahead. Upon entering the building, I'm hit with a gush of cool air and a terrible pungent smell that makes me shrink in disgust. Sweat. So much of it.

I search for room seven when I notice everyone in the hall is staring at me. Men. Lots of men. Mostly shirtless.

*Great. Just great. I had to land in the spotlight.*

Ignoring their gazes, I spot the room and dash toward it. I'm about to open the door when a guy around my age gets in my way.

"Hello." He smirks and gawks at me.

Suddenly I feel self-aware in my jeans and thin beige warmer. The clothes are baggy, but the way he peculiarly studies me, I might as well be naked.

"I need to go." I try to side-step him. He whistles and steps closer to me.

"I've never seen you here before. What's your name?"

I swallow hard and make a list of reasons why I thought coming here was a good idea.

Sebastian should've escorted me inside. I had no idea there'd be so many curious men, otherwise, I'd never come.

"I asked you something," he says in a curt tone.

I shiver but don't back down. "Please step out of my way."

"I will once—"

"Once I knock your fucking teeth then rip your fucking tongue out. Would that be enough for you to step the fuck away from her?" A cold, ruthless voice comes from behind me and everything and everyone stills.

Heath's warm presence burns my back but shields me from every pair of eyes looking at me. I don't feel exposed anymore.

The guy gulps hard and raises his hands "Woah! I didn't know she was with you, man." Fear lingers in his eyes, and he quickly backs away.

"That shouldn't have mattered. She asked you to fucking move, didn't she?" Heath comes around and gives him a strong push. He hits the nearest wall and groans.

With a glare, he spits out, "Calm the fuck down. There are rules."

Heath corners him. The guy spares me a glance and Heath pins him to the wall by his throat.

"Look at her again and you'll see how *quickly* I'll break the fucking rules for her."

*Oh no. This is getting worse.*

Feeling the temperature rise I grab his hand. His attention instantly moves to me, and he backs off. Opening the door, I pull us in. When I shut the door he traps me against it.

We're close. *Too close.* An inch further he'd be able to feel my heart thundering inside my chest.

"What are you doing here?" His voice is low and husky.

"I..." my eyes lock with him and I forget the words.

Slowly, his hands move closer to my waist, but he doesn't touch me. He stays there. Too close yet too far.

Heath cocks his head to one side as he watches me. "I asked you something, Rose."

A wet strand of his dark brown falls over his forehead and my breath falters.

He's handsome. *Really* handsome.

I've seen guys, but no one is as beautiful as him. The way every curve and contour of his face is carved makes every man I've ever dreamed about less. He tops every fictional man I've ever had a crush on—and they are perfect. He is just on another level of hot.

*Rose.* He called me by my middle name. I've never told him.

"How do you know my middle name?" I ask.

A frown embeds between his eyebrows. "I didn't."

"Then why did you call me Rose." *He gave me a nickname. That only happens in books. I'm having a book moment right now.*

His frown deepens. "I have my reasons."

"That's not an answer."

"I know, but it's the only one you're getting."

"But—"

"Now, what are you doing here?" I suppose he won't tell me.

"I brought food," I say.

A smirk lifts his lips, and he moves a little closer, but never too much where I start panicking. Somehow, he knows how to find the perfect distance.

Heath gently pries the bag from my hands. "What did you bring?"

I can't speak.

Moving back, he opens it. "Chow mein? I'm not a fan of Chinese, but I guess I'll eat it just this once."

Am I stupid or is Heath flirting with me?

"It's very tasty." *Oh my God. Why did I say that?*

"Are you bribing me, Rose?"

"Huh?" I can't focus on anything but the way his teeth sink into his bottom lip.

What is happening to me? I've never noticed that about a guy before.

*There was no guy before. Only fictional men.*

"Come here." Taking my hand, he leads me to the end of the small room.

Thick blue mats cover the entire floor. A black punching bag hangs from the ceiling at one side of the room. The walls are cream and there's a window overlooking the parking lot. There's also an AC. A table rests near the door that has his keys, wallet, and a gym bag. I assume this is his private room because it's just as clean and plain as his room.

We sit on the floor cross-legged. Quickly opening the takeout bags, I hand him the boxes and he watches me with a playful expression.

"What?" I offer him a fork.

"You bought it all, didn't you?"

I smile. "I thought it'd be different." Picking up my box I say, "You're always buying me food. Now that I make a little money, I wanna return the favor."

Heath shakes his head and takes a bite. "You didn't listen to me."

Disappointment stirs inside of me. "I..."

"Next time, save it."

We eat in silence. From the multiple glances I cast his way I can see he's enjoying the food, though he doesn't say a word.

"How did you know I was here?"

We've wrapped up the empty boxes and are sitting against the wall next to each other.

"Sebastian drove me here. He said this is where you are when you're not at home. I went to your house first."

He scowls. "It's not safe for you to be here."

I couldn't agree more. "I know now. I'm sorry that you had to...step in. I had it covered though." I give him a confident look.

Heath watches me, then chuckles, for the very first time. My eyes quickly focus on him, so I don't miss it. A film reel records the view and the sound like a memory to look at later.

Wearing only a black shirt and shorts, he looks young and carefree. And as he laughs, he's never looked more alive before. I like this look on him better than the grumpy, angry one.

He shakes his head. "You had it covered? I could see that." He bends his legs to his chest and sets his arms over his knees. His eyes set on me.

"I had a plan," I tell him.

A smile lingers on his lips. "Let's hear it."

Hugging my arms, I say, "I was going to escape and then text you."

"How would you have texted me?"

Right. I don't have his number.

"I could've asked Sebastian to text you." I shrug nonchalantly.

Heath retrieves his sleek phone from his pocket and hands it to me. "You want to talk to me, *you* text me yourself."

I put in my number and send myself a message. My phone pings and I quickly save his number.

"Done."

"Yeah," he whispers, not taking his eyes off me.

My head hurts from the claw clip, so I take it off. My hair falls in waves. I don't have long hair, but it reaches below my breasts if I bring it to the front. I'm about to tuck a few strands behind my ear when he catches my hand.

The air in my throat hitches.

All that I've read about these moments in books happens to me. *Racing heart. Shallow breaths. Butterflies.*

Letting my hand fall into my lap, *he* tucks the few strands of my hair behind my ear in a loose manner—they'd come in front if I moved even a little. His hand lingers on the side of my face, but he doesn't touch me.

"You have wavy hair," he says in a low, deep voice that draws every bit of my attention to his mouth.

"Not from the roots. It's straight then goes curly in the middle and at the ends," I elaborate as if he doesn't have eyes.

His eyes assess my hair from top to bottom as if memorizing it. "I can see that." Then his gaze finally meets my eyes. "I like it," he says.

We stare at each other. There's very little distance between us. We can kiss—

His phone starts ringing and breaks the moment.

I glance at the screen that shows the contact name 'Dad.'

Heath lets his phone ring. The call ends and then rings again, but he switches off his phone and jumps up to his feet. "Let's get out of here."

Fifteen minutes later we're in a department store parking lot with a list of things he wants to buy for his diet plan. Apparently, it costs a lot to have a body like his.

*And he has a body. A great body. Mouthwatering body.*

"You don't have to come if you don't want to," he reminds me for the third time.

"No, it's all right."

After that little moment in the gym, I'm certain we're inching toward a line that isn't supposed to be crossed. We've just started being friends and I'm already on the verge of ruining it by catching feelings for him.

Heath gets a trolley. Together we enter the store and move toward the section that has these massive bottles of protein powder. Seriously, they're quite big.

He dumps four of them in the trolley with ease.

I watch him with an open mouth. They must weigh a ton.

"What?" he asks with a serious face.

"Do you need this many?" I eye him and the bottles.

"Two of them are for Sebastian."

I smile at his reply.

Next, we move to other sections. I push his cart and reach for the products he tells me to. This oddly feels like what friends would be doing. So, I don't think too much about how he stands next to me whenever there's a guy nearby or how he only tells me to get things that don't make me stretch my arm to the moon and flash others.

*He's being considerate.*

We're in the fruit and vegetables section when a voice raises goosebumps on my body.

"Why the fuck are apples so expensive? Do you get them from the black market or something?"

I see Dad's side profile. Instantly fear grips me.

"What do—" Heath leans over me. I jerk away from him.

He pauses.

"What is it?" he asks as his eyebrows scrunch together and he studies me.

I don't answer him. Instead, I search for my father.

I spot him a few feet away with his back turned toward us.

I need to go before he sees me.

If he saw Heath with me he'd kill me.

Not thinking clearly, I dash out of there. Going around Heath's car I sit on the ground with my back leaned against the trunk.

My head fills with his words.

*What are you doing here with a boy?*

*You pathetic girl.*

*Your mom told me you're friends with boys.*

*Is this where you spend your time not studying?*

*I'll tell her how you're wasting time.*

*He would have slapped you.*

*Make a scene.*

*Scream at you.*

The voices get louder. I can't stop the tears that fall from my eyes. All these words and sentences are vague images made up by my mind because I'm scared. I'm so very scared.

That morning when he fooled Mom and moved back home, I didn't miss the evil glint in his eyes or the wicked smile he sent me. That look haunts me at night. I know something big is coming.

My body is trembling. Nothing has happened but my overthinking mind has sent me into a place where I keep spiraling and losing control.

Someone crouches in front of me.

Blue eyes. They are the first thing that I notice, despite the tears.

I don't look away from him and neither does he as he slowly takes my hand and squeezes it.

"You're safe now. I'm here," Heath says to me softly, contrary to how his eyes blaze in fury.

"I'm fine." I don't want him to worry about me. I quickly wipe my eyes.

He arches an eyebrow. "You're telling me that you weren't having a panic attack?"

I shake my head adamantly. "I'm fine."

Realization dawns on me, that if it weren't for him, I'd still be stuck in my mind and thinking about scenarios that are all made up. How sick is that?

He stares at me with the heat of a furnace. "You're *not* fine, Hope."

I'm not. I know that, but he doesn't need to.

"Are you done with your grocery shopping?"

My attempt goes to the drain when he glares. "What happened? Did someone do something?"

"No." I look down in my lap.

We're sitting on gravel, and I've never felt more comfortable before—it's because of him.

"Then?" He probes the matter with determination.

"I saw someone and..." My next words would change everything between us. It's too soon for me to tell him that my father abuses me.

"Who was it?" he asks.

I shake my head. "Please let it go."

"Hope—"

I stand up and dust myself off. My way of putting an end to this conversation.

He joins me and says, "You can tell me."

*I don't want to be a burden.*

"We should go home."

Heath scoffs, but he doesn't push the matter for which I'm grateful.

# 24

## HEATH

I shouldn't care, but I do.

I shouldn't worry about her, but I do.

I shouldn't give two fucks, but I do.

*I just fucking do.*

Sitting in Business class, I'm more concentrated on Hope than the lecture. I can't think of anything else *but* her.

Something doesn't add up, and it keeps circling my mind.

*Who was she afraid of?*

*Who was the person that made her cry?*

*How did I miss the face of that fucker?*

*Why was she so fucking scared?*

*Was it the same person who put marks on her?*

*Was it—*

"Heath." Sebastian pushes my shoulder. I turn to glare at him, but he jerks his head toward Mr. Nathan who's looking at me with a displeased scowl.

"I asked you a question five minutes ago," he says with a displeased tone.

I glance at the whiteboard. "What was the question?"

The whole class stares at me and a few laugh as I sit clueless.

Mr. Nathan points toward the board. "I want you to explain the trend of it."

One more glance at the board and I know the answer.

Despite the fact that I give the correct answer, Mr. Nathan says, "Pay more attention next time."

After the class, Sebastian is onto me as we sneak up to the roof to skip a class. I hate Biology anyway. But more than that, it's *Sebastian* who suggests it. I know it has to do with me zoning out in the class. He's worried about me, which wasn't my intention. Fuck it.

"Did your dad call?" he asks, leaning back on his hands.

He and I both know he's the source of my pissed-off mood half of the time, but this time it's someone else. A girl. A pretty girl who loves to read romance books.

I look up at the sky and act nonchalant. "He calls every day."

"Then why were you looking like someone was scratching your heart out?"

That's one way to put how that pretty book nerd makes me feel.

With a sigh, I lie back on the concrete and close my eyes.

My head spins with these new feelings that float me in and out of reality.

Is this how feelings work? You're trapped in a haze of thoughts about this other person and think about them all the fucking time.

Wait a fucking second? Did I just say *feelings*? I don't have feelings for Hope. Nope. Nada. None fucking at all.

Sebastian shoves me hard, and I almost hit my face against the cement floor.

Anger flares me up and I turn to him with a glare. "What the actual fuck?"

"You were zoning out again. What is wrong with you today?" He runs his eyes all over me in worry.

"Nothing's wrong with me. I'm fine," I mutter.

*Pot meet kettle.* No wonder it gets on my nerves when Hope says the exact same fucking words.

He scoffs, not buying my bullshit. "Yeah, right. It's every day you're lost in your thoughts and stare at the sky. You don't even *like* the sky."

I don't. It reminds me of how Emery is up there and looking down at me ruining my life.

*No thanks. I don't need the fucking reminder.*

I steer my gaze toward the hills. I'm always so calm when I'm up there. Nature manages to quiet the utter chaos in my head.

"What are feelings?" I ask and avoid looking at him. One glimpse at me and he'll know what's going on with me.

Sebastian has a rare talent for calling me out on my bullshit.

"Feelings? Are we talking about someone whose name starts with H and ends with E?" he teases.

Never mind I shouldn't have fucking asked.

"I can ask someone else if you can't answer the fucking question." There's no way I'm asking someone else.

Sebastian smirks knowing damn well I won't. "I'd like to see you try."

I groan. "Bash. Just fucking tell me, would you?"

With a chuckle, he agrees. "Fine. I'll answer."

He crosses his legs and his face gains a seriousness that I don't see often.

"Everyone will say something different, but I'll say what I've experienced. Feelings are emotions you've *never* experienced before. They hit you like a train. You can't stop thinking about this person. In every thought, conscious or unconscious, they sneak up on you, and no matter what you do, they don't go away. Feelings are like water. They fill in the nooks and corners that have been empty, and at the same time are enough to drown your heart. You have this overwhelming surge of desire to be with that person all the time, and risk anything to make them happy. Feelings make you do stupid stuff, nothing wise ever. You become selfish and protective. But at the same time, you are willing to let them go if someone else makes them happy." He ends with a knowing smirk directed right at me. "You can't get rid of feelings."

*For fuck's sake.*

"What if I direct them *toward* someone else?"

Sebastian sighs. "Did you *not* hear a word I said?"

"You made it sound like I have a terminal disease."

"Well, that's one way to put it."

I swivel my head to the sky instead of avoiding it like I have for the past year.

I have no idea if Emery can see me right now, but I hope she knows I'm hanging in there even when I don't want to. However, with the way things have been, one pretty girl might be the death of me.

Leaning against my car, I wait for Hope to step out—she's always the last one.

I fight the urge to smoke a cigarette, especially with the way she's had my head in pieces lately.

One side is yelling 'you like her' in Sebastian's voice—which is disturbing—and the other is telling me that it's not worth it.

In a few months, I'll be off to college somewhere far away from this town and the memories that haunt me here. Of course, I'll miss my sister, but I hate living under the thumb of my father who gets information about me. I don't want anything to do with him. I want to live somewhere where he can't track me down or call me.

After what feels like a decade, Hope steps out carrying a stack of thick textbooks in her arms. Wild strands of her dark hair fly in front of her face, and she has a pen stuck to the side of her ear.

She's such a nerd.

That thought disappears when I see *what* she's wearing.

A plaid skirt, black stockings, and a white warmer. Underneath she's wearing her usual Converse. She looks sexy with the way those stockings hug her legs. Has she always had such long, beautiful legs, or am I fucking blind for not noticing before?

Standing in front of me she smiles at me. I clench my jaw and use every bit of my control to not look down at her sexy legs.

*For fuck's sake.* I've never been interested in legs before.

"How many?" She shifts those books in her arms. Without thinking, I take them from her and put them on the roof of my car.

"Thank you. They were quite heavy." She tucks her hair behind her ear.

I like it when her hair frames her face.

*Fuck.*

I need to get fucking therapy. This feelings bullshit is getting out of hand.

"How many what?" My voice is scratchy as it comes out.

"The orders. That's why you were waiting for me, right?" Her light brown eyes brighten up.

I lie for the life of me, so it doesn't dim. "Yes."

Handing her my phone, I see the grin that etches onto her lips like a freak. There it is. That beautiful fucking smile.

"I got seven orders." She smiles.

She got less than before and she's still happy.

"We'll take more pictures to post and increase interaction. How many followers do you have?"

"One hundred and seven," she says with a grimace.

I don't like that sad look on her. "Not bad. Save the money and we'll use it for ads and promotion."

Hope grins at me. "You're so good at this."

"Of course, I am."

With a laugh, she opens the door and gets inside—before I can do it for her—while I watch her. I'm in so much fucking trouble.

We arrive at my house after mailing the orders. Hope is ecstatic as she gets the money from her last orders. Since she isn't eighteen she doesn't have a bank account and takes cash on delivery. I'm half tempted to ask Marie to make her a fake offshore account, but I know that shit doesn't end well. I'd hate to do that to her when she works so hard to make money.

We're on the porch when I see a big package sitting next to the door with my details on the top. I pick it up and take it into the kitchen and ask Hope to step into the living room.

"What's that, sir?" Derek comes around and scrutinizes me as I open the damn box.

"A box of—none of your fucking business." I glare at him to back off. Of course, he doesn't.

He frowns. "I believe it is my business."

This man gets on my fucking nerves.

Ignoring him, I cut open the box and peek inside. The entire collection of Harry Potter series sits in the box. I might have gone a little overboard and bought two sets; one is illustrated and the other is original.

Derek peeks over my shoulder. "Since when do you read children's books, sir?"

Immediately I close the flaps. "Step back, Derek."

Derek eyes me skeptically like he can see right through me. It annoys the shit out of me. I don't want him to see too much and figure out how certain emotions are flying inside of me when Hope is near me and how my pulse quickens. He doesn't need to know any of it.

Taking the box with me, I ask Hope to come with me upstairs. I don't like how Derek watches Hope. Last time he even dared to interrogate her. I'm sure Father Dearest already knows about Hope.

*Fucking great.*

I click in the lock and suddenly the air thickens.

*I'm alone with Hope in my room.*

The fact shouldn't bother me when it isn't my first time, but it keeps coming to the forefront of my mind like a warning sign.

My heart races. *Calm the fuck down.*

I place the box on the coffee table. "This is for you."

Her eyes widen. "For me? What is it?"

"See for yourself."

"You didn't need to."

"You won't be saying that after you see what's inside."

I watch as she approaches the box and looks inside.

A gasp leaves past her lips. "No... you didn't."

Retrieving the two sets, she takes out every single book.

I notice her hands are shaking.

Instead of a smile, there is a shift in the air that slows the blood flow in my veins.

*Did I get it fucking wrong?*

*Never mind. I'll just order it again until I get it right.*

Hope turns to me and tears are glistening in her eyes.

That doesn't look good. I'll get her new ones if they aren't what she wants. I'll get her—

Running up to me, she knocks straight into my chest like a lightning bolt. Electric shocks jam every single nerve in my body. I can hardly breathe.

*How the fuck does breathing work?*

I'm still processing her proximity, when her thin arms wrap around my waist tightly, and her body is pressed flush against mine.

I feel my heart jump, but she decides it's not enough fucking damage, so she lies her head over my shoulder. Very close to my fast-beating heart.

Lavender scent. Warm body. Soft skin.

My heart skips beats like one does when jumping through a pond over stones.

She sniffles and my chest tightens.

My hackles rise. "What's wrong?"

"Everything."

"Tell me. I'll fix it."

"You already did."

I'm beyond confused. "A little more fucking clarification please."

She rests her chin on my chest and looks up at me with her teary eyes. "You got me the entire series. I've been waiting for it since I was eight."

I stay quiet. Too stunned by her reaction.

"Why did you do it?" she asks.

"It was on sale." The lie rolls over my tongue so smoothly even I'm impressed.

I did it because *she wanted it*. When she told me, all I could think about was getting her those books. They cost a lot, but it doesn't matter. Nothing else matters when it comes to her.

Hope doesn't reply, and I'm in doubt whether she's caught my lie.

My arms stay plastered to my sides. This isn't how a hug is supposed to be. Maybe I should return it.

On that vague thought, I lift my arms and hesitantly put them over her back. At the feel of her body, my hands twitch.

I gulp hard to swallow the fountain of emotions climbing my throat like a damn viper.

Fuck. This feels good.

Hope sniffles on my shoulder. "Thank you so much." Long gone are her tears—thank God, I don't know how to deal with them—and instead, there is a smile that hits me straight in the heart.

"It's nothing."

"It's something."

Stepping away from me—much to my dislike—she hurries to her new stack of books, flipping through pages and running her hands over the covers.

A dreamy look flashes across her face.

*She really is something.* I've never seen anyone look at books the way she does. It's like they're a breath of fresh air, or perhaps the most beautiful artifact of the world that she'll treasure for the rest of her life.

I can't put into words what she looks like when she holds books, but there *is* a word I can use for her.

*Enchanting.*

I stare long at her and realize how serene I feel when she's doing something as mundane as reading a book.

"The illustrated covers are so pretty," she gushes as she aligns them over the table.

"I guess," I murmur, not knowing what else to say.

I don't find books as enchanting as she does. But I find *her* enchanting.

"Look at these original covers." With giddy happiness, she brings the book to my face and forces me to look at it. A month ago, I wouldn't have thought my life would come to this.

"Old is gold."

A giggle pulls out of her, and she doesn't comment on my dry humor.

With each book she picks up, more life descends into her, and I'm standing here, thinking how the fuck did I get myself into this mess?

# 25

## HOPE

It's late in the night when I step inside my house, only to halt when I see Dad pausing in the hallway on his way from the kitchen. He pins me with a hard stare as he takes me in from head to toe.

An unwelcoming chill hits me and freezes every organ in my body.

"What are you wearing?" he asks, looking deep into my eyes.

"Clothes." I don't think he'll like my smart remark when I'm coming home late. It's past ten p.m.

"What'd you say?" Striding toward me in a few steps he gets in my face.

"N-nothing," I stammer with my heart in my throat.

"You're dressed like a fucking hooker." His breath stinks of Whiskey.

I'm not dressed like a hooker. I'm wearing an outfit I saw online and found cute. It's September, the official season of Autumn. I used the things I already had to make up today's look. I did it for myself and not for anyone.

"Are you fucking—" he bangs his hand on the door, a few centimeters away from my head. I jostle in shock. "—lying to me, girl?" he slurs and gets closer to me.

I lean back but the door doesn't allow me.

For that reason, I come face to face with Dad who looks at me like he hates me.

How did we get here?

Where did this hatred come from?

Why does he hate me?

"Look at this damn skirt. Are you whoring around?"

"No!" I blanch in disgust.

"Then why are you coming home so fucking late?"

"I was with a friend. She needed my help with her studies." I feel terrible for bringing Marie into this when it was Heath I was spending the time with. We watched Lucifer and ate dinner. I can't believe he has a personal cook who makes such good food for him.

"Don't you fucking lie to me." Red eyes stare at me with rage and hatred, and all my confidence and bravery crumble to the floor in a heap of sand.

"Let's set a few ground rules, shall we?" Hauling me by my throat he takes me to the kitchen and brings over the whiskey bottle.

I close my eyes at the pungent smell of it. *I hate it. I hate it so much.*

"First, from now on you're going to come home at eight. If you're a second late, I'll punish you."

My eyes widen in shock. I try to get away from him, but he tightens his hold on me.

"Did you hear me or not, kid?" He yells in my face and tears cloud my eyes.

Why today? Why did he have to traumatize me today out of all the days?

I nod and he loosens his grip for me to inhale.

"Second, I want you to keep your mouth shut about the times I've visited before. Are we clear?"

I quickly nod so I can get away from him.

"I mean it. Don't tell your mother anything."

I nod again.

"Third, I don't want to see you dress like this again."

After that, I zone out.

*Focus on studies.*

*Stay at home.*

*Cook meals.*

*Clean the house.*

The list goes on and on. I store every point, so I don't slip up and get punished. Dad doesn't elaborate on that but I'm sure it'll be worse than choking.

He lets me away, after making me get him another bottle from under the bed in their bedroom.

Stripping off my clothes, I take a hot shower and shed all the tears I was holding back earlier. I sob until I'm weak and light-headed. The happiness from earlier is drained out of me. By the time I lie down on my bed in my pajamas, I'm half-dead.

Everything inside my body hurts, and my stomach churns in painful cramps. I'm spiraling so I do one thing that distracts me. Reading.

I get the set box of the Harry Potter books and take out the first one.

From there, time is a distant thought as I fly through pages and enter a world that's as magical as it could be.

I have to thank Heath. A hug and a few tears must've been an indication of how much it meant to me. Still, I want to do something big and meaningful like he did.

It's hard to give someone something when they have everything in the world.

I still can't believe he got me the Harry Potter series. *He remembered.*

No one has ever done something so nice for me.

I pick up my phone and pull up his number. I quickly take a picture of the book and send it to him.

**Hope: My current read.**
**Hope: Thank you for buying me this series. It means so much to me.**

A minute later dots appear.

**Heath: You should stop thanking me.**

I smile big.

**Hope: Can't do.**
**Hope: 'shrug' emoji**
**Heath: Then I'll make you.**

I quickly sit up. *What does he mean by that?*

**Hope: No. You can't.**
**Heath: Is that a challenge?**
**Hope: Yes.**
**Heath: Be prepared to surrender, because I don't fucking lose.**

I giggle and roll over to my other side. My book is long forgotten.

**Hope: You just have to bring the f-word in everything.**
**Heath: It's my fucking specialty.**
**Hope: I believe it's your favorite word.**
**Heath: Agree to disagree.**

My fingers stop. I don't know what else to say. I see dots appearing and disappearing on his side.

**Heath: What's your favorite word?**
**Hope: I don't think I have one.**
**Heath: For the record, *fuck*, isn't my favorite word.**
**Hope: So we both don't have a favorite word?**
**Heath: Seems like it.**
**Hope: Tell me when you find a favorite word.**
**Heath: You'll be the first to fucking know.**
**Hope: You didn't say it, but I'll also tell you first when I find my favorite word.**
**Heath: You fucking better.**

I've never found reciprocation sweet, but in this moment, Heath Travon makes me realize that it's the sweetest thing ever.

**Heath: Is the scar-boy in magic school yet?**

I burst into a fit of laughter.

**Hope: His name is Harry.**
**Hope: I haven't gotten that far.**
**Hope: I've only read two chapters.**

Heath is quicker with replies.

**Heath: Already fucking bored?**
**Hope: No. Not at all.**
**Hope. I've waited for this for years. I'm taking my time to enjoy it. I don't want it to be over in a matter of days.**
**Heath: It'll be fucking over when you want it to be.**

He's not wrong. I want to stretch out my time reading this series for as long as I can. I want to remember this moment so that when I look back, I know I had an incredible time reading it.

**Hope: You're right.**
**Hope: Don't you want some things to last a little longer because they're too perfect to be over soon?**

It takes him two minutes to reply.

**Heath: The sooner it's over the better it is.**
**Hope: I don't believe that. I like it when something that feels good lasts for a while. I don't want the magic to disappear.**
**Heath: At this rate, you might get a letter from the magic school.**
**Hope: It's called HOGWARTS!**

**Heath: Could you write it in capital letters? I couldn't fucking see that.**

**Hope: By the way, I'm five years late to get my letter.**

**Heath: I feel fucking sorry for you.**

**Hope: Me too. I could've been an awesome wizard but I'm a muggle.**

**Heath: What a grave fucking tragedy.**

**Hope: Indeed. Anyway...back to our previous topic.**

**Hope: Someday you'll want a moment to last forever.**

**Heath: I highly fucking doubt it.**

**Hope: We'll see.**

**Heath: Marie is rubbing off on you.**

**Hope: She is.**

**Heath: 'grumpy' emoji**

**Hope: I'm off to finish reading the book that YOU got me.**

**Hope: Thank you once again.**

**Heath: Shut up.**

I pick up my book but I'm too distracted to continue. I keep thinking of our chat and Heath. For as long as I can remember books have always managed to occupy my mind, but for the first time, all I can think about is a guy.

It's Saturday morning, and I dread it already. Usually, I spend the day at the library with the excuse of studying to avoid my parents, but Mom insists that I stay home today.

As I enter the kitchen I find my parents kissing with pancakes getting burned over the stove.

Ignoring their smooching noises, I turn off the stove and get rid of the burnt pancakes.

"Oh shit." Mom steps back with flushed cheeks.

"It's only pancakes. We'll make more." Dad assures her by rubbing her back. He looks at me. "Hope, why don't you make them?" The harsh look in his brown eyes makes me agree.

"Okay."

Mom steps in. "Oh, you don't have to, honey. It's all right I'll make—"

"Let her do some work. You come with me." With a smile, he steers her toward the living room, and she lets him.

I watch the scene with sheer confusion. It's like I'm trapped in a dream that feels real. I'm perplexed by how easily Mom is letting Dad in. He's touching her, kissing her, and ordering me around, but she's too beguiled with his charms. It's almost like he's cast a spell on her when he isn't even a wizard... or maybe he is. *No! He's definitely not.*

While making the batter I catch glimpses of them. Mom looks happy. And Dad, he looks at her a *certain* way. I can't pinpoint what it is, but there's something that doesn't feel right.

He walks in through the doors and Mom just takes him. How is it possible? What did he even say to her? Did he apologize for the way he's treated her for years—and how he almost killed her that night? Has he told her how he's drinking and abusing me? He's leaving marks on my body and he's an entirely different person. I don't recognize him anymore. There's nothing familiar about him, so what does Mom see in him?

Now his eyes are laced with layers of drunkenness, slightly yellow teeth, and his physique is lean. He's lost weight and it's so obvious he's sick. I don't hear Mom complaining or noticing.

All the times he's been drunk, Mom hasn't been home. It's always been me. He must spend the night like that and get sober by the time she comes home. With touches and kisses, he hypnotizes her in whatever webs he's been weaving.

I feel sick and confused.

I don't know what is real or not.

After I serve them breakfast, I return to my room with the excuse that I have a test on Monday when all I want is to leave the house.

It's sometime in the afternoon when Mom comes up to my room with a stern face. "We need to talk."

I quickly close my biology textbook. "What is it?"

She sits on my bed and stares at me with worry. "What is going on?"

"What do you mean?"

"Between your dad and you."

I look away. "Nothing."

She sighs. "I see you tiptoeing around your father. You avoid talking to him and you barely stay in the same room as him for more than five minutes. What's the matter? Aren't you *happy* he's back?"

I lift my head with a frown.

*Happy?* Why would I be happy that he's back?

Has she really forgotten the years of abuse he put her through? And all the other stuff?

"I'm not," I say.

Mom frowns in disbelief. "Why not?"

"Have you seen him? He's been drinking."

She shakes her head. "No. Alex won't do that to me. He's promised me that he quit."

"No, Mom, he hasn't. Every night when I come home he's drunk and yells at me. He's even hurt me physically." I'm about to show her marks but she stares at me as if I'm crazy.

"Hurt you? Yell at you? What are you talking about?" There's disgust and surprise on her face.

"I'm telling you the truth. You can even ask Nadina. She saw him drunk and breaking into the house a few weeks ago."

Mom sighs heavily. "I know about that. He told me. But he's also promised me that he won't go back to his ways. He wants to change. He wants to be good to me and make up to me. I think we should give him a chance. I love him."

Just like I suspected, she is hypnotized. She discards everything that I said. She won't care if I show her how he's been abusing me. Even last night.

I have to try. I have to show her that he's not different. "He's lying to you."

The worry in her eyes disappears, and anger appears. "I know him better than you, Hope."

I nod in sympathy, trying to not let my emotions get the best of me. "I'm sure you do, but you have to *see* that he's not okay. He's hurt me, Mom. I swear."

"He will never hurt you," she dismisses my words.

"How are you so sure? He's hurt *you* before."

She glares at me. "That was before. The time we spent apart has changed him."

"No, he's not. Last night he made up some stupid rules and he asked me to follow them. He told me how to dress and—"

Exasperation flashes across her face. "I know. Alex told me you were dressed like a hooker."

"No! I wasn't," I protest. She knows what kind of clothes I wear.

"From how he explained the outfit to me, I believe him." She shrugs carelessly like my words don't even matter.

"But you don't believe me?" My voice breaks.

Mom sighs and stares at me in sympathy. "I do, Hope. But your father and I know better."

Anger flares through me. "The father who left us four months ago right after he choked you."

Mom stands up and glares at me. "Watch your tongue, Hope! I won't tolerate disrespect next time. Your dad is back home and he's going to stay. You can either deal with the fact or move out."

What?

I can't breathe.

She... she kicked me out? Even after I told her he's hurting me.

She chose to not believe me.

I...

My throat grows thick. "M-move out? W-what are you talking about? I don't have—"

"That's what I thought. When you live under my house you live by my rules."

Emotions overwhelm me to the point they suffocate me, so I burst out. "I just told you how he's treating me, and you don't even believe me."

"It's not that I don't believe you."

I look away from her. Tears sting my eyes, but I keep them at bay. It hurts that she tossed away my words as if they hold no credibility.

"I'm happy he's back for you, but don't expect me to make up with him. You either believe me or you don't. I've told you what he's been doing to himself *and* me, but if you don't want to believe it then I can't do anything."

"What you should be doing is studying."

I lift my head and look her straight in the eyes. "I am, and I'd like it if you leave me alone. I have plenty of tests next week."

Mom's displeased scowl doesn't hurt more than her not taking my word.

What's the point of telling this to someone when they don't believe you?

# 26

## HEATH

"So, how's the friendship going?" Marie asks with a grin.

"What fucking friendship?" I sip my beer.

"With Hope, who else?" She rolls her eyes dramatically. If Marie wasn't a computer geek she'd make an excellent actress.

"That's your fucking business how Blondie?"

"You're my best friend. So of course you're my business."

"She's right," Sebastian chirps in with a smirk.

I study the bar, specifically, the teenagers talking and drinking. Seems like we're not the only ones who got fake IDs. The chatter floats in the air over the soft tune of some 80's music playing on the jukebox.

The sun is going down coloring the sky in beautiful hues. There's a tranquility that comes with it.

"Both of you—" I cock my bottle between the two of them, "—get off my fucking back."

"Can't do." Marie shrugs and dives for the onion rings.

"Then I'm leaving." I'm about to stand up when Marie's next words glue me to my fucking seat.

"Hope is two minutes away."

Right at the moment the door opens. Hope stands there doe-eyed. Black jeans, a maroon top, and Converse. Her hair is pulled in a loose braid with a few strands falling on the sides of her face. Everything is simple about her but to me she's fucking special.

"Here!" Marie excitedly waves at her. Hope and a few others look at us.

With an annoyed sigh, I lean back while Sebastian watches me with a smile. My best friend is having a blast in this feeling-situation I'm stuck in.

The pretty book nerd quickly crosses the room, avoiding the drunk idiots who try to bump into her. I'm seconds away from shoving them right across the dance floor. Fucking assholes.

Since we're sitting in a booth the only seat left is next to me. She takes it after greeting my best friends who send her beaming smiles like they've known her their entire lives.

Then it's finally my turn. "Hi."

"Hi," I say.

My gaze stills over the faint marks around her neck. This is the third fucking time I'm seeing them on her and I'm fucking pissed. Whoever this fucking person is, I will beat the living shit out of them when I get my hands on them.

We're staring at each other, and I don't even want to stop.

"Hope, what would you like?" Marie asks, making Hope look away from me.

"I'm not hungry."

"Bullshit," I murmur.

Sebastian watches me closely, but I don't give a fuck.

Marie moves her basket toward her. "You can have my onion rings." Reluctantly Hope takes one.

Wanting to put an end to this I ask Hope to move so I can get out. At the counter I order French fries and a coke can for her. I pay and turn around only to see Marie waiting for me.

"What is it?" I ask with agitation.

"Nothing." Her smile broadens.

"You look creepy with that smile, Blondie." I check on Hope who's talking to Sebastian. She looks relaxed and even smiles.

Marie sits on the stool while I lean against the counter, waiting for the order. I feel the heat of Marie's stare on me.

So, I turn and glare at her. "There isn't anything going on between us."

"I didn't say anything." Marie sips her coke bottle. Because of Sebastian, she avoids alcohol, not that she was a big fan of it before. She doesn't even take a beer.

This is my first time drinking in a while, otherwise, I avoid it too, especially in front of Sebastian. Even though he's quit and been through rehab and knows not to dive head-first into his urges. As a friend I don't want to resurrect a part of his life he's buried and moved on from.

Although tonight my head is a mess of thoughts about a girl who crosses my mind so often. Everywhere I go I'm thinking about her. All the fucking time.

She *lives* in my head.

On instinct, I check up on Hope for the fourth time

"She's fine, Heath," Marie says, noticing me.

I'm getting addicted to her, for fuck's sake.

"Thanks for telling, not that I care," I say in a curt tone.

"I know you don't." Marie pauses. "I think you should ask Hope out."

I almost break my neck when I turn toward her. "Excuse me?"

"You like her, it's so obvious. So why waste time?"

I watch Marie with astonishment. "We're friends, Marie. I don't like her."

She ignores me. "I see the way you look at her."

My eyebrows pinch. "And *what* fucking way is that?"

"Like she's the only girl you want in the whole wide world."

A dry chuckle leaves my mouth. "She's not my type."

"She's everyone's type," Marie says with confidence, then gets closer to me. "Look around the bar. So many guys are checking her out."

Running a glance at every guy in the bar, my blood boils when I find a number of them staring at Hope who's smiling and sipping Sebastian's orange juice.

Marie pats my shoulder. "Don't worry you'll find your type."

I glare at her. "I don't want a girl."

"Well, good luck dying *single* then." With a wink she abandons me.

A woman drops off my order. I take it back to our table and put it in front of Hope.

I sit down next to her, and she whispers, "You didn't have to, Heath."

Blood rushes through my veins and heats my skin. In a T-shirt, I'm sweating when the AC is working to its fullest. It's happening just because she said my fucking name.

I gesture toward the food. "Eat."

Hope smiles.

I finish my beer and see Sebastian and Marie grinning at me. I roll my eyes and check my phone to catch up on my emails and other work stuff. I like earning money so I can do things freely. One day I'm going to be as rich as my dad, and none of my wealth will be connected to his.

The music stops and Marie jumps up. "My turn! My turn!" Hurrying toward the jukebox she slides in the quarter. I know the song even before it starts playing.

'Shut Up and Dance' by WALK THE MOON pours out of the speakers. Marie's favorite song that she's played so many times I've gotten sick of it. Not Sebastian.

Sebastian joins her and they dance in the middle of the floor while laughing at each other. Their moves are absurd, and they look awkward in a group of people who at least know how to dance, but none of that shit matters to them.

Bodies close, and eyes locked, they're lost in each other as the world around them fades away. It's been exactly like that since they met each other. To them only *they* matter and no one else.

"They're so in love," Hope says.

"Yeah."

I can feel Hope's gaze on me. "Do you believe in love?"

"I don't." Despite those words, I feel a weight on my chest, as if I've lied to her which is confusing.

I meet her gaze. "Do you?"

She shakes her head. "It only exists in books." *She's lying.* There's a flicker of longing in her eyes as she watches our best friends.

"You're a hopeless romantic. You're supposed to believe in it," I argue, wanting to dig deeper for God knows why.

She eats fries as if she's stalling, but I wait for her.

"I *do* believe in love, but only when it's in the fictional world. Love feels real and safe between the pages of a book." With a sad smile, she adds, "Marie and Sebastian contradict my belief. I mean just look at them. They are in love, and it exists in the outside world."

She stares at them, and I stare at her.

Her brown eyes are so beautiful when they're filled with emotion, or the way the golden light of the bulbs in the bar gleams in her eyes.

I realize she steals every molecule of my breath and owns every beat of my heart.

I've never been enamored by a girl this fucking much.

At once she glances at me. Her lips part in surprise when she finds me not looking at anyone but her. Clearly, she has no fucking idea what she does to me.

The black in her eyes dilates and a bright flush adorably covers her cheeks.

I can't help myself as I lean down. I press my lips to her ear and pick up her hand from her lap.

My fingers find her pulse that's fluttering under her warm skin. And fuck, she smells like a field of lavender. Lately, it's become my favorite fucking scent.

"How many chapters have you read?"

*Seriously. That's what came out of my fucking mouth?*

She shivers, then says breathlessly, "Ten."

*Good.* Seems like I'm not the only one who forgets to breathe in our proximity.

A smile dances on my mouth. "Taking it slow so it lasts longer?"

"Yes."

I breathe and her lavender scent attacks me like rain on a pleasant summer day.

I was right, this girl will ruin me, and I'll let her.

"Text me as you read the books. I want to know everything." I'm desperate.

"Okay."

Pulling back, my eyes find hers. I can see so many emotions crossing through them. Then my gaze drops down to her lips and a desire to kiss them marches above my logical thoughts.

*Fuck.*

*Those lips look fucking inviting.*

I've never wanted to kiss someone before, but here I am craving to take one taste.

Lust clouds my mind and body. I can barely see through the haze that blinds me.

*What the fuck is wrong with me?*

"Heath, what are you doing?" Her sweet, scared voice breaks my train of thought.

Fuck. I don't want to scare her by showing her how badly I want her. I'll never take anything she's not willing to give to me. If she gives me nothing I'll make peace with it and learn to live with it. As long as I'm close to her.

"You're safe with me," I tell her instead, wishing she believed me.

I caress the side of her neck, and she winces.

Fuck.

"I'm sorry," I quickly say and rub circles over the inner side of her wrist.

*I keep fucking up, don't I?*

*It's the last thing I want to do.*

I need to be better. I need to be good to her.

"It's all right." She gives me a tiny smile and doesn't pull away from my touch. But I do.

I can never bring myself to hurt her. In fact, how can anyone? She's delicate and pure and there's a monster who's physically assaulting her.

"Another incident with the straightener?" I inquire, keeping my voice quiet so she can't sense the rage flooding through my senses.

"Yes." Her eyes steer away from me as she lies.

I know her because it's so easy for me to read it.

She reads books and I read her.

Squeezing her wrist gently, I nudge her to look at me. "Do you want to leave?"

"Now?"

"Yeah."

"But—"

"Marie and Sebastian won't mind."

"Are you sure?"

"Yes."

Hope finally nods.

We slip out of the booth and bid goodbye to Marie and Sebastian who are dancing to another song now. They don't ask us questions for which I'm grateful. I just want to get out of here with her.

Getting in my car, I drive us around the town as my playlist plays in the background. We sit in silence and it's comfortable.

For her sake, I keep the speed at forty which isn't my usual. I like to drive fast—live on the edge—but then I don't think she'd feel safe with me.

The sky gets darker as I drive us to my secret spot that's slowly becoming *our* spot. The place where I would be lonely is now accompanied by her presence.

Parking the car near the edge of the hill, I help her out of the car.

She sits on the hood of my car, while I grab something that I specifically bought for her.

Leaning against the side of my car, I look at her. "This is for you."

She gasps and meets my gaze. "It's chocolate!"

"Your favorite kind."

"How do you know?"

"You told me."

"Yes, but I didn't expect you to remember."

I fold my arms over my chest. "I remember everything you tell me. You *just* have to tell me."

She smiles and it hits me right in the chest. "Thank you."

I stay silent, fully captivated by the sight of her. The way her teeth bite a little chunk as if she's afraid of finishing it, or the way she melts the chocolate in her mouth, devouring every milligram of sweetness in it.

I feel my body heat up like a furnace. I swear I'm fucking sweating through my T-shirt.

For fuck's sake.

And if that's not enough, my dick strains against the zipper of my jeans.

"Fuck," I harshly whisper as I rake a hand through my hair.

Hope quickly looks over. "What's wrong?"

"Nothing."

She nods, not one bit aware of *what* she does to me. "Can I ask you something?"

My chest tightens. "Go ahead."

Hope gulps hard. From that alone I know something is bothering her.

Slipping the empty wrapper into her jeans pocket, she says, "Why do you think people don't believe victims?"

My body coils in ropes of tension, making me sit straight. My hard-on is long forgotten.

Well, that worked perfectly.

Lots of answers race through my mind. I need to say the right thing, especially when I already have suspicions about her.

"Maybe because they don't want to come to terms that it's happened."

Her short laugh turns into a sob that shakes her entire body. "That's a good excuse."

My heart beats violently against my chest.

Without thinking, I come around and stand in front of her.

"Hey." I approach her in a gentle voice, keeping my hands to myself.

She quickly wipes away her tears. "I don't want to cry in front of you again."

What fucking nonsense.

I ignore her and take her hands which she keeps using to rub her face. However, her tears don't stop. They fall, fall, and fall.

"I think we're way past that."

"I never wanted to." She lifts her shoulder to wipe her eyes. Before she can. I do it for her.

Using my thumb, I wipe away every tear that falls as she cries hard.

It's breaking my fucking heart.

"It's done now," I reply.

Shaking her head, she sniffles. "I should go."

She starts getting off the hood, but I hold her back by grabbing her thighs.

"Stay." There's no way in fuck I'm letting her leave until I know she's okay.

She chews her bottom lip. "I have to be home by eight."

"Then I'll drop you home by eight." Picking out my phone, I show her the time. "It's six-thirty now. We've got time."

"I don't know."

Even in the dark, I see how miserable and scared she looks. For fuck's sake, she's shivering.

"You're staying." I decide for her.

Unlocking my car, I get her in the backseat, then grab the black blanket from the trunk that I keep with me at times I sleep in my car to avoid going to an empty home. It used to happen a lot last year after Emery's death.

I hand it to Hope and then turn on the AC and music from my favorite band. Coldplay.

Hope bundles up in my blanket and looks so small and vulnerable.

She is trouble to my heart.

She has the power to wreck everything in me with her eyes and I'll be a goner. Yet I can't seem to avoid her. *I should. I really fucking should. But I can't.*

"Come here." I've lost my fucking mind, but that's not new. I lost my mind the day she collided with me and turned my world upside down with her pretty eyes. At this point, there is no going back. I'm too fucking invested in her. Fuck, I don't even want to go back.

Hope scoots over to me and cuddles in the crook of my arm. Her head rests on my chest and I'm certain she can hear the fast rhythm of my heart.

"Who doesn't believe you, Rose?" I finally ask her when one song ends and another starts playing.

"No one." She holds the edge of the blanket to her chin.

"I'll believe you."

"Because you're my friend?"

"Yes."

Right, of course, how could I forget we're just friends and nothing else?

"So, then who—"

"I don't want to talk about it."

Later then.

"What's the scar-boy up to?"

A laugh bubbles out of her, and the sound is the sweetest fucking thing I've ever heard. It thaws the ice around my heart and makes it warm.

If I could, I'd record her laugh and play it on a loop on nights when death seems like the only option. I believe this sound can make me stay a day more.

Hope elbows me in the ribs playfully. "His name *is* Harry. You know that."

I do know that, but I enjoy it when she corrects me.

"Harry or scar-boy, what's the difference?"

She gasps as if I've killed her favorite character. "*Big difference,*" she protests.

"What's happening in there? Tell me."

Just like that, she gives me a run down and I listen to every word. I cling to her like a survivor does to a lifeboat. Midway her voice gets slower and quieter and her body molds more into me.

I bet she's about to sleep on me, and the strangest part is, I'll let her.

"I'll tell you more tomor..." The word barely passes her lips before she dozes off on me.

I stop breathing and my body goes still. I don't want to move a single muscle that'll wake her up.

The low hum of the engine and the melody of the song fill the car.

I check the time and it's 6:45 p.m.

Not two minutes later she jostles awake.

"I'm not asleep." She stirs and looks around with sleepy eyes.

"I never said you are." I scowl as she sits up straight but doesn't move away from me.

"I need to go home."

"It's not eight yet." I gesture to the screen in the front.

"It's better if I leave now."

"Or not."

I draw her back to my chest, surprising the both of us. Then she lies her head on my chest and looks up at me.

"Only for ten more minutes."

I like the sound of it a lot.

She snuggles into the blanket. The temperature isn't cold, but it is for her. The AC is blasting air through all its vents.

I lean over to turn the dial down, but she puts her hand over my arm. I pause.

"You don't need to do that. It's okay."

"You look cold."

She raises the ends of my blanket to her chin. "Your blanket is quite warm, *and* it smells like you."

I frown. "Is it a good thing or a bad thing?"

She smiles. "Definitely a good thing. You always smell good."

"Good?" I smirk.

She blushes and it's all I need to know.

I move back and relax next to her.

I face her and find her staring at my neck. "What?"

She reaches up and touches me. "You're always wearing this silver chain."

"My sister gave it to me."

Silence extends between us, despite the music and hum of the engine in the background. The world quietens as if to share a moment of silence for the death of the person I loved so dearly.

"I'm sorry about her."

"You already said that to me."

"I know," she whispers. "I can't imagine how it must feel to lose a sibling."

It takes me a whole fucking minute to get the words out. "It feels like the end of the world."

I hear her suck in breath.

After a minute she asks, "What is her name?"

I almost smile. She used *is* not *was*. It's a small detail, but I notice it and it makes me feel better—she knew how much it would mean to me.

"Emery," I say, feeling like I'm sharing a piece of myself with her.

"That's a beautiful name."

It indeed is a beautiful name, or perhaps I'm being biased, but I don't fucking care.

"It is." It'll always be.

My throat closes on me. I know it's time to end this topic. It's only been a year but it's fucking hard to move on in life without her by my side.

When I'm six feet above ground, she's six feet under. The distance is small, but enough to keep our worlds separated with no mode of communication. Nothing.

The only thing I believe in is that she's not in pain anymore and is in a better place where no cancer or any form of disease can ever get to her. Even if it comes at the cost of me not seeing her ever again.

She's at peace.

It sounds stupid in my head, so I never share it with anyone. Those idiotic reasons are the only ounce of assurance I have.

I feel a hand rest over mine. Heat sears me like a bullet cuts through the air. A trail of tingles erupts under my skin and burns my arm in a way I've never been burned before. It's a good kind of burn. The kind where I want to keep burning.

"You look sad." Hope drops the blanket and gets closer to me.

"I'm fine," I grumble, feeling vulnerable like she's cut me open and can see everything that I hide from the world—all my fucking emotions on display.

"Is that *our* way of avoiding a topic?"

"You tell me."

"I don't want you to do that. We're friends. You can talk to me."

I arch an eyebrow. "Kinda hypocritical of you when you don't tell me stuff."

She plays with the ring on my finger. I don't think she's aware she's doing that. *But I am.* I can barely focus on anything but *her* and the *touch* of her cold skin.

"If I could, I would."

"You can."

Shaking her head, she whispers, "I really can't."

I take her cold fingers and squeeze them gently. "I know I said I won't offer you my help but forget about it. I will help you *no* matter what. If someone is hurting you, I'll hurt them a thousand times worse. I will protect you."

Hope watches me. She watches me for a long time and says nothing—she doesn't have to. Her eyes say it all. She's afraid *for* me.

Throwing her arms around my neck, she hugs me. This is not the first time and I sure as fuck don't want it to be the last time when she hugs me out of nowhere. She does it without thinking. I'm sure it's the only thing—the best thing—she doesn't think about.

I feel her body shiver in my hold. I wonder if it's because of the AC or something else.

This time I don't waste a second and wrap my arms around her waist and press her body to mine.

Because I just can't fucking help it.

Emotions, feelings, little-thoughts-bugging-my-heart-and-mind, or whatever the fuck you want to call them, surge high to the point I feel my own body vibrating. Whatever she's feeling, I'm feeling it too.

No words get exchanged between us. In silence and cold I hold her in my arms, and she clings to me.

I've never held a girl in my arms before—a girl I have feelings for. She's the first, and surprisingly I want her to be the only one who hugs me, and I hug her back.

"You're a good friend, Heath."

"I could be a better friend."

She pulls back but I hold her tight. *Don't fucking go so soon.*

There's little distance between our faces. If either one of us moves even a little bit we'll end up kissing.

The world stops moving, and nothing is in my sight except for her. She's the only one I can see.

Her brown eyes bore deep into mine. Her hands are on my chest and mine around her waist.

"You don't need to be a better friend. You make me feel safe and happy. It's more than enough."

"Your standards are pretty fucking low."

A smile tugs on her delicate lips. "I'm fine with it."

*I'm not fucking fine with it.*

After a moment she adds, "My standards for men are quite high."

My arm tightens around her waist instinctively. "Men?" I croak out in confusion.

She nods. "Yeah. The fictional ones that I think of as a boyfriend or crush."

*Boyfriend.*

*Crush.*

I've never hated those two words more in my life before. More so in one sentence.

Annoyance drips from my next words. "So, you have a checklist for your dream boy toy?"

"He won't be my boy toy."

"I see." *I don't like this fucking conversation at all.*

Hope gets off me and stumbles into the passenger seat. Turning back, she adds, "It's seven-thirty. We should go."

With a clenched jaw and rage bubbling in my head I get in the driver's seat.

On the way, I ask the question because I can't just fucking help it. "So, what do you want your boy toy to be like?"

She turns red. Red like a rose.

Here I thought only I could do that.

"Stop calling him that. He won't be...that."

My hands hold the steering wheel to the point my knuckles turn white. I press hard on the brakes and slowly drive—I don't want to let go of her so quickly.

"Will you just answer the question?" I grit out in frustration.

"Actually, I don't know what I really want."

"You don't have one thing in mind?" I probe the matter like an obsessive dickhead.

"That's the thing, I don't want one thing. There are quite a few." Hope hides her face in her hands. "This is all because of the books. If I hadn't read books I wouldn't have standards in the first place."

Right. Books. Fictional characters. *Fictional fucking men.*

"You must have a favorite."

"The list is long, Heath."

Whenever she says my name a blissful feeling spreads wings in my stomach. I know it sounds stupid, but it is what it is.

"How long?"

"Very long."

For fuck's sake.

"And we can't spend the whole night together where you tell me about every single one of them." I drawl out.

"Exactly."

I pull up to her street. Just like before, she asks me to stop ten houses away from her house.

I find it odd. But if I ask she'll shut down, and she seems to be in a good mood right now. I'd hate to ruin it.

"At least give me one." I can't help not knowing.

She giggles and I like that look on her so fucking much.

I'm losing my fucking mind.

Turning in her seat she pins me with a serious look. "Promise me you won't mock me about him."

*Him. I already hate him.*

"Promise," I say *very* sincerely.

"All right." She says some dude's name. I print it on my mind in red.

With a smile, she gets out and walks down the street without looking back.

I switch off the headlights and tail her.

At this point, I don't even know how fucking deep I am into this feelings-mess.

# 27

## HEATH

"Who is Adrian Hayes?" Sebastian leans back, sipping sweet coffee calmly like it's Sunday morning and nothing is fucking wrong in the world.

"A prick Hope likes," I grumble and drink the protein shake.

"But didn't you say he's fictional?"

"Does it matter?" I snarl at him.

He slowly nods and drinks the coffee. I want to splash it in Adrian fucking Hayes' face. What kind of absurd name is that?

"She said there are more," I tell him, wishing the burn in my chest would abate, but it only flares up brightly. I've never felt like this before. For fuck's sake, I've never even cared who liked who, certainly not some girl.

My best friend was right. She's not some girl to me.

Sebastian chuckles and it annoys the hell out of me. "This just got interesting. Who thought the shy book nerd has—"

One glare from me and he shuts up. Clearing his throat he says, "Well, they're all fictional so it doesn't matter if she likes them."

"It fucking matters," I argue.

Sebastian smirks. "Unless you like her."

I pin him with a glare. "I don't fucking like her."

Rolling his eyes, he sighs and runs his gaze across the parking lot searching for someone. His girlfriend. Marie Anderson. When he doesn't see her, only then he turns to me

"So, this Adrian guy, what he's like?"

"Asshole."

"Heath," he drawls out in a dry tone.

I sip my shake. "Google didn't write much about his attributes, so I don't fucking know."

"Is he a guy or a man? Wait, are there men or there can be guys too in books? You know, under eighteen."

"I don't fucking know."

"I'm sure you wish you did."

"He's some famous golden soccer player at school who's loved this girl since they were children. Have a nickname for her and shit. And he's always only loved her."

I see Sebastian grin from the corner of my eye. "You know a fucking lot."

"Google mentioned it."

"What else did it say?"

"Nothing." That was the annoying part. I have no idea who this Adrian fucking Hayes is.

"So, from what I see he sounds like a good guy. Loves the girl, only wants her, and has a nickname for her. I see the appeal."

"Are you fucking serious?"

"What's wrong?"

"How about we start with *he's fictional.*"

"No threat to your reign, your majesty."

Exasperation clings to my nerves. I'm seconds away from slamming his face into the window and making him realize how much it bothers me that Hope likes this guy.

With a chuckle, he playfully punches my shoulder. "Look, it shouldn't matter when you have no feelings for her. She can like a tree for fuck's sake because *you don't like her.* So why fret over some fictional guy or man? You continue being her friend."

Friend. Right. It's better if Hope and I stay friends because nothing good will come out if we—

Why the fuck I'm thinking about going beyond friendship? I don't want that.

Besides, she needs a friend, someone she can confide in because there is something very wrong in her life. If I want to help her, save her, I can't ruin what little progress we've made as friends.

"Look, here they come." Sebastian gets out of the car, and I follow him.

The second Marie steps out of her car he's holding her by her waist and kissing her deeply.

Hope watches them with a small smile, then comes over to me. Today she's wearing a light sweater and jeans and Converse. As usual, there's a book in her hand. I inspect it closely, it's Harry Potter and the Chamber of Secrets.

I cock my head to the book. "Book number..."

"Two." Life fills her eyes.

"How was book one?"

"Just like I remember. Great." Her smile widens.

I can't stop looking at it.

"You didn't update me," I complain, much to my surprise.

"Oh, I thought you didn't mean it seriously—"

"I always mean what I say, Rose. You should know it by now."

She stares at me with an open mouth. Amusement fills me, and I gently tip her mouth to close it.

I decide to go easy on her. "You haven't read this one before?"

"No. No... um...not at all," she stutters, and my brain believes that it's because of me. "I haven't even watched the movies because I didn't want to spoil it for myself." She hugs the book tightly to her chest.

The school bell rings and the four of us enter the school building. The moment we step inside, people stop and stare at us. As we move along the hallway, I hear the snippets of whispers which I ignore. But that doesn't stop them from talking about us.

Suddenly we're the center of attention on a Monday morning.

Sebastian and Marie have their locker side by side—Sebastian somehow got it done—so they drift away from us.

I don't keep much in my locker except for snacks or spare notebooks and pens. There are no photographs or things like other students have.

I lean against the locker next to Hope's and study the inside of her locker. Like me, she hasn't decorated it. But hers has a row of textbooks, pens, and a hoodie.

"Why is there a hoodie?"

"In case of emergency."

"What about pants?"

Blush tints her cheeks. "There's shorts underneath it."

Hoodie and shorts. An image of her wearing them flashes through my mind. Her long, sexy legs in those shorts.

For fuck's sake. I need to stop thinking about her like that.

"Did I get any orders over the weekend?" She closes her locker and looks at me with her light brown eyes.

"See for yourself." Handing her my phone, I watch as she opens the app.

Averting my gaze from her, I notice the number of eyes on us. Almost everyone is taking a double take at us as if we're dressed as clowns. Motherfuckers.

I search for Marie and Sebastian who are nowhere to be seen. Those two always leave me alone with Hope. Intentionally.

"I got three orders." A deflated smile clings to her features.

"It's something."

Just like that, her gloomy smile changes to a beautiful, bright one. "You just said what I say to you."

I didn't realize.

I fold my arms over my chest. Her eyes quickly drop to my muscles that stretch the material of my black shirt. Her gaze traces my entire arm, then reaches my broad chest.

She's openly staring at me with fuck-me eyes. For fuck's sake.

"See something you like?"

"Yes." Her eyes widen and she cups her mouth in shock.

A smirk itches my lips. I did not expect that.

"*No.* I meant no. Big no. Big fat no," she babbles, looking at me all nervous and shy. Her cheeks further turn red.

"Are you saying I'm ugly?" I tease her with a passive face, not letting her know that I'm enjoying the fuck out of it.

"Ugly? What! No. You're not ugly from any angle." She roams her eyes all over me.

Heat crawls up to the back of my neck and then spreads everywhere. The more her gaze drills into me the more I become self-aware. It's not long before I feel the heat traveling somewhere it's not supposed to. I straighten up.

Insects and heat weren't enough, now I'm getting a boner. Fucking wonderful.

Without thinking, I bend down to her ear and catch her sucking her breath. *Interesting.*

"I suggest you stop looking at me like that, Rose." I linger by her side as her flowery scent draws me to her.

"Why?" She looks up with her innocent eyes at me, which are not so innocent.

"You don't want to know," I whisper, my gaze dropping to her mouth.

Pink full lips. I've never seen lips so tempting before. Fuck. I've never even looked twice at lips before. But right now, I can't stop looking at them.

*Kiss her.*

*Kiss her.*

*Fucking kiss her.*

The shriek of the bell removes the blanket on my senses, and I pull back from her with every bit of self-control I possess.

Her eyes are big and peer up at me with surprise and... something else. I don't like that look one bit. It's tempting.

Turning around, I climb up to the roof to smoke a cigarette.

There's no fucking way I'll be able to concentrate when *full lips* and *brown eyes* are all I can think about.

Four cigarettes later and I'm still thinking about her.

# 28

## HOPE

"Why do you think I got a D?" Marie is beside me the second the Chemistry class ends.

I start gathering my things. "I'll need to see your test paper."

With a huff, she looks through her backpack and pulls it out. She makes a bitter face. "I swear I hate Chemistry. It's the most annoying subject ever."

I stifle a smile, knowing my amusement won't help the situation. Clearly, we have different opinions—it doesn't bother me that much, my weakness is History. I hate remembering the timelines and the many series of events that happen in between those.

"You scored a B when I gave you the notes."

With a snap of her fingers, she points at me. "Hah! Yes! That's the key. *Your notes.* Your amazing, superb notes."

I laugh at her exaggeration.

Averting my gaze to her test paper, I look at the mistakes she's made. So far, there are a lot of big ones that are related to concepts and some minor ones in the calculations. A few study sessions will fix them.

We're in the hallway walking to our next class when someone knocks their shoulder into me. The collision makes me miss a step and I almost stumble. Marie quickly reaches for my arm and steadies me.

"Oh my God! You okay?" Marie asks, worry thick in her tone.

I give her a nod and turn around only to see a smiling Shian looking at me.

"Missed your step I see," she says with a proud smile.

Before I say something, Marie gets in front of me. "You did that on purpose."

Shian scoffs and sizes up the two of us like we're nothing compared to her. We're probably not. She's got her friends standing behind her like a shield. Four of them against us two. Yeah, we're not winning this battle.

I study her and almost gasp when I find my bracelets on her wrist.

"I don't have time for you two weirdos." She walks away, deciding we're not worth her time. I bet it's not that but the regulations against bullying that'll result in immediate expulsion. I don't know what happened last year that made the principal take such a step. I'm not aware of the incident because at the time my parents were fighting every day. It was a mess at home. To escape reality, I read books. The outside world just disappeared and became nonexistent to me. I hope whoever was the victim is doing okay.

Marie gasps. "Weirdos? Us? She's the weird one. I'm not. And neither are you, Hope. We're both not weird ones. We're the cool ones. Well, more like mysterious ones and I'm fine with it. And you're fine with it too. Anyway, she shouldn't have said that. Not that I care but still. I mean—" she turns to me and stops talking.

"What's wrong?" she asks.

"Nothing."

"Tell me, you look happy."

Leaning down to her ear—Marie is an inch shorter than me—I whisper, "I saw her wearing my bracelets."

"Your bracelets? The ones you..."

I nod eagerly.

She giggles and I join her, sharing a secret that only the two of us know in this entire town. Well, Heath and Sebastian know, too.

"And she called *us* weirdos."

I shrug, not really caring about it.

"This just made my day."

"I think everything makes your day."

She thinks for a moment, then nods. "Yeah, you're right. Everything makes me happy, but Sebastian ranks in first spot."

"Because he's your boyfriend."

She hums in a dismissive tone. "Yes, but it's more than that. He's my best friend and I just love spending time with him. I can spend a lifetime with him and not get bored. We usually play games or make out. Either is fun, as long as I'm next to him. He has this calming aura that puts my super-energy to rest. All I want to do is curl up against him and relax."

Just like how Heath makes me feel comfortable.

Heat rises to my cheeks, as I remember snuggling in the backseat of his car with him. That was the safest I'd ever felt in so long. The hardness of his chest, the rhythm of his heart, and the intense heat of his body—everything about him is perfect. I can't believe he let me get this close to him. I'd like it if it happens again.

*Wait what?*

Marie snaps her fingers in front of my face. "Hey, where did you go?"

Shaking my head, I disperse those stupid thoughts.

Gosh. I'm developing feelings for Heath—not like the ones I have for my fictional men.

This is different.

These feelings are *real*.

"I..."

She holds up her hand. "How about you hang out with me at my place after school? We can study and you can tell me what you were thinking about."

I don't have any reason to decline. Dad has a deadline of eight o'clock. I'll hopefully be home by then. Until then I can hang out with her and tell Dad that I was at the library. It's not like he's going to search for me—or maybe he will since I've become his punching bag lately.

"I need to be home before eight," I tell Marie, hoping she doesn't ask too many questions.

Instead, she frowns. "Wait? You have a curfew too?"

More like a death threat, if you ask me. "Yeah."

She rolls her eyes. "Here I thought my dad was the only paranoid one in the town. I have a curfew too. Same as yours. If I'm a second late he looks disappointed, and I hate disappointing my dad."

"Oh, so he doesn't... get mad?"

"Mad? No. Never. My dad has never gotten mad at me. Well, there was this one time when—" A dark look crosses her face, and she shuts up. It's the first time I've ever seen Marie look like this. "—all he did was lecture me, but that was it." She recovers quickly.

I wonder what happened. I don't think she was abused... well... I've never seen a mark on Marie, so I don't think she's being abused, but then again, when people want to hide things they do it so well that you'd be surprised.

Look at me. None of the three friends that I have know what happened to me. I don't blame them for not knowing. I'm glad they don't. It's not their burden. I don't want them to worry about me and try to help me because it'll all end in vain.

"Anyway, we'll go to my place after school. Done?"

I give her a nod before going to my next class.

Marie is filthy rich. The kind of rich that competes with Heath on every level.

Like him, she lives in a beautiful mansion. The cobblestone driveway is lined with trees and flower plants and a sprawling garden on one side. A gardener is working on a bush with hedge shears, giving it a definite shape. Two bodyguards in suits linger around the main gate, keeping a watchful eye on us as we move down the driveway.

Parking her car in a huge marble-floor garage with recessed ceiling lights, she gets out. I follow her and stifle a gasp when I see the other luxurious cars.

"C'mon."

Marie grabs my hand and leads me up the porch steps to the glass door that has an intricate design on it. Swinging it open, she pulls me inside into the foyer. A massive chandelier hangs above, adorned with crystals that bounce off the golden light. Nature paintings, colorful vases, and antique pieces decorate the entrance, setting down the fact that everything here costs thousands and millions.

"Mom. Dad." Marie calls out while dragging me to the living room that's as lavish as the rest of the house. Victorian sofa sets sit in the center of the room with a glass table in between them. There are magazines, a vase with fresh flowers, and packs of biscuits on top of it.

Heels click on the floor.

"Marie, you're home, love." A feminine voice speaks, and then a tall, slim woman with dark brown hair appears in the doorway. She has light blue eyes that resemble the color of the sky, and facial features that are closely similar to Marie's. She looks stunning in a beige dress and white heels that click on the marble floor as she makes her way into the room. She's graceful.

I'm staring at her when Marie meets her halfway with me by her side.

"Mom, this is Hope." Marie quickly introduces me before I have any time to recover.

Marie's mom turns to me, and she smiles—much like her daughter, with it reaching her eyes.

"Hope Hanson, the girl who loves reading books, makes bracelets, scores A-plus in every subject, and makes *perfect* Chemistry notes." She grins. "I feel like I already know you. My daughter has told me everything about you. It's so nice to finally meet you. I'm Marie's mom. You can call me Camila, no need to stick with Mrs. Anderson."

I'm too stunned to speak.

Marie's mom is a carbon copy of her. No wonder she's always so positive, smiling, and just a ray of sunshine.

"I... it's nice to meet you, too," I sputter out a complete sentence. I should pat myself on the back.

Her eyes brighten. "You have no idea how much Marie talks about you. It's all she's ever—"

"Mom!" Marie protests with a face as red as a tomato.

I'm focused on the fact that she's told her mom about me. When I told my parents they didn't believe I could have friends.

The irony.

Camila laughs. "It's the truth, love. We don't hear about your games anymore. It's been months since you told me how far you've made it in the Elden Ring."

"That's not important anymore," Marie says.

Camila nods in agreement. "Exactly. Hope is more important. Your first girl best friend in the world."

Marie flushes at those words and I can't help but smile. *She's my first girl best friend in the world, too.*

"Now, how about you two rest a bit in your room and I bring you snacks?" Camila offers, looking excited.

I quickly shake my head. "Oh no. You don't have to Mrs—I mean Camila," I whisper.

"Yes, stick with that, love." She gives me a thumbs-up.

I only manage to give her a nod.

Marie jumps in. "Mom, please bring that chocolate you got from London. Hope loves chocolate."

My jaw hangs.

*Oh my God.*

*I want to disappear.*

*Evaporate out of existence.*

In sheer panic, I croak out, "No. I don't. I don't like chocolate."

Marie frowns. "What? That's not true. I know you love chocolate. Heath told me."

"Heath was the one to find that out, huh?" Camila asks with a smirk.

Marie turns to her. "Yeah. He knows everything she likes or doesn't like. Because he likes her."

*Because he likes her.* That's the only bit I focus on.

Camila grins. "Finally. You and I have been waiting for it."

"Yeah."

I don't have to look in the mirror to know I'm as red as blood because all the vessels in my face have exploded from embarrassment.

"That's not true," I say.

Both Marie and Camila turn to me. Their smiles and eyes filled with optimism.

Marie speaks first. "He does."

"I agree," Camila adds.

Before I can ask them more, a woman interrupts us, and Camila leaves with her to bring us snacks.

Marie turns to me. "Why'd you say you don't like chocolate? You love chocolate."

I fold my arms over my chest to make myself as small as I can. Sometimes, I wish that was possible. I could hold myself and become invisible. The invisibility cloak forever rests on my shoulders, so whenever I'm feeling like it I can quickly hide under it.

"I don't want to bother your mom," I say, feeling my chest tighten with guilt.

Marie rests her hand over my shoulder. "Trust me, you can never bother my mom. Especially when she loves you. I've told her so many things about you and she always asked me to bring you around. She loves the people who love her people. Because of me, she loves Sebastian and Heath. You know how grumpy Heath is, but even he softens under her kindness and love. She's just that amazing."

"Like you," I blurt out.

She shakes her head, a sad look flashing across her face. "I'm not half the person she is. She's way too perfect."

I take her hand off my shoulder and squeeze her fingers. "After seeing you two, I'd say you're very similar. Maybe you're not like her, but you're also not less than her. I see a lot of her in you and maybe that's why I will be able to get comfortable around her like I did with you."

Instantly a wide smile plasters on her face, and she nods.

"Let's go. I'll show you my room." Marie takes my hand, like it's second nature to her, and leads me to the staircase that has an elegant metal design handrail.

I knew Marie was rich but seeing it with my eyes it's different. I'm reminded of the fact how different we are. Family wise, money-wise, and even as individuals. I don't deserve her, much less be her best friend.

We walk down a hallway and finally reach her room. Pushing the door open she bounces on her feet as she pulls me inside and shuts the door.

Her room is five times bigger than mine—it's huge. The walls are painted in a soft pink and the white ceiling has a small crystal chandelier hanging from it that looks beautiful. The king-size bed is neatly made with pink pillows arranged against the white headboard and a matching duvet that sits folded at the end. There are nightstands on either side of the bed; the right one has a white journal and pen next to it and the left one has glasses and a laptop with white headphones set on top of it. There's a vanity set near the tall windows overlooking the garden with every makeup accessory and jewelry put together in little cups and boxes.

"C'mon, let's lie down," Marie says as she dumps both of our bags on the floor and plops on the bed with a heavy sigh.

I stand next to her bed, not sure if I should join her or wait for her to tell me what to do.

Marie turns her head at me and rolls her eyes. She pats the spot next to her. "Join me."

Removing my shoes as quickly as possible, I lie down beside her.

"Your room is beautiful, Marie. It looks straight out of a magazine."

She breaks into a fit of laughter. "That's interesting because it is indeed straight out of a magazine. When I started therapy—" she freezes.

"I didn't know you went to therapy," I mumble.

Breaking free from the shock, she takes a deep breath and doesn't speak for five minutes. I watch her inhale long breaths, hold them in, then let them out. It appears to be a breathing exercise that helps her because she starts to look like herself.

All the while I stay quiet and give her the space to be okay. I want her to know she's safe with me and she can trust me—kind of a hypocrite, but I will get there someday.

When she opens her eyes, she looks better. "I still go to therapy. Once a month because I'm doing much better now."

I smile at her.

"I haven't told you this, the therapy part and the things that led to it because it's still fresh. I mean I started therapy in January, and it's been a couple of months, but it's helped me so much. I was lost, sad, depressed, confused, angry, erratic and so many other things. I didn't know what was wrong with me. I truly thought I was going crazy and there was nothing that could save me. I..." She gulps hard as if the next words are difficult for her to speak. "I thought about dying. I thought about it every single day for months. I visualized how everyone would feel if I just left. I felt good for myself because then I'd be free from this pain, ache, hollowness, and emptiness I carried around with me. But I also saw the faces of people who'd be devastated to lose me. My parents, my brother, Heath, and Sebastian. Five people. Five lives that'd change because I decided to die."

Tears are rushing down my eyes.

I can't believe it.

Marie thought about dying.

If she died, then I wouldn't have met her.

Somehow, that feels like the greatest loss of my life.

Nothing would have been the same.

Her gaze is focused on a random spot on the bed, not aware of my tears and the pain I'm feeling for her. Is this how friendship works? You're able to feel each other's emotions as if they are your own. If this is friendship then I'm glad I have friends who make me feel this way. I want to share their pain and make them feel better. I want them to know they aren't alone.

There's so much I want to do to save them—anything.

"My dad was the one who encouraged me to go to therapy. He talked to me every evening about it, he knew how I felt and there was nothing he could do. He wanted to save me, he just didn't know how to. But he understood that someone else could. In two weeks, he visited multiple doctors until he was satisfied with three of them. He went with me to each of them until I decided on Ivanna

Onley who saved my life. If it weren't for her I wouldn't be here. But I guess the credit goes to my dad before her. Every weekend he took me to her office in the city. I went to her on Friday and Sunday. For those three days, we stayed at an apartment he rented out and spent time together. He talked to me for hours and gave me all the reasons why I needed to stay because people loved me. Sometimes Mom came with me too, and she was equally supportive and loving. My parents saved me, and I love them so much."

A sob breaks out of me and instantly catches Marie's attention. Her own eyes fill with tears.

"You don't need to cry. I'm fine now. I promise. Geez, you're like Sebastian. He started crying when I told him everything. You both are cry-babies." She wraps her arms around me and consoles me.

"I'm so sorry that you felt that way. It's terrible and hurts so much," I tell her in an annoying voice between my hiccups.

She rubs my back. "I know but it's not terrible anymore. I'm good. I'm fucking incredible."

"Do you really mean that?"

"Yeah. I really mean that."

Assured with her answer, I wipe away my tears and wrap my arms around her. I hold onto her tightly, letting her know that she means a lot to me, more than I could ever put into words.

A knock on the door separates us, a few seconds later Camila walks in holding a tray with two mugs, biscuits, and chocolate packets.

My stomach grumbles at the sight of food. I missed lunch because I didn't want to spend the little money I earned. As Heath advised I want to invest so I can make more money and be able to do something in case Mom kicks me out.

With how aggressive Dad is getting toward me, I want to leave. I want to get away from the place they call home. It hasn't been that in years. When I was little I was too naive to understand what fear was, but now that I'm old I know what it feels like, and I don't want to live every day in it. I want to be safe. I want to be okay. I want to be alive.

Marie quickly opens a chocolate bar and hands it to me. Her eyes fill with excitement, and she squeaks. "Try it. Try it, Hope!"

I take it from her. The sweet taste of the hard chocolate swirls into my mouth before it melts away.

"It's the best chocolate ever," I say, taking another bite and covering my mouth so if the little bits fall off I don't embarrass myself.

"I know you'd like it. Mom got an entire box for you. Right mom?" Marie looks about ready to start jumping in happiness.

Camila smiles widely. "Of course I did." She turns to me. "I'll give it to you when you leave. Enjoy it but don't eat too much at the same time, love."

I only manage to nod.

"Now I'm gonna go. If you girls need anything, let me know. Hope, would you be staying for dinner with us?"

"No. I have to be home by eight."

"Curfew I see."

"Yes." *More like a death threat.*

She gives me an understanding smile. "Maybe some other day then. I'd love to prepare a meal for you."

"It's not a big deal. I'll eat anything."

She chuckles and backs up until she's in the hallway. Before closing the door she says, "I bet, but Marie will make sure I prepare a banquet for you."

"Yeah. Hope loves a banquet." Marie pipes in.

My eyes bulge out. "N-No! That's not true. I'd eat anything. I don't need a banquet."

Camila leaves with a laugh.

Marie hasn't told me what happened to her, but I have a feeling something devastating happened to her. Something that changed her completely. It made her want to die. I can't imagine how bad it was. My only assurance is that she's doing better now, though I wish to know her even better so I can help her in any way that I can. I want to be there for her and hug her when she wants to hide in the darkness or cry in the shower. I just want to be her best friend in every sense.

"Marie!" I send her a mean stare—I'm not an expert like Heath but I try regardless. "Why'd you do that?"

She falls back in laughter, her arms curled around her stomach as she watches me between her closed eyes. "I was joking."

"It was a bad joke. I hope your mom doesn't believe you."

"She won't. Anyway, what is your favorite food?"

"Anything Italian. What about you?"

"Chinese and Thai. I also like Indian."

"What about dessert?"

A silly smile takes over her face. "Ice cream. What about you—wait I know. Chocolate!"

"Yeah."

"What's your favorite color?"

I don't think. "Blue."

She smirks. "Like Heath's eyes, huh?"

Heat brushes over my cheeks. "Not really... I mean..."

*There's no I mean.*

*I like Heath's eyes.*

*It's the most perfect shade of blue to ever exist.*

"No need to hide the truth. You're starting to *like* him. Admit it."

My eyes widen. "W-what? No! I—"

She waves her hands in my face. "Don't lie. Not to me or yourself. Definitely not to yourself. My therapist says the first step to anything is acceptance."

Trying to distract myself I reach for the mug. I've never tried tea before. The only drink that is frequent at my house is alcohol.

Hesitantly, I take a sip. I love it. Eagerly I drink some more.

"I'm trying to understand what I feel. Feelings are complicated."

"Then let's un-complicate them together." Marie picks up her mug and clinks it against mine.

"How?"

"Well, how do you feel when he's close to you?"

"Safe."

Marie nods in agreement. "That's a perfect start. What else do you feel?"

"Comfort."

"Keep going."

"I also get butterflies."

Marie squeals, but then takes a deep breath and composes herself. I half-believe she's trying to imitate her therapist right now and running a feelings-diagnosis on me.

"Butterflies. Love them." She grimaces. "*Loved* them."

Clearing her throat she meets my gaze. "This question is important. Think carefully. Do you want to spend all your time with him?"

"I... I don't know."

"Hah! Your feelings are new then. Get back to me when you figure that out. We'll discuss it in our next appointment."

I stifle a laugh. "Okay."

By the end, we're both laughing, and it feels good. Really good.

Soon afterward we delve into studying. I give her my Chemistry notes and also explain them to her in great detail. We do many questions and exercises until I'm satisfied she's got the concepts right and deep into her memory.

Time flies by so fast. Before I know it's seven-thirty and I race to leave her room. She offers to drive me, but I decide to walk home.

Just like that, the loneliness I didn't feel with her creeps back inside of me.

I'm reminded of how empty it makes me feel.

# 29

HOPE

It's Friday night, almost a week after I went to Marie's house. It's evening and I'm writing an English paper when my phone pings.

> **Heath: Come outside.**
> **Hope: Why?**
> **Heath: No time to ask fucking questions.**
> **Hope: What does that mean?**
> **Heath: It means I'm fucking waiting to take you somewhere.**
> **Hope: What?**
> **Heath: I don't have the answer to that.**
> **Hope: Are you really outside my house?**
> **Heath: No, I sent my fucking copy.**
> **Hope: Where's your original body?**
> **Heath: In your room.**

I search my room like a dumb person, even though I know Heath isn't there. I've lost my mind. I mean if he were here, I'd know. My body reacts when he's close to me.

> **Hope: I checked. Your original copy isn't here.**
> **Heath: Did you look under your bed?**
> **Hope: Wait a sex.**
> **Hope: Sex.**

**Hope: SEC. I MEANT SEC.**
**Hope: Freaking autocorrect.**
**Heath: Are you sure?**

*Oh my God.*
*What does that mean?*
*Is he flirting?*
*What should I reply?*
*I hope he doesn't think I want sex.*
*I DO NOT.*

**Hope: Yes. It was a mistake.**
**Heath: Come outside. I'm not going to wait for you all night.**

Getting off my bed, I stumble on my way as I hurry to the window and peek outside. Heath is standing against his black car and looking up at my window. He's parked in front of Nadina's house who's staring at him from the front porch.

**Hope: I can't go with you.**

After I came home from school Dad was leaving with some men. I've never seen them before, so I don't know who they are and why they came to our house. It's been two hours since he left, he'll be home any minute now. If he doesn't find me in my room, I can only imagine what will happen to me.

Heath reads the text, glances up at me, then starts typing.
My phone pings in my hand.

**Heath: I'll get you home by 8.**

My first thought is to think about the scenarios if I get home late. All end with the same results. *Bruises*.

A shiver runs down my spine and a chill settles deep into my bones. Fear.

**Hope: Where are we going?**
**Heath: Get in the car and I'll tell you.**
**Hope: That's not assuring.**
**Heath: Do you trust me?**
**Hope: Yes.**
**Heath: Then get your ass down here.**

Much to my reluctance, I shuffle away from the window to get ready. After spending time with Marie at her house, I've realized I like it when I'm with these people. They are nice to me and make me laugh. I have a good time with them, despite how short our moments are and how fast they go by. When I'm with them I feel less lonely.

I don't know when I decided to not feel lonely anymore. I want to be with people—these people. I want to be surrounded and not be alone in my room.

Opening my closet, I grab some nice clothes and quickly change into them. When I stand in the bathroom I make an effort to look pretty by applying mascara and a bit of lip gloss.

*You're doing this because Heath is picking you up.*

Maybe I am. I'm not a hundred percent sure how he feels about me, or how I feel about him, but there's something and I want to find that out.

Racing downstairs I leave the house as quickly as possible and check the street multiple times in case Dad is walking home.

When I stop in front of Heath he straightens to his full height that towers over me. Like always he's in all-black attire; black jeans, black T-shirt, and black Converse. And as always he looks deadly and handsome.

He locks eyes with me, then runs them all over me.

When I shiver because of his steady gaze he opens the door for me, and I slip inside.

I look over at Nadina, but she's focused on Heath. She gestures to him to come forward and he complies. She talks to him and all he does is nod his head.

Five minutes later he joins me. As he pulls out of my neighborhood I try to make myself small, so Dad doesn't see me in passing. If he caught a glimpse of us, I'd have hell to pay.

It's only when we're a couple of blocks away that I'm able to breathe properly.

"What was Nadina saying?"

"Why were you hiding yourself?"

I smile. "I asked first."

Heath rolls his eyes. "I can't tell you."

My smile drops. "All right. Can you at least tell me where we're going?"

"Bowling alley."

"Really?" Excitement fills me.

"Yes."

"I've never been to a bowling alley before."

"That's what I thought," he mutters under his breath as he parks the car in the parking lot that's filled with cars.

Since we live in a small town, it takes us little time to reach places which is a good thing because I travel mostly on foot. If I were to walk to school that was thirty miles away I'd pass out somewhere in the middle for sure.

I'm counting money in my small wallet when the door to my side opens. I look up at Heath who gestures at me to get out. So impatient.

I slip my wallet into my jeans pocket and get out.

"Marie and Sebastian are already inside," Heath informs me before he starts walking ahead of me.

We walk inside the building that's big and lit up with neon strips and fluorescent lights. It's so bright and loud inside. Music is playing over the hum of the boisterous crowd of teenagers that fill the place.

I see groups of guys lurking in corners sipping cans and checking out girls. A few of them turn my way and I immediately go all red.

*How quickly can I hide?*

On instinct, I move closer to Heath and bump into his shoulder. He stops walking and looks at me with a frown. "What's wrong?"

"Nothing," I mutter. Not knowing how to tell him that I feel uncomfortable because a group of boys are leering at me. My social anxiety kicks in and all I want to do is find a corner and read my book—become invisible.

His gaze runs over my head. I notice how his eyes darken, and he sends a death stare to the group.

I startle when I feel his hand touch mine. Slowly, one finger at a time, he holds my hand until our palms are pressed together and my hand is engulfed in his big one. My breath hitches and my pulse skyrockets to the sky.

"Let's go." He leads me deeper into the hall.

The warmth of his skin and the feel of his big hand are all I can focus on. I feel his rough calluses from fighting and working out. I also feel his thumb running back and forth on the back of my hand in assurance.

It probably means nothing, he's being considerate, but still, my mind decides that he's doing it because he cares about me.

"Here you are." Marie advances for a hug the second she sees us. When her arms wrap around my body, Heath lets go of my hand.

I twitch my hand, missing the heat and safety it provided me.

A single touch shouldn't be able to affect me this much, but it's Heath we're talking about. He's affected me since day one. There's just something about him that makes me feel like characters do when they catch feelings for their love interest.

I know it so well, after all, I've read so many romance books. When it comes to myself I become as clueless as a non-reader which is a shame.

If only I could read his thoughts and understand him. It'd make it so easy for me to listen to the words he doesn't say or read the words that hide behind his eyes.

I decide I will understand him.

I want to.

Like he understands me.

"It'll be fun," Marie squeals. "Let's go and play."

I've never been anywhere except for school and the library. My whole life only orbits around those two places and nowhere else. Now being able to hang out with these three people, I feel like I've missed out on so much in life. I might as well be the last one in the race while everyone else is so far ahead of me.

Truth is, that distance has never bothered me. Books took me to places, and I lived voraciously through them like I was the main character. I've been to countries, cities, towns, and places all the while sitting on my bed and reading the words. *Words.* I know how powerful they are—they can fly you anywhere in the world *or* other worlds like a ride on a magic carpet. You get to see everything and experience every adventure and feel emotions that you've never even thought about.

I do feel bad about not living enough like others have, but I've also lived in ways that they haven't. I suppose that counts for something.

I check the time on my phone. 6:15 p.m.

Marie and Sebastian hurry to the counter to pay, leaving Heath and me behind like they normally do. I notice how they're always trying to bring us closer which works every time. Like right now.

Heath stands beside me with a brooding face. His blue eyes look cold as they lock on me.

"You okay?" he asks.

"Yes, I'm fine." I shoot him an assuring smile, despite the turmoil swirling inside of me.

I'm worried about what will happen to me once I get home.

Heath stares at me as if he can read my mind. I quickly look away.

"What book are you on?"

I smile. Books are my favorite thing in the world, and he knows that.

"Book four."

"And are you enjoying it?" Heath leans against the wall and folds his arms. The black material of his T-shirt stretches across his arms and chest. I miss his question. All my attention seems to move over his fit, lean body.

Tilting his head to one side, he says, "You're giving me that look again?"

"Huh?" I look at him, feeling my mouth dry.

*Oh my. I was drooling over him. What is wrong with me?*

"The look," he states in a gravelly voice that I feel deep in my stomach.

"What look?" I frown.

Striding toward me, he stops in front of me, then bends down so his face is a few inches away from mine.

"*The look*, Rose."

"I don't understand."

With a smirk playing on his lips, he tucks my hair behind my ear. "The fuck-me look, Rose."

*Wait what?* I open my mouth to deny him, but no words come to me.

*Oh my God. This is worse.*

*Say something.*

*Anything.*

"I...I..."

Slowly he pulls back. "Don't worry. I'm not fucking you until you ask me to."

My jaw opens in surprise.

"We got it guys," Marie speaks from behind us.

The spell breaks and I step away from Heath, but his gaze follows me.

"We also placed the food orders." She points to a lane. "That's for you and Heath."

"Aren't we all going to play solo?" I ask her quietly.

She smiles and I see the speck of mischief in her hazel eyes. "We are going to play in duos. Since Heath and Sebastian are good and we both aren't. Sebastian will play with me and Heath will play with you." She frowns in worry. "Is that okay with you? If you want I can play with you—"

"No, it's fine." Seriously. There's no way I'm separating her from her boyfriend. She told me she likes spending time with him.

Besides, it's not like I don't like spending time with Heath. In fact, I like it. More than I should.

Sebastian comes beside Marie. Squeezing her ass, he kisses her forehead. Love shines brightly in his green eyes as he looks down at her reminding me of a certain couple I've read in one of my books—Ethan and Stella from Love in Notes.

Heath clears his throat. "We are here to have fun and not to witness a make out session."

Marie rolls her eyes.

"The word *fun* exists in your vocabulary?" Sebastian comments, with a smirk.

"It does. I just don't take the definition you do." Heath scowls hard.

Marie ignores him. "Hope, have you been here before?"

"Never."

Her features soften. "There's always a first time for everything. Don't worry. We'll practice a little and then play a match. Whoever wins will get a chance to give a dare to the losing team." Marie claps her hands excitedly, and Sebastian kisses her temple.

"What kind of dare is allowed?" Heath smirks, looking at Marie.

She jabs her finger in his chest. "Don't think about scaring me with frogs. You know they freak me out."

He nonchalantly lifts his shoulder. "That thought didn't even cross my fucking mind."

Marie glares at him, and when it doesn't work, she turns to Sebastian. "Promise me he won't scare me with frogs. You know I get—"

"Of course he won't, babe. Relax." He rubs her shoulders in assurance.

Heath groans. "Way to kill the vibe, Bash. If I remember correctly, it was fucking fun, and you were laughing your ass off."

A smile splits on Sebastian's face, but he stifles it when Marie stares at him wounded. "It won't happen again, Marie. I promise. You can always trust me."

Marie grins and turns to Heath. "Hah! You heard him."

Heath turns to me. "What are you afraid of?"

I stiffen. *My dad.*

Of course, I can't say that.

"Um...spiders...lizards and mice," I tell him.

"Why?"

"Uh, because when they see you, they come at you," I say as if it's pretty obvious.

"She's so right!" Marie adds quickly.

Heath's stony face breaks and a tiny smile dances on his lips. "That doesn't fucking happen."

"It does," I argue.

"You have it fucking wrong."

"No. She's right." Marie jumps to my defense. "Also, Hope and I both have a curfew so we should start playing. I don't want to leave without beating you." She sends me an apology.

"I'm not losing to you, Blondie," Heath replies, confident as ever.

Before they can talk further, Sebastian steers her toward their lane that's a few lanes down from us.

"Looks like it'll be us."

"You okay with that?" I ask, looking up at Heath.

At the same time, he looks down at me. "Why wouldn't I be? You're not half as annoying as others."

A laugh bursts out of me. Only Heath would compliment me this way.

"Only half? I thought I'd be more than that since we spend so much time together."

He rolls his eyes and starts walking toward his best friends. "Don't get ahead of yourself now, Rose."

*Rose.* He's called me that eight now and each time the butterflies in my stomach have soared.

"Let's go."

The chances of us losing are high considering I've never been to a bowling alley before. There's no way I'll be able to land a perfect strike—it's just impossible.

With low spirits, I trail behind him like a kid lost in the crowd.

We stand at our assigned lane and Heath takes a black ball—no surprise, black is his favorite color. Getting in stance he throws the ball in one smooth move and straightens. I watch as it hits the pyramid of pins and knocks down every single one of them.

"That was perfect."

"I know."

Turning around he picks up a blue ball and hands it to me. I stare at it, clueless about which finger will go in which hole—okay that sounds dirty but it's not. Books might've messed me up.

I put the wrong fingers in the holes and Heath shakes his head.

Without hesitating, he guides my fingers in the right holes but doesn't let go of the ball as it's heavy.

Really. How do people make it roll like it doesn't weigh a thousand tonnes?

"If you let go it'll fall on my feet," I warn him.

"You'll get used to it." With that, he lets go.

Surprisingly, my fingers manage to hold it. I shoot him a proud smile. "You were right."

"I always am."

"That's not true."

"It is. Now concentrate." Placing a hand on my back he leads me to the lane and stands close to me. "Bend down and swing your arm back and forth. Once the ball comes forward, release it onto the lane with full force. Got it?" he asks with his lips dangerously close to my cheek. I nod. Although, I won't lie. I didn't listen to a single word of what he said as his hot breath was fanning over the side of my bare neck.

"I'm right here with you. Don't think about winning or losing. Just focus on getting it fucking right." He backs away from my face.

I'm able to take a breath that isn't filled with the intoxicating cologne he wears all the time.

I let out a deep breath and focus on the pins and the long lane.

*Focus.*

*I can do this.*

Following his instructions, I did as he told me. The ball travels down the lane and I get quite excited, but it only hits one of the pins and disappears.

"I don't think I can do this."

"We've just fucking started. This is your first time."

Heath runs a hand through his dark brown strands that look effortlessly styled. Even messy they're pointing in the right direction and only add to his appeal.

Taking my hand, he leads me to the ball rack where the ball I rolled appears.

"Try every one of them and tell me which one feels the lightest," he commands.

I'm busy trying out the balls as he watches me intently. I make eye contact with him and the moment our eyes lock I quickly look away.

Heath has always watched me with such a deep look in his blue eyes. It almost feels like being submerged in the bluest waves of the water and suddenly drowning doesn't seem like a bad idea.

One by one, I try different balls and weigh them until I find one that feels easier to hold.

Before I can tell him he's by my side and his eyes are glued to me.

My heart starts racing.

I press the ball to my ribcage and wrap my arms around myself.

"You look tired." He runs his gaze all over my face.

My lips part in surprise. I've been feeling weak lately. First I thought it was because I've been studying hard and writing assignments and completing homework, while also doing house chores, but I think it's more than that. I'm getting weak mentally. At school, I'm overthinking about what will happen when I get home and once I'm home I face the man who brings me pain and misery. I tried talking to Mom and that turned out so well—she told me to move out if I had a problem.

All this time I've been keeping all my secrets, fears, and sadness inside of me. Maybe now it's showing on my face and body. I can't hide anymore.

"I'm fine," I say.

"That's not what I fucking asked."

I give him a weak smile. "I've been staying up late to study. It's our last year. I want to get good grades."

"You already *have* good fucking grades, Rose."

"They can slip away."

"Not with you. You're smart as fuck."

This time, I smile genuinely. "Thanks."

"It wasn't a compliment, just a fucking fact."

I laugh. "What about your grades? Are they good?"

"I have A's in all of my subjects, except for Biology."

*He has A's.*

*How come I didn't know?*

*He's indeed a mystery.*

I move toward the lane, and he follows me with his black ball. We stand side by side and he goes first since his name comes first on the board above our head.

*STRIKE!*

I'm amazed by how skilled he is at almost everything. Is there something he isn't good at? Biology.

Then it's my turn. Only two pins down.

As I wait for the ball to appear, I turn to Heath who's waiting next to me when he can go for his turn.

"Um...I can help you with Biology. I can give you my notes or explain the chapters to you. Whatever it is...that you prefer." I'm so nervous.

"I'll be fine, Rose."

I freeze. "Oh... okay." I pause. "Yeah, sure. I...just thought—"

"You should help me?"

I nod.

Tilting his head to one side, he gives me a look. "How about you let *me* fucking help *you*?"

*What is he talking about?* "I don't need help."

"With those fucking marks, I mean. Tell me and I'll make sure your fucking straightener doesn't fucking choke you again," he says in a deep voice that's filled with rage.

The ball almost slips out of my hands as I stare at him in complete shock.

Words disappear from my head. I don't know what to say to him.

*It's not my straightener, it's my dad.*

Heath looks about ready to kill someone. His blue eyes are heated, and his face is set in a granite-hard look that promises vengeance—just because someone hurts me.

"Will you tell me what really happened?"

I avoid his gaze. "It doesn't matter," I say and fiddle with the ball.

His hand catches my wrist, and he gently squeezes it, nudging me to look at him.

"Why doesn't it fucking matter?"

I think about all the reasons that it won't matter to him like it didn't matter to my mother. He won't believe me. Like she didn't. I'll be a burden for him. A situation he can't help me with but pity me.

I don't want his pity or worry.

I want him to like me without my burden.

"Because what happened doesn't bear any importance," I repeat the words that perfectly sum up how my mother made me feel about abuse. *It. Is. Not. Important.*

Heath stiffens. Tension radiates off his body in waves and hits me.

Then his thumb begins swiping over my skin. Back and forth. Back and forth. The action surges my numb nerves with electricity that bursts sparks into my blood, making warmth flow through me.

"It *is* fucking important, and it fucking *matters*, to me. You matter to me, Rose," he says softly.

*I matter to him.*

The shock from his words jostles me. I slip my hand out of his hold. "We...should practice."

I go first even though it's his turn.

I just can't stand in front of him when my heart is beating painfully fast, and my head is repeating his words on a loop. *You matter to me, Rose.*

Like before no pins hit the ground and I'm reminded just how terrible I am at this game—the absolute worst.

Heath is gazing at the pins. With a sigh, he moves his attention to me.

Striding closer, he gets behind me and my body immediately straightens. Gently, he grips my wrist with one hand and circles my waist with the other. A quiet gasp leaves my mouth.

My entire focus is on him and the way he holds me, so close and softly against his body.

"Relax," he whispers into my ear.

*How am I supposed to relax when you're so close to me?*

I try to loosen my muscles and lean more into him. At once, his hand on my waist tightens and his fingers dig into my skin lightly.

"This isn't relaxing, Rose."

"I'm trying," I murmur.

"You feel like I'm holding cardboard and not a pretty girl."

"Hey!" I turn to him and right there is his face. So close to me.

"I won't hurt you," he says.

"That's not it." It's the truth. I'm not afraid of him. Not even a little bit.

"Hmm. I find that fucking hard to believe."

I laugh. "I've never met anyone who uses the f-word this much."

A hint of smile delicately touches his mouth, and his eyes lose the heat from before as they drop to my lips. "I've never met anyone with such a beautiful laugh."

My breath hitches just as his fingers grip me a little tighter around my wrist.

He clears his throat and breaks the thread of tension between us.

"I'm going to teach you, so watch fucking closely." Heath lifts my hand that's holding the ball. He brings my right arm out, then swings it forward, and I release the ball. We both stare as all the pins hit the floor.

*STRIKE!*

"Oh my God. Did you see that?" I look back at him and find him staring at me rather than the pins.

"I did," he murmurs.

"I managed to land a strike. A strike!"

"Now you can easily take me down."

"You're better than me."

"Hey guys, are you done?" Marie is beside us.

I give her a nod. "Yeah."

"Let the games begin, then." Marie grabs both of our hands and takes us to Sebastian who has already set up the game with our names—well not exactly with our names. I'm sure it was Marie who got them down because they just reflect her.

*Butterflyvenom (Marie)*
*Stormash (Sebastian)*
*Prettygirl (me)*
*Fuck (Heath)*

"Why do I have a stupid name? Blondie," Heath asks.

"It's your favorite word," Marie replies.

Sebastian and I hold our smiles as Heath glares at her and she looks at him like there's nothing wrong.

"You could've used my gaming username, *black shadow*," Heath argues with a scowl.

Marie shrugs. "I don't like that username."

"Too bad it's not yours."

"I wouldn't want it anyway. Mine is cool."

"Butterfly venom is cool?"

"The best."

"It's the most uncreative fucking name ever."

"I like it, and I don't care if you don't."

"Get my name changed."

She shakes her head with a goofy grin and instead picks up the ball. Before Heath can stomp over to the counter she's already rolled the ball, and it knocks down eight pins making my jaw hit the floor.

Heath forgets about the name change and instead meets my gaze with a knowing look. *We have to fucking win.*

"All the best losers," Sebastian teases as he walks past me. He's someone I don't talk to much. I mostly interact with Heath and Marie, but in our little interactions, he always smiles at me and is nice to me. It's enough for me to accept him as a friend.

When Sebastian swipes the floor with a smooth strike, I realize Heath and I will lose.

"You'll be fine. Just remember what I taught you," Heath says in a quiet, assuring tone.

I peek at him. "I'm sorry."

His expression hardens. "Don't fucking think about it, and instead have fun."

Walking up to the lane, I pick up the blue ball that is light in weight and is easier for me to throw. Gazing down at the lane, I do as Heath taught me. I manage to hit seven pins.

I glance back at Heath who gives me a nod.

"Nice ass." One of the boys from the group near our lane shouts at me. Others whistle and stare at me with big grins.

I freeze in my spot.

"What the fuck did you just say to her?" In a second, Heath strides to the guy, grabs him by his collar, and yanks him to him. "Stop looking at her, you asshole! You're making her uncomfortable."

The guy replies to Heath but I'm far away to hear what he says to him.

Sebastian rushes over to them and pulls back Heath who looks about ready to kill him. His fists are curled tightly, and his body is filled with tension. I can only see his back, but it's all I need to see to know he's ready to throw in the first punch.

"Hey, are you okay?" Marie stands next to me and holds my hand.

"I'm okay," I lie, but my fingers shake in her hold, and she looks at me.

"Boys are stupid. Don't mind him, okay. We all are here for you." She squeezes my hand.

We both turn to the group that steps back, as Heath exchanges a few words with them, and then returns to us. Sebastian says something to him and grins.

"Sebastian shut up!" Heath scowls at him.

Sebastian looks at me. "Are you okay?"

I give him a nod.

"If you aren't, you can tell me—"

"She can tell me," Heath interjects.

Sebastian grins.

"Heath, it's your turn. Hurry up," Marie says impatiently.

"Good luck," I mumble to Heath.

"I don't need luck." With that, he gets in stance, rolls the ball, and straightens. It all happened fast, but in my head, it happened slowly. I watched his muscles move and shift under his T-shirt, reminding me of the perfect body that hides beneath it.

A shot of him half-naked enters my head.

*Don't think about his naked body.*

His movements are flawless. I'm not surprised when he knocks down all the pins.

The game continues and our scores fluctuate.

Marie and Sebastian are good, winning points after points and increasing their total score. Between Heath and I, it's obvious he's great and I'm not. That luck I had for my first shot, disappears for the rest of the game. The rest of them are either gutter or cheap shots which drop our score.

Heath doesn't remark on how we're losing. He only gives me tips to get better. Even when I hit a few pins he gives me a nod which in Heath's language is a proud thumbs-up—I think.

Soon it's time for the last round and we already know who's going to win.

"Watch this, James," Sebastian tells Heath.

*STRIKE!*

I'm next and I knock down a few pins which makes me very happy.

When it's Heath's turn, he effortlessly lands a strike and pushes up our total score.

The game ends and the four of us stare at the scoreboard with various expressions. Marie grins, Sebastian smiles at her, Heath looks annoyed, and I feel bad for being terrible.

"We won!" Marie wraps her arms around Sebastian and hugs him hard. Then they share a sweet kiss that prolongs making me look away.

I turn to Heath. "I'm sorry that we lost."

"Did you have fun?" he asks, instead.

I grin big. "So much fun." It's true. I did have fun.

"Then it's a win," he says softly.

My lips part in surprise. That was not what I was expecting from him. Not at all.

"We are the winners, you are the losers," Marie sings.

Heath scowls in irritation and glares at her. "No need to rub it in our fucking faces."

"Let's go, the food is here," Sebastian states.

# 30

## HEATH

We lost.

If there's one thing about me, it's that I *hate* losing.

I can't recall a single time when I've been beaten at a game, much less by my best friend and his girlfriend. But I don't even fucking care that I lost. All I can focus on is the smile on Hope's face. She looks happy. A look that I want to stay on her face forever.

I watch her talking to Marie who's listening to her and eating fries.

"You can't seem to look away from her," Sebastian mumbles from beside me.

"I'm making sure she's okay. I'm being a good friend." Even my words sound shit to my ears.

"Yeah, sure." He rolls his eyes.

"You don't believe me." I steal from his plate, and he glares at me. He hates it when I do it. More reason for me to do it.

"Not one bit."

"What's there to *not* fucking believe?"

"Everything."

"Stop talking in code words."

"I'm glad we have a secret language. Strengthens our friendship."

I sigh heavily. "Sebastian, get to the point."

"All right. What I'm *trying* to say is you've got feelings for her. Why don't you do something about it?"

"Do something about it? What exactly do you suggest now?"

"So, you admit you have feelings for her."

I scowl. "No, I don't."

"You're one stubborn fucking horseshit."

"That's the best you've got?" I smirk.

"Shut up."

I chuckle and look away only to witness a guy slipping a note near Hope's plate and walking away.

"Oh my God. That was so smooth," Marie squeals.

"I know right," Sebastian joins in.

"Check what it says." Marie encourages Hope who looks conflicted.

Her light brown eyes look at me. I stay still and stare right back at her, mainly because I can't look away from her. She's just so beautiful.

Marie grins. "He gave you his number and he called you gorgeous."

I scoff and everyone looks at me.

"You disagree?" Marie shoots daggers at me.

"No," I lie and look at Hope and my breath gets lost somewhere.

She is not gorgeous. She's beautiful. So, fucking beautiful that she steals my breath away.

"Good." Marie turns to Hope. "You should text him right now."

"Wh-what? I shouldn't. I don't know him," Hope replies nervously.

"He's looking at you."

I follow their gazes and fair enough a lanky guy with glasses is gazing at Hope with a stupid smile. He looks like a geek, perfect for Miss. Nerd here. His looks are average and he's not too tall either.

My chest burns like it's on fire and smoke fills every corner of my lungs.

I can't breathe as silly ideas of them together occupy my brain and rile me up.

"He's a loser," I grumble.

"He's not," Marie argues, then looks at Hope who smiles at the guy.

What the fuck?

Marie continues, "Don't listen to Heath. I think you should text him and see how things go."

"Do you really think so?" Hope looks hesitant.

"Yes, of course. Life is about experiences."

"I'll think about it." Hope spares me a glance.

I want to fucking punch someone or let them punch me. Either will do as long as I don't feel my chest burning with fire.

Marie turns to me. "Seb and I won. Now we have to give you guys a dare."

"I'm done here." I stand up, but Sebastian pulls me down with so much force that when I sit I shake the whole table.

"Sit down, she's speaking."

Running a hand through my hair I suppress a groan. "What's your fucking dare?"

"I don't have it in mind yet. I'm calling a rain check."

"That's now how dares work, Blondie."

She frowns. "Why not?"

"I don't know."

"Then it can work like that."

"Whatever. I'm fucking out of here." Before any of them can protest, I exit the building and let the cold air of the evening welcome me.

Leaning against my car, I smoke a cigarette and watch a group of men checking out women outside a local bar that's brimming with a drunk crowd. One of them, a tall man with dark hair, smacks a woman's ass and then squeezes it. She shoots him a smile over her shoulder, and he leans down to kiss her.

I contain my disgust and light up my second cigarette.

The more I smoke the quicker my chest unfurls with tension.

I can breathe again without feeling like my chest is on fire.

I hate this fucking feeling. I've never felt it before with anyone.

For fuck's sake. I've never cared about a girl texting another guy. Yet, here I am, thinking about Hope contacting that sorry excuse of a guy and going on a date with him.

The thought makes me want to punch a wall.

*For fuck's sake.*

This is all so new to me. I've never let anyone, much less a girl, get under my skin.

I'm head-deep in the sea of thoughts that is her. I don't even want to fight my way up to the surface and breathe air. I just want to drown in her.

*Maybe you do like her,* my heart whispers.

I stop breathing.

*Do I like her?*

I care about her as a friend, and I'd do anything to make her happy. I like spending time with her and talking. I even like it when she rambles about her books. Listening to her brings me silence and calm. I enjoy it more than I enjoy smoking. Is that how it is when you have feelings for someone?

I'm still thinking about it, when the door flings open, and Hope storms out. She frantically looks across the street, stares for a minute, then turns around. When her eyes settle on me, she runs toward me and my heart skips a beat.

Throwing her arms around me she hugs me tightly. Her erratic heartbeats thump against my chest and I can feel her anxiety seeping out through her skin.

She's afraid. So fucking afraid.

"I need to go home. Take me home. Now!" She rushes out.

"What's wrong?" I discard my cigarette and fight with myself to not cup her face in my palms.

"I-I just need to go home," she stammers.

A tear falls and I quickly wipe it away.

*Who made her feel this way?*

*Why is she shaking?*

*What the fuck scared her so much?*

So many questions pop up in my head and I can't answer a single one. She won't either. All I can do is hold her and do as she says. This is the only way I can help her.

Marie and Sebastian see us as they stumble out. Their gazes lock on us and I give them a nod. *I got this. I got her.* They steer toward Sebastian's jeep but don't leave.

Hope trembles against my chest.

Hesitantly I put my hands over her waist. My touch immediately pulls her attention, and she tilts her head back to meet my gaze.

"I'll take you home once you stop crying," I demand in a cold voice, masking my emotions well.

"What if I can't stop crying?"

"Then you're staying with me."

She stays quiet for a long time, her eyes dropping so many tears, then she murmurs, "I wish."

My hands tighten on her waist, and she steps closer to me. Her lavender scent invades my senses, and the familiarity throws a blanket of calm over my raging state.

Hope sniffles and then wipes her eyes. I hold the car door open for her.

During the ride, she barely speaks a word to me.

I'm mad. So fucking mad. At *her* for not telling me stuff. At *myself* because I can't seem to figure it out. At the *universe* for making me catch feelings for her when I wasn't supposed to.

How am I supposed to deal with any of this? I'm lost, confused, and livid.

I pull the break and park a little away from her house, just like she wants. If I ask her she's going to give me a stupid answer.

We sit in the car and watch the road. I wait for her to make a move, but she sits still. So incredibly still that it makes me worried.

"It's seven-thirty," I speak, breaking the ropes of silence tied around us.

A nod is all she gives me as she looks out of the window.

I open my mouth to say something, anything, but nothing comes out.

She has a curfew. *I can't keep her with me, even if I want to.*

She has to go. *I don't want her to go.*

My phone pings with a text message. Hope and I both look at it at the same time.

**Mom: Happy birthday, son.**

I quickly shut off my phone.

"It's your birthday?"

"Tomorrow."

I don't like my birthday anymore. It was the one day Emery made a big deal out of. From decorating the living room with a horrendous rainbow of balloons to getting a custom-made cake. She went all out like it was a carnival. She was annoying and unbearable most of the year, but on my birthday she tried hard to make it the absolute best for me. We were the only family for each other, and we were happy. We were enough for each other.

"You should've told me," Hope says in a feeble voice.

"It's not my birthday yet. And it doesn't matter. I don't celebrate my birthday since..."

"Since Emery's death."

"Yes," I rasp out.

Hope stares at me like she can see right through me. All that I hide from the world because I can't bear their sympathy and pity, but it's there, all of it. Grief, anger, guilt, regret, love, sadness, emptiness and so many other fucking emotions.

"It's like any other day. Forget about it," I gruff out roughly, and look out on the street that's lit with a few houses where people are moving around casting shadows on the curtains.

"I can't just forget it. You're my friend. It's your special day, so it's a special day for me, too."

*Friend.* I needed this reminder after *how* I've been thinking about her lately.

"You should go. It's almost eight."

"I should." But she doesn't make a move to leave.

I look over and find her staring at me with a tiny smile. "Meet me at the library tomorrow morning."

My eyebrows furrow. "Why?"

"You'll see." She shrugs with a smile.

"I told you I don't celebrate my birthday."

"I never said a thing about celebrating your birthday." *She's good.*

"If you want me to read books with you at the library then don't bother. They bore me."

Hope gasps but a shadow of a smile dances on her lips. "I'll pretend I didn't hear that. And no, we won't be reading books or doing anything book related."

"Then?"

"It's a surprise."

I roll my eyes. "Blondie is rubbing off on you."

"I love Marie."

"Clearly."

"I gotta go now. See you tomorrow."

Just like that, she's out of my car.

# 31

## HOPE

I saw Dad last night. He was at a bar with friends who looked as drunk as him. But the worst was the sight of him slapping a woman's ass, and then kissing her. It was disgusting. I can't believe he so easily cheated on Mom. I watched it happen right in front of my eyes.

However, when he looked at the window of the bowling alley, I swear it was like my soul left my body.

Luckily, I got home before him. He came in late, and I heard him fumbling around the place, probably looking for a bottle. But he didn't make it up to my room. Perhaps, he couldn't. Whatever the reason was, I'm glad. It'd be a lie if I said I had a good sleep. I haven't had a good sleep since our first encounter a month ago. He haunts me in my reality and dreams. A couple of hours is all I can manage which leaves me tired all day.

I'm at the library, reading the fifth Harry Potter book, but I can barely concentrate. I fight back another yawn as I look out the window for Heath's car. He's supposed to be here by now. It's ten a.m.

*Maybe he isn't going to come.*

*He probably has something to do.*

*He could be asleep.*

*What if he forgot?*

Doubts pop into my brain and the sadness grows.

My eyes trace the words on the page, but I can't pay attention to a single word.

I read it again, but it doesn't matter. Heath is all I can think about.

A horn blares outside and my head turns to the window.

Right across the street, leaning against the black McLaren is Heath. Black shirt, jeans, and Converse, he's dressed the same as every day, yet the sight of him makes me forget how to breathe. He's so breathtakingly handsome.

He peeks inside and our eyes meet. We stare at each other for what feels like minutes, but actually, it's only a couple of seconds.

He tilts his head to the side and gestures for me to come out.

Grabbing my bag, I throw in my book and hurry outside to not make him wait.

Heath straightens when he sees me. His blue eyes fix on me as I cross the road and stand in front of him.

The bitter smell of the cigarette wafts off him strongly. With the way he looks so calm and collected, there's no doubt he's had a couple of them.

"Hi," I say, stepping back because I can't handle the bitter smell.

"Hi," he says softly, but his eyes are anything but that. The hue of his blue eyes is just *blue*. There's no emotion in them. Nothing. Just emptiness.

He's not the Heath I know.

The realization painfully tugs my heartstrings. But I plaster on a fake smile. Maybe what I have in mind will cheer him up.

"C'mon. We should go. It's Saturday. The place will be packed."

The lack of response and emotion dims me, but I promise myself that I'll make this day good for him.

I ruined it.

Remember what I said earlier? Forget it.

I didn't make his day *any* better.

I thought going to an arcade would cheer him up, but it did nothing.

Heath is extra quiet today. At the arcade, he barely said a word to me and made no effort to join me in games. Instead, he stood behind me and watched me play all the games.

By afternoon, we exited the arcade. I took us to a diner where we—I—ate food. Heath just sat back and looked out the window. For every question I asked he either gave me a short answer or silence. No facial expression. Nothing.

The whole time I felt like I was having a one-way conversation. He didn't participate even a little bit, which is so unlike him. He didn't even ask me what Harry Potter book I was on.

His bleak face and soulless eyes were the highlight today.

I slump downhearted when we walk out of there.

My parents think I'm at the library studying for some big test. It was the only way I could get out of the house with a valid excuse.

Dad watched me closely and I almost had a nervous breakdown.

However, from the looks of it, Heath had more fun staring at the sky than going to an arcade with me.

We're on the curb when he goes to open the door for me, but I grab his hand. He stiffens but he doesn't pull away from me.

"What's wrong?" I ask.

Cold blue eyes turn to me. "Nothing."

"I know you said you don't celebrate your birthday, and it's nothing special. I just thought..."

"You could make it special?"

I nod. "Yeah."

Heath stares at me, then laughs. A laugh that has no humor in it.

He rips his hand out of my hold and runs it through his messy dark hair.

With a hard scowl, he says, "You're like everyone else. Trying to change me."

"Change you? No. I just want to help—"

"I don't need your fucking help." He raises his voice as he glares at me.

Every part of me shudders at his icy tone. It's the first time he's talked to me this way.

Digging knives at me through his piercing stare he moves closer. "I'm not broken, damaged, or whatever the fuck you think I am. Just because we're friends doesn't mean you know me. You know shit."

That detached voice slashes through my heart.

When I say quiet in surprise, he continues, "Arcade, lunch, what the fuck were you thinking dragging me to those places? You think I'm two?"

I shake my head, feeling horrible and embarrassed.

He shakes his head. "I can't believe I wasted half of my day doing this crap. You made it worse than it already is. Leave me the fuck alone."

Tears fill my eyes, but I keep them at bay. I fight really hard to not let a single one drop.

Reaching inside his car, I get my bag. I'm about to close the door when I remember his present. The present I spent a lot of time on.

Taking it out, I put it on the dashboard and start walking toward the library.

Heath doesn't stop me. I don't want him to.

This was a terrible idea. What I didn't know was how badly it'd backfire on me.

Yes, all that we did today was not out of this world. I went an easy route. A simple place and diner that would make him happy because it usually does. But I was so stupid. So very stupid.

I should have known this. After all, I haven't had friends. I don't know the first thing about being a friend. Much less how to make someone feel special on their birthday.

I enter the library being a mess.

Luckily no one is around.

I shuffle to my corner in the back. I hide behind a book rack and bring my knees to my chest.

Marie's call lights up my phone screen but I ignore it.

# 32

<hr />

## HEATH

September 25th is the last day I want to spend in the living. The day consists of twenty-four hours, but it might as well be a thousand hours with how many memories it carries with it.

I hate how this day holds so much power over me.

My mind feels like it's trapped in a labyrinth of memories from the past. I escape one and enter another. Every passage has ten more. I can't look at something without thinking about my sister.

This town reminds me of her. Part of me desperately wants to abandon this place. Never return here. But the other part knows I'll hate being away from my sister, or whatever is left of her now.

Sitting on the hill, I look down at the town that shimmers with lights.

*It's beautiful.* I've lost my goddamn mind. I've smoked more than four cigarettes. I'm not sure just how many.

I'm out of my senses tonight. Too much calm. Too many chemicals in my veins.

I used to do weed but Sebastian got me to lay off of it. Now it's just nicotine for me which works like shit but at least it's something. A year ago, I also consumed alcohol, too much of it, until I saw Sebastian go to rehab for it. I stopped after that, deciding that rehab was the last place I wanted to be.

My phone rings for the tenth time. With a groan, I pick it up.

"Where the fuck are you?!" Sebastian roars.

"What do you need?"

"The list is long, but I'll start with *get your ass home right fucking now.*"

Fuck. He's raging.

"I'll be there," I murmur.

"Don't make me wait or I swear I'll—"

I hang up.

I start driving to my house. My hands tighten around the steering wheel in tension as I speed through the roads. For once, not even the rumble of the engine or the speed affects my mood.

When I reach home, I see Marie's car in the driveway, and I already know they're waiting for me inside.

Fuck.

I walk into the living room and find Marie and Sebastian cuddled up on the couch with a cake on the table.

Marie quickly sits up and looks behind me. "Uh, where's Hope?"

My stomach rolls in uneasiness. "Why would she be with me?"

Marie arches an eyebrow. "She had plans for you."

Right. Of course. Her boring plans.

"She didn't show up," I lie.

Marie looks bewildered, but Sebastian looks like he can see right through me.

"That's strange. She was really excited about it. We talked for an hour. She told me all the things you guys would do. Especially that punching game. She thought you'd love it."

I send her a frustrated glare. "Like I said. We didn't go."

"Oh…" her smile falters and the light in her eyes dim.

Sebastian notices and kisses her cheek. "Babe, why don't you get Hope and let me talk to Heath."

She looks up at him and they talk through their eyes.

"Okay." Pressing a kiss on his cheek she leaves.

The moment the door shuts, Sebastian pulls me to him by my collar and sniffs me.

"I knew it." He pushes me so hard that I miss a step and fall on the sofa. "You're high." He glares at me.

"I'm not high. I don't smoke weed."

"But you smoke enough to lose your fucking mind."

Getting on my feet I push him, but he doesn't budge. "Sebastian, leave me the fuck alone."

"Can't do. Unlike you, I know how to be there for a best friend."

*What the fuck?* The words are a low blow that hits me straight across the chest.

"Fuck you asshole!" I grit my teeth.

With a scoff, he punches me so hard out of nowhere. The surprise evaporates when my ears start ringing and dots appear in my vision.

"Fuck you too asshole!" he yells in my face.

"What's your problem?" I lunge at him, but he easily tackles me to the ground and straddles me. His heavy weight presses down on me.

His green eyes darken. "You listen to me. And you better listen to me good."

"Piss off!" I roll us over and punch him across the face, knowing damn well Marie will have my head on a platter for ruining his face. But I don't give a fuck. He's the one who started it.

"Not my face you dickhead!" He warns me.

His arm reaches for me, and he hits me across the jaw. Pain bursts through my skin and I groan at the sting.

Annoyance and rage, the two emotions I've been keeping at bay, blend well into a delicious cocktail.

Before I know Sebastian and I are onto each other like wild cats.

I'm oblivious to the count of punches, kicks, curses, and words we exchange. All I know is he's trying to fight off something broken and damaged inside of me. Trying to reach me.

We're a bloody mess by the time Derek pulls us apart. Our faces are covered in bruises and blood.

"Can you act civil for a moment so I can grab the first aid kit?" Derek asks me, his stern stare promising a long lecture later.

Sebastian shrugs. "I can. Can't say the same about Heath."

"You want to go at it again?" I take a step toward him, and he copies. We stand face to face and stare at each other with so much baggage and stuff to unload, but there's also a calm now. The spike in my emotions is lowering slowly and I feel like I can breathe again.

Marie and Hope's voices fill the hallway.

Derek smirks at us. "I guess you two will be just fine."

Marie enters the room first and curses. Hope looks at Sebastian and then at me.

"What the hell happened here?" Marie approaches us, dragging Hope along with her.

Putting her hands on her hips she sizes up the two of us. "I left for twenty minutes and you two look like you had a wrestling match of your own."

"Yours truly started it," I grumble.

"And you nicely reciprocated," Marie rebukes me and I shut up.

"Look babe, I'm sorry. I swear—Ah!" Sebastian holds his jaw, his face morphing into pain.

"Sit your ass down right now."

Ignoring the three of them, I take the stairs. Derek passes me in the hallway with a questioning look, but I spare him no glance.

In my bathroom, I remove my shirt that's stuck to my skin because of sweat. Leaving my pants on I look in the mirror and find a few bruises on my stomach.

*Asshole.* I hope I left some on him, too. Though Marie would be on my ass for hurting him.

My split lip is bleeding, and my knuckles are scraped.

There are a hundred ways this evening could've gone, but none of them involved Sebastian and me fighting like animals. He landed good hits. Not that I'd ever tell him that.

My phone vibrates on the nightstand. I see Mom's name flashing across the screen. She's called me ten times today, but not once I felt the desire to hear her voice. While Dad hasn't called me yet, I know he will. He calls me every day even when I don't pick up.

There's a knock. No one will have the courage to face me right now. Everyone knows I'm in a bad mood and won't hesitate to bite their head off.

I fling open the door, ready to yell, but the sight of Hope stops me.

She's wearing the same dress. White summer dress with strawberries on it. It fits her tall, skinny figure perfectly and ends a few centimeters below her knees leaving her long legs exposed. She's wearing sandals, earrings, and her bracelets.

She looks beautiful. Just like she did when she stepped out of the bookstore and stole my breath away. She was everything my eyes wanted to see, and so did my heart.

Hope blushes and her eyes wander all over my upper body. I look down and realize I'm half-naked.

I clear my throat, and she meets my eyes.

"What are you doing here?" My temper gets the best of me.

Hope doesn't look offended. After my afternoon outburst, I can't fathom how she's here. I made her cry, for fuck's sake. I feel awful about it. It's why I've decided I should stay away from her. I want to hurt a lot of people, but she's not one of them. Intentionally or unintentionally, I never want to be the person who makes her cry. For fuck's sake, when she cries it's like acid seeps into my skin and burns me.

"I thought you might need some help," she says.

She doesn't give up.

"I don't need help. I'm fine." Turning around, I walk back into the bathroom, not expecting her to follow me. I can't be alone in peace even on my birthday. Who the fuck did I piss off?

"You should go," I say, leaning against the sink and folding my arms over my chest.

"I will after I clean your wounds."

"You're stubborn."

Hope doesn't reply. Instead, she looks through the cabinets until she finds the first aid kit.

Grabbing a ball of cotton, she stands in front of me and looks up at me expectantly. "I can't reach you."

"I don't want you to reach me."

Lifting on her tiptoes she steps closer. My body turns hot, and my arms drop from my chest as I stare at her in surprise.

The cotton ball presses against my split lip that aches like shit. But with Hope standing so close I can barely focus on the twinge of pain. All I can think about is how extraordinary her brown eyes are and how much I like them.

Her adamant gaze hits me as she says, "I will always reach you because you'd do the same for me."

"No, I won't."

Hope smiles. "Liar."

"That's the truth."

"You're right. It must be. I don't *know* you."

The slash of her words makes me grimace, reminding me of how I behaved earlier.

"You do know me," I whisper.

"Then why did you tell me otherwise?"

"Because I'm a fucking asshole."

She bites her lower lip to hide her smile.

Dabbing off the blood on my lip she patches up my knuckles and bruises. Once she's done she takes a bit of cream and applies it to my lip. The way her finger touches my lip makes heat crawl across my chest and travel downwards.

When she keeps rubbing it I know I can't fucking take it anymore. The girl is giving me a fucking boner.

I attempt to move away but in doing so I make her lose balance and she falls on me. Our fronts press together, and she holds my biceps for support. With a groan I tilt my head down, only to see her looking up at me.

Brown eyes. So fucking perfect.

My gaze drops to her lips. Pink full lips with a delicate cupid bow.

"I'm sorry," she whispers and tries to step back, but my arm circles around her waist and keeps her close to me.

I don't want her to go. For this moment she's managed to quieten my thoughts.

Using my other hand I brush away the loose strands of her hair that fall on the sides of her face. Her beautiful, sweet face. When I first saw it I thought she was pretty, but she's much more than pretty. She's beautiful, selfless, kind, considerate, and the sweetest person I've ever met. It's not just her beauty that attracts me to her, it's those other things too.

I look at her lips, fighting everything in me to not press mine against hers and see if she tastes as sweet as herself.

*I bet she does.*

Very slowly, I lean down, adamant to kiss her but I stop when I'm a few centimeters away. I feel shallow breaths leaving her mouth and her body stiffening in my arms. I search her eyes, but they're closed as if she's blocking out what's about to happen.

My heart dives straight into the pit of my stomach and dread fills me.

Hope is terrified.

I don't know what or who. She's willing to act like it's a passing thing rather than live in the moment. It's now how I want our first kiss to be.

I touch her lower back, and she jumps. Wide eyes and a face as white as a sheet stare back at me.

We stare at each other until she frees herself and runs out of the bathroom.

I grab a shirt and put it on as I follow her.

She stands beside the window holding herself in her arms and looking at the same view I do every night.

"Hope—"

"Have you forgotten about today? Especially after the way you treated me. You hurt me with your words and those mean glares you send to everyone else. I shouldn't even be talking to you after the way you made me feel. It feels awful."

I stay rooted in my spot after hearing those words. *I hurt her.* That realization hurts me more than anything ever has. Those punches Sebastian landed on me feel deserving now. Maybe he should've done more, because I fucked up royally.

Hope continues when I stay silent in guilt. "I know it's hard for you—"

"You have no idea," I whisper and sit down on my bed.

She sits beside me. Her beautiful eyes stay glued to my face as I gaze at the floor trying to push the words out of my mouth, but they feel too heavy.

My throat tightens and my mouth dries up.

Finally, I feel the weight of today pressing down on me, and it rips my fucking breath away. My lungs go empty with air, and I struggle to breathe.

Fuck. It can't be happening here. Not in front of her.

I clench my hands that rest in my lap, but really, nothing helps.

"I..." I start, hoping I'll be able to talk to her, but what comes out is a raspy sound.

*What is fucking wrong with me?*

*I need to get my shit together.*

A warm hand lays on top of mine. I look down and realize that my hands are shaking.

"It's okay. I'm here for you," Hope says in her sweet voice that manages to slither through the haze I'm stuck in.

Her other hand goes to the back of my head, and her fingers play with my hair.

"Just breathe." She encourages me in a soft voice.

Fuck.

Fuck!

FUCK!

Why am I having a mental breakdown right in front of her? I've never let anyone see me like this, except for Sebastian. If he weren't helping me all those times when I was on the floor heaving for air, I wouldn't have made it this far.

He's my best friend, but Hope has become more.

"I'm fine," I wheeze out.

Turning my head, I look at her, and fuck, she's a sight to behold.

I remember that day so clearly, the moment I collided with her. Her brown eyes and bony face blinded me with how beautiful they were. I was thinking, how had I missed seeing a face like hers in school? How had I not seen her before?

Distracted, because I can't look away from her, I feel her open my fist and intertwine our fingers. She gives it a gentle squeeze. "I see you like you see me. You don't need to hide from me."

She adds, "Now, take a deep breath and let it out slowly."

I do as she says—that's how it is with us, she tells me things and I just fucking do them.

Inhaling a deep breath, I keep it inside, then let out in small breaths.

"Again."

I do it again, again and again, until I can finally breathe. My lungs relax and my chest unfurls from whatever ropes it's bound with.

I'm free.

But my head feels heavy. Without thinking, I lean my head over her shoulder and sigh.

Hope stiffens. I hear her breath hitch. She also stops playing with my hair and for some odd reason, it fucking annoys me.

"Don't stop," I murmur weakly.

She resumes playing—or whatever it is she's doing—and I close my eyes. "Better?"

"So much fucking better."

After a few minutes she says, "You get panic attacks too."

"Quite often."

Her hand stops. "What do you do, then?"

"Don't stop and I'll fucking tell you."

She laughs and continues doing those finger-movements she does. I relax more. Being this close to her I can smell her lavender scent that drives me fucking crazy. Out of all the things in the world, a flowery scent is my demise. Who would've fucking thought?

"Usually Sebastian helps me, but if he's not here, then I pass out or—"

"You pass out?" She holds my hand so tightly, it hurts. I don't think she's aware that she's cutting off my blood supply.

I look up at her and she looks down at me. Her face is so fucking close. I can easily kiss—

After that last attempt, I need to make a plan. Spontaneity won't work on this one. I need to prepare her beforehand, which I don't mind one bit.

*I want to kiss her. I really want to kiss her.*

"Heath, tell me!" There's urgency in her voice that pulls my complete attention.

"Yes. I pass out. Like you were about to in that alleyway, remember?"

She gives me a weak nod. "I'm sorry that it happens to you."

"It's life."

She doesn't say anything. I decide it is best to tell her now why I acted like a dick.

"Last year I spent my birthday sitting at her grave. The one before it was in the hospital by her bed. Emery always made a big deal of my birthday, but I haven't celebrated my last two birthdays. Now it's become a habit. In countless ways today is associated with her. I can't get her out of my fucking head. A grave visit does nothing to make me feel less lonely or less..."

"Sad."

She looks down at me, knowing she's right.

"Yes."

"I don't think you're damaged, but I think you're broken."

The muscles in my body strain in denial. "I'm not—"

She stares at me with a grave expression that shuts me up. "Emery's death broke some part of you. It hurts you deeply, but you refuse to admit it."

"That's fucking bullshit," I grit out.

"Or maybe I can see right through you."

I roll my eyes. "Since when did you get annoying?"

A smile kisses her lips. "Since we became friends."

"You're good at this friendship thing."

"Really?"

"Yes," I say in a heartbeat.

Hope blushes and my heart rapidly beats inside my chest. I'm starting to notice it does that a lot in her presence.

She clears her throat. "We should go down. Marie got a cake for you."

"I should just stay here."

"It has chocolate," she chirps excitedly.

"I *hate* chocolate."

"Maybe you'll like it."

"Very fucking unlikely."

"It's sweet."

"I hate sweet things."

"You haven't found the *right* sweet thing."

I glare. "You're fucking impossible."

She grins.

Lifting my head from her shoulder, I stretch to loosen my tight muscles. In doing so, I notice Hope's attention on me, and it makes me smirk. "See something you like?"

"I..." she falters.

Those fucking red cheeks make me chuckle.

"You're fucking adorable," I say without thinking.

We both stare at each other in surprise, but I won't fucking take it back.

I meant what I said.

Together we enter the living room where Marie and Sebastian are bickering over something. When they see us, they grin like hyenas.

"Finally! You guys are here," Marie says.

Sebastian gets up and comes my way. He looks as bad as me which makes me smile a little. He returns it.

Marie brings in my cake with a beaming smile. She reminds me of Emery in that regard, and I realize why I care about her. In some ways, she's like a younger sister to me.

Picking up the knife, I cut the cake and the three of them eat it, but I don't, because I don't like chocolate. Also, I'll have to work extra hard to lose those calories.

Sebastian doesn't have a care in the world as he munches on the cake like a starved man. Great. Now he's also becoming a chocolate addict.

"You want some?" Hope asks with a bit of chocolate on the side of her mouth.

"No."

"Try it." She advances the plate toward me, but I have something else in mind.

I lick my thumb and graze it over the chocolate mark, slowly getting it off. Pulling back, I taste the chocolate off my thumb and for once I don't mind the sweet taste.

Hope watches me with an innocent gaze that tightens the knots in my stomach. Her mouth parts making me want to kiss her.

*Fucking hell.* For the past hour, all I can think about is kissing her.

"I think I like it," I say.

"Yo-you do-do?" Her gaze drops to my mouth for a second.

"Mhm."

Her throat moves delicately and fuck I want nothing more than to touch her and kiss her—

What the fuck am I thinking? She's my friend. She trusts me. I can't fucking do it.

To distract myself, I look over at the obnoxious couple. They're dozing off, cuddled in each other's arms. An imposing sleepover *again* I guess.

Hope and I clean up while Sebastian and Marie get some rest. We're in the kitchen washing dishes—despite Kelly asking to do it, Hope gets her to agree to let us do it.

"Did you open my present?"

*She got me a present.*

"No." I dry the last plate and put it in the cabinet above.

"Oh." Her facial expressions turn dull.

It fucking bothers me. "Give it to me."

She closes the tap and dries her hands with a washcloth, then faces me. "It's in your car."

What? When did she put it there?

I leave the room in a hurry and Hope follows me.

Reaching my garage, I unlock my car. A small blue box sits on the dashboard. It's covered in a simple white ribbon with a little note on the top.

*Happy birthday, Heath.*

*– Hope*

I untie the ribbon and open the box. A simple black bracelet is inside.

Taking it out, I move around the beads with my thumb. A blissful feeling erupts in the center of my chest.

I know how much effort it takes for her to make bracelets. I've seen it. Fuck, I've even helped her. She spends hours on it to make it perfect.

The fact she did it for *me* is what has my blood rushing through my veins.

"Do you like it?" Hope asks, tucking a strand of her hair behind her ear.

I nod. I can barely find my voice as emotions climb up my throat.

"Can I put it on?" Her fingers are restless as they fidget with each other, but she's plucking courage for me. She wants to do it.

"I bet you won't take no for an answer," I drawl out in a dry voice.

With a smile, she takes the bracelet from me and steps closer. Gently she ties the thing around my left wrist. "It looks cute on you."

*Cute.* That's the last thing I want to be interpreted as. But the way she lights up at the sight of her bracelet on me, I don't even care about it.

"Thank you," I mutter, avoiding her stare.

"You're welcome."

The longer I stare at her, the more the heat swirls inside of me. My veins surge with warmth and lust.

My self-restraint weakens when I remember how the chocolate tasted off of her. I bet it'd be a hundred times better if it were her mouth. Her gorgeous, alluring mouth that's making me lose my mind.

Hope is unaware of the chaos she's havocking inside of me.

If she knew my thoughts she wouldn't be standing here alone with me.

I'm about to step closer to her and hold her when her phone buzzes. Whatever's on the screen turns her face pale, and her posture goes rigid.

"I need to go home." Without waiting she makes a run for the door, but I run after her and catch her wrist.

When she looks back I can sense her fear more than I can see it in her eyes. Her pulse is going crazy under her flesh, and her skin starts to get cold.

"I'll drive you."

"No!" She blanches, trying to free herself.

I gently pull her to me. "What's wrong?"

"Nothing," she says immediately.

I want to push her on the matter, but she beats me to it.

"I need to go home now."

Like always I toss away the conversation and comply with her request.

Ten minutes later we're near her house. My body is stiff with tension.

Something is terribly wrong in that house. I know it deep in my bones. But I don't know how to figure it out.

The reason why I became friends with Hope was to help her, but I seem to suck at it. Instead, I'm catching feelings for her. She's all I can focus on. In school, at home, at the gym, and in the middle of a fucking match. Her eyes and face are all I fantasize about—among other very explicit things.

She's wearing a dress that has a favorable neckline, giving a sneak peek at her cleavage. The material curves generously around her small breasts.

"So..." Hope starts, fidgeting with her fingers.

I arch an eyebrow.

"Was it a good day for you?"

"It was." I don't have to lie. Even though I didn't participate in the arcade and acted like an asshole. Watching her smile and laugh made me content.

She hesitantly nods her head.

I feel awful. "It was better than any other day I've had."

"You disagreed earlier."

I almost smile at her attempt to set me straight.

Leaning over the console, I whisper, "I was being an idiot."

"A big one."

"Oh yeah?"

She nods.

"I'm sorry," I say sincerely. When she doesn't say anything I feel even worse.

Running a hand through my hair I blurt out. "I'm really fucking sorry for the words I said to you and the way I acted toward you. It was a dick move and I feel terrible. I hurt a lot of people, and I don't care about half of them, but *you* are

not one of them. You'll never be. I never want to fucking hurt you. Like ever."
Taking a deep breath I continue, "All the things I said today, I didn't mean them
when I didn't even try to have fun with you. You planned a day for me, and I
turned it into shit. For that, I'm sorry, so fucking sorry."

Three heartbeats later she wraps her arms around my neck. I place my palm
over her back and keep it there.

"I'll make it up to you."

"You don't have to."

"I will."

That night she leaves without saying goodbye.

# 33

## HOPE

I'm bleeding.

I stare at the red liquid on my fingers.

Standing up with the help of my bed, I weakly stumble into the bathroom.

My vision blurs and black dots appear in front of my eyes. I barely make it inside on my two very imbalanced feet.

Turning on the light, I take in my disheveled state.

My hair is wild, and my eyes are puffy and red with the tears I shed in the past five minutes. But nothing is as horrific as the handprint on the left side of my face, and the gnash on the side of my head from hitting the edge of the bed.

Everything inside of me hurts. My skin, my bones, my heart, my soul, even the blood in my veins is searing hot like lava.

The door opens downstairs and a few minutes later the unmistakable sounds of pleasure phase through the walls. I gag and try to hold back the storm of sickness brewing in my stomach.

I can't believe Mom can let him touch her. He was drunk when he attacked me.

*I enter the room with my heart beating out of my chest. I press my hand against my skin to keep it in. I truly believe Heath was going to kiss me. The way his blue eyes darkened as they stared at my lips, and his breathing turned ragged. Erasing those couple of centimeters between us, he could have been my first kiss.*

*The thought gives me butterflies as I step on the porch with an excited smile.*

*I feel something for him. Somewhere deep inside my heart, under layers of fears and doubts, there is something that blooms whenever he's near me. His proximity makes me feel safe.*

*And gosh, the way he looks at me. I feel his stare in my bones. Like he can see right through me—which is scary when I'm hiding secrets from him. Even knowing that he doesn't look any different at me.*

*I'm still thinking about him when I step inside the house and come face to face with Dad. He's in a white tank top and jeans. A cigarette hangs between his fingers as he exhales the smoke in my face.*

*I wave my hand around to brush away the smoke.*

*"Where are you coming from?" He stands in front of me.*

*"I was at the library," I lie.*

*He smiles. "Funny you say that. I was at the library earlier and Anastasia said you weren't there."*

*Air whooshes out of my chest. "I left early."*

*Sweat builds on the back of my neck. I'm nervous. So nervous.*

*"Interesting." He smothers the cigarette against the wall and throws it on the floor near my feet.*

*When I look up, he grabs me by my hair and drags me up to my room. His grip is tight, and he yanks my hair out of roots as his strides are long and mine aren't. I can barely keep up with him.*

*Shoving me inside my room he slaps me so hard my ears begin ringing.*

*For a second there my brain stops working.*

*"You're stupid if you think you can lie to me, and I'll let you go." Yanking me up by my arm he shakes me. The smell of alcohol is on him and his eyes are red.*

*"Where the fuck were you?" He raises his voice.*

*I try to cower away from him. But he's too strong and big compared to me.*

*"Let me go, please," I beg him with tears streaming down my eyes.*

*My cheek hurts so bad from the sting of his slap.*

*"I asked you a question." He pulls my hair.*

*"Where were you?" he asks again, gazing at me with his dark, menacing eyes.*

*My lips tremble from the pain. I'm in so much pain.*

*"Dad, let me go."*

*"I'll get the truth out of you, bitch. I bet you're whoring around the town thinking I won't find out. But I will. And when I do I'll kill him."*

*Chills race down my spine at the thought of him hurting Heath.*

*My face must've shown my worry because a smirk splits on his lips.*

*"I knew it. There is an asshole you're fucking."*

*"No!" I fight him but he tightens his hold on my hair.*

*"I can see it in your eyes. There is a guy. Tell me his name."*

*I shake my head. So hard and so fast I lose balance and stumble, but he keeps me in place.*

*"You're a fucking cunt who spreads her legs for the first guy she saw. Do you need attention, Hope? Is that what it's about?"*

*"No."*

*"Whoever it is, stay away from him, or else you won't like the consequences."*

*"Don't hurt him," I whisper, my eyes closing from the pain in my head from all the hair pulling. I'm half unconscious.*

*"I fucking knew it." Dad slaps me again. I fall and hit the side of my head against the edge of the bed.*

*I slump on the floor.*

*I don't know when he leaves, but the shift in air allows me to catch my breath.*

I clean myself and then curl up on my bed. Lying on the side, I look out of the window.

The hills hide the view of the other side. I wonder what it's like out there. I've never been to the city before. From the whispers of the townspeople and the knowledge I've gained from books and TV, I bet it's wonderful there.

I've never wished to go to the city before. But tonight, I do. I wish to go away from here.

In more than a month Dad has traumatized me enough to be afraid of sleep. He's breaking me little by little. I'm losing pieces of me. Or maybe he's already broken me.

Tears drip down my chin and wet my T-shirt.

I'm in pain. So much pain.

The thing is, I don't even know why he's abusing me. Ever since he's come back, I've become his target, and Mom has become his biggest supporter. Everything has taken a three hundred and sixty turn around. I can't make sense of anything.

Dad threatened Heath. I can't let him hurt the one friend I care about the most. The person who makes me feel safe. The person I can share stuff with. The person who cares about me.

Heath is a good guy, despite what the school says. I don't even care what anyone says.

I see him, and I know he sees me too.

The mere thought of him accelerates my heart. The kind I've read about in books when a character starts to catch feelings.

Am I catching feelings for Heath?

*You can't,* my mind warns me.

After what Dad did tonight, I can't.

I care too much about Heath to get him hurt because of me. I won't allow it. Even when the idea of being away from him makes me weep hard.

The next day at school I avoid Heath at all costs. It starts with the locker and then our first class together which is Math. I take the furthest seat from him, but he moves the guy sitting next to me and takes his seat. His stare burns my face throughout the class, but I refuse to acknowledge it.

Luckily we have different classes. I'm in AP classes for most of my subjects so I don't see him until physics. Like before, he sits next to me but I'm quick to change the seat. The lecture starts before he can do anything.

Marie and Sebastian don't say a word during lunch, but they know something is up.

By off time, Marie pulls me to her car.

"What's up between you two?" she asks.

"Nothing." I tightly hold my book to my chest.

"If there's something, you can tell me." She touches my arm, and I flinch.

She frowns. "What was that?"

"Nothing." I smile.

She shakes her head. "It wasn't nothing. You *flinched* when I touched you."

"Just a stupid body reaction," I say, hoping she believes me.

"But—"

I start to back up. "I should go. I have to be home to make dinner."

"You want a ride?"

"No, thank you."

She nods and watches me as I hurry out of the school.

I don't want to hurt Marie. She's my friend. But I also can't burden her with my worries.

# 34

## HEATH

Hope is ignoring me.

She thinks I'm a fucking fool if I don't notice, but I do.

I notice everything when it comes to her.

So, it amuses me when she thinks she's invisible, but she's *all* I can see.

She tries to blend in the background, but I'd pick her up even in a kaleidoscope of colors. She's anything but a shade that's supposed to not capture your attention. My attention.

It's been three fucking days.

Three days of absolute shit.

I can't concentrate on shit. In the two classes that we share, I try to meet her gaze, but she refuses to look at me.

I haven't looked in her eyes for three days and it's driving me fucking insane.

No one has ever affected me this much. No one.

The pretty book nerd has me going insane over her.

I know her routine by now; she arrives late at school, sits away from me, spends lunch in the library saying she has tests, and then leaves school early.

It's the same shit every day.

Today, I'm putting an end to it.

I'm going to ask her *what the fuck is wrong?* She thinks I don't notice how one side of her cheek is a little swollen and red, and the way she keeps her distance from everyone and doesn't say a word when she's with us.

Entering the mass of students in the hallway, I glare at a few to clear my path. They all cower away from me.

Thursday is as busy as every other school day. The hallway is filled with people who can't stop talking.

Marie and Sebastian are standing next to Marie's locker, keeping an eye on me. Marie is also worried for Hope and has been driving Sebastian and me crazy with her plans to help Hope. I swear, if she comes to know about my abuse theory, she'll be raging a storm on the two of us.

Leaning against my locker, I narrow my gaze on Hope who's collecting books from her locker. She's in a white sweater and jeans that fit her ass perfectly—yes I'm fucking staring at it. Her hair is down, and the dark tresses frame her face, hiding that red cheek from my view. *Good.* Otherwise, it'd piss me off.

The second she slams her locker shut, I'm striding in her direction. She never sees me coming, which works because she can't run away from me like she's been doing lately. I take hold of her wrist and slip us into the nearest classroom and close the door.

Turning around, I face her, only to see her wide eyes and pale face. That's not how I wanted her to look at me after three fucking days.

I put distance between us to prove my point. "I'm not going to hurt you, Rose."

"I know," she says, holding tightly to the Harry Potter novel. I have no idea what book number it is because she hasn't updated me. That worsens my mood even more.

She's supposed to tell me about the books she reads.

"Then why do you look fucking terrified?"

"I'm not. I'm fine."

"You are not fucking fine," I burst out in frustration.

Instantly, she looks down at her shoes.

Fuck. This was not what I wanted.

Striding toward her, I stop when I'm right in front of her. There's a little distance between us that I want to erase, but I won't until she gives me a sign.

Putting my index finger under her chin, I lift her face so she's looking at me.

"Why are you ignoring me?" I ask.

"I—"

"Stop ignoring me. It fucking bothers me."

A shaky breath leaves her lips and falls over my finger.

"It...bothers you?" Her brown eyes peer up at me in surprise.

Fuck. I adore those fucking eyes.

"You have no fucking idea just how much," I say.

"Why?" she asks, her eyes trained on me, searching for answers.

I lean down, slowly, waiting to see if I'm making her uncomfortable. When she doesn't step back, I proceed until I'm a few inches away from her face.

"Because I fucking care about you, Rose. Don't you already know that?"

"I..."

"Tell me what's wrong so I can fix it."

She falters, but I catch her by holding her arm. "Wh-what?"

"Whatever it is that's bothering you, I'll make it go away for you. I'll do anything for you. You just tell me what's fucking wrong. I'll take care of it, Rose."

I can't stop myself from calling her Rose. It's *my* nickname for her.

She shakes her head. "You can't. *You just can't.*" She sounds defeated.

Ignoring her words, I caress her red cheek tenderly, so I'm not hurting her at all.

"Does it hurt?"

"Not anymore."

"How did you get this one?"

She begs me with her eyes. "Door."

Bullshit.

"I didn't know a door could have fucking hands."

She slips from my hold and puts distance between us. *Not fucking good.*

"I need to go."

I block her path. "We need to talk—"

"There's nothing to talk about."

I take a step forward and she takes one backward. It continues until her back hits the desk and she has nowhere to go. Putting my hands on either side of her waist, I trap her. Her fingers tighten around the book but her eyes stare at my chest.

"Will you please look at me?" I ask, lowering my voice.

Hope tilts her head back and meets my gaze for a second, then looks away.

Deciding to put an end to this bullshit, I lift my hand to tip her chin, but she flinches.

Tremors shake her body as her hands shield her face.

Stunned, I push back from her.

My brain short circuits.

For fuck's sake.

*Someone is physically abusing her.*

*I was right.*

"You thought I was going to hurt you," I grit out.

The shock makes my breathing stutter.

Her teary eyes and heaving chest make my knees weak.

Everything in me wants to step closer, but I know it'll set her off in the worst way possible. She'll think of me as a threat and try to escape—

Too fucking late.

Side-stepping me, she rushes out of the room, while I stand there and watch.

I can catch her.

But I don't.

In the evening, I arrive at the underground, burning with the desire to fight someone.

My mind can't rest. I'm certain I've lost it with how irritated I am tonight.

My opponent lands a few sloppy hits on me, pulling my attention to him.

Usually, the shouts and cheers of raging men are a blur when I'm in the ring. My opponent is the only thing I can focus on. Tonight, that's not the case.

When he aims for my stomach, a dull ache permeates there.

Shooting him a glare, I swing my arm and break his nose. Blood droplets follow through and he stumbles back.

I don't stop.

With hit after hit I turn him blue and black until he signals the speaker who calls off the match.

I'm still heaving in anger, itching to get another fight, when Sebastian's peculiar gaze from the crowd puts a stop to my plan.

The speaker makes my victory announcement, I walk out.

Sebastian follows me silently to the room, but I can feel the tension radiating off him. He's worried for me—the last thing I want him to be.

I sit down on the floor and chug down an entire water bottle.

I'm burning with heat. The erratic beats of my heart roar in my ears like a drum. Still, my mind is unable to steer away from the teary brown eyes I saw today. Whenever I close my eyes, they appear right in front of me.

The way she flinched, stiffened, and refused to meet my gaze.

I can't stop thinking about it.

I want to punch the bastard who hurt Hope. I want to break his bones and make him feel the same way Hope does. For the first time, I want to use my strength and fighting skills to hurt someone.

I won't feel one bit of remorse. I never do.

Some people don't deserve kindness or mercy. Unfortunately for him, I won't grant him either.

I don't know what I'll do if it's a woman. She won't be receiving mercy from me though. I'll get Marie to beat her or better yet hire someone. I'll make her pay for hurting Hope. I'll make anyone pay for hurting her.

Sebastian takes a seat next to me. "For the first time, I don't like the look in your eye."

I break out of my thoughts and realize that my hands are shaking.

I'm on the edge of getting to the bottom of this matter without asking Hope. I just want to know.

"I'm fine," I grumble.

"That's not what I said, is it?"

"That's my fucking answer."

"What's wrong?"

"Nothing."

Sebastian puts his hand on my shoulder and squeezes. I'm half tempted to break his wrist, but I swallow the urge. He's looking out for me like he always does.

"You know, I'll always stand by your side. You're my best friend, James." Sebastian only calls me by my middle name when he's dead serious about something. He knows I hate it because Emery used to call me that all the time. But on occasion I let him slip up. Maybe because I miss being called that.

Looking over at him, I give him a confident nod. "I know."

"Then what's up?"

"Nothing."

"You're a tough dough."

"It's cookie."

"That's reserved for sweet people. You're bitter."

"I'm not bitter," I grit out.

Sebastian arches an eyebrow. "Don't get offended now."

I sigh and look away.

He bumps his head against the wall and sighs heavily. "How many times do I have to ask before you surrender?"

I smirk. "A million."

"Challenge accepted." I hear the smile in his reply.

Just like he said, he eats my brain all the way home. I thought he'd shut up, but he kept chanting 'what's wrong' in my face.

My patience snaps. I end up telling him everything.

His stupid idea of befriending Hope and gaining her trust isn't working. That idea sank worse than the Titanic. Of course, it would have. It was Sebastian's idea, after all.

I was right. I should've dealt with this matter head-first. Now things have gotten worse.

Hope has created a shell around her. A concrete exterior that keeps growing day by day.

I can't understand how anyone can hurt Hope. She's the sweetest and kindest person I know. I've been an asshole to her on occasions—about which I feel terrible—but she always tries to help me.

On my birthday when I made her cry, she still returned. She's *that* good.

Sebastian sits down on the couch. We're in my room so we can have this conversation without anyone bothering us or eavesdropping on us.

"Why don't we invite her here and just ask her?" he asks.

I shoot him a glare. "She doesn't tell me, what makes you think she'll speak in front of you guys?"

"Maybe she'll see that we are there for her."

The thought of Hope telling him and Marie upsets me. It sounds selfish but I want to be the one she confides in.

"I don't know." I run a hand through my hair.

"You really like her, James."

*I don't.* The words are right on my tongue, but I can't get them out. I just fucking can't.

"Do you have a point asking that?" I ask indignantly.

With a teasing smile, he shakes his head. "No. Not at all. I just needed to see something."

We stare at each other, and I know he can see it all in my eyes. He knows what I feel for this girl. How long I've fought to not feel whatever it is that I'm feeling. He understands why she matters to me and why I'm at war with myself about protecting her.

I clear my throat. "It's late. You should go home."

"Marie is busy tonight. So, I don't have a reason to go home. If you want me gone, I'll go."

No. I don't want him gone. I never want him gone.

I stand up from the bed and grab my gloves from the desk. "Let's spar then."

Sebastian grins evilly. "Want to get beat up?"

"You wish." I scowl.

"I do. I wish for it badly."

"That's all you'll ever do."

"Don't get cocky. You're not that good."

"Fine. I challenge you to touch me."

"I have a girlfriend, Heath."

I close my eyes in frustration. "Dickhead."

"I heard that."

We enter the gym and wrap our knuckles. Stepping onto the mat we're at each other. But still, a certain book nerd is all I can think about.

# 35

## HOPE

I've always wondered how people are so good at pretending—I'm not.

My flushed cheeks and minimal eye contact give away that something is up with me. I bet anyone in Bellmare can tell I'm pretending. But they can't say the same about my dad. He's so good at acting, even I believe him.

Sitting at the table, I watch him shower Mom in sweet nothings and kisses.

The sight appalls me in every disturbing way possible. My stomach can't stop churning at the marvelous act he puts on in front of her.

I wonder if she can see what I see, or if she bluntly chooses to ignore it, just to keep him. She's missed him the entirety of those three months he was away. She got drunk frequently and sent me texts about how she wished for him to come back. She mourned his departure when she should've been relieved that he was gone.

For heaven's sake, he tried to kill her—the part she has conveniently forgotten. That's not it. He's physically and mentally abused her for years, but looking at her now, it's like she's hidden all that mess behind a beautiful painting.

"Why don't we have a nice dinner over the weekend?" Mom suggests with a twinkling smile.

Dad pauses and frowns. "Dinner?"

She hums. "Yeah. You and me, somewhere nice like the old times."

I keep my eyes on my breakfast. I wanted to leave, but Mom dragged me here from my room to sit with them and eat a meal. There's been more PDA than eating.

Dad smiles. "If that's what you want, sweet."

Not a second later kissing noises fill my ears and the one pancake I've eaten rises to my throat.

I want to be anywhere but home.

So, I slide off the stool. "I-I need to go to the library." I run up to my room and grab my bag and phone.

On my way to the door, I can feel Dad's piercing glare on me.

"Be home on time, honey," Mom hollers.

"She will be. Don't worry." Dad assures her with conviction just as I close the door.

After what he did last time, he has all the reasons to be confident. He terrorized me to the extent I can't stand human touch.

Piece by piece I'm breaking apart. Terror and fear are making a permanent home in me.

Since he's returned, he's made *me* his target and is giving affection to Mom. I'm not jealous, only dejected that he's hurting me. I don't even know what I've done to deserve it.

I was doing well before him. I wasn't the happiest girl in the world or anything, but I was normal—as normal as an introverted, shy girl can be. More than that; I was okay; I was safe.; I was comfortable.

Now he's ruined *me* for *me*.

My heart feels heavy from carrying this sadness. I just want to let it all out and feel light. It's strange how *one* emotion can be so heavy.

On the short walk to the library, I think about the good things in life. One of them being my small business. Since I've been ignoring Heath for the past few days, I haven't been able to check his phone for orders. At some point, I'll have to talk to him and see if I have any orders to fulfill.

Talking to him won't be easy. He'll ask me questions that I can't give him the answers to. It'll create tension between us which isn't something I want.

Today's Friday. I should be at school, but there are competitions happening that I'm not a part of. Marie's entered a computer science project, so Sebastian is there to support her. As for Heath, he's not the type to participate in anything—kind of like me.

We are both loners and introverts.

I mean he has two best friends, but I've seen that he also likes his alone time. Like going to that secret spot on the hill. That's his place to hide from everything.

For me, that place is the library.

I greet Anastasia, the librarian and the owner, and rush upstairs. It's not her fault what happened to me, I don't blame her. If she knew I'm sure she'd protect me, but I'm too much of a coward to tell anyone and burden them.

I'm low maintenance. I don't like to bother people. I've been this way since I was a kid. My parents have never had an issue with me. That explains why I want to be the best at everything and just not cause them to worry. It's drilled into my brain.

However, I do have high standards when it comes to fictional men. I mean, it's not like I'll ever have a real boyfriend.

Who would date a girl who loves books with her entire being? I'll always love books before him.

I know that sounds awful, but books have been my longest relationship, and nothing will ever change that.

*Wait. What if I stop reading someday?*

*I know that won't happen. Ever. But still.*

Walking down the shelves, I find my secret spot. No one comes here. It's quiet and lonely—exactly what I need.

Sitting down, I pull my knees up to my chest, making a makeshift table for myself. I open the last book in the series that's become one of my all-time favorites.

Taking out the bookmark, I run my fingers over the page. The feel of a book always makes me feel better. Bringing the book to my nose I sniff the addictive scent of it. It calms my senses instantly like a spell.

If someone were looking at me they'd think I'm insane. Lucky for me, no one comes here.

"I see you're on the last book."

I jostle in shock at the sound of his voice. I can recognize it anywhere.

I spot him leaning against a shelf. He's wearing a simple black T-shirt and jeans with black and white Converse—his usual attire. I'll be amazed if I see anything besides those clothes and colors in his gigantic walk-in closet.

Heath looks breathtaking. One side of his face is hidden with shadows, and the other is bright due to the sunlight that's streaming from the window, heightening his sharp features. His blue eyes look unreal—they've never looked as beautiful as they do now.

I've read about so many fictional characters, but no one comes close to Heath—even though I create them in my head from words on a page. He's the most handsome guy I've ever seen.

But that's not why I'm drawn to him. I mean, it is one of the reasons, but there are other reasons too. Like how he shows his care in little things; buying me food because I'm hungry, turning the AC fans toward me because I'm wearing a turtleneck and feeling hot, calming me down when I'm overwhelmed, and asking me about book updates because *I* love books.

When I sit tight-lipped, he steps away from the shelf and strides in my direction. Without breaking eye contact, he sits down beside me and leans his back against the shelf. He bends one knee and sets his forearm on it while his other leg stretches long. Sometimes I forget how tall and muscular he is. He has a great lean athletic body. No wonder he's a great fighter.

Tilting his head to one side, he says, "It's rude to stare, Rose."

I blink and quickly look away. "I... I wasn't staring."

"Sure." His voice is husky as if he's just woken up and decided to come here.

I hold the book tightly. "What are you doing here?"

"I was waiting for you." He stares deep into my eyes.

Red climbs up my cheeks and clings there with the promise of not coming down.

*Excellent.* Because it's so romantic to look like a tomato in front of the guy you sort of like.

"Why?" I mumble.

"You've been avoiding me."

"Not really." *Okay, so maybe I was hoping that he wouldn't bother after our last confrontation.*

After a long moment he says, "You're lying a lot today."

"No—"

He arches an eyebrow, and I shut up.

Putting away my book, I hug my knees and set my chin on top of them. All to make myself as small as possible. Invisible.

I stare at a random spot on the floor. "How did you know I'd be here?"

"You love reading."

"Yes. But how did you know I'd be in this spot? Not a lot of people come here."

"Precisely *why* you'd be here," he replies in a sure tone like he knows me from the inside out.

"How do you know me so well?"

"Because I watch you and learn everything." Then he adds, "I want to know you, so I can understand you better."

My heart jumps.

I look at him, surprised by his words.

For a minute I don't even know what to say to him.

We sit in silence for minutes like it's the most normal thing for us.

Finally, I say, "I like the quiet and loneliness here. It's peaceful to me."

"I understand."

"You do?"

He nods.

Lifting his hand, he caresses my injured cheek. His touch is gentle and feather-like, quite contrary to how rough the calluses are on his fingers.

"It isn't red anymore," he murmurs.

His entire focus is on my cheek, knuckles running back and forth over my skin, but I feel his attention on every inch of my body. "If I ask you something, would you tell me the truth?"

My breath hitches and my heart beats frantically.

*Oh my God.*

*Is this it?*

*This is it.*

I stare at him, begging him to not ask me what I know he's going to ask.

I want to look away from him, I really do. But something in his gaze keeps me tied to him.

*You don't ask for hugs. You take them.*

Moving forward, I wrap my arms around his neck and bury my face in his neck. Tears pour down from my eyes as my heart breaks into pieces in silence. The destruction makes no noise, yet it brings about pain.

I'm so scared. So helpless. I don't know what to do or where to go. I feel stuck. Like time has frozen me in place. I can't escape, I can't hide, I can't leave. *I can't do anything.*

I snuggle against him, seeking refuge in his arms, because at the moment he seems like the only place I can unburden myself.

Heath wraps his arm around my waist and with the other, he holds the back of my head. His fingers tangle into my hair and reach my scalp. With tenderness, he kneads and squeezes me against him in a tight grip.

We're so close I can feel his strong heartbeats thumping against mine.

"You're always stealing hugs from me," he whispers against my ear.

"Do you mind?"

"Fuck no."

Heath holds me as I silently cry in his arms. He doesn't ask questions or push me away.

Last time I couldn't wait to get away from him when he cornered me in the classroom and today I'm pressed against him and feel the safest I've ever had.

It's strange that I feel like this with him. A guy like him should make me stay away from him, but I can't.

The night Dad choked Mom, I promised myself I wouldn't let myself develop feelings for a guy. I would keep my distance and never let myself fall in love or catch feelings. I promised myself over and over that night as I lay in bed shivering and crying.

I guess it's too late now.

I have feelings for Heath.

Shakily, I pull back from him and almost crumple by his intense stare.

Before I can, he wipes away my tears and cheeks, removing any trace of sadness.

"You shouldn't cry."

"Why not?"

"You look awful when you cry."

I laugh.

If there's anything I've learned about Heath, he's rough around the edges, but within that boundary lies a good heart that he doesn't let anyone see.

I see my bracelet around his wrist and butterflies soar in my stomach. It looks like he hasn't taken it off since I put it on him.

Heath follows my gaze. His expression turns serious, and he clears his throat. "I...on my birthday...we..."

I grin.

It's funny how confident and sure he acts, but now he can't seem to get the words out of him.

"What is it?"

I watch as he clenches and unclenches his hands as if tension is whirring through him and he can't seem to get rid of it.

Slowly, I lay my hand over his and he goes still. His eyes focus on where we're touching, and he takes a deep breath. "Do you want books?"

I stagger with shock. "What?"

"I want to buy you books," he says with a seriousness that leaves me bewildered.

"Books! You want to buy me books. What? Why?"

An exasperated sigh leaves him, and he rolls his eyes. "Do I have to answer all those questions?"

I gingerly nod.

Running a hand through his mess of dark strands he fixes me with an intense look. "I didn't like the way I treated you on my fucking birthday. You planned a good day, and I fucking ruined it. It won't happen again. But I feel irritated for being a fucking asshole, so let me make it up to you."

"You could just say you're sorry, which you did."

"Let me buy you books." His throat moves undeniably slow in a sexy way. "It'll make me feel better."

"I forgave you."

Heath's eyes brighten as if he's been struck with a lightning bolt idea. "Mailbox then."

Confusion clouds my mind until the meaning settles in.

I gasp. "No. Don't do that!"

"Then let me buy you books right now."

"But—"

"Stop arguing with me." He sends me a glare, but it doesn't faze me.

"Okay, but there is an issue."

"What now?"

"The books I want aren't available here."

"We'll buy them online then."

The sound of 'we' makes another flock of birds take flight in my belly. Only this boy can make me feel like this.

I can barely hold my giddiness as he pulls out his phone.

I place orders of three books on his Amazon account, but he pushes me to make it ten. When I try to fight him, he takes matters into his own hands and orders books that are similar—book cover-wise—to the ones I read.

I can't believe he pays me this much attention. My parents have never cared about what books I read. They're always criticizing my hobby, sometimes making me believe it's stupid. But I know it's not stupid.

Reading is the only thing in the world that makes me the happiest. And nothing that makes you the happiest is very stupid.

Chocolate comes second.

"They'll be here by next week," Heath informs just as he proceeds with the checkout.

"I forgive you again for being an..."

His eyes are on the phone but his mouth twitches. "Asshole."

"Yes."

"I feel so much better now," he says in a dry tone.

I smile, and he scowls.

That's just how it'll be between us.

# 36

## HEATH

A few days later, we go to my secret spot after school.

September is on the verge of goodbye with Autumn in full effect. An array of trees crowding the slopes and feet of the hills are in shades of yellow, orange, and red. It's a whole color palette down there with the town sitting ahead of it.

"How do you know so much about Instagram pages, and managing a business? It's one thing to study something and another to know exactly what to do."

I lean back and turn my neck to look at her. I *always* need to look at her.

"I manage a few Instagram pages for various stuff."

Hope criss-crosses her legs and gazes at me with all her attention "Such as?"

"Some are niche pages that I grow an audience on so I can sell them later. The others are businesses like drop shipping, merchandise, and stuff."

"You create merchandise?"

"Marie creates. I work on the marketing aspect."

"When did you guys do it?"

I smirk. "We have never done it, Rose."

"What—"

My smirk deepens, waiting for her to catch the innuendo.

Her cheeks turn rosy and those innocent eyes dart away from mine. It's a delightful sight.

"You know what I meant," she whispers.

"I don't," I joke, finding her uneasiness entertaining.

"Don't make it say it, please."

I laugh hard. My chest shakes in a way it hasn't had in a long time.

Hope watches me with a cute smile.

"What?" I ask.

"That's the first time I'm hearing your laugh."

"Hm. What do you think of it?"

"That I like it, and it's my second favorite thing about you."

"What's your first favorite thing about me?"

"The way you make me feel."

"How *do* I make you feel?"

"Safe."

I stiffen. It's exactly what I've wanted her to feel when she's with me.

Clearing her throat, she says, "So, um, when did you and Marie start this business?"

I take the hint. "We made it a little after Sebastian went to rehab. She was depressed and distraction is the antidote to sadness."

Her mouth opens in shock. "Sebastian went to rehab?"

I go rigid as the memories play in my head.

"Last year," I answer quietly, fighting to block that dark time out of my head.

"Is he okay now?" Hope asks in a concerned voice.

"He has his days, but now he can get through them."

"That's good for him."

I inhale a deep breath. "It was difficult to see my best friend destroy himself, all because his mom didn't know one thing about being a parent. She destroyed him in ways no one could heal him. But therapy and Marie have healed him."

Hope stays motionless beside me, absorbing everything.

"Don't mention any of this to Bash. He hates talking about it," I warn her.

"I won't," she promises me. "So, the merchandise. Why didn't Marie tell me?"

I rest my head against the hood of my car and set my forearms over my knees.

"I made her sign an NDA," I tell her.

"Why?"

"So she wouldn't tell anyone else. Sebastian knows. And now you."

"Thank you for telling me."

Her phone pings and I see the name Elliot across the screen.

Picking up her phone she replies, then puts it down.

"Made a new friend?" I ask casually, when on the inside I can feel my chest burn at the name Elliot. What a stupid name it is.

"He's that guy from the bowling alley."

"So you texted him, then."

"Yes."

She fidgets with her fingers. "Actually, we're going on a date."

I sit upright. "What the fuck?"

Hope flinches and I feel like a dick.

I take a minute to cool myself down, but nothing helps. The thought of some guy spending time with her drives me crazy when it shouldn't.

"Why the fuck are you going on a date with him?"

"Because he asked me on a date," she whispers.

"And *not* because you want to?"

"I want to. He's sweet and it's nice talking to him."

I scoff.

"Marie supported the idea," Hope adds and now I want to kill Marie for suggesting this stupid idea.

"When is this fucking date?" I ask.

"He's picking me up at six tomorrow."

Maybe it isn't too late to leave town. I can book a hotel for the weekend and escape. It's better than staying here and witnessing Hope going on a fucking date.

Shortly after I drop her home, I drive to Marie's house.

I knock on the door impatiently. Seriously! What the fuck was she thinking?

The door opens and Issac Anderson, Marie's father, steps out in a white button-up and dark gray slacks. He's as tall as me and has a lean build.

He greets me with a warm smile. "Heath, it's nice seeing you. It's been a while. How are you doing?"

"I'm fine," I mutter irritatedly.

This man looks at me with such affection. I don't like it one bit. He adores both me and Sebastian—him more than me because he's the boyfriend of his daughter. He's an incredible father to Marie. I've seen it from time to time. He'll destroy anyone who makes Marie miserable—he almost did.

Between Marie, Sebastian, and I, she's the only one who has the most caring and loving parents.

Issac holds the door open. "Why don't you step inside, son?"

*Son.* The word always gets to me when he says it. Maybe it's the longing, knowing my father and I will never be close like he is with his two children.

I take a step back. "I should go."

"Sit with me for coffee."

"I have something—"

Giving me a playful glare he warns me, "Don't make me drag you inside, son."

Deflated, I follow him to the living room which looks straight out of a magazine. The decor is simple and elegant in a homey way. Everything is expensive and meaningful. Like the white plush rug under the coffee table, Marie begged for it because she loves soft things. Or the red cream curtains with self-prints because Camila likes them. Marie has told me so many stories when I used to come here to keep her company because Sebastian was in rehab.

Issac motions for me to sit. "I'll bring your black coffee with no sugar."

I open my mouth to argue but he sends me another glare causing me to sit my ass back down.

I've never been able to fight off Issac Anderson. The way he treats me or talks to me gives off this fatherly energy. And because I crave it in life I smother under it like a sunflower in the sun.

I can say *fuck off* to anyone, even my father, but not to this man. He's as good as his daughter. Like patches torn from the same cloth.

Issac returns with my coffee and sits across from me on the sofa.

Taking a sip of his coffee he studies me. "So, what brings you here?"

"Is Marie home?" I get to the point.

"She will be in thirty minutes. Camila took her and Sebastian shopping."

"I'll see her tomorrow, then." I stand but he gives me the look. The daunting businessman look.

I glue my fucking ass to the couch.

He leans back. "Want to talk about what's bothering you?"

*What the fuck?*

*How does he fucking know?*

"Nothing is bothering me."

Issac smiles like he knows something is up. I suppose it's parental instinct.

"Then you shouldn't mind giving me a run down. It's been months since I've seen you."

"Miss me or something?" I ask drily.

"I do. So, tell me."

"It's the same as before. School and boxing." *And Hope.*

Issac watches me with a knowing smirk as if he can read my mind. "No new thing or someone, perhaps?"

"No."

Issac chuckles and puts away his coffee mug. The Rolex watch on his wrist shifts, and I'm reminded of the million-dollar empire he's built around the world but keeps that world separate because he loves Marie so much that he moved here for her sake. He takes her to therapy and spends time with her. He's the epitome of a perfect parent. I don't envy Marie at all, but her parents are something else. The moment you enter this mansion, you realize it's more of a home than a magnificent place worth millions.

"That's interesting because Marie has been raving about this girl Hope and how she's her best friend. I believe our whole neighborhood knows about her at this point. My wife had the pleasure of meeting her and now both of my girls are singing her praises." He sighs in mock sadness. "Unfortunately, *I* missed the opportunity to meet the person who brings so much joy to Marie. I want to see that smile on her face."

"*Everything* brings joy to Marie."

He shakes his head. "Not everything, Heath. You and I both know that."

From the moment I met Marie, I saw loneliness and sadness in her. But more than that, she's always wanted to have friends, but no one wanted to be her friend. I've watched her cry, complain, and cry some more, because all she's ever wanted is for people to accept her.

"Yeah," I whisper.

He nods. "She mentioned how Hope and you have been spending time together."

I stiffen and hide my face behind the mug of coffee. "As friends."

His hazel eyes, identical to Marie's, watch me. "I see. That's where everything begins."

I scowl. "Nothing is fucking beginning."

"Getting defensive now, Travon."

I hate being cornered.

Issac gives me a teasing smile. "Hope and you are friends. How's it going?"

"Fine."

"Told her about your sister yet?"

"Yes."

Issac studies me. I know if I give him a second more he'll see what I'm hiding.

"I'm getting late," I say but make no effort to stand up.

"You like this girl, don't you?"

What the fuck is up with everyone? Is it tattooed on my face or something? How can anyone know what's inside of me?

"You're crazy," I reply in a tense tone.

He arches an eyebrow. "Am I? Because I believe I called your bluff."

I glare at him, and he calmly stares back with a smile that's the same as Marie's. There's no doubt that they're blood. Genetics aside, he has the habit of probing me for details just like his daughter.

"Does it matter if I like her or not?" I grit my teeth as I ask.

He nods. "Yes, it does. *Your* feelings matter, son."

"Not enough since she's going on a date," I burst out.

For a moment there's silence, then he says, "Have you told her how you feel about her?"

"No." It's too late now.

"You should. Maybe she feels the same about you."

"I highly fucking doubt it."

Issac places his elbows on his knees and leans over. "Why do you say that?"

"If you don't know it already, I'm not the epitome of a good guy."

"Sebastian wasn't either, but he's dating my daughter. Why? Because he loves her. No man will ever love my daughter like he does."

Love. That word creeps me out. It's like one of those spells you'll never recite fearing it'll come to life.

"I don't love Hope. I'm sure of it."

"But you *like* her."

I look away feeling vulnerable for the first time in my life.

"You should tell her," he suggests.

"I don't think so. She seems to like this other guy," I tell him in a rough voice. How fucking pathetic.

Issac laughs. "You're jealous."

I glare at him. "What the fuck are you talking about? I'm not fucking jealous."

Issac gives me a look. "Tell her before it's too late."

Before I can fight him, the door opens, and chatter fills the hallway.

Marie and Camila appear smiling and carrying tons of bags.

"Oh, Heath is here. What a surprise. How are you, love?" Camila asks in a motherly tone as she comes my way.

"I'm fine." I stand up and move toward Marie.

Marie stares at me in shock. "Heath, what are you doing here?"

I point my finger at her. "You and I need to talk, Blondie."

She nods. "All right. Let's go up to my room."

I start walking out of the house before her parents can make me stay for dinner. "Meet me outside."

Two minutes later she steps out with a concerned look on her face. "What's up?"

The rage I smothered a while ago lights up with full force.

I glare at her. "Why did you tell Hope to go on a date with that platypus?"

Marie frowns, then starts laughing and my annoyance only gets worse.

"Platypus? That was funny."

I grimace. "That guy isn't for her."

"And you know how?"

"I just do." I grind my molars with how mad I am right now.

"You told me she isn't your type, so I don't understand why you're interfering."

"I'm looking out for her as a friend."

"Are you sure that's the only reason?" She arches an eyebrow. Her eyes are as curious as her father's.

"I'm done here."

I drive home all the while thinking about Hope and that average-looking guy on a date. I can't get the image of them laughing and talking out of my head.

I fucking despise it.

Fucking platypus.

I hate it so much that I'd give anything to *not* have her go out with him.

The truth I've been hiding from everyone hits me across the chest in bold italic big letters.

*I. Like. Her.*

*I. Fucking. Like. Her.*

I don't know *how* or *when* it happened, but somewhere in her beautiful brown eyes and pretty rosy cheeks I started feeling something. I have no interest in books, but when she talks about them I just want to listen to her. The way she looks when she talks about her favorite characters or the smile that hangs on her lips at the cute moments, it's enchanting.

The thought of someone hurting her evokes the killer instinct in me. I've never wanted to kill anyone. But I want to kill whoever lays hands on her and terrorizes her. I'll go to jail for her just so she feels safe.

Never in my life have I felt this sort of pull toward someone. It's stronger than the magnetic force of a planet or opposite poles. There's no way I can resist it.

I like her. I like her so fucking much that it hurts to not be with her all the time.

Sitting in my car, I hear my rapid heartbeats echoing in my ears.

She makes my fucking heart race.

Fuck.

I want her. I want her so badly.

# 37

## HOPE

My parents decide to go away for the weekend.

I don't know how Dad managed to save money when he has no job, and he spends every cent of Mom's money on alcohol. The thing that surprises me the most, is how Mom can't see any of this. The empty bottles and the change in his behavior. The telltales are right there. Somehow, she makes me believe it's all in my head and I'm delusional.

Somehow, I still believe, the worst is yet to come. This isn't it.

Friday arrives, and I'm so glad that it's the last school day and a weekend awaits me. At school, Heath ignores me in all our classes together and glares at me whenever our eyes meet. He's mad about the date thing, which I don't understand. He's the one who said we should be friends and has never made me feel otherwise. While I've been feeling anything but *friendly* toward him lately.

When he simply looks at me, my heart jumps in excitement, literally sky-rockets to the sky. When he talks to me—in that soft voice—I feel butterflies fluttering around in my stomach like a field of flowers has grown in there. When he touches me, I forget to breathe.

There are so many other things, too.

His eyes are always gentle when they look at me, like I'm the most delicate thing in the world and he'll never think about breaking me. His big arms wrapped around me make me feel safe. So easily, he manages to vanish every dark thought out of my overthinking brain when he presses me against him and calms me down when I'm having panic attacks.

*I like him. I like him so much.*

Everything he does makes me feel exactly how it is in books. He makes me believe in all that I've read about.

All my life I've thought what happens in books can't happen in real life. Love is easy in a fictional world but not in reality.

Heath makes me believe in love, that perhaps it can happen to me, too.

However, it's too late now. I have a date with Elliot, who seems too nice to be stood up. He told me I'm the first girl he's ever asked out. I can't do this to him. I know I'd hate it if some guy did it to me.

When I come back from school, my parents leave, informing me that they'll be back the next day.

I hate this new arrangement. I've made my feelings clear on the matter, but Mom doesn't believe me and Dad, well, he'll be staying here for a long time. With how much he's making an effort to swoon Mom off her feet there's no doubt he's staying.

The only silver lining is by next year I'd be out of here. Until then, there's no place of refuge for me.

Around five p.m. the doorbell rings.

Marie is standing on the porch, holding many shopping bags. "You have a date and I'm here to help you."

I lean against the door. "That's nice of you, but you didn't have to."

I'm so glad she's here when my parents aren't home. I'd resent myself if Dad pulled an act in front of her or hurt her in any way. I already know I won't think twice about throwing myself in front of her to protect her.

"C'mon, let's go to your room. These bags are quite heavy."

I notice the five bags she's carrying—all designer brands—and she looks like a model herself. She's so beautiful it amazes me sometimes, that she considers *me* her best friend.

I let her inside. I think about how my house is nothing compared to the mansion she lives in. Her home is beautiful and safe, unlike mine.

Inhaling a deep breath, I show her my room and she carefully looks around before turning to me with a beaming smile. "I can't believe I'm seeing your room. Heath must be so jealous."

I blush. "Um... he's seen it before."

Marie whips around to me with a shocked expression. "When?"

"It was raining one day, and he dropped me off. Then there was a power outage, so he stayed with me for a while. It's then I told him about the bracelet business."

Marie groans. "I can't believe he has one over me."

I laugh a little as I shut the door behind me. "Is it a competition?"

"Not really," she murmurs and sets her makeup supplies on my study table and all the other things she's brought with her.

"So, what should I do first?" I ask, fidgeting with my hands.

Marie looks at my hair and sighs. "You'll need to take a quick shower."

"Frizzy hair?"

"Greasy hair."

"Yucks."

"Indeed, but don't worry. I'll make it better." She gives me a confident thumb-up.

Taking a towel, I rush into the bathroom, turn the taps, and wait for the water temperature until it is warm. I have to wait for ten minutes because of the broken heating system, but it's better than showering in cold water.

This is happening. I'm going on a date. My first date.

I'm getting all those pre-date sparks in my stomach and I'm nervous.

Elliot studies in another school that's out of Bellmare. It's a bit of travel, but it's fine with him because his friends live here, and he also accompanies his father in dealings.

From the conversations we've had, he seems to be sweet and funny. We talk about studies and bond over movies. But he doesn't make me feel sparks or butterflies like Heath does. With Elliot, it's the comfortable kind of connection, the one I need. But with Heath, there's fire beyond the comfortable connection, the one I want, but I won't get. Because I don't know how Heath feels about me.

I wash my hair and body. I don't know why but I shave too, even though I know nothing of that sort is going to happen between us. I'm not yet ready for it.

When I come out in a T-shirt and shorts, I see Marie has laid dresses over my bed with shoes and accessories.

"Marie—"

"I should have brought more. Don't worry I can call—"

"It's enough. You didn't have to. I've got something I can wear tonight." I cast a nervous glance at everything that's on my bed. Probably worth hundreds.

She grins. "It's your first date and you should look the best."

"We're going to a local diner. Nothing fancy."

"*Still,* you should look the best. We don't know what might happen."

"What do you mean—"

"We're getting late!"

After what feels like an hour Marie is done with my face and is halfway through curling my hair at the ends. We don't talk in between because Marie said that she can't do makeup while talking.

"How was your first date, Marie?"

A deep blush covers her cheeks. Clearing her throat, she peeks at me with a smile. "Sebastian took me to laser tag first. It had just opened up. We had so much fun there. Afterward, we went to a diner and had pasta which was the best I've ever had. Then we sat on a roof and talked until sunrise. He kissed me a lot, too."

"What were you like before Sebastian? How did he even meet you? I've always wondered but never asked you."

Marie sets the curling rod aside and adjusts the curls with her fingers. "You know I'm an over-talkative girl, so guys stayed away from me. They thought I ate their brains with my long speeches. I had lost hope that I would ever find a guy who would love me and care for me. I was that girl who had no friends and when she tried to make some, people would just make excuses and leave. I was alone. My parents and Kevin, my older brother, were all I had. I wasn't alone at home, but at school I was. And that made me sad." She explains with a forlorn face.

I take her hand and squeeze.

She squeezes back. "You remember that botanic garden trip?"

I nod. I didn't go because my parents couldn't afford a four-hundred-dollar trip.

"I was sitting alone on the bus. Mr. Nathan was about to close the doors when Sebastian hopped in. The only seat left on the bus was next to me and he took it. I didn't talk to him because I was sure if I uttered a word he would just get annoyed. Also, he was so handsome, and I got nervous. I was hesitant to make any small talk. Out of the blue, he started talking to me. I began to ramble, and you know what Hope? He listened to every word and even smiled. That's how things started between us. One thing led to another, and we became friends who fell in love with each other." She winks.

"Marie." She hums in response. "How did you know Sebastian was the right guy?"

Marie focuses on my hair, thinking deeply about the question. She parts it from the middle with two tendrils on the front. Then, she makes a twist on each side and pins it with some black hairpins. Satisfied with her work, she styles the rest of the strands.

"That's the thing, Hope. I didn't know he was the one, my heart did. When he kissed me for the first time, I got the *butterflies*. I felt those *goosebumps*. I still get them. They never go away."

Looking at me in the mirror, she says, "You never know who's the right guy and that's why you have to be careful."

I look at myself in the mirror. A beautiful girl stares back at me, with a face covered in minimal makeup and hair that looks perfect. There's a little blush on my cheeks and a light shade of pink gloss on my lips. My light brown eyes look prominent because of my eyelashes which are coated with layers of mascara.

"Marie," I whisper.

"You look beautiful, I know. Let's get to the dress." She squeezes my shoulders.

I wear a summer dress that I bought a few days ago. Marie hands me a thin shawl as it gets cold in the evening.

"This dress looks beautiful on you. Where did you get it?" she asks, adjusting the shawl on my arms.

"A local shop close to the library. You like it?"

"I love it. Maybe we should go shopping sometime."

"Only if you let me pay too."

She shoots me a smile but doesn't say anything. I already know she won't let me, just like Heath.

At the mention of his name, my insides swirl in an uncomfortable feeling that I can't put my finger on. He didn't talk to me at school or text me. I wish I knew what was wrong with him. The wall in front of his heart is far thicker than me. Sometimes, it's impossible to read him or understand him.

I slip my feet into a pair of pumps because I don't own a decent pair of heels.

"Hey, wear this!" Marie holds a pair of white heels that are just my style if I had them.

I shake my head. "Oh no. It's fine. I can just—"

"C'mon, take them. Shoes are important."

"Are you sure?" I ask in a little voice, feeling like I'm imposing on her.

She nods. "Ten thousand percent. They'll look good on you and go with the dress."

With an uncertain heart, I hesitantly take the heels from her and put them on.

*They look amazing.*

"Looks amazing, right? I know." Marie reads my mind with a knowing grin.

Grinning at her tactics, I put on some earrings and bracelets that I made myself.

"Let's take some pictures." Marie pulls me against her and starts taking pictures on her phone. In almost every single picture we're smiling or giggling.

Once we're done, Marie peeks outside the window. "He's not here."

"Five minutes are left."

"You're right, but he should be early." She huffs.

"Any piece of advice?"

"Have fun tonight but not that kind of fun. What the hell am I even saying?" She face-palms herself. "Just don't panic and if you need my help either text or call me, and I'll be there in no time. If you want, I can go as an undercover agent and keep an eye on you guys, so he doesn't try anything. Look I—"

Without thinking I hug her, and she stops talking. "If I need you, I'll call you."

She relaxes in my hold and wraps her arms around me. "I charged your phone."

A smile tugs on my lips at the gesture that's so small but means so much.

When the doorbell rings we both pull away.

Marie stares at me with a knowing look that I can't decipher. "First date. I wish it were with someone else, but life is full of experiences."

"You mean Heath?"

She nods excitedly.

I fidget with my fingers, nervously. "He has to ask me out... I mean if he wants me in that way which I don't think he does but—"

"Time will tell."

We get downstairs. I pause at the loneliness and the quietness floating in the space that was here four months ago—I miss it now.

My hand on the handle shakes and my pulse is out of my control.

Taking a deep breath I open the door.

## 38

### HOPE

Elliot is standing there in simple jeans and a white T-shirt with flannel on top. His blond curls fall over his forehead and his brown eyes look soft behind the pair of thick glasses. He looks cute in a nerdy way. Someone who'll understand me, perhaps.

"Hi. You look pretty." His eyes check me out in a subtle way.

I tightly hold the door. "Thank you. You look good too."

He shoots me a smile and it's adorable.

"Are you ready?"

I nod. "Yes."

Just then Marie comes down and wedges herself between the doorframe and me. "It's Ethan, right? Look after—"

"Elliot." He corrects her before I can.

My eyes train on her but she's busy staring at me and avoids my side-eye.

*Seriously, what is Marie doing? I thought she was okay with him.*

"Ethan, Elliot, same thing, isn't it?" Before he can reply, she brushes him off with a wave of hand. "The point is, look after my best friend and don't you dare try something or I will make sure you don't see the next sunrise."

My lips open in shock, and I grip her arm. "Marie!"

Elliot chuckles and raises his arms in surrender. "It's *just* a date."

"I hope you remember that." Marie glares at him.

I'm frozen in place by the switch in her attitude. This is the first time I'm witnessing this side of her and God, she is scary when she's acting protective.

Leaning down to my ear she whispers, "Text me when you get home, or I'll drive here to make sure you're okay."

I only manage to give her a nod.

Dragging her bags out of the door, I say goodbye to her as she glares at Elliot before driving away.

Once she's gone, he turns to me. "So, that's your best friend? She's scary."

"I'm sorry—"

"I don't mind."

We walk to his car. I pause, thinking he'll open the door for me, but he strides around to the driver's seat without looking back at me.

My heart sinks. Heath always opens the door for me.

*NO!*

*I can't think about him when I'm on a date with another guy.*

*Just go with it.*

When I get inside he's already started the car.

A country song plays, as he slowly maneuvers the streets to the diner he plans on taking me to.

Silence fills the car, and we don't talk at all which makes me really nervous.

Usually, I don't mind the silence but when I'm with someone—except for Heath—it drives me crazy. I'm thinking of all the topics I should start, that can turn into long conversations and won't end no matter how we talk over it—okay that's crazy but the point is to not be silent.

Fortunately, we soon arrive at a local restaurant that's well-known in Bellmare. People frequently eat here because it serves the best food and has a beautiful setting. The moment we walk inside, I notice the lights that are wrapped around the ceiling and the small origami figures hanging from the ceiling in different colors and shapes. The tables have white cloth, with a vase of fresh flowers sitting on top. It's romantic and a cute place, especially for a date.

Elliot chooses the table by the window, and we sit across from each other. A young waitress asks for our order, and I freeze, much like I do every time. Luckily, Elliot notices and asks for pasta and water.

The waiter goes away, and he turns to me. "So, you don't like to order?"

"It makes me nervous."

"That's odd." He laughs a little as if it's silly.

I swallow. Again, then again. Still, I feel the pinch of his remark right in my stomach.

"Do you have any plans for college?" I change the topic to get over the hurt before I start overthinking about it like I do with most things.

He shakes his head. "I'll be helping my family business." Leaning over the table, he says, "What about you? What are your plans?"

My mother's words come to me and a burden the size of a mountain rests over my chest.

"Med school. I'm going to be a doctor." My tone is detached and empty, even to my ears. Is this what I become once I get there? Someone who's lost themselves?

Elliot leans back. "That's a long road."

"I know." My lips lift in a half smile to uplift my mood. *Poor attempt.*

"You love medicine?"

"I'm good at science."

He chuckles. "Ah! You're one of those."

"One of what?"

"One of those people who follow a path because they're good at something."

He's not wrong. Mom seems to strongly believe in that idea and won't listen to me *if* I try. I mean, it's not like I possess the courage to talk to her about it. She'll get mad, so mad. I fear she might disown me.

"Yeah," I whisper and fidget with my fingers in my lap.

My anxiety increases as I think about the future that I don't want for myself, but I can't do anything to change it. People like me, who love stories about adventure and bravery, are the ones who lack it in real life. The reason *why* we read that kind of book is so we can experience them in the confines of fiction while also feeling like we're that character.

Everything that I'm afraid of—love, friendships, adventure—is what makes me read books.

The waitress from before puts down our food with a lovely smile. I look up at Elliot only to catch him staring at the girl's ass.

My stomach drops ten feet down and tension swirls like a tornado inside of me. *This isn't right.*

Instead of confronting him, I choose to ignore it and focus on the food that tastes delicious.

Elliot looks back at me. "You told me you like books. What genre do you read?"

"Romance." I try to be honest. He should know the real me, even though it makes me nauseous when I tell people that I love reading about love.

Elliot laughs. "Love. You believe in that?"

"I do," I reply in a strong tone instead of feeling insecure. I won't let him make me feel that way.

"Seems boring to me. How uninteresting is it to read about characters falling in love? It's like watching a cheesy movie but with words."

Only one thing is true out of all that he said.

It is cheesy reading about characters falling in love. But to *me,* it's magical and sweet.

All my life I've seen the uglier and messier side of love. The side I shouldn't have seen because it's altered my opinion on the matter. Despite reading so many romance books, the foundation my parents have laid in my head is unmovable.

The truth is, I'm scared of falling in love. I don't want to fall in love knowing the other person won't have the guts to catch me. And if he does, someday his mind will change, and he'll let me go.

I've seen people fall out of love over time. It's only in books I see people falling in love more each day. It's fiction and it doesn't matter. But something heals inside of me when I read that fake reality.

Books are the best escapism. Only those who escape in its worlds would know.

I hold my head high. "It's interesting to me."

"That's the reason why you have a book in your satchel right now."

I put it there to show him some of my annotations, in case he was interested in me and wanted to know me more.

"I carry a book with me everywhere," I say.

"Why?"

"It's a habit."

We talk about other things including family, siblings, friends, and summer break.

Elliot seems polite, but some of his comments set me off. I endure them and counter back when necessary, but I don't feel great. He and I share different opinions on things and that can only go a long way. I respect his perspective, but his point of view on my choice of books isn't something I can ignore.

I love books and if I ever fall in love with a guy, I want him to understand how much I love them. Maybe it's too much to ask for when guys don't like romance books and steer clear of girls like me because we have high standards. In reality, we don't. We ask for care, attention, love, and understanding. Aren't those very simple things to be able to give?

On the ride back home, we don't talk except for the occasional glances we throw at each other.

My neighborhood is dark and quiet at seven p.m. The lights are off in almost every house and an eeriness wanders the street like a ghost.

Elliot walks me to the porch steps and lingers as if he's got something to say.

I turn to say goodbye, but instead, I find him standing close to me. His mint breath caresses my skin, and I quickly step back.

"Thanks for tonight." I smile.

I turn around to go back inside when his hand clasps around my wrist. Before I can think, he pulls me back and I stumble into him.

"What are you doing?" I ask in a shaky voice as I look into his eyes.

Elliot looks down at me. His eyes are filled with a strange emotion that doesn't make me feel good. I want to move away from him, but my body won't move.

Touching my cheek with his warm fingers, he leans down, and whispers in my ear, "Aren't you forgetting something?"

Without waiting for a reply, he leans closer. Just an inch more and his lips will be on mine.

*His lips on mine?*

*I don't think I'm ready for that.*

*Not with him.*

I start, "I don't think—"

"Shh. I need the kiss," he murmurs in a raspy voice that raises goosebumps on my arms.

"No," I manage to say and try to move but my body won't cooperate with my plan.

*What is wrong with me?*

*Why does this always happen to me?*

*Why can't I move?*

Anxious thoughts start pouring into my head. My breathing drops to shallow breaths.

"Stay still," he warns me.

"What are you doing? I don't want it," I remind him again.

Before I know it, he's moving in my direction.

Suddenly he's ripped away from me. "She said fucking no."

Heath punches Elliot straight in the jaw and he stumbles back and hits the nearby tree.

Elliot glares at him as he holds his jaw. "Who the fuck are you?"

Heath looks murderous as he glares at him. "Someone who'll beat the shit out of you if I see you near her again."

"She doesn't have a boyfriend."

"She doesn't want one."

"We went on a date. She owes me a kiss." Elliot looks at me as if I'm his prey.

Heath steps in front of me, blocking his view. "She owes you nothing, asshole."

Elliot tries to hit Heath, but he easily dodges him and lands three more hits on him with a precision and strength that can break bones. When he stands straight, he isn't even breathing hard.

With a groan, Elliot backs away from him in pain. He has a bleeding nose and split lip.

"Fuck it. It was a stupid bet." With that, he's out of sight while I'm standing there thinking about his words.

Heath faces me and his sharp eyes lock on me before moving down my body, looking for an injury. Taking long steps, he reaches me. "Are you okay?"

I'm so stunned I can hardly speak a word.

His eyes narrow as he searches my eyes. Taking my hand, he says, "Rose, you need to tell me. Are you fucking okay? Did he do something?"

I shudder. "No...he...didn't do anything," I finally answer.

His thumb rubs circles over my wrist, exactly where my pulse is strumming at a rapid speed.

"Good," he whispers.

"Why did you do that?" A gush of cold wind sweeps past us. I withdraw my hand from his and wrap the thin shawl around my shoulders.

Heath stares at me but doesn't answer. He has this hard, cold look on his face that reflects how angry he is.

"Why are you even here?" I ask.

He frowns hard. "Because he doesn't deserve you."

"And you do?"

For a long moment, he just stares at me and then shakes his head. "No, I don't."

I step back from shock or hurt—I don't know exactly.

"So, I don't deserve anyone," I murmur, feeling awful.

Stepping forward, he places his index finger under my chin and tips back my face. "I don't deserve you, but I'm too selfish and obsessed with you to not become the person that you deserve."

*Oh my God.*

*Heath Travon wants me.*

My breath hitches.

I don't know what to do next.

Should I inhale or exhale?

He gets closer, and just like that he manages to suck all the air around us.

I've never felt like this with anyone. There has always been something about him. That first meeting changed everything. *He's* changed everything.

I trust him. The thought scares me, but my heart says it's okay for me to take the leap if it's *him* I'm falling into.

"Breathe, Rose. You need to breathe," he says softly.

"I'm...breathing," I pant.

A smile appears on his lips. "Not like this."

"Then...how?" I speak between quick, short breaths.

Lifting his hands, he cups my face and looks deep into my eyes. "Take a long, deep breath then slowly let it out."

Keeping my eyes locked on him, I do as he says.

"Good girl," he rasps.

My insides melt.

Then, he cups the back of my neck and slowly leans down as if allowing me time.

Anticipation and surprise curl my toes in a delicious manner.

"Wh-what are you doing?"

"I'm going to kiss you."

"R-right now?" I whisper.

"Right fucking now."

Before I can ask him more questions, his warm lips meet mine.

A gasp leaves my mouth, and I stiffen.

Pulling back, he leans his forehead against mine and breathes out, "What's wrong?"

"I've never been kissed before."

Moving his hand to my lower back, he pulls me flush against his body.

"You'll learn with me." With that, his lips are on mine again.

Sparks explode into fireworks that warm my body.

The butterflies in my stomach flutter around urging me to lean more toward his body. His tall, strong build presses against mine, and I feel like I can hold onto something as gravity begins to loosen its grip on me.

Only one thought crosses my mind. *Heath is kissing me.*

Once the initial shock dissolves, my lips start to move along his.

We find a rhythm.

Heath kisses exactly like himself. Confidently. Every stroke of his mouth brings me closer to the edge. Before I know it, I'm falling into him.

Pulling away, he lets me suck in the air, then attacks me again. This time he takes the lead with possessiveness as if he can't stay hungry any longer.

I can't either.

I want him.

His kiss is not at all the same as those I've read in books but laced with a passion that ignites every inch of me. There's sweetness, but also the primal affection that he wants me badly.

Heath bunches up the material of my dress to bring me closer to him.

*Wait. What are my hands doing?*

I realize they are limp against my sides.

*I'm such an idiot.*

Lifting them, I place them over his chest where I can feel his racing heart.

I smile into the kiss, realizing I'm not the only one feeling this way.

Heath tugs on my lower lip before backing up.

I open my eyes and find him already looking at me.

"We kissed."

"We fucking did."

A smile hangs on my lips. He leans down and pecks me which isn't what I wanted.

I want more from him.

My heart is racing too fast, and my head is spinning with thoughts.

We kissed. Twice. Thrice if you count that little, short kiss, too.

Happiness sinks in, just as a wrecking ball hits me with a memory.

*Whoever it is, stay away from him, or else you won't like the consequences.*

My smile drops.

An abyss of sadness grows in the pit of my stomach, swallowing every bit of emotion I was feeling a second ago.

"I..." I step back from him like he's fire and I'll burn. Only it's the other way around. He'll get burned if he gets closer to me. He'll get hurt because of me.

Heath frowns and reaches for me, but I flinch.

"Hope, what's wrong?"

"Everything," I whisper.

He frowns harder. "What do you mean?"

Shaking my head I start to back away from him. "I need to go."

"Wait. Talk to me!"

I run inside, lock the door, and lean my back against it. I place my hand on my stomach and try to contain the ball of anxiety that is a second away from rolling down and taking me with it.

Sometimes, we don't get what we want, no matter how much we want it. It's painful how much life is different from the fictional world.

I go to my room and curl up on my bed in a ball.

My body shakes with tremors as Dad's warning loops my brain on repeat.

That's how much he's ruined me. I've had my first kiss with the guy I like, and I can't even relish in the joy of it because he'll find him and hurt him.

In the middle of the chaos, I see that pair of blue eyes staring at me, and slowly the feeling of his lips on mine takes over.

My first kiss was perfect.

# 39

## HEATH

With a bang, my locker shuts, and I inhale a harsh breath.

"So, you punched her date and kissed her."

I roll my eyes. "Do you and Marie ever *not* fucking share everything?"

"We don't. Not because we can't keep a secret but because we love talking to each other."

"I can see that," I say, exasperated.

Here I thought what happened on Friday night would always be a secret, but I should have known. Hope confided in Marie and she in Sebastian. These two can't keep anything under cover. Since that night Sebastian has been on my ass about the matter. It was indeed a long fucking weekend.

He leans against my locker. "Why did you do that?"

"Why wouldn't I? The guy was a fucking tool."

Sebastian sighs heavily. "You intervened. That's not—"

I chuckle. "You're the one to talk Mr. We Are Only Friends."

Sebastian's face turns red. "Shut up."

"You wanted to be more than friends with Marie. I want the same with Rose."

He smirks. "You have a nickname for her. How cute."

Before I can reply to him, my eyes finally catch her—the person I've been waiting for the last ten fucking minutes.

*That kiss. Fuck.*

I've kissed girls before, but they don't matter. Hope is my first real kiss because everything about it was perfect. She's also the best kiss of my life, despite the fact I only got to kiss her twice—which is not fucking enough. I want more kisses. Thousands and millions of them.

Hope walks in through the doors in a soft blue sweater and jeans, looking beautiful. The sweater is loose on her skinny, tall figure, but the jeans are tight around her curves and long legs. Her hair is loose as it sits on the front in wavy curls—I can't wait to get my fingers lost in them—and her face is deep in concentration over a book. Like always she's not watching where she's going.

I'm about to clear her fucking path and glare at anyone who tries to trip or knock her but stop.

Marie greets her from behind and both of them grin, then share a hug. Together they walk to Hope's locker as Marie fires words at her. Hope opens the locker with a sweet smile that slips into a laugh.

I can't stop looking at her.

For the first time, my heart has climbed up to my throat and I can hardly breathe.

It's fucking unbelievable how much this girl affects me.

She must have felt my stare as she turns her head and looks straight at me.

My fucking heart flies right out of my body.

*Fuck, she's so beautiful and I really fucking like her.*

Her hand tightens around the book.

I'm about to go to her when she looks away from me and walks in the other direction with Marie.

Sebastian makes a disapproving noise. "Wasn't she supposed to walk *toward* you instead of *away* from you?"

I grind my teeth, angrily. "I don't know what's going on."

"Then ask her. I remember after our first kiss Marie walked straight up to me."

"I was there." I watched him dive his tongue down her throat like a hungry animal. He made out right in front of me. The sight still creeps me out.

He arches an eyebrow. "Did you tell her you like her?"

"I didn't get the chance. She ran inside."

"Fuck off, Heath."

"It wasn't my fault."

He gives me a pointed look. "Clearly."

"It wasn't."

"Maybe you used too much tongue."

"I did not—"

"See? I told you to have a little practice because now you've fucked up. You might have just shoved your tongue *too* deep."

"Trust me. Not deeper than you."

"Will you ever listen to me?"

"Never."

Sebastian scowls. "I'm just helping you."

"I know *how* to kiss."

"Sometimes people forget."

I give him an incredulous look. "What do you mean?"

He clears his throat. "What I'm saying is maybe something happened. Talk to her today and tell her how you feel."

"I don't think so."

"Why the hell not?" He gets in my face.

I run a hand through my hair, growing nervous and frustrated with the conversation. "Maybe I'm the only one who feels this way and she doesn't."

"She does," he protests.

Now it's my turn to arch an eyebrow. "How do you know that?"

Sebastian rubs his face. "Bless my soul I survived rehab, otherwise no one would help you."

"I'm sure your ghost would be there."

He nods in approval. "You're right. We're best friends for eternity."

"How do you know she feels the same way about me?"

"It's her—" The bell rings and Sebastian shakes his head in panic. "Oh shit. I have a class. I'll tell you later."

"Get your ass back here, Bash!"

He's already jogging away from me just to piss me off.

I check the library and infirmary, but Hope is nowhere to be found. Eventually, I go to the Math class knowing she'll be there.

The strangest thing happens. Hope skips the Math class.

Later, I wait for her at the cafeteria but she's not there as well. Marie is missing too, meaning they're together somewhere.

**Heath: Where's Hope?**

Marie leaves me on read which annoys the fuck out of me.

**Heath: Is she with you?**
**Heath: Will you just fucking tell me?**
**Heath: I need to talk to her.**
**Heath: Fine, don't tell me. Just let me know if she's okay or not.**
**Blondie: She's okay.**

I release a breath of relief that I didn't even know I was holding in. Since the girls are missing, it's only Sebastian and I like the old times. We talk about anything but Hope and the kiss. I prefer to steer clear of that topic until I've talked to her.

I'm pissed that she's ignoring me. She kissed me back which means she's into me.

Also, one kiss was all it took for her to turn me on. I've never been that hard in my life.

It took every bit of self-restraint to not kiss her until my lips went numb or I was drunk off her taste. I knew it would be too overwhelming for her and that's the last thing I wanted. Still, I stole a small kiss at the end just to savor her sweet taste for later.

I've kissed girls at the underground before. But nothing compared to the one I had with the pretty book nerd on Friday night. It was special in ways I can't understand or describe.

Her lips, her touch, and her taste are stitched on my skin.

Whenever I close my eyes I can imagine her. The touch of her lips still lingers on my own.

*She's marked me.*

Because she's all I can think about all the fucking time—and it's driving me nuts—Kelly had to repeat the same thing three times because I was zoned out thinking about Hope.

I'm so fucking down for this girl. I can feel it in my bones.

She thinks books are where you escape. She should take a tour of my mind.

She's the owner of my every fucking thought where I find escape.

*She's my escape.*

After a long fucking day, the school day ends. Surprisingly, I've been attending all my classes lately, and don't pick fights with anyone. I want to be good, someone who's more than just his bad reputation and cold attitude—for her.

The parking lot is filled with guys and girls, and some of them turn and look at me. Several groups of girls are checking me out with their seductive smiles.

Not. Fucking. Interested.

The only girl I'm interested in always has her head buried in a book while walking.

Sweeping my gaze on the property I search for her, but it's like she's disappeared.

Raging in frustration, I stride to my car to get away from here, when I see her leaning against it. A romance novel is in her hands and she's busy reading it.

Relief washes over me, but then hot white anger blinds me. "I've been looking for you all day."

Hope jostles in shock. Her fingers start fidgeting with the pages of the book—she's nervous.

"Why are you ignoring me?" I near her because I want to be close to her, but she steps back.

"I think we should stay away from each other."

I frown hard. "Are you fucking kidding me?"

Hope shakes her head and refuses to look at me. She's staring at my chest with a determined face.

"No, I'm not joking," she says.

"Look at me."

"I can't."

"Why not?"

"Because then I'll forget what I want to say."

I almost smile. "You'll forget?"

"Yes."

"That makes no fucking sense." I pause. "Look at me."

"Please, Heath." Her feeble voice pierces through the fog of my anger.

However, I stand my ground. "Will you just fucking talk to me for once? I'm getting tired of you ignoring me and not telling me stuff. It's fucking hard for me too, but I try. You don't even do that."

Her eyes brim with tears. "Because I can't!"

I take a step in her direction. This time she doesn't step back which is a fucking relief.

"Can't or won't?" I ask.

"I can't."

"Fucking bullshit."

A tear falls down her cheek and my anger slips away with it. Without thinking, I wipe it away and keep my thumb over her cheek.

She brushes away my hand and wipes away her tears. "I'm so sorry."

I sigh. "What are you fucking sorry about?"

"About everything."

"There's nothing for you to be sorry about."

"There is." Her lips quiver, and another wave of tears advances in her eyes.

I glare at her. "There fucking isn't."

She nods but the tears don't stop.

Which bothers me.

"Come here," I mutter.

She takes a step in my direction. It's all I need. *One step. I'll take care of the rest for you.*

I pull her to my chest. My arm locks around her waist and my chin rests over her head. Gently, I tuck her head over my chest. I realize just how perfectly she feels in my arms and against my body. As long as she is here, nothing will hurt her. I'll make sure of it.

With my other hand, I pry the novel out of her hands and put it over the roof of my car.

"Your heart is racing," she murmurs, but I hear her. I always hear her even when she doesn't tell me anything.

"It's because of you," I admit, tired of hiding my feelings for her or fighting them.

I'm fucking done.

Hope takes a shaky breath and her body trembles. "I thought we were friends—"

"Not anymore."

She looks up at me in shock. "Wh-what are you talking about?"

I bend my head to look deep into her light brown eyes which have become my favorite eyes in the world.

*When did this fucking happen?*

*I don't know and I don't care.*

I cup the side of her face and caress her cheek. That damn blush appears, and I get weak in my knees. "It means that I want to kiss you, touch you, and hold you *wherever* and *however* I want."

There I fucking said it.

Her eyes widen. "But—"

"I think about you all the time." I lean my forehead against hers "You're driving me over the edge of insanity, Rose."

"I am?" She croaks out, puzzled.

I can't help but smile. "I fucking swear."

"Oh."

"I've never felt like this for a girl before." I swallow hard. "I think I like you."

She stiffens in my arms, and the black in her eyes dilates crazily.

I rub circles on her lower back, and she starts to relax.

"Yo-you like me?"

My gaze drops to her lips and the urge to kiss her fills my mind. "Yes."

Her fingers clutch my T-shirt, and I feel her nails scraping my skin. Instantly my body tightens, and my skin turns warm.

Keeping her eyes locked on me, she lifts herself on her tiptoes and catches me completely off guard when she presses her lips against mine.

I stagger but gather myself. *She is kissing me.*

Moving my hand from her cheek to her neck I kiss her back. She's unsure and uneasy in her strokes, but I guide her and keep it slow for her.

I keep my hand glued to her waist, knowing damn well if I touch her anywhere else, she might freak out. When I squeeze her a little, she falls into me.

I sense her getting breathless, so I unlock our lips. She draws in a deep breath, and I smile.

"I like you, too," she says quickly.

"You do?"

In reply, I get her beautiful smile.

"Words. I need fucking words," I plead.

With a spark in her eyes, she inches closer to me. "I like you, Heath."

"Fuck!" I lean my forehead against hers.

A laugh bubbles out of her.

I listen to it, and then I have my lips on hers and we're kissing.

I can't get enough of her lips.

After a minute or so, we pull back and our breaths mingle in the tiny space between us.

"Hi." She smiles.

"Hi." I smile back.

*Yes, I'm fucking smiling.*

*Only for her.*

I know I've lost my mind. But it's fine, as long as it's *her* I'm losing my mind over.

Clearing my throat, I say, "You got some orders."

I give her my phone and she eagerly takes it.

Instead of a smile, she grimaces, and that tugs my heartstrings.

"I can't come tonight to fulfill these orders. Maybe tomorrow?"

Disappointment sinks in me like claws. "What's wrong?"

She chews her bottom lip, and all I want to do is kiss her again. "I need to be home," she mutters.

She's hiding something. I can see it in her eyes, but I let it go.

"I'll pick you up in the morning."

Her eyes go big. "You don't need to."

"I will."

"Heath—"

"Get inside." I open the car door for her and guide her inside. With a huff, she complies. I hand her the novel.

# 40

## HEATH

The crowd cheers and the mixed smell of sweat and alcohol fills the room.

Tonight's match is big because Lex Kent is fighting me. He's as deadly looking as his skills. With long hair, tattoos covering his arms, and a huge build, he is intimidating. He's the same height as me but has a few years over me.

Stepping into the ring, he eyes me with his calculating dark brown eyes. He stands tall and throws some punches around, trying to scare me off.

I heave a breath and get in a stance.

The match starts and he quickly attacks me. He moves like a wild animal, hungry for its prey. His hits are everywhere as he rains them down on me.

I dodge a few hits, but he manages to land some that hurt like hell.

With a glare, I step back and reciprocate his hits.

I throw a combination of a punch, jab, and an uppercut that's too fast for him to see.

As I predicted, he grows restless and careless, leaving his body in the open for me to attack.

With quick moves, I steal those spaces and land some powerful hits. I swing an uppercut, and he knocks down on the floor holding his head in his hands.

I return from the match covered in a few bruises and an aching body.

Ryan hasn't reached out to me again regarding Mr. White and his offer, which is like a deal with the devil. That man is dangerous and someone you don't want to fucking mess with.

When I said 'no' I had half expected his goons to chase me but turns out he's found a replacement. A good fucking thing. I would never work for him.

After a short drive, I get home, biting my cheek due to the bruise on my stomach. Even a little movement causes so much pain.

"Sir, are you okay?"

I close my eyes. *Fuck*. I can't go one day without Derek shadowing me.

"I'm fine. Go to sleep, old man." I throw the words over my shoulder as I climb the stairs.

"I'm not old. And I can see you're not fine, sir."

When he calls me 'sir' I want to bang my head against the wall.

"Leave me alone, Derek."

"Can't do, sir."

I turn around in annoyance. "I don't want you to meddle in my business. In fact, I don't want you anywhere close to me. My parents pay you, not me. So do me a favor and stay the fuck away from me. I don't need a parent."

Derek watches me with a cold expression, but I can see in his eyes that I've hit a spot. But I'm too enraged right now to give a damn.

"Your lip is bleeding. I can get you something."

I rub my forehead only to hiss when I scratch a gash.

Fucking great. More pain, exactly what I needed.

I take a cold shower and then treat my injuries.

I'm applying balm on my lip when my phone rings.

Thinking it's Sebastian who's calling to check up on me I answer. "I told you I'm fine. It's nothing I can't handle."

"So you do answer your phone."

I stiffen at the sound of the crisp, deep voice that's oddly similar to my own.

My father is on the line.

"What do you want?" I grind my molars at the inconvenience that he's got a hang of me.

"What are you doing out late, son?"

Bile rises to my throat at the word 'son.' I'll take any other title over it. Even 'asshole' has a better ring to it.

"So now you care about me?"

After a long moment he says, "I *do* care about you, Heath."

I can't hold my laugh. "Yeah, right."

He clears his throat. "Derek told me you were out late at night and returned home injured. What the fuck is going on?"

"It's none of your fucking business."

"It is my business." The sudden shift in his tone makes me straighten. He sounds as cold as ice.

So I retaliate in the same voice. I suppose some things do run in the blood. "Like Emery was, but you abandoned us. What happened to her is your fucking fault. So don't tell me I'm your business because I'm not."

I can hear the change in his breathing. He's mad, flaring with the twinge of my accusation.

"Are you doing drugs?" he asks sternly.

"I'm doing cigarettes. Alcohol is reserved for special nights."

"You're nothing but a spoiled kid, who doesn't deserve any of the kindness I've been showing to you. I'm going to freeze your credit cards—"

"I don't use them anyway."

"—then where do you get the money from?"

"None of your fucking business."

"Heath, I swear, if I learn if you're doing anything wrong I'll—"

"You will do nothing. We share blood, but nothing else. You have no ownership over me now that I'm eighteen so stay the fuck out of my business and stop calling me."

I switch off my phone.

The silence in my room is overtaken by my ragged breathing.

For fuck's sake.

I don't need my dad, or my mom, or anyone. I'm better off being alone. It's best that way.

Hope pops into my mind, I hang my head down. One person won't hurt. I can keep her and stay away from others. I can keep my best friends, too. They're good people. But others, fuck them.

Getting into bed, I try to regulate my breathing. It takes me a while to fully calm down. The adrenaline from the fight and the rage from the phone call still linger.

Rolling over to my right side, I find a book on my nightstand.

Stretching my arm out, I pick it up and analyze the cover. It's one of Hope's romance novels. The one she snatched from me when I was in her room and in return gave me a boner. I'm amazed how she didn't feel it—it's probably for the best.

Switching on the lamp, I open the book and skim through the pages. She's written her thoughts and emotions and also underlined her favorite quotes in a pencil. There's not a trace of pen on the paper which tells me she doesn't like using pen on her books.

I'm reading her annotations when my eyes spot the name 'Adrian Hayes.' I double-check just to make sure.

Anger consumes me, but so does curiosity.

Flipping to the first page of chapter one, I start reading the book just to know what's so special about him. Hope likes him *a lot*. Which I don't like one bit. Fictional or not, he's another guy that's not me. She's only supposed to like me.

One hour turns into three and then five, after that, I lose track of time.

The story has me captivated by its characters and plot line. Fuck, even Hope's annotations make it interesting.

I've never been interested in fiction books. It's not because I don't like them or they bore me, they're not just my thing.

When I was young, I liked playing soccer. Once I grew up, I moved toward exercise instead. I started working out when I was twelve. I liked running, lifting weights, and doing anything physical. Last year, I found boxing. It's something that brings me great comfort—it sounds strange, but it's true.

The books I occasionally read are nonfiction regarding entrepreneurship, business, and making money. That kind of knowledge fuels my mind and gives me the freedom to not live under the thumb of my father.

The people in his world expect me to carry on his company and legacy, for all I care it can turn to ash.

I have no interest in being his heir and acquiring the control of an empire. The power and money will make me invincible, though, if there's anything I've learned from his life, it's the people you love that matter.

No amount of money can let you buy your way in the past and steal moments with someone. No power can let you manipulate the laws of space and time and have your way. It's all in vain.

I'd rather be poor and spend time with the people I love than waste away my life gathering money.

I do want to be rich. I enjoy the privileges that come with money. But not at the expense of losing the handful of people I have in life.

Marie, Sebastian, and Hope, they're the only three people in my world now. Kelly too, since she's always been nice to me.

The first morning light breaks in through the windows and swallows the darkness in the room.

I sit up and stretch. I'm halfway through the book. So far it's too predictable, sweet, and cringey for my taste. There's too much love and shit in this book. Cute moments and sweet nothings.

Is that the kind of guy Hope wants?

I blow out a long breath. *I'm not that kind of guy. I'll never be.* I don't know the sweet words or the cute things.

So where do we go from here?

We've kissed and admitted that we like each other, but it feels like we've only reached the first mark of a long journey.

My lack of experience is regrettable because now I don't know what to do.

Should I kiss her every time I see her? *I did tell her that.*

Should I ask her on a date? *I've never taken a girl out on a date.*

Should I ask her to be my girlfriend? *Fuck. It's too soon. We've only reached first base.*

My head is a mesh of thoughts and questions. I feel overwhelmed.

However, at the thought of her, some weird shit happens in my stomach. *Strange.*

Rubbing my eyes, I lean back against the headboard. Folding an arm behind my head, I continue reading. This Adrian Hayes guy better give me some clues.

# 41

## HOPE

Dad hit me again.

I thought he wouldn't.

For some silly reason, I believed that perhaps he had a good time with Mom on their trip so he would let me off the hook. Turns out, he couldn't afford to pay the bill and got into a tussle with the waiter and then the manager kicked them out of the restaurant. In the end, Mom paid, and it angered him.

Yesterday, he cornered me the second I stepped inside. He recited the whole incident to me while he was drunk. He slapped me twice, bruised my wrists, and then pushed me so hard I hit the wall and hurt my left shoulder. He also called me names and said awful things.

I cried in my bed for half an hour and took a long shower only to hate myself. There are prominent marks on my pale skin. I can't hide them with anything, except maybe makeup. And then there's the pain shooting everywhere in my body.

I dreamt of getting away from here. So far away that he couldn't reach me or hurt me. When the morning came, and the light fell on my face I knew it was wishful thinking. How could I escape him?

School goes exceptionally slow. My shoulder hurts badly and I can't move it at all. When I try, a trail of hot lava spreads under my skin.

Marie is busy with a presentation and later she has an extra class for her elective computer science. So I barely see her.

Heath and I share Math, but he doesn't talk to me. However, his attention burns holes in my face. I know he knows something is up. Even Sebastian suspects something.

I'm walking down the hallway with him when someone knocks into me. I wince and hide it by biting on my lip real hard.

"Are you okay?" Sebastian watches me with his curious green eyes that feel like they can see through me. Just like his best friend.

"I'm fine," I say weakly.

Sebastian doesn't believe me. His gaze falls to my shoulder that I'm holding. "Despite the fact that we don't talk too much, you can always talk to me. Anyone who's Marie's best friend is my best friend."

"I'm fine, Sebastian," I repeat, hoping he'll believe me.

With a smile he says, "No wonder he likes you. You two are the same."

A deep blush rises to my cheeks.

"C'mon, I'll walk you to your next class."

Later in the day, I try to get Tylenol from nurse Anna. But she's absent, and the infirmary is locked. Just my luck in play as usual.

By the end of the last class, all I want to do is get home because I'm in too much pain.

When the bell rings I'm the first to get up. Collecting my things I rush out and make a quick spot at my locker to put away all my heavy textbooks.

I step out of the school when a familiar black car pulls up in front of me.

Heath rolls down the window. He looks striking in a black shirt and jeans—his usual attire. I never get tired of how handsome he looks in it even if he wears it every single day.

Knowing he won't take no for an answer, I walk over to the passenger side.

He drives us to a drive-thru and orders food for me. At this point, I don't even fight him over it. It's no use. He does what he wants.

The AC is working efficiently but sweat collects on the back of my neck. I shouldn't be feeling hot in the October weather.

I squirm uncomfortably, having no idea what's happening to me.

Black dots appear in my vision and my head starts spinning like a dice on a board.

*What is wrong with me?*

I inhale a deep breath, but no air enters me.

*What is wrong with me?*

Nausea builds up in my throat and I hold the dashboard. I cup my mouth to keep it inside. It disgusts me but I can't puke in Heath's car. He keeps his car neat. He'll kill me if I don't hold it in.

"What's wrong?"

I hear him speak. It's like a whisper over my tumultuous state.

I want to reply but it might result in a vomit. I'm scared of opening my mouth.

A gut-wrenching cramp pumps my stomach. I seize it inside with everything I've got.

*What is wrong with me?*

I keep asking myself that question, but no answer comes to me.

I was feeling just fine five minutes ago, then suddenly my body started acting up.

Reaching for the handle, I push the door open and stumble outside.

Frantically I search for a trash can that is nowhere in sight.

*No!*

*I can't puke in the middle of a parking lot.*

*Oh my God.*

Heath comes into my view and frowns hard. "Will you tell me what's going—"

An agonizing wave hits my guts. I can't help but turn my head and puke on the asphalt.

Another wave hits me, and I empty my guts out.

*Invisibility cloak better reach me now.*

*Wherever you are in the world, come to me.*

Vomiting is humiliating, especially in front of the guy you really like.

I hug my stomach to contain the rest, but my body doesn't get the notion. It's decided to make Heath never kiss me again.

*Oh my God.*

*What if he never kisses me again?*

"It's okay. You're okay." Heath gathers my hair and rubs my back in a gentle manner. His touch is warm and light as if he's afraid to hurt me.

*You can never hurt me.* I want to tell him.

Once I'm done, I wipe my mouth with the back of my sleeve feeling every bit disappointed that I'm not like Harry in any way. The invisible cloak would've saved me from a major scene of embarrassment today.

On shaky feet, I stand but quickly lose my balance. Before I can fall, Heath holds me against him.

"I got you," he murmurs in my hair.

"I'm fine, really," I whisper and lean into him as exhaustion takes over me.

*Seriously. What is wrong with me?*

I feel his lips against my temple. "Can you walk?"

"I think so."

"Not fucking good enough."

In the next second, he lifts me in his arms as if I weigh nothing and holds me close to him. Without thinking much, I lean my head against his shoulder and close my eyes.

Exhaustion lures me in like a spell and I fall under its magic.

I'm tired. I'm so very tired. Not just physically. My mind is empty right now, and when it's not, there's a storm of thoughts in there. So many voices speak. I can't escape them. I can't mute them. I can't do anything.

I'm losing a battle. One I can't see but only hear.

Heath sets me down in the car and bends over me with eyes flaming with anger and concern.

"I'm going to get you something to drink," he says.

"Water. I need water," I tell him, hoping he can hear me.

"Okay." With that, he shuts the door and leaves.

I lean my head against the seat and look out. The sight of my pool of vomit disgusts me.

*Oh my God. I can't believe I did that.*

The worst part is that Heath saw it. He saw all of it. I believe there's nothing more embarrassing that's left to be seen by him. He's seen me cry, sob, have a panic attack, and now puke.

I want to dig a big hole, throw myself in it, and never climb out. This time even the invisibility cloak can't save me. I just want to disappear.

*Oh my. I'm so incredibly embarrassed.*

The same mouth he's kissed just retched up in a parking lot. I bet he's sworn to never kiss me again.

With a groan, I cup my face in my hands.

I loved our kiss. It was the only good thing in my life. Now, it won't happen again.

*Why did I have to ruin it all?*

Well, I'm not sure what really happened.

One minute I was okay, the next minute I was nauseous.

Heath appears with two bags. He opens one and gives me a water bottle.

I quickly take it from him and drink a quarter of it. The cold water goes down my throat and washes off the remnants of the mess I threw up.

"How do you feel?" he asks.

I look over and find him watching me.

The streaks of warm orange rays from the setting sun, lovingly kiss his face. The hue of blue resembles the waves of a calm ocean touched by the last light of the sunset. Under that soft glow, his features emerge more strikingly. The perfect cut of his face, the sharp jawline, the strong nose, and the contours of his cheekbones. Every curve and edge look sharpened.

He smiles. "Are you lost in my eyes again?" he asks, in a raspy, deep voice.

"I...I..." No words come to my mind.

A chuckle breaks out of him and when he sobers up, his eyes stare at me so softly. Like all the tenderness and gentleness has collected in his eyes just for me.

Lifting his arm, he tucks my hair behind my ear, then cups the side of my face. "I asked, how are you feeling?"

"I'm better." Somehow, I manage to say, even though all I can think about is his hand cupping my cheek.

"You promise?" His thumb caresses my cheek, and his eyes never look away from me.

Has he always ever looked this much at me?

*Definitely not.*

Ever since we first kissed, he looks at me with these long stares that don't end, even when I look away. It's like his eyes love me or something.

It's probably something, not love obviously. I mean—

My nose twitches when I feel a kiss there.

I startle in shock and find Heath very close to my face.

"What are you cooking in that pretty little head of yours?"

"I...You..." That's all I can utter.

"What about us?" He looks amused.

My cheeks burn in embarrassment. Of course, I can't tell him what I was thinking.

"Nothing," I whisper.

"Tell me. I want to know what you were thinking about us."

"I'm sorry," I say instead.

That word changes his expression, and he backs up.

Heath narrows his eyes on me with a hint of anger in them. "What the fuck are you sorry about?"

"For puking and causing you all this trouble."

With a sigh, he looks away. "What you should be sorry about is not telling me what's going on. Seriously! What was that? Were you *that* sick the whole day at school? Or is there something else?"

He asks too many personal questions—inching closer to scraping off the last layer that's holding all my secrets.

"I don't know," I cry out, feeling confused and vulnerable all at once.

I want to talk about what happened yesterday, but I can't. Knowing Heath, he will confront Dad, and a fight will start between them. Possibly him getting hurt worse than at that illegal place he fights at.

I can't let anything happen to him.

I want to protect him.

Heath is like my favorite book out of the five hundred and ten books I've read so far.

He's the best thing that has happened to me.

I'm scared of Dad hitting me, but I'm terrified of losing Heath.

I've always wondered why people in books keep a secret when they can simply tell the other person. Now that I'm in the same position I understand why the big reveal doesn't happen until the last few chapters. It's because, like them, I don't want things to change between us. It's going good so far. Even when my secret looms over us like an evil eye.

"You don't trust me," he says harshly.

"That's not true."

I trust him, but not enough to talk about my family.

He arches an eyebrow "Isn't it? You hide things from me—"

"I don't know about your family. You never talk about them."

Heath's jaw flexes in response. I've hit the mark with those words. He knows I'm right, just as I am.

With a scoff, he replies, "I don't talk about them because I don't want to."

I gulp hard. The air is dense between us due to tension.

"And I don't talk because I can't."

"You keep saying that Hope. I'm fucking sick of it."

I look at him with tears burning my eyes. "I'm sick of it too. But sometimes you have to risk something to keep someone."

Heath stares at me for what feels like hours when in reality it's only been minutes.

I watch the sun set in his eyes and I watch the dusk arrive the same.

I could look away. I should. But I don't. Because in his eyes I find all I've been searching for.

A shift in air happens when he moves forward and cups the side of my neck. Gently, he pulls me to him. I go without a struggle. Pressing his forehead against mine he says, "You think I don't see the marks on you, but I do."

His hand takes mine, and he pushes up my sleeve revealing the bruises. "I know your arm hurts. I've been watching you all day. I only wished you'd tell me about it yourself."

"It hurts a lot."

His eyes soften, the anger from earlier dissipating a little. "Is there a bruise there?"

I nod.

"Did you take medicine?"

I shake my head.

"What the fuck am I supposed to do with you?"

"Don't leave me." I pause. "I don't want to lose you. *Not you.*"

"I *won't* leave you. All I ever really think about since I've met you is *you*, Rose. I think about you all the fucking time. It doesn't matter if we're talking or not, you are there. Silence in my alone moments, or chaos in my mental breakdowns. In the middle of it all, you are there. You are always there."

"You are there too, in my chaos and silence. You're always there. Right in the middle of it."

His expressions turn serious. "You can trust me with anything. *Anything.* Whatever's going on that's causing you pain, I'll end it. I promise you. Just tell me. Talk to me."

"He's stronger than you," I whisper.

Realization sinks in until it's too late. I just told Heath. I gave him a hint.

I search his eyes and sure enough he's trying to piece it together.

His lips thin. "It's a man."

I don't speak a word.

He closes his eyes. "Fuck! I knew it. I knew there was someone."

"Heath, please let it go. I'll be fine—"

He turns to me with a dark look. "Fine? Hope, he's leaving fucking marks on you. Do you know how violent he must be—"

"I *know* how violent he is," I burst out.

My chest burns with heat, but I continue, "He hurts me. He hits me. Pushes me. Slaps me. Chokes me. He does so much to me, so believe me I know. I know how violent he is. You don't have to say it. It hurts a hundred times more when you say it."

He breathes heavily. "Tell me who he is, and I'll swear I'll bury him six feet under. You won't ever have to be afraid of him."

I hate how much it hurts when I talk about that monster. He isn't a human to me anymore.

My phone buzzes with a phone call. I retrieve it and see Mom's name.

I let it ring until it gets sent to voicemail.

A minute later, a message pops up on the screen.

**Mom: Hope, where are you? I told you there would be a family dinner tonight. Why aren't you here?**

**Mom: Get home right now.**

**Mom: Your dad and I are waiting.**

I switch off my phone with trembling hands.

Right. The dinner. It's why I vomited earlier.

A stare burns the side of my face. I know Heath is watching me closely. I bet he can read my emotions right off of my face as I do with books.

The panic starts to bubble under the surface, but I diminish it. I can't have another breakdown after having one just minutes ago.

I clean my face and sit up straight. "I need to go home."

"Home? Is that where he is?" He pauses. "You told me you live alone with your mother."

*He's back.* Two words. Certainly, they shouldn't be this difficult to speak—they are.

"I..." Silence follows.

Heath stares at me with patience. "Tell me what's going on? Who is this man that hurts you? Is this a man your mother is seeing or something? Give me something, Hope."

My phone buzzes again and I see another text from Mom.

Turning to him I say, "I need to go home. Now. Please."

He looks torn between interrogating me or taking me home. I understand the dilemma since I'm stuck in one myself. I want to tell him everything but protect him too.

Starting the car, he gives me a hard look that says *I don't want you to fucking go.*

"Will you be okay?"

I could lie to him—I *should* lie to him. But he's the last person I want to lie to anymore.

"I think I will be. I'm here, aren't I?" I give him an encouraging smile, wishing it raises his spirits.

It has no effect on him. If anything, he looks more infuriated.

"What if—" he bites his lip and closes his eyes.

*What if you aren't?* He's thinking about Emery. The sibling that he loved and cherished, then lost.

For once it's me who cups his cheek. His eyes shoot open and gaze at me with a magnitude of sorrow and grief—it almost buries me.

"I will be fine. I promise you," I assure him with a bright smile.

His eyes drop to my lips then return back to my eyes. He scowls. "That's what I'm fucking afraid of. You being *fine.*"

"Don't worry about me," I tell him.

He narrows his eyes on me. "I will *always* worry about you. It's not something I can just fucking stop. I don't think there's a stop button in my system."

I nod slowly.

His tone softens as he says, "I care about you a lot, more than the fucking limit."

"I care about you, too."

He gulps hard as if it physically hurts him. "If anything happens, call me. I will take you away from that house. I will come for you, no matter the time or day. I will come for you. You just fucking call me and I'll be there. You understand?"

Tears well up in my eyes. *You just fucking call me and I'll be there.*

Those words move my heart with an indescribable emotion. "You will come for me."

"Always."

Heath drives slowly as if prolonging the little time so I can't get home. I'm sure he's thinking about everything that I said to him. I gave him all the clues except for one.

I should feel better now that Heath knows a little, but all I seem to experience is anxiety.

I'm worried for him.

I can only wish he doesn't look into things deeply. If he does, I know it's a matter of time before he unravels the rest of it. I'm unprepared for that moment. I don't know what I'll say or do. What I do know is that everything we've built will splinter into pieces and my heart will be one of them.

# 42

## HOPE

There is no family dinner because Dad isn't home. Mom tricked me.

We sit in the kitchen, eating the meal she made for the three of us but there's only the two of us.

"I don't know why he isn't home. He promised me he would be."

I stay quiet, thanking my luck. I want to stay as far away as I can from him.

"Why do you think he isn't home?" She directs the question at me as if I know where he is. What she doesn't know is we don't talk at all. Ever since he's moved back in we haven't had a conversation that didn't end with him hitting me.

"I don't know." I shrug and devour the food. It's delicious and I'm hungry—after I puked my guts out hours ago.

To avoid him, I've been skipping meals. All I eat are the remainder of my snacks—which aren't a lot. I had a pack of chips from months ago that I ate for a week. It finished a few nights ago. Now I have nothing in my room. When I took a shower this morning, I saw how much weight I'd lost. I'm all bones now. Skinnier and more tired than I've ever been in life. When I scrub myself, I can count my ribs and feel my hip bones. There's not much meat on me.

I'm deteriorating, and the worst part is that Mom can't see it. She's fixated on him.

All the money I've earned from my little business, I've been saving it. I don't spend a single penny because I want to buy myself books or a nice phone. Who am I kidding? It'll be books.

Mom gives me a warm smile. "Don't worry. We'll have a family meal together one evening."

It takes every bit of my self-restraint to *not* let my true emotions show.

When my silence extends, she says, "I saw that guy who dropped you off. It's the same guy. Does he do that a lot?" Her curious eyes set on me.

This time Heath parked the car two houses down, instead of ten. Big mistake.

"Sometimes," I murmur.

Her gaze turns calculating. "How often?"

"A few times."

"Does he live nearby?"

"No."

Mom looks quite keen on knowing about him. "What's his name? Where does he live?"

These are all the questions I want to avoid. I don't want to tell her about Heath. There might be a chance she mentions him to Dad.

I look into her serious gray eyes. "He's just a friend, Mom."

*Wrong move. I should've been careful with my words.*

Mom sits upright. "He's a boy. A young teenage boy. They *always* want something, Hope."

"He's not like that." I know it's not true. Heath doesn't want anything from me. I don't have anything to offer to him, anyway. All I have, he's got much more and better. For heaven's sake, he lives in a mansion and is so rich.

Doubt seeps in. He has everything, so why does he want me?

*I think about you all the damn time.*

I wonder why he thinks about me at all. I've got nothing but complications and troubles in my life.

Mom smirks. "You really are stupid, honey."

The insult claws my heart in the worst way possible. "I'm not. We're just good friends."

"Your father and I were good friends."

I hold my mouth to not scowl or utter a snide remark.

"Now we're here," she says with a bright smile,

I take a bite to not say anything but Mom's adamant to talk about Heath. "That boy is like every other hormonal guy who is looking for girls like you to prey on."

Anger laces my words as I glare at her. "I told you, it's not like that."

Mom doesn't take heed. "Be honest. Has he touched you?"

He has, but not the way she thinks.

He's touched me to hold me. He's touched me to wipe away my tears. He's touched me to comfort me. He's touched me to make me feel safe. He's touched me to give me a perfect kiss that I've only read about in books.

"No," I lie.

The way her lips quirk up in reply, tells me she doesn't believe me one bit.

"Well, that's interesting. I guess I'll tell your dad to have a chat with him."

I jump out of my chair in shock. Blood rushes through my veins, and the loud drum of my heartbeats roars in my ears.

I shiver at the idea of him knowing about Heath, and what he'll do to me.

"I told you we're just friends, Mom," I say.

She rolls her eyes. "I wasn't born yesterday. I know what happens when a guy drives a girl home."

"It's not like that."

"Your father used to—"

"He's not Dad."

Mom glares at me. "And he won't be because I won't let him. When Alex comes home, I'm discussing this with him. You can't be distracted."

"No! Please don't tell him. *Please*," I beg her.

A sick smile plays on her lips, and she's never looked more evil before.

I'm half convinced I'm hallucinating.

Right now, she looks far away from the sweet, friendly mother I grew up with, and closer to a manipulative, clever woman.

She hums. "That boy and you are having sex."

I blanch. "No! I swear he's not touched me like that."

My hands turn clammy with how nervous I am. The wetness makes me feel disgusted. I rub them over my jeans, but they sweat all over again.

I need to convince her, somehow. "We're not having sex. I wouldn't do that. I'm young and I want to go to med school. I would never jeopardize my future like that. You know me."

I speak all that's expected of me rather than what's inside my heart. This is the only way to get myself off the hook.

"Like hell you will ruin your future. I will make sure you won't." Her gray eyes pierce through the air like an arrow, hitting me in the chest.

My lips tremble. "Please don't tell him. He's only a friend."

Mom finishes her meal. She takes her time with every little movement, driving me frantic.

Standing up, she collects the dishes and puts them in the sink.

I stand still, waiting for her to tell me that she won't tell her husband. She and I both know, it won't end well; what she doesn't know is it won't end well for me.

Leaning against the sink, she folds her arms and studies me. "I won't tell your dad if you promise me you'll stop seeing him."

I can hear it. The sound of my heart breaking into pieces.

"I can't do that."

Mom rolls her eyes as if I'm being dramatic and these aren't my true feelings.

She doesn't care about me. Not anymore.

Like him, she's changed.

"Trust me you'll find a better guy than him. One I'll find one for you. For now, you need to focus on your studies."

Heath *is* that better guy.

"I'm getting good grades," I argue.

Mom looks displeased. "That can fall if you hang out with a guy like him."

"He's got nothing to do with it," I almost scream.

Mom glares at me. "Don't take that tone with me, Hope."

I shake my head. "Just don't tell Dad. I will keep my distance from him. He'll get mad at me, Mom. It scares me."

Mom gives me a long look. "Fine. I won't tell Alex. But you start distancing yourself from that boy. And for fuck's sake don't let him drive you home. One day it won't be me who sees him dropping you off."

"Okay."

I don't know what she sees in my eyes, but her eyes soften, and for a second I see love flashing through them. She reminds me of the good days when we were close. Now we're only drifting apart like two ships moving in opposite directions.

"Finish your dinner and then go up to study."

I agree eagerly.

Mom watches me. I feel stupid for letting her see how relieved I am that she won't tell him. She can take advantage of the weakness.

I can only hope she doesn't.

# 43

---

## HEATH

Why Marie and I are best friends is beyond me.

We are opposites in every fucking way. I knew it the first time I met her. She is too fucking bright for my taste. From her looks to her accessories and clothes, and her smile and energy. She's a walking sunshine throwing light into everyone's life, doesn't matter if you're a stranger or someone she knows.

I've always wondered why Sebastian loves her. She talks *too much*. Jumps *too much*. Gets excited *too much*. Smiles *too much*. Everything about her is *too much*. Nothing is mundane or bland when it comes to her.

Marie is like a paintbrush made of rainbow. She strokes it across your canvas and turns you into shades of colors. Perhaps, that's why Sebastian loves her. She paints him in colors he didn't know existed.

Marie presses a pink, short dress to her body and looks at me. "Does this look good?"

I give her a nod so we can get it over with.

She rolls her eyes. "Heath, you're supposed to give me a little more than that."

I scowl. "It looks fine."

Marie groans like a toddler. "*Fine* is not the word I'm aiming for."

With a bored expression, I lean against the nearest wall. "That's all you'll get from me, Blondie."

She pauses, thinks for a moment, then says, "Try giving me a synonym."

I roll my eyes. "I only have five minutes—"

"It's for Hope."

Just like that, she has my undivided attention, and she relishes it.

Her hazel eyes brighten up in delight. "Aww. That's so cute. You like her."

I glare at her. Marie knows how to get on my nerves. Besides, I feel like this is just the beginning. There's an eternity of teasing waiting for me from both Sebastian and Marie. They won't ever shut up about my first crush *and* the first girl I ever wanted.

For fuck's sake.

Pushing those thoughts away, I ask her, "Why are we getting a dress for her?"

Marie stares at me deadpan. "Are you serious?"

I arch an eyebrow.

She seems annoyed that I don't know the reason. I mean, Christmas isn't around the corner. Also, it's not Hope's birthday. It's in November.

Marie sighs. "I'm buying this for the fair. We're all going."

I fold my arms over my chest and fix her with a serious look. "I thought you wouldn't go this year."

At once, sadness soaks her bright light, and her face tightens in melancholy.

I hate myself for reminding her of that night.

What happened that night is what pushed Sebastian to go to rehab, he put the one person he loved in danger because of his mental issues and addiction. Marie also decided to join therapy and get better. It was an unfortunate event, but it resulted in both of them getting the help they desperately needed.

"I don't want to. Well... maybe you're right. I shouldn't go. It's stupid."

I feel like a dick for making her feel sad. It's never my intention to hurt her in any way. Yes, we bicker like siblings all the time, but I fucking care about her. I never want anything to hurt her, especially after I've seen her struggles and listened to her cry. Her sadness brings me pain.

She starts putting back the dresses on the rack when I approach her. I stop her by holding her wrist

"It's not fucking stupid," I say softly.

She shakes her head. "You're always right. After that night I shouldn't bother with going out this year. It's still too fresh—"

"And in the past. Let it fucking stay that way. New year means—"

"New memories." She smiles. "You told me that."

"Did I?"

"Yes, you did. You were drunk when you found me crying and talking depressing shit. I remember you saying that."

I sigh. "I don't think—"

Marie swats my arm. "You did."

"Sebastian is rubbing off on you."

She turns pink and a smile etches onto her face. "I mean—"

"Just forget I fucking said that," I grumble.

A laugh bubbles out of her, and her sunshine energy is back in full force, which makes me happy. I want her to always stay like this. Sadness doesn't suit her.

I cock my head toward the dresses. "Now let's find a dress, shall we?"

She grins and starts walking down the aisle. "Of course. We're buying it for *your* girl after all."

I follow her.

I'll kill Sebastian for bailing on me—because he had to work at the cafe—and forcing me to go shopping with Marie. Again.

I hate shopping. And shopping with Marie is unbearable. She drags me to hundreds of stores only to return empty-handed and indecisive. Also, I look like a complete idiot carrying her bags and following her.

"Heath, look at this." Marie shows me a blue dress. It's simple with a modest neckline and doesn't look that short. All I can imagine is Hope wearing it and making me lose my mind more than I already have.

"Get it," I demand.

Marie assesses it critically. "It's a local fair, not a club night. We should keep moving."

I snatch the dress and buy it, while she watches me with a mischievous grin. When I return with the bag I say, "What?"

Marie sighs dreamily with a grin and fans her face with her hand. "Ah! I love phase one."

I frown hard. "What's phase one?"

"Falling in love."

"I'm not falling in love. I only *like* her."

"We'll see."

I'm half-tempted to swing the shopping bag in her face.

After ten minutes, we walk out of the shop. "Can we leave now?"

Marie gives me an exasperated look. "Of course not. We've not bought *my* outfit yet."

"You have plenty of—"

"Come on. We're running late."

After two hours we've got everything she needs. Marie hides the bags, so I have no idea what they're going to wear to the fair. She asked me to wait outside while she bought all the stuff.

I don't give two flying fucks what Marie wears, but I give all the fucks what Hope wears.

The element of surprise is killing me. I try to peek inside the bags, but Marie is so strong and attentive that she doesn't even let me touch them. She's ready for my every move.

Sebastian is a dick for teaching her everything. I lose every battle against the two of them because they're my best friends and know me too fucking well.

I drive her home and carry her bags inside with her. She's smart enough to not hand me the ones that contain stuff she bought for Hope. And she's not open to any bribe I'm willing to offer to her.

I set down the bags in the living room and glare at her. "Just so you know, you're not a good friend."

Marie smirks evilly as she sits on the sofa. "You'll eat your words when you see Hope."

"I won't." *I will.*

Whatever she wears, I know she'll take my breath away. I'll be beside her all night to keep the other guys away from her and if anyone whistles or catcalls at her, I'll punch them in the fucking face.

"Challenge accepted," Marie says confidently.

I smirk. "Be prepared to lose, Blondie."

"I never lose."

"That's not decided."

"It is."

"It isn't."

"It is."

"It isn't."

Fuck it. She can win.

Leaning my head back, I think about what Hope told me a few days ago. She gave me a hint. A man is hurting her, but she won't tell me *who*. My only assurance is that she said she'd call me if something happens. I should trust her to ask for my help, but I don't. She's never one to ask for help even when she's suffering.

*Like me.*

We both like to endure our struggles on our own, not wanting to bother the people around us.

I glance at Marie who's drinking pumpkin spiced latte, her favorite seasonal drink of Autumn. For every season she has a specific drink that she orders. A smile is on her face, and she looks happy and excited—her usual self. I can't fathom telling her about Hope and worrying her. She'll march down to her house and demand it to make it right for her. Since she was bullied, she knows what physical and emotional abuse can do to someone.

My fists curl in anger and I want to wrap Hope in my arms and just fucking protect her.

Knowing Marie, she'll move heavens and earth to be there for her. I'm surprised that she hasn't figured it out already. I mean Hope is shit at lying.

Marie catches me staring at her. "What are you frowning about?"

"I wonder how you drink that obnoxious fucking drink."

"It's delicious."

"And fucking sweet."

"That too." She shrugs nonchalantly.

Standing up, I grab my car keys and turn to her. "I'm gonna leave now."

Marie quickly comes up to me and gives me a short hug. She frees herself before I can do it for her.

Thanks for fuck's sake.

The only hugs I can tolerate are those I get from the pretty book nerd. She can steal as many as she wants, I don't mind at all. With everyone else, I want to detach myself as quickly as possible.

"See you at the fair."

I stride into the foyer, and she follows me like a younger sibling.

"I'm not going," I tell her. A fair is not my scene.

"Hope will be there."

*I'm going.*

# 44

## HOPE

It's Wednesday and I'm sitting in the loud cafeteria waiting for my friends. In two months these three people have made me someone who likes to sit in a boisterous room rather than in a quiet nook of a library—I mean I still like that, but if I have to choose, I'll choose them.

Marie barrels to our table in excitement with a grinning Sebastian following her, his eyes fixed on her and filled with love.

"We're here," she announces as she puts down the bags of takeout food and sits across from me.

"You were quick," I say.

"I placed my order during the class." She purses her lips in thinking. "I should do it more often. It saves time."

"Totally."

"I wanted to talk about something."

"Yeah, sure." I put aside my novel and wait for her to open the bags.

I missed breakfast because my parents were in the kitchen, and I had no desire to get in their way if I could avoid it.

Marie opens the bag as if she can read my mind. I start with fries and almost smile at finally finding something to eat.

Sebastian presses a kiss to her forehead and thanks her when she gives him his bucket of chicken tenders. It reminds me of Heath. He loves them too.

Marie turns to me, blushing hard. "What was I saying?"

"You were going to tell me." I add, "You looked excited."

"I can't remember." She taps her head hard and turns to Sebastian. "Your kiss just made me forget it."

He chuckles. "Now you know how *I* feel."

She frowns. "What do you mean?"

Smiling softly, he says, "When you kiss me, I forget everything else. Only *you* exist in my mind."

With a grin, she nods. "That's exactly what's happening to me right now."

"I love you, my silly girl."

"I love you too, my brainwasher boy."

"You guys are like a book couple," I end up saying because they're so cute.

Marie's grin widens. "Thanks. We try really hard."

Laughter escapes me and soon the three of us are in a fit. A lot of heads turn in our direction with curious eyes and whispers that haven't gone away, even though it's been months since we've been hanging out. Sebastian and Heath attract the attention of everyone—the girls—and Marie and I are the invisible ones which is fine by both of us.

"Have you ever been to the fair?" Marie asks.

I know about the annual fair that takes place in October and is a big event. There are rides, food, drinks, and a variety of stalls selling handmade and local things to the tourists and the newcomers who specifically come to attend it.

The fair is a blast and the talk of Bellmare until Christmas. Everyone attends it no matter what.

I've never attended it. I'm not an enthusiast of places that are crowded and noisy. It isn't my scene.

"No."

Marie looks stunned. "Tell me you're kidding."

I shake my head.

Of course, it's odd that I haven't been to an event that's so famous, but I have my reasons. I chose to not go. But now, after meeting these people, I want to go.

I feel him before I see him.

My heart starts racing and blood rushes to my cheeks, even before the chair next to me scrapes against the floor drawing the attention of a lot of people around us.

*Don't look at me, people.*

*I'm not here.*

When I check, sure enough, girls and guys are gazing at the two of us while talking to their friends. I wonder what they're saying. Scratch that. I'm anxious about what they're saying about us—me.

Heath sits next to me and just like that, he's the only one I can focus on.

I tilt my head to meet his steady stare that's now perfectly aligned with mine.

"Hi," he says in a deep voice.

My throat goes dry, and my head goes blank.

*What's the word for greeting?*

"Hi," I reply in a scratchy voice that isn't cool at all but makes his lips quirk up in amusement.

We stare at each other and the entire world fades away. Only he and I exist.

Marie snaps her fingers between us. "Love birds focus!"

Blush rises to my neck.

Clearing my throat, I look away from him, but he doesn't as if he physically can't.

"I can't believe you haven't been to the fair. Everyone attends it."

I resume playing with my hands underneath the table, feeling embarrassed that I haven't been there, not even once.

"Some just don't fucking attend, Blondie," Heath counters back in a stern voice.

Something passes between them. Then Marie turns to me. "You can attend with us this year."

My breath hitches. "Are you sure?"

She beams. "Of course. I'd pick you up from your house so we can get ready at my place."

*Oh no. Not my house.*

I don't want Marie anywhere near my dad. Even if the driveway is a good several feet away from the front porch. There's a chance he'll pounce on her because of me for some delusional reason. I can't let that happen.

"I'll go to your place," I say instead.

"Or we can get ready at Heath's place. He lives near me." Marie bats her eyelashes at Heath who shoots her a glare.

"My house is not a fucking salon," he grumbles.

"It'll be easier for Hope. She knows the route to your house."

Heath looks down at me. "Will you be able to get there, or do I have to pick you up?"

"I'll get there."

"I'll pick you up."

When I open my mouth to fight him, he narrows his eyes.

Marie breaks the tension. "It's decided then. We'll all meet at Heath's house and then drive to the fair together."

"Is anyone left? Or maybe we should bring the whole fucking town to my place," Heath says sarcastically.

Marie snaps her fingers. "That's a great idea."

Heath rolls his eyes. "It's fucking not."

"You'll have fun," Sebastian assures me, then turns to Marie. Both of them talk in quiet voices.

"You aren't eating," Heath points out.

Well, I can't exactly tell him that I ran out of fries and it's the only thing I'm craving right now.

"I'm not hungry."

Heath looks irritated but rummages through the bags, takes out the fries, and hands them to me. "Eat."

"You didn't have to."

"If you are not going to feed yourself, then I will."

"You aren't serious."

His arm rests on the back of my chair, and he leans in closer. "I'm always serious when it comes to you."

I turn my head away and a strand of my hair comes to the front, concealing me from his view.

*Perfect timing hair strand. Hide me.*

The way Heath looks at me with sheer concentration makes my heart beat a thousand miles per minute and my mind forgets how sentences and words are made. I swear I forget the English language.

He breaks my thoughts by holding that hair strand and gently tucks it behind my ear. His warm fingers slide over the side of my neck like silk mixed with gravel because of the calluses he's got from fighting. It's a strange combination of soft and rough, yet in the perfect proportion.

Bending down to my ear, he speaks in a low, dark voice. "I see you."

My pulse pounds loudly in my ears.

If he presses his skin against mine, he'll be able to feel the beats of my erratic heart or how warm I am despite the cold temperature in the room.

After a long moment, he moves away, and I want to protest. As much as his closeness unsettles me, I want it because it's the good kind. I'm not afraid of him because he'll hurt me, but what he might make me feel if we cross the line. I'm nervous but excited too because I trust him. I trust him with myself.

Heath puts a book on my lap. I look closely and realize it's my copy.

"How do you have it?" I pick it up and flip through the pages. I see annotations that are in a different handwriting *and* in pencil—those are his thoughts.

"You left it in my room."

When I see remarks on one of the spicy scenes, I want to dig my own grave and bury myself in it.

*He's read those scenes. And he even left comments.*

I can't handle the shame.

"I did?" I ask in a squeak high voice that makes him smile.

"You sure did, Rose."

*Oh my God.*

*What's the quickest way to escape this situation?*

*I need it right now.*

Whatever little courage I possess, I gather it to glance at him. All I see is humor swimming through his eyes and lips that twitch from holding back a smile—he rarely gives me those smiles.

I don't have to ask. I know he's read it. And he knows that I know he's read it.

What I'd give to erase this moment from the timeline; I'd give anything.

Minutes pass and I don't say a single word.

His arm on the back of my chair touches my back. "Look at me."

Closing my eyes, I take a deep breath and do as he says.

With a pleased look, he curves in his chair so he's completely facing me.

"I read the entire book in one fucking night," he says.

"Huh?"

He smirks. "I feel like I can understand you much better now."

I want to die. Drink a cup of poison or fling myself off a cliff. I'll choose any option that'll make it easier for me to die than to have this conversation with him out of everyone in the world.

I clear my throat. "Like how?"

I want to slap myself across the face.

Why did I ask that? *Because I'm curious.*

He nods in deep thought. "I know who Adrian Hayes is."

"He's perfect, right?" I ask with a smile. "He did so many cute things for her."

"*And* steamy things."

Red burns my cheeks and I know I must look like a tomato.

I slip the book into my bag and try to pretend that we don't know each other at all.

"We'll talk about it later." Heath smirks tight.

"There's nothing to talk about."

Heath looks at me with a heated gaze. I know this conversation is far from over.

"So, um, how are you?" I divert the conversation.

He frowns. "I should be asking you that. Are you hurt?"

"Not at all."

"You aren't fucking lying to me, right? You can talk to me. I'll listen to you and help you."

A true smile appears on my lips. "I'm not lying to you. I'm really fine." I get nervous staring into his eyes, so I look at his chest instead. "You can talk to me, too. I'll listen to you and help you, well, I don't know if I can help you like you can help me, but I'll try."

Heath sighs loudly. "My face is up here, Rose."

I keep staring at his chest. "I know."

"Then why aren't you looking at me?"

I gulp. "I thought I should give my eyes some rest, you know."

*You make me nervous with those beautiful blue eyes of yours.*

*Really. Why are they so pretty?*

"By staring at my fucking chest?" I can hear the confusion in his tone.

"It's nice."

"And my eyes aren't?"

That makes me look at him and I'm bewitched by his stare. He looks at me as if he'll never get tired of the view.

My stomach fills with butterflies.

"No. Your eyes...they're beautiful. Really beautiful."

A muscle jumps in his jaw. "I'm going to kiss you."

I startle. "W-what?"

He frowns hard as he moves closer to me. "Is there something fucking wrong?"

My gaze runs across the room and catches the stares of so many people who are looking at us, observing us, and talking about us. My social anxiety kicks in hard, and my nerves quiver.

His hand cups my chin and draws my face toward his. "What's wrong?"

My lips tremble. I'm on edge from all the attention that I don't want.

"Can we do it when it's just the two of us?"

"Is someone making you nervous? Tell me their name—"

I grab his hand and shake my head. "No. It's no one," I assure him. "I'm just nervous here with so many people watching us."

Understanding dawns on him and he pulls my face closer to his. Bending his head down, he whispers against my cheek, "I'm taking you to my secret spot after school." Then kisses my cheek.

When he moves back, the butterflies in my stomach are soaring.

Marie squeals and pulls my attention.

"He kissed her," she tells Sebastian who's giving Heath an amused look.

"I saw that, babe."

"That was so cute."

"Indeed."

Heath scoffs. "Don't you two have other things to do besides watching us?"

Marie scrolls through her phone and shows us the screen. "I took a picture of you two." She captured a moment where we were lost in each other's eyes as Heath held my chin up.

Heath pulls out his phone. "Airdrop it to me right now."

A few seconds later, he has the picture on his phone and we both stare at it. Then, he sets the picture as his wallpaper and my heart claws my chest open to come outside.

Switching off his phone, he turns it back on and we both see the picture that's on his lock screen and home screen.

"I like that you're looking at me," he murmurs.

# 45

---

## HOPE

"You read spicy books?"

I hide my face in my arms that are hugging my knees that are pressed up to my chest.

Just like he said, after school Heath took me to his secret spot.

"No," my reply comes out weak and muffled, opposite of what I intended.

"It fucking seems like it," Heath remarks in a witty tone that says he won't let me off the hook so easily.

"There's romance."

"And sex."

My stomach rolls in a wave of heat that shouldn't come from him saying the word 'sex.'

Of all the fake scenarios in life, I never expected him to read my book—specifically the one with explicit scenes. I should've been more careful with hiding them.

My torment doesn't end. "Here I thought you were fucking innocent."

I peek at him through the little gap between my arms. "Everyone knows that kinda stuff."

Heath smirks as he looks down at me. "*You* more than the others."

He isn't going to let it go.

I groan. "Will you stop?"

"Why? Am I making you wet, Rose?"

I swat his arm. "Stop it."

He chuckles. "Fine."

"What's your middle name?" I ask.

"James."

I smile hard. "If only your name was Jack. We would be Jack and Rose."

"Then we'd be doomed."

I gasp in utter shock. "You've watched it?"

"Who hasn't?" Heath arches an eyebrow.

"I haven't."

His eyes narrow. "You're fucking kidding me."

I shake my head.

"Fuck!"

"My parents urged me to focus on my studies." Another layer of me slips away. It feels strangely good to tell him about my life, but at the same time also scary.

"Did you watch cartoons growing up?"

I nod eagerly. "All the time. My dad would be at work and Mom would do house chores. It made it easier for her if I was occupied."

A sad smile touches his lips, and he stares at the sky. "Emery and I fought over shows every single time. In the end, I'd always let her choose because she was one whiny kid."

"Or you were a good big brother."

"I tried to be."

"I'm sure you were. You're so caring and attentive. That's what a sibling needs."

"Apparently, not enough. That's why she isn't here today."

"That's not—"

He straightens. "Your parents, tell me about them."

I welcome the change of topic but also dread it. I don't want him to know too much. He'll be quick to join the dots together and see the bigger picture that I've been hiding from him all along. He'll know it's my dad who abuses me.

I look away to escape his scrutinizing gaze. I stare at the dusk sky, the way it stretches to miles till your eyes can't keep up.

"I was very close to my mother growing up. We went to the park every day where she'd swing me and make sandcastles with me. She'd also let me help her in the kitchen and we made cookies every Sunday. But once I got into school we started to drift away. She got strict, mean, and controlling. Perhaps she was always like that, and I didn't realize it until recently. The closer we were, the further we are now. It's not the same. Nothing ever is, I suppose.

"Then my father left because..." I pause. "And she got more distant. She missed him and wanted him back. She also started drinking which I don't think helped her to cope with the pain. If anything, it made her more sorrowful. I tried to be there for her, but she wanted him, not me. She pushed me away and I..." My throat grows thick. "Then she started working. I don't see her very often."

I look at him. "There's little room for bonding when no time is spent together."

Heath takes in everything that I said.

Before he can ask about my other parent I turn the question on him. "What are your parents like? You never talk about them."

Heath leans his head back against the tree. His jaw ticks with tension and his body goes rigid beside me. "What's there to talk about? They were never there for us."

"You have no memories with them?"

In the past two months, he hasn't mentioned his parents much. All I know is it's a sore topic for him.

I know they don't live with him. Perhaps they live in the city. But that doesn't explain why they don't ever visit him. All those times I've been to his house I haven't seen them once. There aren't any pictures around the mansion. It's like they don't exist.

"None I can recall." His voice is bitter.

Silence extends between us and tension turns the air thick.

Heath takes out a cigarette and lights it up. Taking a long drag, he puffs it out in a smoke cloud away from my face.

Biological facts loop my mind in warnings. The chemicals in cigarettes ruin the human body, especially the lungs. Those gruesome images of the side effects flash across my eyes. I can't stomach the thought of the same happening to him.

"You shouldn't do it. It's so dangerous for your health."

Heath exhales the smoke.

I watch him continue doing it and before I know he's halfway done with it. The smell is thick around us.

"Why do you smoke?" I ask to understand him better.

He looks visibly relaxed and at peace. Not his usual, grumpy angry self that only knows how to glare and scowl. "It calms me."

"I feel the same about books."

He chuckles. "Then we both have addictions."

I smile. "Mine isn't dangerous to my health."

He turns his head. "Any addiction is always dangerous."

My eyes drop to slightly pink lips. The desire to kiss them overwhelms me.

I know how they feel.

I know how they move.

I know how they taste.

"You're giving me that look again," he rasps.

"What look?"

"The look that says you want to fucking kiss me."

I lick my lips. "Maybe I do." Then I rush out, "If you want, that is."

Heath stares at me for a few more seconds, before stubbing out the cigarette against the dirt and throwing it away from us. He cups my jaw and pulls my face closer.

His breath fans on my lips. "I've been wanting to kiss you since the last time I kissed you."

"That was days ago," I breathe out.

His hold tightens. "Exactly. It's been a fucking torture for me."

"You can kiss me now."

"I plan to." His firm lips are on mine and he's kissing me. The bitter taste of the cigarette is hard on his lips, and I decide I hate it. I hate cigarettes. But I enjoy the way he kisses me.

There's a gentleness to his movements but a dominance to his strokes as he devours me.

I still have no idea how to kiss, but he takes the lead and isn't bothered by my lack of experience. He pulls me even closer and goes deep.

My hand reaches forward, and I grip his T-shirt. It's warm from the heat of his skin.

We break away with our breaths filling the space between us. I pant heavily, while he looks like he can go on for hours.

"Cigarettes taste really bad." I grimace.

He chuckles.

"I won't kiss you if you smoke."

The way his gaze drops to my mouth and his fingers caress my jaw. I can see the wheels turning in his head. Bending down he pecks my lips. "I won't fucking smoke then."

"Really?" I ask in disbelief.

He kisses me. "Yes."

"I thought you liked smoking."

He kisses me again. "I like you more."

Before I can say a word, he cups my neck and fuses our lips in a tight lock. My hands shoot up to his arms and I hold onto him tightly as he deepens the kiss. I feel it in my bones, knowing I'll be feeling it all night long.

He guides me gently and slowly, getting me used to the feel of his mouth. He hasn't used tongue, which is good because I don't know how I'll deal with it.

I've read about it, and it doesn't sound fun to me.

Our lips unlock with a little noise.

"Are you okay? Is this fucking okay?" he asks in a husky voice.

I smile at him. "I'm more than fine. It was perfect."

"Tell me if you ever don't like something I do or want to stop."

I nod then ask, "Will you... ever use tongue?"

He frowns. "Do you not want it?" He pauses. "If not, tell me. I'll remember it."

"No!" I startle and he frowns harder.

*Okay, I'm not making the situation better.*

"I haven't done it before. I mean I've never kissed someone before you, which is pretty clear, but I just meant, it scares me a little bit."

"Then we won't fucking do it." He decides. "I don't want to do anything that makes you uncomfortable. It's not fucking worth it."

My heart swells. "What about you? Do you want it?"

His thumb rubs my lower lip. "Do *I* want it? *That* means a lot of things for me, Rose."

"Like what?"

Inching closer to my mouth he whispers, "I think you already know since you read those spicy books." He presses a kiss to the side of my mouth. "You're not as innocent as I thought."

Well, he isn't wrong.

His breaths come out heavier as they lay over my skin. "Do *I* want to use tongue? Yes. But it doesn't matter what I want. What matters to me is what you want. And if it's off the table then it's off the fucking table."

"We can try it once."

"If you want."

"I want to see how it feels."

"Then we'll do it once."

Heath swings his arm around my neck and brings my body to his chest. His chin rests over my head, and I snuggle against his warm, hard chest that makes a great pillow.

We sit in silence until he whispers, "I fucking like you."

I grin. "I like you too."

The breeze of wind greets us on the way, and I shiver.

Heath holds me tight, then quietly he says, "Not more than I do."

# 46

## HEATH

Derek watches me with sheer interest from his spot across the room.

I move left and he follows, I move right, and he follows.

Eventually, my meter blows up, and I glare at him. "What do you want Derek?"

"Sir, is that girl your girlfriend?" he asks solemnly.

I narrow my eyes. "Is that Dad asking?"

"No sir." I stand up to talk to him up close. "Yes sir."

Dad lives in Toronto but he's keeping an eye on me from that far. Derek reports back every single thing like an obedient soldier. I suppose it's reasonable when he's paid thousands of dollars for spying on a teenager.

Dad thinks he knows me, but he doesn't. He hasn't heard a good deal of things from his dutiful soldier because I'm brilliant at hiding.

I don't want them to know half the things I do because I want no connection between us. The only connection he and I share is a less than five-minute call. Which reminds me he hasn't called me since that last call. It's unusual for him to not call me. He calls me every day even when I don't attend his call. And now my phone sits without his missed call.

I mean it's not like I miss him or anything. I don't even fucking care.

Before my mood turns sour, I turn my focus on Derek. "You can tell him to ask me himself."

He takes out his phone. "I can call him right now."

Sometimes I forget my butler has no sense of sarcasm.

With a scowl, I say, "It means it's none of his business. I don't want him to know anything about me or that girl I bring home."

His face stays impassive. "Mr. Travon is worried for you. He thinks that girl is manipulating you for money."

What the actual fuck?

Hope can never manipulate me for money. She can't even ask me to buy her food, let alone money.

The mere thought is stupid.

"Trust me she isn't," I reply with a twinge of anger in my tone.

Before I can argue more, Sebastian stands in the hallway. He's in a simple white T-shirt, denim jeans, and sneakers.

"They're getting ready?" He nods to the guest room.

"For the past hour."

Sebastian and I turn on Xbox and get our controllers. We set up a Fortnite match and start playing to kill time. We usually don't talk during the games, but today that isn't the case.

"So, how are things going with her?"

I'm too engrossed in the game, it takes me a minute to answer. "With whom?"

Sebastian's character stops moving. I turn to him only to find him looking at me with irritation. "I'm talking about Hope, you idiot."

Right, of course. It's a top priority for both Marie and Sebastian.

I nudge him to play and reluctantly he does. "We've kissed a few times. And I've told her I like her. She said she likes me too."

"And..."

I give him a confusing look. "What?"

Sebastian looks like he's done with me. "Have you asked her on a date?"

I press my lips together.

This is the fucking issue, I don't know *how* to ask Hope on a date. To be honest, I don't even know how to plan a date. I'm clueless. That book of hers I read did give me an idea. Adrian took Eleanor on a nice, romantic dinner which is something I think Hope would like. I just need to plan it perfectly.

"No," I state curtly.

"Cute."

I send him a glare to drop the sarcasm.

He rolls his eyes. "No seriously! What are you waiting for? *Another* guy to take her on a date so you can ruin it."

At those words, that awful night comes back to my mind. Seriously. *Why the fuck did I let Hope go out with that awful guy? I should've stepped up and confessed my feelings.*

Sebastian continues, "I guess that's what you're waiting for."

I ignore him.

"I know you're a pussy, but fuck. This is low even for you."

I grind my molars.

His eyes set on me and a smile appears on his face. "You're scared."

"I'm not fucking scared!" I burst out, knowing damn well that he's right. I'm scared about planning a perfect date for the only girl I've ever liked. I don't want to mess up. I want it exactly how she imagines it.

Sebastian's grin widens. "I think you are, James. You're scared of asking out your crush."

I'm seconds away from choking him. "Sebastian, I swear if you say that one more—"

"You're scared."

*For fuck's sake.*

I lunge at him but he's quick to get away. In a hurry, he crosses the room and stands next to the archway trying to hold back his laughter.

"I can't believe it," he wheezes out.

I chase him but he's fast. "Get your ass here, fucker," I yell after him.

We make a round through the hallway, only to circle back into the living room. Quickly he gets behind the sofa which keeps me away from reaching him.

He holds his stomach, seconds away from topping over the sofa from laughing.

"Heath doesn't know how to ask a girl out."

"I swear I'm gonna—" My words die the second I see Hope standing in the archway.

She's wearing a soft blue sundress with white daisies all over it. It fits her perfectly and ends a little below her knees, leaving her legs exposed. Underneath she's wearing white pumps that look new. I travel my eyes up and down her body, before locking them on her face. Air knocks out of my chest like someone's punched me hard. Her hair is slightly curled and falls on her front in soft waves—it's wavier than her usual hair. Light makeup coats her bony face, thick eyelashes pop her light brown eyes, and light pink gloss covers her lips.

She looks fucking beautiful.

Her brown eyes bounce from Sebastian to me.

*That's what I was waiting for. For her to look at me.*

The longer I stare, the more I want to keep looking at her. She looks perfect tonight.

Marie appears behind her, looking like a model with her blonde hair set in unruly curls and perfect makeup. She's wearing something black... I don't know and I don't care. I can't look at her when my eyes seem to be glued to someone else.

Sebastian approaches Hope and she smiles as they talk.

"Thank me," Marie says to me as she stands beside me.

I give her a confused look. "For what?"

"The list is very long, but I'll start with tonight." Glancing at Hope, she turns to me with a smile. "I did her makeup and hair. I didn't do much because she's so beautiful—"

"She is."

Marie smiles big. "—and kept everything minimal."

I seek Hope's attention but she's busy chatting with my best friend. What the fuck are they talking about?

"Let me handle this." Marie skips over to Sebastian. When he looks at her, he forgets about everything and eye-fucks her openly.

I'm about to yell *get a fucking room*. If I do, it'll be a room in my house where I can hear them.

Hope stands in the corner, her eyes are fixed on a random spot on the floor as her fingers twiddle with each other—a nervous habit of hers that I find incredibly cute.

Without wasting a second more, I stride toward her. The moment she sees me, her eyes light up and a soft smile appears on her lips.

My stomach fills with creatures that jump around in excitement. *Fucking butterflies.*

There are three steps left between us, which is a fucking lot. I'd very much like there to be no distance between us, but her romance novel taught me boundaries are important. I want her to reach me. If not, then I'm fine with it, too. Just being this fucking close to her is enough.

*She. Is. Enough.*

"Hi," she whispers.

"Hi," I rasp.

She blushes.

My favorite shade of red paints her cheeks, and I'm a fucking goner.

Her red cheeks do *something* to me. She can ask me to buy her all the books in the world and I'll fucking buy them for her. Or she can ask me to read them to her and I'll do it without hesitation.

She brings me to my fucking knees, and I'd gladly kneel in front of her.

Lifting her hand, she tries to push back her hair, but I catch her wrist.

"No, let it be. I like it," I say.

Her eyes widen. "Okay."

I feel her hand shiver in mine. I quickly engulf it in between my palms.

"Are you cold?"

She shakes her head.

"Scared?"

She shakes her head again.

"Nervous?"

She pauses, then nods.

I step closer to her—because I can't help it—and caress her knuckles. "There's nothing to be nervous about when you're with me. I want you to be comfortable. If you're not, then tell me. I'll do anything for you."

"I'm not nervous like that." She takes a step forward in my direction.

One more step and the fucking distance between us will be even less.

"Then what is it?" I ask.

Her blush intensifies and she bites her lip.

Blood travels down my body, to a region it's not supposed to, especially right now.

Moving my hand toward her face, I lean down and kiss her.

*For. Fuck's. Sake.*

She tastes like heaven. Pure perfection.

Slowly, and gently, I go deeper, and she meets my strokes. Her hands wrap around the back of my head, and she grips my hair tightly. When she tugs, I can't help but groan into her mouth. If she continues, I'll be walking around the fair with blue balls all night.

It's fucking clear to me that I want her. Not just emotionally, but physically too. I want to touch her skin and learn the temperature of it. So I can make her feel warm underneath me from all the wicked things that I'm dying to do to her. I want to kiss every inch of her so there's no place unmarked.

I want to take my time and find all the scars on her body and kiss them, so pleasure is all she'll remember. I want to take away her pain permanently.

There's so much that I want to do to her, but none of it matters. What matters is *her*.

*Still too far away.* I slide my arm around her waist and press her against my hard body that's hot from the need to worship her.

When I pull back to give her room to breathe, she pulls me right back at her and I can't help but fucking smile.

*My greedy girl.*

We kiss slowly and sweetly, taking time to memorize each other's mouths and how fucking perfectly they fit.

I've never found kissing special. However, that was until I met Rose. I can kiss her for as long as she'll allow me to.

Kissing her has become one of my favorite things to do with her.

"Guys, quit sucking each other's face off," Marie says from somewhere close.

Hope freezes in my arms and quickly pulls her mouth away from mine.

"Seriously. You were straight up making out," Marie adds.

"Like you don't do the same." I arch an eyebrow at her.

She leans back into Sebastian who wraps his arms around her stomach and kisses her hair, making her laugh hard.

I turn my attention to the most beautiful girl in my arms. "Are you okay? Was that okay?"

"I'm good and it was fine—I mean not fine. No! It was perfect," she stammers timidly.

"Hmm, so which one is it? Fine, good, or perfect?" I muse.

"The last one."

"Yeah?" I smile.

Setting her chin on my chest, she looks up at me with those innocent doe-eyes. "Yeah."

"Good."

"How was it for you?"

"Fucking perfect."

I'm rewarded with a grin that makes my heart race. I'm afraid that she might hear it or feel it but fuck it. I'm not hiding or fighting my feelings for this girl anymore.

I want her and I'll get her. I'll do anything to be with her.

We all saunter toward the driveway. Marie and Sebastian take his jeep and go ahead of us.

I walk toward my McLaren and open the door for Hope.

Her smile widens. "Thank you."

When I join her I ask, "Why did you thank me?"

"Because you opened the door for me."

"It's not the first time I've done it."

"Yes, and that's why I wanted to thank you." Playing with the necklace she says, "I like it when you do it."

I make no move to start the car.

Fuck it. For all I care, we can sit here for the rest of the night and just talk.

I'll be with her, and it'll be enough.

"What else do you like?"

"I like it that you notice little things about me, ask me about book updates, order food for me, calm me down when I'm having a panic attack, take hugs from me even though you don't like them—"

"I like yours," I tell her. "What else?"

"You make me feel safe."

"Because you are."

She nods. "I know."

"Is there more?"

A smile spreads on her lips. "I like you. I like you a lot. Probably more than my fictional men."

I narrow my eyes. "Why probably and not *fucking* definitely?"

A laugh breaks out of her and my annoyance shimmers down.

"It's not fucking funny," I grumble.

"Are you jealous?"

"Fuck yes, I am. Now that you like me, there shouldn't be room for *those* guys."

"I like you the most."

I shake my head. "Not enough."

My heart burns as if it's on fire. Hot, scorching flames rise in heat, all because I'm fucking jealous that she likes other men more than me. Seriously, whoever invented this jealousy-feeling should be sentenced. It's a fucking awful feeling.

Hope cups my face in her hands and presses a soft kiss on my lips. "They are fictional, you're real."

My anger and irritation go away. Fuck them. They don't have her like I do. She's mine.

"I bet they can't do this." Turning her face to the left, I bend down to her neck and press hot, wet kisses that make her breath hitch. There's a spot, just below her jaw that makes her shiver, and another near her collarbone that makes her dig her nails into my skin.

"Heath..." she whispers in a heavy breath.

Stealing a kiss from right under her jawline I move back. "Yes, remember my name, because only I can make you feel this way."

She swallows, then puts on the seatbelt as I start the car.

On the drive, we don't talk, but there's something I have to tell her. So, when we stop at a red light, I turn to her. She's looking out of the window.

I pick up her hand and her attention diverts toward me. "You look beautiful," I say.

Her mouth opens. "Oh... it's Marie. She did everything to—"

"It's *you*." I assert.

Her fingers tighten around mine. "You look great. You always do."

"Always?"

She nods.

I smile a little and look down at my all-black outfit. There's nothing new, except for the thin jacket I threw on because it gets cold in the evening, and while I can stand it, I know Hope can't.

So I'm wearing the jacket for the sole purpose of lending it to her.

The car horn blares behind me and I'm forced to drive when all I want to do is stare at the girl beside me. With a sigh, I turn to the street and speed us to the fair. Like every year it's brimming with life and music. Shouts and squeals carry in the air. Colorful lights are everywhere as they line the paths.

We wait in the car for Marie and Sebastian who left before us but still aren't here.

"Are you excited?" Hope sounds nervous—she doesn't have to be.

"No."

"I am."

"What are you most excited about?"

She gazes at the fair. The multicolor lights glint in her eyes.

"The Ferris wheel." With a shy smile, she turns to me. "I'm afraid of it, but I want to see the view when I'm on the top. How everything and everyone looks small." With a shake of her head, she adds, "But I'm scared."

"I'll go with you."

Surprise flickers across her face. "You don't have to."

"I don't have to, but I want to because you want to."

She looks at me with disbelief and something else.

A knock sounds on the window. I see Marie grinning at Hope.

The four of us enter shortly after we get our tickets and pass the security checkpoint.

Hope walks ahead with Marie, who's explaining everything to her, and she watches it with awe. The look is so innocent and pure that I want to pack it in a box and keep it safe from the fucking world.

"Instead of staring, take a picture. It'll last forever." Sebastian elbows me with a teasing smile.

"Get a hobby instead of observing me," I retort.

"Why would I? This is fun."

I roll my eyes.

Sebastian turns serious. Tipping the coke bottle toward Hope he says, "Ask her out tonight."

I look at Hope who's laughing as Marie fails at throwing the rings around the hoop.

"What if she says no?" I voice my worst fear.

"Then you ask again," Sebastian assures me.

I give him a puzzled look.

"You *pathetically* like her. You can't give up until she says yes."

"That's how you got Marie?"

"You bet your ass I did," he replies with an arrogant smirk.

"Get a life, Bash."

"Get your girl, James."

We follow Hope and Marie from stall to stall. They play games and buy stupid stuff—that's Marie.

Occasionally Hope and I make eye contact, and she always looks away with a smile that makes my stomach fill with strange insects. I'm half-convinced that something is wrong with me the number of times I feel everything move inside me.

Everyone from our school is here and I can sense their gazes on our group. Girls eye me openly as I pass them, a few even make the effort to talk to me, but I ignore all of them. They should get the hint that I'm not fucking interested. If they approach me it's straight-up rejection for every single one of them.

The one I want is walking ahead of me. I only want that one.

"We need to win something," Marie exclaims as we stop at a stall.

On the wall, there's an array of balloons tied in many colors and sizes. Inside the glass counter various stuffed animals, keychains, and other items are organized according to winning points.

"What do you want? I'll win it for you." Sebastian slings his arm around his girlfriend's shoulders and pulls her to him. Pressing his lips to her ear he speaks something that has her smiling hard.

I look down at Hope who's busy staring at an Eiffel Tower keychain.

Putting a hand on the glass beside her, I lean down to her ear, "You like it?"

She meets my gaze. "I love it." A shy smile hangs on her lips. "I've always wanted to visit Paris. I've heard it's beautiful there."

"I'll take you there someday."

She gasps. "You're joking."

I gaze at her with zero hint of amusement. "You know me enough to know I don't joke when it comes to you."

"I don't have a passport."

I cough to hide my laugh. "We'll get it. Now do you want it?"

"I want it."

My eyes drop to her lips and all I want to do is kiss her. Kiss her over the folklore music playing in the background. Kiss her over the noisy boisterous throng of people. Kiss her over the psychedelic dance of colors in her eyes. Kiss her over the roaring beats of my heart echoing in my ears.

I just want to fucking kiss her. Again.

"I'll pay." She takes out money from her satchel and hands it to the man who eyes her oddly.

I make my feelings known by glaring at him when he hands me an air gun.

"Good luck." He might as well be cursing me for failure.

Hope looks at me with encouragement—it's all I need.

With a deep breath, I aim and land a clear shot. Marie and Sebastian chant in excitement but I'm only focused on *her* smile that I can see from my periphery.

I land clear shots without a miss. I would be lying if I say I have never picked a gun, because I have. Last year, I spent quite some time at a shooting range. I thought it'd help, but it didn't. Nothing did.

Then I met the pretty nerd who loves books more than anything, and all the chaos whirring in me quietened into whispers.

Now I'm not angry all the time. I'm not annoyed with everyone—well that's a lie—except for her. When I'm with her, I'm just with her. I'm not phasing out or wanting to get to my room so I can have a mental breakdown. If anything, I smile, talk and laugh with her. I also fight the urge to not kiss her every five seconds.

I shouldn't feel this way. But for fuck's sake I can't stop myself.

I'm moving head-first toward her, and I don't fucking care anymore.

When I burst the last balloon, my friends jump with a hurray, but I only look at the person beside me.

We stare at each other.

She's smiling. *Fucking worth it.*

"So, what's it gonna be?" the man asks.

He scowls at me which I ignore. I point to the keychain, and he retrieves it.

I take it from him and hang it in front of Hope. "It's yours with the promise that I'll take you to Paris someday."

She takes it from me. "Someday."

I glance at Marie and Sebastian grinning from ear to ear like two golden retrievers. I roll my eyes at their enthusiasm.

Once Sebastian wins Marie a unicorn stuffed animal, we move along to the other stalls. We play many games and also get into a photo booth to get polaroids of us four together, all because of Marie. Just like last year, she manages to push me inside, how she does that with her little strength is astonishing.

"Oh, I need to buy something for my parents. Gotta go!" Marie drags Sebastian out of the booth leaving Hope and me alone.

We sit on the stools cramped in the tiny room. My legs can barely fit and so does my frame which makes me bump into Hope.

"Do you want to take a photo?" Her fingers are fidgeting with each other nervously.

"Of us?"

Her cheeks redden. "Yes."

I gulp hard as if I've swallowed a rock.

She presses the screen, and the countdown of three seconds starts.

It snaps a photo of us which isn't good because we're sitting away with sour faces.

"Maybe we should get closer," she suggests.

I comply with her request. My shoulder presses against hers. Her brown eyes quickly shoot up, then soften.

"What kinda photo do you need?" I ask, my voice unreasonably deep.

"Um...a nice one?"

My lips quirk up in amusement. Mischief fills my mind, and I can't stop myself.

I lift my hand and cup her chin. Tilting her head back so our gazes align, I drop my eyes to her seductive mouth that's going to make me a kissing addict.

"Are you ticklish?" I whisper lowly.

"Wh-what—"

I hit the timer with my other hand and then place my fingers on her stomach. I tickle her and she starts cackling. I can't help but laugh with her.

The noise of the snapshot rings and I stop.

Hope is blushing hard, but a smile is on her lips. Wrapping her arms around her stomach she holds it tightly. "Heath!" She attempts to glare at me but fails miserably.

A Polaroid slips out. I grab it and give it to her. "Here's your *nice* photo."

We both look down at the black and white grainy photo that's captured a perfect moment.

"Wow. This is..."

"Perfect."

"Yes."

I hit the timer again and both of us don't notice anything around us because we're staring at each other. A Polaroid slips out and hits the floor.

I let my eyes drop to her lips and the urge to kiss her hits me.

Fuck it.

"I'm going to kiss you," I tell her, just as I click the timer again.

When I meet her lips she goes soft against me and kisses me back like she wants it as much as I do—not a fucking chance, I'm a starved man for her taste.

"I can never get tired of kissing you," I murmur.

We get the photos and exit the booth. Marie and Sebastian are nowhere to be seen so we wander on our own and play games.

It's the most fun I've had since Emery's death. For once, I don't feel guilty for experiencing happiness. I know she wanted this for me, but I rejected it because I thought I was betraying her. Today, I realize, it's okay for me to have a good time.

The crowd gets thicker the darker the sky gets. People bump into each other like idiots and it's full of chaos.

I grab Hope's hand and steer us away to an open space so we can fucking breathe.

"You okay?" I ask, squeezing her hand.

"I'm fine."

She looks back at the crowd. "There are so many people here."

"It's like this every year."

"Did you attend it every year?"

"I haven't since Emery was in hospital, but before that yes."

"What did you guys do?"

I search for an empty bench and find one. Sitting down I stretch my legs and then look at Hope who looks curious about my answer.

"We went on rides, ate the oily food, and bought stupid stuff."

She chuckles. "I can't imagine you buying stupid stuff."

I smile. "You know me well."

"Is it hard coming back here without her?"

I inhale a sharp breath and examine the fair that's the same as it was years ago. Nothing has changed. Same vendors, stalls, rides, heck even the crowd is the same. Yet everything feels different because my sister is dead.

"Yes." I fidget with the purple ring I got altered to my size so I can wear it. I move it back and forth, the motion calms me.

"Sometimes I wish I had a sibling," Hope says.

"Trust me they're nothing but trouble."

"It's better than loneliness."

I stare at her, trying to decipher her. She tries to hide so much inside of her. It irks me because I don't want her to hide from me. She can talk to me about anything, and I'll listen to her. I'll always listen to her. Whether it's about those romance books she reads or her rambling about how chocolate makes her happy. There's nothing I won't ever listen to when it comes to her.

"But not worse than grief."

Hope meets my gaze, and I feel like she can read me.

Looking at the sky, she watches the stars. "I read somewhere that when the people we love die they become a star."

I scoff. "Don't tell me you believe in that nonsense."

She takes my hand and moves the purple ring back and forth.

"Look at the sky." I give her a dry look. "Please."

With a sigh, I lean my head back and stare up at the meaningless sky that I hate so much.

A mass of stars blinks black at me, as they hang on the black canvas, shimmering like glitter.

I take my time and watch every single one of them. Until I stop at one that shines the brightest and is golden. It's away from the cluster, but still, it has a light that no other star possesses.

I know without a doubt that it's Emery if she were a star. Something about it *does* something to me. Like there's a cosmic energy that I can feel. An assurance that she's in a better place. I wouldn't want anything more for her. She deserves that, and so much more.

Tears burn my eyes, and I cough to push down the lump of emotions trying to claw their way up. I rip my hand away from hers. Turning my head to the other side, I take shaky breaths that seem to tear me apart from the inside.

I can feel it. The storm from the past is trying to eat me alive.

My lungs ache with emptiness.

*I hate it.*

*This can't be happening right now.*

*For fuck's sake.*

*What will Hope think of me?*

*She'll think I'm weak.*

*She'll think something is wrong with me.*

*I'm being strange.*

*I wish I were in my room.*

*I can't cry here.*

*What should I do?*

*And why the fuck can't I breathe?*

*I need my mind to slow down.*

*Why are there so many thoughts flooding in my mind?*

*Why the fuck can't I stop thinking?*

*I need air.*

*I need to lie down on my bed and stare at the ceiling.*

*I need that right now.*

The mayhem in my head gets stronger and louder. I hear so many voices; I can't find my own.

"Heath, look at me."

I do as she says.

"Listen to me only." She runs her thumbs over my cheeks. I realize she's cupped my cheeks.

My face is in her hands.

"It's okay," she assures me.

"Take a deep breath with me." She shows me.

I copy her.

"Again," she instructs.

I do as she says, maybe because she's doing it with me.

I'm not alone in this.

Doing it with her doesn't make it seem so difficult.

We do it for a while, I don't know how long, but by the end, a string isn't tied around my chest.

"You're okay," she tells me as she wraps her arms around me tightly.

After a few minutes, she begins to move away but I hold her in place.

"Let me kiss you."

# 47

## HOPE

His lips are on mine before I can think, and maybe that's a good thing. I don't want to think when it comes to Heath Travon. My hands move to the back of his head, and I play with his hair.

He cups the side of my neck and angles my face to one side, making it easier for him to kiss me deeper.

Butterflies fly with wildfire in my stomach this time. Even though the air is chilly, I'm sweltering hot, and buzzing with the energy of a vibrating atom.

We pull away, and he gives me a moment to breathe, but then he kisses me again. I smile against his lips, and he squeezes my waist.

The sound of a camera capturing a picture breaks us apart.

We both turn our heads and find Marie holding her phone while Sebastian is smiling hard.

My skin burns with a flush.

I scramble away from Heath who's glaring at his best friends.

"Delete that photo right now." Heath stalks over to Marie and tries taking her phone but she slips it in her cleavage.

"Do it yourself."

Heath stares at her deadpan. His hands curl into fists.

"I *can't* get the phone," he grits out.

Marie smirks. "I know."

"You're the most annoying person on the planet, Blondie."

"I love you too."

I stifle my laughter.

Marie looks at me. "Want to get cotton candy?"

At the stall Marie and Sebastian split and pay for everyone except for Heath who doesn't like sweet things. I'm not sure that's the case since he ate chocolate off my mouth just fine.

My body heats up. *Right.* That scene still makes me hot and bothered.

We pass the arcade, but it's filled with teenagers. We have no chance of stepping inside let alone for Marie and Sebastian to test out every machine and make new high scores.

As we stroll further, I look at Heath who discreetly eyes my blue raspberry cotton candy.

"Here, take a bite." I hold out the stick in front of him.

"I don't eat sweet things."

I roll my eyes. "That's not true. You ate the chocolate cake."

"Because it was on you."

I blush hard as I pluck a tiny piece of cotton candy and press it against his lips. "Try it."

Heath reluctantly opens his mouth and takes it. I drop my hand and watch him chew it and then gulp it down painfully slow. His throat moves sensually.

It's the last thing that should be sensual, but it's Heath. Everything about him is sensual.

"It's good," he says. Eyes fixed on me.

"You can have more." I try to hand him the stick, but he only plucks a little bit.

On our walk to the Ferris wheel, Heath eats half of the cotton candy. I pretend that I don't notice, but it's hard not to. I just smile and let it be.

For the first time, I'm happy. These three people have suddenly become the most important people in my life. I'm beginning to love them. I always thought it was better to be alone. At least that's what I fed myself because something was wrong with me. Now I realize that nothing is wrong with me. I just didn't find my group of people. And now that I have, I don't ever want to let go of them.

I can't imagine my life without them. I hope I don't have to.

We get to the Ferris wheel and buy the tickets. Marie and Sebastian go first, and then it's our turn.

The sound of the door closing makes me shiver in both excitement and fear.

I seek Heath who's sitting opposite me and has already his eyes on me.

"You'll be fine," he assures me.

"I think I will be. I mean I've never seen someone die on a Ferris wheel, or have they? I don't think I've heard the news. There would be if something like that ever happened. Wait. I think I remember—"

Heath shuts me up by kissing me.

The cabin starts moving up and my heart goes down.

I reach for him, and my hand lands over his chest where his steady heartbeats drum under my palm.

Suddenly, he's all I can focus on.

He tucks my hair behind my ear. "You're safe with me, Rose."

"I know," I say.

"There's nothing I wouldn't do to protect you."

A silly thought crosses my mind. "But I can't protect you."

The Ferris wheel is going up but I'm too engrossed in our conversation to look out.

"You don't have to protect me. I can do it myself. However, you can tend to my wounds."

"I can do that."

"Yeah."

Our gazes lock, and in his eyes, I see everything I wanted to see. Lights, people, town, and the sky. There is everything.

"You're so beautiful," I whisper.

His breathing gets deeper.

I touch his face with my finger and trace his cheek, lips, nose, and forehead. There's no flaw.

"So very beautiful." My finger stops at his lower lip.

I lean forward and peck his lips which taste like cotton candy and warmth.

"Look out," he says.

I stare down and my heart dives into my stomach.

We're so high up that everything looks small. I take in the sky and the stars. In the distance, the hills stand tall and hidden in darkness. It's all so beautiful from up here. I can't believe it.

When our cabin goes down, gravity lurches for my heart. I quickly grab Heath.

"Did you feel the fall?" I ask.

When he doesn't reply I find him staring at me with a dark look that has my insides melting into liquid.

He looks bewitched by me. As if he looks away from me he won't be able to breathe.

No guy has ever looked at me like he's looking at me right now.

I don't want there to be another guy. I want it to be him. Always and only him.

The ride ends and we're the first to get out.

On the sidelines, we wait for Marie and Sebastian who are the last ones.

Sebastian hunches over a trash can while Marie rubs his back.

"Are you okay? Here, drink water." She holds the bottle to his mouth, all the while rubbing his back.

He washes his mouth before saying, "Fuck! I hate it. Why do they have to spin me like that?"

"Come here, babe." Marie wraps him in her arms. Tucking his head in her hair he relaxes.

"The fireworks are about to start. Let's all sit somewhere," Marie suggests.

Every bench is occupied by families or groups of friends. So instead, we settle on the ground, away from the eyes of our classmates.

I yawn and try to find something to lean against but there's nothing.

"Come here," Heath whispers against my temple.

Opening his legs, he helps me sit between them. I lean against him. My head is over his shoulder and my back is against his hard chest.

I sigh in relief and close my eyes. "I get it now."

"What?"

"Why people come here. I never had so much fun." I yawn and try to hide it, but my arms are noodles.

"Sleep, Rose."

"I don't want to kiss the fireworks."

"You can't kiss the fireworks."

"I meant miss. I don't want to *miss* the fireworks."

"You can barely keep your eyes open."

"Is that a challenge?"

He chuckles. "I'm getting convinced you have a split personality when you're tired and sleepy."

"I do not."

"You do."

"Challenge accepted. I won't miss the fireworks."

"I challenge you to sleep."

"Challenge rejected."

Heath laughs, making his chest shake against my back.

"When does it start?"

Just then the noise of the fireworks bursts through the air and a silence falls over the crowd.

I watch the kaleidoscope of bright colors fill the sky and brighten it up. It's a beautiful sight. I can't put it into words.

I further lean against Heath, and he wraps an arm around me.

When the last spark dies out, I turn my head. "Take me home."

# 48

## HOPE

Heath parks in front of my house.

"Good night," I murmur, having no strength to keep my eyes open.

"Get your ass inside," he orders.

Fighting back a smile I stumble to the porch.

I look back and Heath is watching me. I give him a wave and get inside my house as quietly as I can.

I make my way to the stairs through the darkness. Also, it's eerily quiet in the house.

Mom is supposed to work a shift tonight and Dad is out with his friends.

I told them about the fair, and they agreed. Though Mom cornered me later and asked me about Heath. I thought about lying but figured she would see through me. When I told her he'd be there, she lectured me to stay away from him among other things. I half-listened to her scolding—which is a first for me. I respect her too much to not ever listen to her. After Dad left, she put herself to work to provide for me while also saving up for college. She's done so much for me. But she doesn't know Heath like I do. I wish she did.

In the safety of my room, I lock the door and quickly change out of my dress and wash my face.

Wearing my favorite blue pajamas, I slide into bed and retrieve everything out of my satchel.

The polaroids. I love all three of them, but there's one that's my favorite. The way Heath is smiling down at me while I'm laughing has my heart turning into a cotton ball.

All my feelings for him resurface and butterflies wreak havoc in my stomach. I like him so much.

I wonder what he feels for me is as strong as what I feel for him.

A knock on my window pulls my attention. Heath is there, hanging onto the windowsill trying to lift himself off of it. I rush forward and open the window. "What are you doing here?"

"I needed to ask you something."

"You could have texted me."

He gets over the windowsill and shuts it behind me.

"That wouldn't have worked." He grabs the back of his neck and looks anywhere but me.

"How did you climb so high up?" I look under the window and gape at the height. My room is on the second story.

Heath comes behind me and points at the trash can. "I stood on it and then climbed up using the bricks pointing out."

"That isn't safe."

"I needed to see you."

We steer toward my bed. I make room for him to sit. His eyes settle on the Polaroid, and he picks it up. "This picture—"

"Hope, open the fucking door," Dad speaks from the other side.

My heart skyrockets in alarm.

Cold sweat beads appear on the back of my neck and goosebumps sweep over my body.

I look at Heath who's watching me closely. His blue eyes darken, and his face turns serious.

"Is it him?" he asks in a harsh voice.

I shake my head and grab his arm, pulling him to stand up but he doesn't. "Please. You need to leave."

He stands up. "I'm not leaving. I'm going to beat the shit out of him for hurting you."

The knocks get harder and louder.

"Please, Heath." I squeeze his arm, as I try to drag him to my window but he's strong. He barely moves an inch.

"Hope open the fucking door right now," Dad hollers, and my palms start to get clammy.

Heath glares at the door with the intent to burn it down. "He's the man who's hurting you, isn't he?"

I shake my head.

Heath cups my cheek. "I'll protect you. Go hide—"

"No! You don't understand. You have to leave. I beg you," I hiss at him, trying to control my frustration and fear.

"I won't leave you with him," Heath argues and it's certain that he won't leave.

"Then hide in the bathroom please," I try.

Reluctantly, he gets into the bathroom and closes the door enough to leave it a little ajar.

"Hope!" I jostle and don't have the time to fully close the bathroom door.

I run to the door and pull it open with shaky hands. Dad stomps inside and grabs me by the throat. "Who the fuck is in your room?"

"No-no one." I sputter in short breaths.

Dad releases me with such force the side of my head hits the wall and my ears ring.

"I saw the car and I heard the noise. I know someone came up." He glares at me and then surveys my room looking around at the nooks and corners.

"It's just me," I tell him, holding the side of my head that's throbbing.

"Really? Then who's this fucker?" Dad holds up the Polaroid.

The color drains from my face.

Shivers chase down my spine, then curl toward my stomach and freeze every muscle.

*This can't be happening.*

*He can't know.*

*Oh my God.*

*He'll kill me.*

My eyes glance at the bathroom door where blue eyes are watching me. Heath is there. I have to protect him.

"He's a friend," I mumble, my hands shaking with terror.

It feels like I'm stuck in a nightmare and it's all part of my imagination. But the ache in my head tells me it's not. This is happening. This is how everything goes down, crashes, and burns into quick flames.

Dad strides toward me. His hands grip my arms, and he squeezes hard.

"Don't lie to me you fucking bitch," he snarls at me with boiling anger.

"You're hurting me."

"You think I don't—"

Dad's voice fades out as I see Heath opening the door. His face is shadowed with rage and an intense look I've never seen on him before. Even from afar, I can see the tremors moving down his arms. He's shaking with blind rage that's consuming him from the inside out.

I shake my head at him and then meet Dad's dark gaze.

"I knew it! I knew you were whoring around." He yells at me.

I try freeing myself from his hold and he lets me go. I take a shallow breath of air, only to have it knocked out of me when he slaps me across the face. My balance slips and I fall to the floor holding my cheek that stings with searing heat.

Dad yanks my head up by my hair. His fingers pull my hair, and I wince hard.

"Tell me his name. Tell me his fucking name!" He applies more pressure, and I wail out in excruciating pain.

But it lasts for only a moment.

The pain disappears and my head drops.

Moving on my feet and hands I back away from him and hold my scalp that's aching with the sensation of a hammer jamming my head.

Then I hear him, "Heath Travon. That's my fucking name. And now I'll imprint it on your fucking soul so even your shadow is scared of me."

Through my blurry vision, I see two figures. One is hunched over the other and landing punch after punch.

I wipe my eyes and watch the scene.

Heath is holding down my father by his throat and his arm is busy punching him.

Dad looks bloody and bruised. His body is trying to flee but Heath isn't letting him escape. He's holding him down with his weight and knee that's rammed in his stomach.

"You're going to be dead by the time I'm done with you," Heath warns him.

Dad chokes as he flies his hands around.

Heath stands up and kicks him hard in the ribs. Dad rolls over so he's looking at me. His face is covered in blood and sweat, and his eyes are burning with anger directed at me.

I scramble away under his dark eyes.

"Don't look at her!" Heath pulls his head toward him. "Don't you fucking dare look at her. I swear I'll gouge your fucking eyes out."

I'm trembling against the wall. My body is paralyzed by shock. I can't move myself.

"Who the fuck are you, boy?" Dad coughs out. His eyes watch Heath with keen interest.

"Someone who'll go to any extent to protect Hope. Even against her goddamn pathetic excuse of a father."

Dad gives him a cynical smile. "Is that so?"

Heath glares at him. "I swear on it with my fucking life."

For the first time, I see fear washing over my father. He's scared. The same fear he used to instill in me is now what he's feeling.

The eye contact prolongs until I see a little movement. Dad takes out a small knife from his jeans pocket and holds it tightly.

"Heath!" I call out but I'm too late.

Dad pushes it to Heath's thigh, and he groans.

Getting to his feet Dad rushes out of my room.

I run to Heath and quickly press tissues to the open bleeding wound.

"It's not stopping." My hands are trembling because of how anxious I am.

*I don't want to lose him.*

*Why does it feel like I'm losing him?*

Heath cups my chin and makes me look at him. "Tie a piece of cloth around it. I'll be fine. It's not deep."

I tear apart one of my T-shirts and tie it around his wound tightly.

Then I help him stand. "Are you okay?" I run my eyes all over him, searching for any injury.

Heath brushes his fingers over my temple. "You're bleeding, Rose."

He brings his fingers down and I see blood on them.

I should feel concerned, but the only person I seem to worry about is him.

"I'm fine. It's nothing."

Heath looks at my injuries and his gaze turns intense. The black swallows the blue with rapid speed. "Come here." He wraps his arms around me and holds me tightly. "You're shaking."

My head is spinning, and my chest feels heavy from the worry and fear.

"It's okay. I'm here. I'll protect you," he assures me as he rubs my back.

*Protect me. How?*

*He got stabbed because of me.*

*I got him hurt.*

*This is all my fault.*

"Hope?" He looks down at me. "Look at me. I need to see you."

*He. Got. Stabbed.*

*I'm the reason.*

*There was blood.*

"Rose, listen to me!" He shakes me a little until I break free from my thoughts and face him.

His blue eyes hold anger as he says, "Don't get lost in your head."

My lips wobble. "You got hurt because of me. There was blood—"

"It isn't your fucking fault," he hisses.

No. He's not thinking right. He has feelings for me that's why he doesn't want me to feel responsible but that doesn't erase the truth. I got him hurt.

Before I can argue with him, he pulls away and says, "Stay here until I come back."

I panic. "What?"

Heath points to the bed. "Sit."

I shake my head.

"I need to take care of him," he says.

My eyes bulge out in apprehension. "What? No! You—"

With a sigh, he limps out of the room, and I follow him. "Heath, you—"

"Shh..."

Before leaving I grab a thick book, it's the closest weapon I can find. It can do serious damage if I throw it with enough force.

Heath gives it a bemused look and then moves down the stairs with caution. I stay right behind him instead of walking ahead of him like a shield.

*God. How pathetic I am.*

We hear Dad speaking to someone in the living room.

The moment we join him, he gets off the phone and looks at us with amusement in his brown eyes that I inherited from him. I wish I didn't. I wish I didn't look like him or resemble him in any way. I wish we weren't connected at all.

"So, this is your boy toy." His smile is sick and evil. With the blood on his face, he looks truly wicked.

I keep my mouth shut and stay behind Heath who's glaring at Dad with zero ounce of fear.

Dad wipes off the blood from his busted lip. "She isn't worth it. You're stupid if you think she is. Like her mother, she's useless."

Heath goes rigid. His body vibrates with tension. "She's worth it. You asshole!" Heath snaps.

Dad breaks out into laughter and the sound makes me reach for Heath's T-shirt.

Heath takes a step toward him and lashes out at him, "You beat your daughter. How fucking sick are you?"

Dad glares at him. "Now you're going to teach me how to treat my daughter?"

Heath's hands curl into fists by his side and I see them trembling. "*Treat* your daughter? You fucking asshole you beat her blue and purple. I've seen the marks. You choke her, hit her, slap her. How fucked in the head are you?"

Dad straightens and suddenly the air in the room evaporates.

The walls close in on me and the space looks ten times more congested than it already is.

My hand tightens around Heath's T-shirt which seems to help me hold myself together. Otherwise, I'd be having a panic attack.

I can't face the man who's my father. How messed up is that?

I slide further behind Heath, and Dad notices, and a grin appears on his mouth.

No. I hate that grin. It makes me restless because I know something very bad is about to happen.

Just then, the police sirens fill the vicinity. Blue and red lights flash in through the open windows. The noise of cars pulling up fills the neighborhood.

In minutes policemen barge inside holding guns and shouting instructions.

It all happens so fast. I zone out.

I feel like I'm in a nightmare and I can't move.

My eyes take in the scene, but my ears are muffled.

I see it all happen and I do nothing. I *can't* do anything.

Dad points his finger at Heath and screams words I can't hear. He cries with actual tears then shows his bruises and scrapes to police about how he's the victim.

A man comes around me in uniform and handcuffs Heath who's speaking words to me.

I can't hear him. I can't hear anything around me.

*What is wrong with me?*

In panic, I lock my arms around him to prevent him from going away from me, but Dad pulls me away. He digs his fingers into my arms as I try to reach Heath who's screaming words at Dad, but it only makes him hold me tighter.

The police take Heath outside and push him inside the car. Not for a second his eyes avert from my face.

"...yes he hit me like a wild animal. You can see the damage he's done to me. He's a criminal for sure because no normal kid goes around hitting people.

I wonder if he's hurt my daughter." Dad stands beside an officer murmuring words in misery and wiping his tears.

I try to open my mouth and tell the police the truth. I really try. But I can't. It's like suddenly I've gone mute.

I'm stuck in a limbo of fiction and reality where I'm a ghost—my existence is merely a fraction of my soul. Nothing more than that.

*Wild animal.*

*He's a criminal.*

*He's hurt my daughter.*

The voices get louder.

I want to scream at myself.

I want to scream at the policeman.

I want to deny the lies my father spoke and tell him the real truth.

Out of nowhere, courage rips through me and I face the policeman. "Sir, I want to tell—"

"Nothing." Dad slips his arm around my shoulders and squeezes hard. "Right, sweetie?" He looks down at me and the warning shines brighter in his eyes.

I won't crumble. "No—"

"She's still in shock. Don't mind her." Dad assures him who gives us an unbothered look and walks away.

My body seizes into panic.

*No! Come back.*

*Can't you see his fingers digging into my arm?*

*He silenced me and you left.*

It's then I realize that it doesn't matter if I tell the authorities or not. They won't help me. Much like that policeman they'll turn deaf and ignore my words. They'll go blind and not see the signs that are right in front of them. All because they don't care. No one does.

Except for Heath. The only person who stepped up for me, who fought for me, and who tried to protect me.

He's the only one who didn't *ignore* me. Not like my mother or the policeman.

I close my eyes to get a hold of myself. *Breathe in. Breathe out.*

I don't know how long it will take me, but I will pull myself together once again.

The first thing I notice is, I'm sitting on the couch. Dad is in the corner reciting convincing lies to a woman while staring at her with interest.

*This is my chance.*

*I need to get to Heath.*

Standing up, I run outside and hear Dad shouting my name and asking officers to stop me.

My feet hit the asphalt hard as I run in the direction of the police station. It's seven blocks away from my house but I don't care.

I have to get him out somehow. I have to do something.

Sirens blare behind me and alarm bells ring in my head.

However, I don't stop running.

The only thought in my head is Heath. How he's in this situation because of me.

I run, run, and run.

Blood and adrenaline pump through my veins. Hot sweat gathers on my skin.

My breathing is loud and uneven. I can't catch oxygen.

Still, I don't allow my steps to falter.

The only thing on my mind is to reach the guy I know I'm falling in love with.

# 49

## HOPE

I rush inside the police station.

By the time I stop, my head is dizzy, and I'm seconds away from fainting.

I hide behind a car to not let Dad and the others catch me.

Taking out my phone, I text Marie to send me Sebastian's number. She does it in a minute. Dialing his number, I call him, and he picks it up right away.

His warm voice pours out of the speaker. "Hey, Hope. Is everything okay? I can get Heath—"

"Come to the police station please."

"What! What's going on?"

In the background, I hear him moving around and making noise.

"Heath... they arrested him." I choke on a sob.

Sebastian curses and then speaks, "I'm coming. Don't worry. I'll get him out."

"He's in there because of *me*."

Silence stretches on the line. His breathing gets heavier over the engine of the car, and I realize he's already in the car.

"It's not your fault, Hope," he says softly.

It hits me then. *Sebastian knows*. He knows about the abuse. He knows everything because Heath told him.

"You-you k-know." I'm shaken to my core.

Sebastian curses. "Not the way you think, Hope. He told me so I could help him find the person who's hurting you."

I should be mad at Heath. I should be mad at Sebastian. *I'm not.*

All I feel is a weight has been lifted off my shoulders.

"Please come."

"I'm five minutes away."

Before he cuts the call I can hear the screech of the tires. He's surely breaking signals to get here.

I walk inside and see police officers everywhere.

There's a cell in the back where Heath is. He's removed his jacket and is hunched over his knees, his hands locked in place.

I run toward him. "Heath!"

An officer gets in my way. "Hey! What are you doing?" His big, muscular body intimidates me as he looks down at me.

I stand my ground. "Please. Let me see him."

His eyes roam my face and then drop to my chest where my hands are clutched together.

"Fine. You have five minutes," he says.

I thank him, then rush to Heath who stares at me with wide eyes.

"What are you doing here?" He reaches for me through the bars.

"I'm here for you."

"You shouldn't be here."

"You're wrong."

He cups my cheek and sighs. "You need medical treatment."

"I'm fine, I swear."

"How did you get here so fast?"

"I ran."

His face tightens. "The fuck! You ran here. Seven fucking blocks?"

I nod and reach for his hands and lace our fingers together. "I ran for you."

He curses. "I'm rubbing off on you in all the fucking wrong ways."

"No," I whisper. "No, you're not."

Heath holds my gaze, and I see all that I want to. He's angry, worried and scared. For me.

I wish I could get him out of here.

"I'm sorry—"

He glares at me. "You have nothing to be sorry about."

"But—"

"Where is he?" I hear Sebastian behind me.

In a minute he joins me. His green eyes assess the damage on my face and then move to Heath who's glaring at him.

"I told you," Sebastian says harshly.

"I don't want to hear this now," Heath grumbles and looks at me. "Stay with him tonight."

I shake my head. Dad will wreak havoc if I don't return.

Just as I think about him, his voice reaches my ears. "Hope, sweetheart. There you are."

Coming closer, he brings me to him by pulling my arm. I try to wrestle out of his hold but he's too strong. Leaning down he murmurs, "Go along or your boyfriend will spend more than a night in the cell."

I look at him in horror. "Please don't do it."

He smiles. "Then leave with me right now."

I give Heath a last glance, but he's busy shooting daggers at my father.

Sebastian nudges him and he looks at me.

Through thick tears I watch him. I open my mouth to say something, but he beats me to it.

"I'll come for you." Glaring at my father he adds, "No matter who gets in my fucking way."

Dad drags me out of the police station when all I want to do is be with Heath. The only person who makes me feel safe.

"I swear you've gotten fucking disobedient like your mother." He squeezes my arm.

My heart crawls into the pits of my stomach like a little kid sneaking under the covers for comfort and safety.

I can see it coming. The storm promises a thousand nightmares and wounds. All I can do is wait for it to pass and wish that by the end I'll survive it.

# 50

---

## HEATH

I want to kill her dad.

I want to stab a fucking knife through his heart and make him bleed.

For the second time in my life, I wish death upon someone. And I want to deliver it.

My hands turn white with how tightly I'm holding the bars as I watch him take her away from me.

I want to chase them. Rip him apart from her so she's in safe hands. Then keep hitting him until I fucking can't.

I've been taught to not use my fighting skills for evil, but I want to because that pathetic excuse of a man deserves it. He deserved every hit I landed on him.

Sebastian is pissed as he glares at me. "You did it! You just couldn't fucking help yourself."

I glare at him. "Did you see her? She's fucking bleeding!"

"And you're in a cell while she's going home with him. What do you think he's going to do to her now?"

Dread grips my chest like a snake has wrapped its tail around me. It squeezes the life out of me.

I hang my head low. Sweat and heat roll all over my body.

I lost.

She is in more danger now.

Because of me.

Fuck.

I let my guard down in front of Sebastian with ease. He knew it and he warned me. I didn't listen.

Opening my mouth, I push the words out because I need to tell him. "She was screaming when he pulled her hair. I couldn't help myself. It took every bit of my strength to not intervene when he abused her. But when she started screaming, all I saw was red."

Sebastian gives me a sympathetic look. "I'm sorry you had to see that."

I think about his words. "I don't think I'll be able to sleep now. Her screams will ring in my ears. I'll never forget her teary eyes and frightened face. She was terrified of him. Her fucking dad."

"He looks pure evil."

"He is. The way he fucking looked at her..." I swallow. "He hates her. He truly hates her."

"Wow, talk about similar parents."

My eyes shot up to him. "Your mom—"

He grimaces. "Look like she's cut from the same cloth as Hope's father."

I grind my teeth remembering all the shit that he went through and never told me about. He's the kind of person who'll go through the worst and still find it in himself to smile and be fucking optimistic about life. The reason why I never learned how fucking brutal it was for him. And I couldn't be there for him. But every time I needed him, he was. He still is.

He leans against the bars and smirks. "You fucked him up good. Well done!"

I chuckle. "I was going to do much more, but he pulled out a fucking pocket knife and cut me."

He straightens. "Where?"

I point to my wound that's wrapped up in cloth but needs medical attention. Fuck it. I don't care about it right now.

"I'm surprised that he called cops on me and spun the fucking story," I complain.

Sebastian stays silent in thought for a minute. "He's smart, Heath."

"I don't fucking care. I'll protect her." I push away from the bars and sit down on the bench. "I need to get out of here."

Sebastian nods and walks to the officer behind the desk. They get engrossed in a deep talk which accelerates into a loud argument.

I zone them out and think about Hope.

When I close my eyes I see her red face and teary eyes.

Anger fuels me like gasoline ignites fire.

I want to go to her house this hour and beat him some more. Perhaps break his arms and legs so he can't hurt her anymore. That would put my mind at ease. But if he dies I'll thank the heavens.

I've seen shitty people, but he's something else.

At the underground, there's a variety of dickheads, but I'm sure no one comes closer to him.

*He beats his daughter.* The sick part is he enjoys it. I saw it in his eyes. He loves violence.

That guy should be in a psych ward rather than a house. Everything Hope told me about not being able to talk whenever I asked her, comes to my mind. I understand now why she couldn't. She was petrified of what he'd do to her. And me. She was worried and terrified for me.

How that son of a bitch turned the story around and made me the suspect is clever. I didn't expect that.

I should have.

He's smart and knows how to cover his tracks.

Which makes me wonder if Hope's mother knows. What if she's just like him? I wouldn't be surprised. That woman is onto something too. I saw it the way she watched me from the window. Something is seriously fucked up with her parents.

The one girl I have feelings for has crazy ass parents who hate me.

Fucking great.

I look down at the bracelet she gifted me. I run my fingers over it and somehow it makes me feel better.

I have big fucking feelings for Rose. I don't know what they are or how big they are. But they run deep and consume me like a drug.

I can't stop thinking about her. I can't stop worrying about her. I can't stop liking her. There's no stop button. Frankly, I'm glad there isn't.

What I feel for Rose is real and fucking good.

Every laugh, smile, and talk with her is my good moment. I haven't had those in a long time. She's my good moment, and I don't want it to ever end.

Her father said she's worthless. But he's wrong on every letter of that fucking word.

Rose is worth everything.

Sitting in this cell, because I beat the man who's been hurting her for God knows how long, feels satisfying. I don't regret it one bit. I'll do it again just so she gets a few days off without someone banging her head against the wall or yanking her hair.

Sebastian walks toward me. I look at him in question.

He leans against the bars and starts tugging the band on his wrist.

I sense it before I see it. Something is wrong. He's anxious.

"What is it?"

He looks distressed. "You might have to spend the night in the cell."

"Why the fuck?"

"Alex Hanson has made serious allegations about you. They have proof too. You fucked him up and threatened to kill him."

"So what?"

Sebastian sighs exasperatingly. "You need a lawyer."

I laugh. "Yeah right."

"You're eighteen and you have some serious assault charges, Heath."

I grimace at the reality of the situation.

"Get me a lawyer then."

Sebastian scratches the back of his neck. "That's the part I was working on."

"And..."

"He said he'll bring one."

I frown. "Who?"

Sebastian takes a deep breath. "Don't kill me."

I narrow my eyes. "What did you do?"

Sebastian meets my gaze. He looks nervous as he says, "I called your father."

**To be continued...**

# LEAVE A REVIEW

*Thank you so much for reading Collided. It means a lot to me that you took a chance on my book. I hope you had a great time reading it.*
*Please leave a review on Goodreads, Amazon or any other platform of your choice.*
*I'd be grateful to you.*
*Love*
*Mary*

# Upcoming Releases

*Book two is called 'Mended' and it comes out soon.*

# KEEP IN TOUCH WITH MARY

Instagram: itsauthormary

TikTok: authormary

Sign up to my newsletter using the link on any of my profiles.

# ACKNOWLEDGEMENTS

To my Wattpad readers — Thank you so much for sticking around for this long. Gosh, I can't believe I wrote Hope and Heath's story in 2020. Four years later, and now you're holding it in your hands. You guys have been my longest relationship and my favorite friendship. From the bottom of my heart, I'm grateful for all your support and love.

To Katie — Thank you for everything. I met you on Wattpad and now we're such great friends. You're the first person I send my every manuscript to and it's always a joy to hear back from you. You edited and proofread this book, for that I'm so grateful to you. You make me believe that online friendships are the best.

To Sasha — You're my ride or die. Thank you so much for everything.

To Bri — Thank you for the formatting. Without you, this book wouldn't have reached the readers. You're the best and I'm so grateful for everything you've done for me.

To my brother — Damn, without you I wouldn't be here. My therapist, my best friend, my favorite person in the whole wide world. Thank you so much for being my number one supporter.

To my alpha readers — Thank you so much for all your feedback. It really helped me shape this story for the better.

To the Book Community — Ah! You guys have changed everything. The sheer amount of support and love I got from you in the two weeks before the release will always be one of my favorite memories. I can't thank you enough for your posts, messages, Instagram stories, edits and reviews. You guys are the best and I'm so glad that I got to meet you. Thank you so much.

Love, Mary

Made in the USA
Coppell, TX
28 January 2025

45077762R20261